PRAISE FOR *THE PORNOGRAPHER'S POEM*:

"At heart, *The Pornographer's Poem* is a randy and radical coming of age tale, which follows a young man's journey from childhood to the demimonde of downtown. It's a familiar journey for anyone who has read such books as *Catcher in the Rye*." — *The Globe and Mail*

"Time twists, memory lane detours and honest eroticism should draw everyone to this brilliant book ... Turner's deft plot and narrative voice anticipates the reader's every response. Minus of course, the one in your own head that marvels at how this book plays like a movie in your mind." — *The Province*

"Three novels lurk in the pages of *The Pornographer's Poem*: a conventional rites-of-passage recreation of school, a paean to the pleasure and riches of cinematography and, toward the end, an Elmore Leonard-like tale of hustlers, betrayals and deals gone wrong. Michael Turner handles all the genres with considerable skill ... Very few novels manage to be funny, moving and true: Turner is capable of hitting some very difficult notes." — *National Post*

"In *The Pornographer's Poem*, Michael Turner smashes what is usually considered the crude genre of pornography against the kinder, gentler young adult novel. But once the initial blow has fallen, all kinds of delicate particles drift down." — *The Vancouver Sun*

"Turner's clear-eyed technique is a unique combination of hard edge and poignancy." — *NOW Magazine*

"Michael Turner is simply one of the best writers in thi Reading *The Pornographer's Poem* is exciting in a way rarely are." — *The Georgia Strait*

"*The Pornographer's Poem* is a relentlessly intelligent k of very high accomplishment." — *The Globe and Ma*

"By turns both hilarious and achingly sad, *The Por* is also a book about narrative — about the produ — *eye weekly*

THE PORNOGRAPHER'S POEM

Also by Michael Turner

Company Town
Hard Core Logo
Kingsway
American Whiskey Bar

THE PORNOGRAPHER'S POEM

a novel

Michael Turner

VINTAGE CANADA
A Division of Random House of Canada Limited

VINTAGE CANADA EDITION, 2000

Copyright © 1999 by Michael Turner

All rights reserved under International and Pan-American Copyright Conventions. No part of this book may be reproduced in any form or by any electronic or mechanical means, including information storage and retrieval systems, without permission in writing from the publisher, except by a reviewer, who may quote brief passages in a review.

Published in Canada by Vintage Canada, a division of Random House of Canada Limited, in 2000.
First published in hardcover in Canada by Doubleday Canada, in 1999.

Vintage Canada and colophon are registered trademarks of Random House of Canada Limited.

Canadian Cataloguing in Publication Data

Turner, Michael, 1962–
    The pornographer's poem : a novel

ISBN 0-385-25848-8

I. Title.

PS8589.U748P67 1999   C813'.54   C99-931394-0
PR9199.3.T87P67 1999

Passages from The Sadeian Woman *by Angela Carter, copyright © Angela Carter 1979. Reproduced by permission of the Estate of Angela Carter c/o Rogers, Coleridge & White Ltd., 20 Powis Mews, London, England W11 1JN.*

Cover photograph by Suzanne Opton / The Image Bank
Cover design by Bill Douglas @ The Bang
Printed and bound in Canada

Visit Random House of Canada Limited's website: www.randomhouse.ca

TRAN   10   9   8   7   6   5   4   3   2   1

THE PORNOGRAPHER'S POEM

1.1

Sixteen years old. My first porno. Pornos, really. There were three: *The Blue Balloon*, something starring Clint Westwood, and another one whose name I can never remember. Cut together. And continuous. From noon to midnight. Seven days a week.

So: first porno was pornos. About fifteen minutes' worth. The cops threw me out before I knew what I was watching. But which one out of three? Does it matter? You'd think it wouldn't. But it does, in a way. I think.

This is what I know I saw:

EXT. THE VENUS THEATRE. NIGHT

A brick building. Her busted marquee. Purple curtains in the windows. Posters, too. A Hindu woman (40) stares from the booth. I approach, camera-right.

                              WOMAN
          Five dollars.

I give her the five, she tears off a ticket.

1

INT. THEATRE

A small lobby dressed in pink drapes. A popcorn machine with a CLOSED sign taped to the counter. An older Hindu man (70) sits at a card table. In front of him, a shoebox. For the stubs.

He reaches out. I give him my ticket. He rips it in half, then points to a slit in the drapery.

>   MAN
>   There.

Static pops. Low groans. Some "oh" sounds. And some high-sucking "ahs." Snippets of dialogue. But they are so muffled, so scratched, the voices seem sexless, indistinguishable.

>   INDISTINGUISHABLE VOICE #1
>   Can you feel it?

My heartbeat. Beating harder. In 2/4.

>   INDISTINGUISHABLE VOICE #2
>   Yes.

I step into the light. The silver light. Hundreds of seats. The backs of ten heads. Silhouetted. I adjust, though I'm slow to focus. I think: Silver makes the darkest shadows. I still can't see. But I end up front-and-centre. A mystery to me. To this day.

>   INDISTINGUISHABLE VOICE #1
>   Here ...

The brightness of the first row. Skin completely white. The pores of my flesh. The stiffness of each arm hair.

This big guy takes the aisle seat. To my right. Creaking. An old guy. Fifties. The speakers hang above us. His crunchy coat like thunder.

>   taste it.

An interior scene. A woman and a man. She shuts the door. Not a crack of daylight. Just a candle by the nightstand.

INDISTINGUISHABLE VOICE #2
I'm gonna wanna smell it first.

The guy on the aisle. He crosses his legs. Then he uncrosses them. Then he crosses them again. And again. The heat off his body with each uncrossing. The salt in the air. From his lap. Different from the rest. I mean the others in the building.

IV #1
Okay.

His hands in his pockets. The whole aisle creaks. A sustained creaking. Then this ticking. Like a metronome. Then a note ascending. Chromatically. This tick ... tick ... ticking.

IV #2
Okay, then.

Soundtrack. Bass first. For two bars. High-hat. Then a close-up on her face. Eyes. Wow! Organ fills. Horns. Then wah-wah. Fuzz. And him. So funky.

His hands grip the armrest. The aisle creaks. The bolts strip. I feel me. Sliding down to see. To where I can't be seen. I scratch my cheek to see. Him. Leaning. Arching. Toes pushing out. Heels dangling down. His pushing pushes me. Jiggling my seat.

IV #1
Oh ... *ohhh!*

His eyes closing. His breathing. With my fingertip, touching. I trace the outline where I've grown to be. The strain against my jeans. And me. Leaning. Into this moment. Creaks. Everything.

IV #2
Ah-ah-ah.

An exterior scene. A blast of streetlight. His coat slides away. He pulls from his body. This monster. Holds it forth. The boldest I've seen. To this day. Mottled. Uncut. Big balls bobbing. Jumping for something. Right out of his goddamn pants!

IV #1

I'm coming.

In spurts. Three. The first between his feet. Then one straight up. Disappearing. The last one a drop off the top of the stage.

IV #2

Yeah. *Oh yeah!*

An interior scene. Pitch black. The lighting of a match. A cigarette. Mumbles. Chuckles. One voice high, trailing off at the end. Suggests a question. Then another. Low. Monotone. Not inclined. Bored.

IV #1

You'll have to go now. You know you can't stay here.

IV #2

I've got a feeling you're right.

He adjusts his coat. Gets up. Goes.

IV #1

Do you think I'll ever see you again?

Footsteps.

An exterior scene. A car pulls away. From an old brick building. He's gone.

NEW VOICE

Young man?

ME

Huh?

Can I see some ID?

Two cops. One talking. One holding the flashlight. Asking me to leave. The flashlight in front. His partner behind continues ...

TALKING COP
It's for your own good, son. These people — they're perverts. You never know what one of them's gonna do in the heat of the moment.

EXT. THE VENUS THEATRE. NIGHT

Outside. The talking cop. His lecture. To the woman in the booth. She nods. Looks barely there. A ghost car pulls up, jumps the curb. The flashlight cop makes the OK sign. Talking cop calls out ...

Detective!

The guy from the aisle seat. He gets out of the ghost car. Looks right through me. To the talking cop, the detective says ...

What do these kids see in this shit?

And from the flashlight cop ...

If we knew, we'd be detectives.

1.2

— Sorry. I've forgotten the question.

— We asked you how old you were when you saw your first pornographic movie.

— Oh.

At school the next day. Friday. Early. By the smoke doors. In the snow. Students sliding down the hill. In twos and threes. Laughing. I could see better. Having seen things they hadn't seen. I could see the muffs on girls I hadn't been with. I could see the cocks on guys I hadn't played ball with. I began to imagine them together. Unlikely unions. Cheerleaders with science nerds. Rugby players with Job's Daughters. Everyone was getting it on. No wallflowers. No disc jockeys. No monitors. This time.

Shawna Kowalchuk. Her gimp leg. She's naked, except for the boot-brace, lowering herself over Bobby Galt, team captain, braggart, waiting for his limp prick to inflate. Her working it straight, having dispensed with the condom for fucking's sake. "Just get this thing in me and we'll be okay." Bobby's face blushing, swollen with blood, miles from the end-zone victory rush. Shawna submits to the bag on her head. Her pussy is sweet. "Yes," Bobby agrees. "Then why, you wimp, can't you put it inside me?" Shawna chews a hole through the Safeway paper, to suck on Galt's cock. But it just stays the same, a worm-like thing that won't go away. "Lick my sweet pussy!" Shawna demands, her weight on the good leg. "If you want me to, Shawna. If you think it's okay." She thinks it's okay that he's behaving this way. She knows that he'll never make fun of her again.

Or:

Jeffery Smith-Gurney, physics magician, discovers an island after floating at sea, sees Cindy Carruthers, Shaughnessy pom-pom, dissatisfied rich bitch, on the rocks bawling 'cause she's run out of make-up, with no one to rag on. Up floats Smith-Gurney, naked from the waist down, his cock the size of an August zucchini, avoiding the rocks, meek greetings to Cindy, and into the bush to make a skirt from some palm fronds. As followed by Cindy: "Can I touch your weenie?" Her titties bananas, her pussy a peach. Smith-Gurney is hungry. But Cindy's insistent. "I want the whole thing." Keeps bouncing right back after umpteen attempts. Cries 'cause she's dry, 'cause she wants it so badly. Smith-Gurney is starving. Asks, "Is Shawna K. handy?"

1.4

— Thirteen. I was thirteen when I saw my first pornographic movie.

— Do you remember the name of it?

— Yes. It was called *Circle Jerk '76*.

— Do you remember what it was about?

— Yes, very clearly. It was about five boys who go out into a cornfield with a jar of Vaseline and a stack of *Hustler*s.

— Would you characterize this film as heterosexual or homosexual?

— Neither.

— When you say "neither," don't you really mean bisexual?

— No. They brought their dogs with them.

1.5

Bobby Galt asked me where I was the night before, why I didn't show up for biddy-ball. I lied and told him I was at home reading Pushkin. He told me I shouldn't be reading "that communist shit," and that I was lying 'cause he phoned me three times. "Your mother said you'd gone to the movies." I told him that's what I tell her when I want to be alone. "Oh, so your mother's a liar, too!" "That's right," I told him. "I come from a long line of liars."

1.6

— We have reason to believe you've been lying to us.

— Based on what?

— Based on our review of your memory.

— You mean your memory of me.

— That, too.

1.7

Galt shook his head.

I hated this behaviour, this dumb family trait. His dad did the same thing! Such lame disappointment. The dumb-ass goofs. Fucking Galts! But whatever. Bobby, though — faking his hurt like that. With that look. That look I'd grown up with. A look so tired and second-hand, so televised, a look that cried out for inquiry, whining to be broken by my qualification. So: "I'm not playing, Bob." And Bobby, all dumb-faced, knitting his brow into phoney abstraction. "What are you thinking about when you look at me like that, Galt?" Another Huh? "Honestly, Bobert, what are you thinking?" Bobby's confusion when he thinks he's sincere. He says, "I'm just wondering what's happened to you. I mean, you know, you used to be such a *guy!*" I give him my *and?* look, my best *please continue.* But Bobby plays troubled, distracted by a lack. We pause for the Kowalchuks' Nova, still without a muffler.

Bobby's new angle: "Well, you know, you used to come out for sports and stuff. Parties. Go in on bags of dope. And, well, you just don't do those things any more, do you?" Wow, the honesty. "Well, Bobby, what's happened to *you*? I mean — you used to be so cocky, so confident. Now you're all gushy and sentimental. I guess we've both changed." Galt shook his head again. Tsking. Then, with a finger to the Nova, he bails on the topic: "You know, if you put a bag on Kowalchuk's head, I'd fuck her in a second."

1.8

— What happened at the Venus Theatre on November 26, 1978?

— I don't remember.

— According to our records, you were sixteen years old and you saw your first pornographic movie.

— Pornos, really.

— There were three. *The Blue Balloon*, something starring Clint Westwood, and another one —

— Whose name I can never remember.

— Called *Adventures in Amber*.

— That's right!

— Cut together.

— And continuous!

— From noon to midnight.

— Seven days a week!

2.1

I hated high school. Not always, though. I was a popular kid. I excelled in all the right things: good looks, grades, athletics, humour. And I took delight in this. As if that's all there was. But something happened when I turned sixteen. I can't really explain it. Something just kicked in, something deep inside. And the next thing I knew I had this intense resentment towards my friends. Not so much because of who they were but for what they represented. Where they came from. Where we all came from. The wealthiest end of Vancouver. This place called Shaughnessy.

One of the best movies I ever wrote was a parody of Shaughnessy. I called it *Rich Kid Gang Bang* and it was really mean-spirited. I even used people's real names. All the people that pissed me off: classmates, teachers, neighbours, whatever. Our distributor hated it. Too much dialogue, they said. Apparently they used to joke about it, said it was gonna be their worst seller ever. They'd call it our "contribution to science" film because it was the closest thing they'd seen to a cure for insomnia. They even wanted to put a big sticker on it: WARNING: CONTINUOUS VIEWING MAY CAUSE DROWSINESS. Stuff like that.

But a funny thing happened. *Rich Kid Gang Bang* became a hit. Not a big hit, like *Deep Throat* or *Devil in Miss Jones*. But a little hit. According to the distributor it did surprisingly well in small towns like Madison, Ann Arbor, and Chapel Hill; and yet it bombed in big cities like Los Angeles, New York, and Chicago. All of which got me thinking: Why is it that certain films do well in some markets but not others? So we did some research. We even hired a demographer. What we came up with could've changed the way we made our films forever.

2.1a

The Original Synopsis for *Rich Kid Gang Bang*

> *Rich Kid Gang Bang* is the story of an encounter between wealthy teenagers and a group of loggers. The film begins with the teenagers talking about how they're going to pass the summer. They talk about how bored they are, how everything has become the same (and they do this in a particularly snotty way, making them instantly dislikeable). So to spice things up they decide to drive up into the mountains for a beer blast. Once in the mountains, they find a cosy spot by a creek and start drinking. After every beer, the guys casually chuck their empty cans over their shoulders into the flowing waters; and with each beer the guys become more and more aggressive. After all the beers are gone, the guys start groping the girls. At first the girls resist. But that takes too much effort. Eventually they give in. (They're so fucking bored they can't think of anything better to do!) As a means of coping with their boyfriends' behaviour, the girls begin to fantasize about what they'd rather be doing. And we follow these fantasies. Some of these fantasies involve being crowned Miss America, some of them revolve around finding cures for cancer. And some of these fantasies are sexual. Some involve older men — movie stars, construction workers, black men, white men ... And some of these men are each other — that is, some of these men are

women, the women these women are with. Then along come the loggers, a group comprised equally of men and women. They're doing some kind of conservation work, which consists for the most part of picking beer cans out of the creek downstream. They spy on the teenagers, all the while remarking on how bored the girls look and how clumsy the guys are. They decide to "educate" the teenagers. What follows is a gang bang. The film ends with the teenagers, under the supervision of the loggers, planting trees on a mountaintop, all laughs and smiles, naked from the boots up.

2.1b

The Demographer's Letter

June 6, 1979

Dear Sirs,

We are just completing the study of the markets you requested information on pertaining to the popularity of your film, *Rich Kid Gang Bang*. Although we can't yet include a complete set of statistical correlations, our preliminary findings indicate that your film has done particulary well in small college towns that draw on large populations of upper middle-class students and are supported by equally large working-class populations.

We hope to have a complete statistical breakdown next month.

Ordinarily we don't release the results of our preliminary findings until we are satisfied that the results have undergone rigorous testing. However, in this case, we've made an exception: a clear pattern emerged early. And since it was consistent with your initial hypothesis, we thought it wouldn't do you any harm to pass this note along.

Sincerely,
Doug at Culturesearch

— The film you ended up making looked nothing like your original synopsis.

— Which version of the film are you talking about? As I recall, there were two.

— We're referring to both versions.

— Yeah, well, the idea was basically the same. That's the main thing — the idea.

— So when did you start making films?

— I'd been making films all my life.

2.3

For as long as I can remember my mother had cameras. All kinds of cameras. Brownies, Polaroids, Instamatics. She even had a movie camera. A regular-eight number. A hand-wind.

When I was eleven years old I found a big cardboard box in the basement. It was filled with photographs. I remember spending a whole Sunday afternoon going through that box. Oh yes. It was wild. My mother took pictures of everything. A mom's-eye-view of my entire life! And it's funny — you know, looking back — how I remember weighing those photos she so obviously chose to save against memories that I, at the time, was trying to forget. Yes, I remember feeling pretty adamant about some of those photos. So you know what I did? I took all the photos I didn't like and I burned them. I remember thinking: She'll never notice.

The following Friday my mother picked me up from school. It was really embarrassing 'cause she never did this. And even when she did — if, say, I had to go to the doctor's or something — we'd usually arrange it so I wasn't, you know, within sight of my friends. Anyway, she was waiting for me, in our rusty old Falcon, honking the horn, smiling, waving, putting on a show — "I'm here! I've come to pick you up!" ... And I was just coming out the gym doors with my friends and I was totally in shock and my friends immediately started teasing me and, ugh, it was pretty awful. So I think I said to them: Oh, that's right, my mom's taking me to get some new skis or something. Then I quickly waved them away and jogged off like some cool goof towards the car.

I was so pissed off. And I was pretty sure I was gonna let her have it this time. But when I got in the car I could tell from the position of her lower lip that she was even more pissed off than I was, which pissed me off even further 'cause it totally wrecked my anger. Staring straight ahead, and without a word, my mother put the car in gear. We were off.

It wasn't until we turned the corner, away from school, that she asked me, very calmly: "What have you done with my photos?" Huh, what photos? "The photos in the basement; I noticed a bunch are missing." I felt a chill. I knew there was no point in lying. She probably noticed I was looking through them. "I guess I misplaced them," I told her, trying to be casual about it, like they're only photos or something. "Okay," she said, like it was resolved. We turned another corner. She began again: "What were you burning by the compost the other day?" Shit! This was classic mom: Allow for the truth, right off the bat, then, if the truth doesn't come, counterattack. "Okay, I burned them," I told her. "I burned the photos." "That's all I wanted to know," she said, as we turned up the driveway, home.

I went up to my room, sat down at my desk, and stared out the window. It's what I always did when I got in shit like this. I would replay all the events leading up to being caught, then try to determine the punishment. It always seemed to happen like this: get home from school, get interrogated, then sit in my room till dinner. I'd get the silent treatment during dinner, then I'd voluntarily clear the table when I figured the meal was over, usually after my father got up. Then, like a good little suck, I'd wash the dishes. And then, as I was polishing the last plate, my mother would come into the kitchen and announce the punishment. The punishment was always foreshadowed by my father's whereabouts: if he was in the den, I'd be grounded; if he was in the backyard, it'd be corporal. But this time was scary — because it was the first time I'd fucked up since my mom kicked my dad out.

Just before dinner there was a knock on my door. It was my

mom. I felt really stupid when she asked my permission to enter. Stupid because I thought it was understood by now that I deferred all rights to her when I fucked up like I did. So: Yes, come in.

I remember not turning around, that I would wait for her to start talking first, so that when I did turn around I could do so as part of my response, that it would give my defence a bit more weight, that it would be a lot easier, for some reason, that way. The door creaked open. I listened for footsteps. Nothing. I was waiting. It seemed like ages before my mother said my name. I was beginning to feel mad. The same kind of madness, I suppose, that caused me to burn those photos in the first place. Then she said my name again. And right after that: "Why did you burn my photos of your father?"

I don't remember turning around, but I do remember holding my mother. I remember holding her for what seemed like a very long time. And I remember my sister joining in at some point, and how I thought my sister was being stupid because she was way too little to know what this was all about, other than the fact that Mom was crying because she must have hurt herself or was scared by something or was lonely. When my sister finally began asking my mom what's wrong — "What's wrong, Mommy?" — my mother sniffed and, composing herself, said, "How about we all go downstairs and watch some movies?"

My mother had a movie projector set up in the den. And beside it was a giant metal canister. The tape around the canister said: 1960–1969. She told us to get comfortable, that we were going to have hot dogs and tomato soup for dinner, and that we were going to watch a movie. This was getting a bit weird. We never ate in the den, especially since my mother had always been so paranoid that we'd spill on her gold sofa. And what about my punishment? I really wanted to get that one over with. "The name of the movie we're going to watch tonight is *The Story of This Family — So Far*," my mom said, a bit of the cry still in her voice. "And even though we haven't been making much of this movie lately, it doesn't mean that it won't" — sniff, sniff — "continue."

She had ten years on one reel and we watched it all: my mother and father, before they were married; my parents' wedding day; me, when I was one week old, all sickly after surgery to correct a diaphragmatic hernia; my sister, who was born a few years later, coming home from the hospital, all pink and crinkly. Vacations. Birthdays. Relatives. You name it! Sometimes my mother would narrate, sometimes she'd just cry — sometimes both. We'd laugh at my granny smoking a cigar or wow at my father diving off a cliff somewhere along the Oregon coast. I remember seeing footage of my father's father, a man I'd only heard about, lighting a cigarette on the beach at Big Sur. Occasionally mom would stop the projector to set up a story or to finish one or even just to talk about something completely different.

Well, all this went on till late, late, late. And I remember being kinda shocked when I found out how late it really was. I don't think I'd ever been up past midnight before. But I didn't feel at all tired. In fact, I was kind of dreading having to go to bed. Then my mom told me to wait for her while she took my sister upstairs and tucked her in. When she returned she told me flat out that I wasn't going to be punished, and that she understood how I felt about things but that was still no excuse for burning her photos and then lying about it, and that just because I may not want to look at something doesn't mean I have the right to take away somebody else's right to look at something. She also said that there would be many more examples of this in life, and that as I got older these examples would become more and more complicated, and that I should try to keep an open mind, and that these situations can usually be resolved by talking about them, and that certain situations that begin as negatives often get turned into something positive. And then she kissed me. And then I kissed her. And then I went to bed.

2.4

— How did your mother support you and your sister after your father left?

— He didn't leave, he was kicked out.

— Very well. How did your mother support you and your sister after your father was kicked out?

— She worked. She's always worked.

— What kind of work did she do?

— Cytology. My mother's a cytologist.

— Cytology: the study of cells.

— Cells and cell behaviour, yeah.

— And who looked after you while your mother was working?

— We looked after each other. The Cancer Institute was progressive enough to allow my mother to work around our school hours.

— Was your mother a religious woman? Did she bring you and your sister up in any particular faith?

— Yes. Both my sister and I were confirmed in the Anglican church.

— Our records indicate that your church attendance was very poor after you were confirmed. Is there any particular reason for that?

— My mother told me that once I was confirmed I was old enough to make my own decisions about the church.

— And so you chose only to go to church for christenings, weddings, and funerals.

— Look, I don't see the point in all this. I really don't. You already seem to know the answers to all the questions you're asking. So what's the fucking point?

— There are some things we just don't know about you.

— Like what?

— We can't tell you that.

— Y'know, if you'd only just ask me the things you don't know, and not the things you do know, then we'd be out of here a lot quicker, right?

Two weeks after my twelfth birthday I returned to school only to find that the greatest teacher in the world, Mr. Gingell, had retired over the summer. This seemed a little odd given the fact that Mr. Gingell was nowhere near as old as Mr. Cavanaugh, who, though nowhere near as popular, retired amid great fanfare two years before. So naturally there was some confusion amongst the student body. And many of them, including myself, began to ask questions. Why didn't Mr. Gingell get a big retirement assembly like the one Mr. Cavanaugh got? Or even more to the point: Why didn't Mr. Gingell tell us he was retiring? Doesn't he care about us? Later that day Mrs. Smart, the neighbourhood know-it-all, forced her busybody self through our front door and dropped the bomb on my mom: Mr. Gingell had been fired. It happened last year, on the last day of classes. He'd been caught with his hands down Timmy Waite's pants.

This was disturbing news. Very strange. Most of us had known Timmy and Mr. Gingell since kindergarten. And it was because of them that most of us could grasp concepts like *special education* and pronounce words like *cerebral palsy*. And it was always Mr. Gingell who would charge onto the playground and defend Tim's right to be there, that he should somehow be integrated into our games, and that if we just used our imaginations, we could all have fun together. So it seemed perfectly logical, after overhearing Mrs. Smart tell my mother that Mr. Gingell allegedly tried to defend himself by arguing he was only helping Timmy go to the bathroom, that Mr. Gingell wasn't doing anything out of the ordinary. But it wasn't until the last part of Mrs. Smart's story, after having reduced my mother into a series of *oh dears* and *oh nos*, that my brain blew up, that I was forever imprinted with the voice of Mrs. Smart: "I mean — good God! — who helps somebody go to the bathroom in a broom closet anyway?"

I had real mixed feelings about this. All summer long I had been looking forward to being in Mr. Gingell's Grade Seven class. He was easily the best teacher, certainly the most popular. Everybody loved his sense of humour, his enthusiasm. And his field trips — whether they be to the aquarium, the planetarium, the bird sanctuary — whatever — they were legendary. But now he was a child molester. And as much as that troubled me, I still wished he was teaching Grade Seven and that I was front-and-centre in his class.

I remember telling all this to Mrs. Leggie, the district guidance counsellor. It was during our first week back and she had been assigned to meet with us individually to talk about our future plans. I think I spent my entire fifteen-minute visit rambling on about how I felt about Mr. Gingell and what had happened to him. And all I remember, the whole time, was her leaning back in her squeaky chair, tapping her pencil against her teeth, looking at me like I was out of my mind, like I was somehow complicit in all this.

3.2

— This Mr. Gingell — did he ever touch you?

— No.

— Did he ever touch any of your friends?

— No.

— So Timmy Waite — he wasn't your friend?

— Mr. Gingell never touched Timmy Waite.

3.3

During our second week back, Mr. Stinson, the vice-principal, who had been doing a thoroughly boring job of sitting in for the fallen Mr. Gingell, introduced us to our new teacher, Ms. Singleton. I had never met anyone like Ms. Singleton before. First off, she was black. This in a school where almost everyone — except for the grocers' kids, who were Chinese, and an Indian kid named Josh Peter, who kept getting kicked out for smoking — was white. And we're talking a large elementary school here of about five hundred kids, in a city that was closing in on a million. Second of all, Ms. Singleton was probably ten years younger than Miss Conroyd, the librarian, who had once confessed to Margie Stott, the relentless snoop, that at age thirty-four she was at least fifteen years younger than Miss Turpin, the next youngest teacher. But third of all — and this is what really fucked a lot of people up — Ms. Singleton had a very proper English accent — even more refined, Mrs. Smart would joke, than her husband, the good Judge Smart from Oxford.

Mr. Stinson's introduction was typical Stinson — awkward, overblown, an uncomfortable dance of hand-wringing, exaggeration, and dry coughs. I think he even farted at one point. But as bad as it was, it did tell us a lot about our new teacher. For during Mr. Stinson's intro all eyes were on Ms. Singleton, where we could see for ourselves, from the subtle tics and winces, that Mr. Stinson was clearly describing someone who was not only unfamiliar to himself but to Ms. Singleton as well.

Obviously Stinson knew little of Ms. Singleton, as he knew little of everything else, which only served to endear us to our new teacher ever more. So we laughed. And Ms. Singleton laughed, too. And then Mr. Stinson, thinking he was on the verge of becoming the next Bob Newhart, he started laughing as well. Which was where Ms. Singleton so gracefully stepped in, smiling a thank you to Stinson, before telling us that although she didn't really come all this way over from England just to teach our particular class, she hoped, nevertheless, that in the end she would be willing to say that if she hadn't, she most certainly would have wished that she had. Or something like that. But whatever. She thanked Mr. Stinson once again — this time with words — before reminding him, by way of telling us, that she preferred to be addressed as *Ms.* and not *Miss*, once again directing her smile at Stinson, pressing it against him until he clued in that it was time to leave us be.

Once Stinson closed the door — to a smatter of polite applause — our new teacher took a small step forward and told us, in a very soft voice, still smiling, that she knew how much we loved Mr. Gingell, and that if we worked really really hard this semester, she would tell us as much about what had happened to him as she possibly could; but that we had to work really really hard, and that we had to all really really trust each other, because what we were going to do in her class wasn't going to be easy, and that it was going to be far different from what last year's Grade Sevens did — indeed, far different from what anyone else in the city was going to be doing in Grade Seven that year. Then, stepping back, she reached over to her desk and pulled from her handbag something that looked totally space age, like a weapon from a movie set somewhere in the future. We were totally impressed.

3.4

— A movie camera!

— That's right. It was a Nikon. A super-8. And it was so much more sophisticated than my mom's hand-wind that I didn't even know what it was when she pulled it out.

— She was going to teach you how to make movies?

— Yes. And we made them.

3.5

Where I went to elementary school, most of your three Rs were taught by your home-room teacher. And Grade Seven was the year where all those classes were taught in the morning — with Art, Music, and Physical Education in the afternoon. Right away Ms. Singleton proposed that we combine the three-R classes into one big class, and that we use movie-making as our theme. As soon as Ms. Singleton suggested this, Margie Stott's hand shot up: "How, then, Miss Singleton, do you suppose we could do Arithmetic when we're talking about movies?" Ms. Singleton smiled. "Simple," she replied. "If I send you out with three super-8 film cartridges, with each cartridge consisting of three minutes and forty-seven seconds of film, and a camera that shoots twenty-four frames per second, and then I ask you to edit that film down using a three-to-one ratio, how many frames will your movie have?" Silence. "Oh," said Margie. And everybody laughed.

Well, it was like that. Ms. Singleton was amazing. Probably the most amazing teacher I've ever had. For the next two months she had us immersed in film. We'd be watching about two hours of film a day. All kinds of film, too. Not just feature-length stuff. Short films, advertisements, training films, experimental films — you name it. I know all this sounds pretty slack, but I don't think I've ever worked so hard in my life. Every film required a report, a written assignment that was sometimes as big as five hundred words. Plus there were all these terms we had to use. Film-talk stuff, like *montage* and *vérité*. And the amazing thing was we were all so into it. Because Ms. Singleton made it all really fun, super interesting. But it wasn't easy.

One time, while we were watching *The Battleship Potemkin*, the door swings open and in walks Stinson. It was at the exact same moment where the baby carriage starts rolling down the Odessa steps. At the end of the sequence, a flustered Stinson asks Ms. Singleton if he could have a word. "But we're right in the middle of a proletarian uprising," replied Ms. Singleton. We all laughed, applauding. "Besides, I think I belong with the people right now," she added, matter-of-factly, to even more applause. Stinson hit the lights, blinding the class. The people winced. Somebody booed. "The revolution's over, Miss Singleton. In my office!" And as if to underline his point, the asshole storms over to the projector and actually kicks the plug right out of the goddamn wall.

Ms. Singleton wasn't gone long. Long enough, though, for the class to have a few laughs replaying Stinson's kick at the wall socket, which took him two tries. When Ms. Singleton returned it was clear that she was now as pissed off as Stinson. I could tell because she did the same thing with her lower lip as my mom. "Mr. Stinson has told me to inform you that as of tomorrow we will be returning to the regular curriculum; so, beginning at nine o'clock, we will be starting with Arithmetic, to be followed by Science, to be followed by Social Studies, to be followed by Language Arts," Ms. Singleton said, gesturing towards the open door, where Stinson hovered, nodding, moving slowly backwards into the darkened hall. Groans. "However, class," Ms. Singleton brightened, shutting the door, "tomorrow will also mark the beginning of our own films. So I want you all to start thinking about what we've been watching lately, what you like and don't like in a film. And when you go to sleep tonight I want you to dream about the kind of film you'd like to make. It can be about anything you want. And that's your assignment for Language Arts tomorrow: one hundred words that best describe your film."

After school I walked home with Bobby Galt. He was in the other Grade Seven class. Mr. Tomlinson's class. Bobby was going on about how great Mr. Tomlinson was, how easy he was, how he never checked anybody's homework assignments, and how he never asked any of the students any questions, so you could just sit there and read a comic book all day or doodle in your notebook if you wanted and he wouldn't care. I told him about what we'd been doing in Ms. Singleton's class, and then he told me he'd heard all about it from his

21

mom, who was also friends with Mrs. Smart, who knew Miss Murray, the school secretary, and how everybody thought it was a bad idea, watching films all day, and that he agreed it was stupid, and that none of us would learn anything, and that none of us would know how to factor when we went into high school next year. I told him most of us already learned how to factor and that he was full of shit, and that what happened to Ms. Singleton that day was really cruel and super unfair. But Bobby didn't care. In fact, he'd already heard that Ms. Singleton wasn't going to be coming back after the Christmas holidays.

3.6

— But you made movies. We know that you made movies.

— Yes.

— And Ms. Singleton — did she come back after Christmas?

3.7

First of all, I think it's important to consider where Ms. Singleton was coming from. Remember, this was 1974. And a lot of what was happening in the sixties, all those radical ideas about what education was, well, all that stuff was only just beginning to get tried out in the public schools. Except nobody had tried anything different yet in our school — until Ms. Singleton came along.

Penny Singleton and her husband John McKinney were both graduates of the University of Edinburgh in Scotland. Although both were in education, they did a lot of work in film. John's Ph.D. thesis was on film education, while Penny's was on the effects of television on the primary grades. Upon graduation John was offered a position at the University of British Columbia, a couple of miles down the road from our school. Unfortunately, no such offer was forthcoming for Penny Singleton, so she made plans to forward her résumé to the Vancouver School Board in the hope of getting work as a substitute teacher.

Penny and John arrived in Vancouver the Sunday before Labour Day. After spending all of Monday scrambling to find accommodations, they took up temporary residence in the Sylvia

Hotel, in Vancouver's West End, until something came up in October. On Tuesday Penny phoned the school board to see if they had received her résumé. They had. And they were very anxious to interview her. Indeed, one of the school board secretaries remarked it was a rare sight for a municipal school board to receive a résumé for substitute teaching by a Ph.D. in Education — and from the British Isles, no less. Anyway, they told her they wanted to meet with her right away, but that they were in a terrible disarray because of the city's teacher shortage, and that all hiring personnel were either out in the classroom filling in or off recruiting in the other provinces. Then they asked Penny if she would be interested in full-time work, and if she was, would she be available for a phone interview at lunchtime the following day. Penny told them that she was and that she would be, but then had to ask when lunchtime was in Canada.

The next day, just before lunchtime, Penny got a call from Stinson. He told her that her résumé had been forwarded to our elementary, and that it was very impressive. Some years later, Penny told me that Stinson's interview was really more like a monologue: twenty minutes of complete incoherence, occasionally marked by loud discharges about how important Grade Seven was given the fact that "the children's bodies would be changing before your very eyes," or how thankful he was that Ms. Singleton was British at a time when Canada was "being overrun by immigrants." Before Penny could say a word, Stinson finished his jag by telling her that he would recommend to our principal, Mr. Dickson, that she be hired. And with that, he thanked Penny, and promptly hung up the phone. Five minutes later the phone rang again. Once again it was Stinson. But this time he was phoning on behalf of Mr. Dickson to congratulate her on being offered the job. Penny, incredulous, accepted.

3.8

— You seem to know quite a bit about Ms. Singleton.

— Yes. I did.

3.9

Penny was to start as soon as she'd settled, which turned out to be the middle of the second week. When she arrived in the office that morning, she was told by Miss Murray that all janitorial positions had been filled and that any further inquiries should be directed to the school board office. Penny told Miss Murray that she was delighted to hear that all janitorial positions were filled because she couldn't imagine teaching in a cold, dirty school all year. Miss Murray looked puzzled. Penny quickly introduced herself, then asked Miss Murray if she wouldn't mind showing her where her mail drawer was. A stunned Miss Murray pointed to a large cabinet beside a door marked MR. DICKSON: PRINCIPAL. Penny opened the drawer marked MISS SINGLETON. She pulled out a thick manila folder. The folder contained three copies of her contract. Penny sped-read the top copy, then began signing her name next to Mr. Dickson's when Mr. Dickson's door suddenly swung open, trapping Penny in the triangle created by the cabinet, the wall, and Mr. Dickson's door. "Miss Murray," Dickson began, unaware of the trapped Penny, "could you please phone the school board and tell them we are still two janitors short. I'd like to get this matter resolved as quickly as possible."

Through the rippled glass of Dickson's door, Penny could see Miss Murray motioning towards her, in an effort to get Mr. Dickson's attention. Penny recognized the motions as pointing, but to her they looked as though Miss Murray were throwing something, for the motions were repeated, calisthenic, almost hysterical. Penny giggled at this. A startled Mr. Dickson swung the door around. Penny stepped out of the alcove, peeled off the bottom two copies of her contract, and handed them back to Mr. Dickson, who took them. "I'm Penny Singleton," she said. "You must be Mr. Dickson." Dickson stood stupid, the contracts bowing flaccid in his hands. "Oh. Oh yes, of course! Nice to ... uh ... meet you, Miss Penny," he said, via Miss Murray.

3.10

— How do you know all this?

— Word got around. Some of it I heard from Penny herself.

— Can you distinguish between what "got around" and what Penny told you?

— Not any more — no.

Ms. Singleton — she was amazing. She was the most amazing teacher I've ever had now that I think about it. And how she got to be our teacher was just as amazing. But even more amazing was how she was able to put up with all that bullshit from the people she was supposed to be working with. I mean, isn't the toughest part of a teacher's job supposed to be motivating students? I reckon most of the staff were jealous of her. After all, this smart young woman — who happens to be black — comes out of nowhere to a school where most of the staff are white and in their fifties, only to have her entire class eating out of the palm of her hand. And that English accent! She was way more British than any of the others could have ever hoped to be. And yet they treated her as if she was beneath them, as if she was almost fraudulent. In some ways I wish I was old enough then to appreciate the conflict, 'cause as kids it really didn't seem like that big a deal. I mean, it wasn't that different from what we were seeing on TV at the time.

3.12

Movies, though. We made movies. Our assignment for the remainder of the year was to make two movies. The first movie we were to make ourselves. The second movie we were to make as a class. But it wasn't like, Here, take this camera and a roll of film and come back when you're done. It was way different, much tougher, more like the way films are really made. Because Ms. Singleton stressed from the beginning that it was just as important to know how films get made as it was to learn how to make them. So, on the day after *The Battleship Potemkin* incident, at the start of Language Arts, Ms. Singleton announced that as of now we would be referring to our class not as Language Arts but as the Language Arts Film Collective. We were all declared independent filmmakers, and Ms. Singleton would be relinquishing her role of Language Arts teacher in favour of the more appropriate title, executive producer in charge of funding and distribution — or EP, for short.

The first thing we had to do was write, on a single piece of paper, a story — or what is known in the biz as a synopsis. Once all the synopses were completed, we were to put our names in a box. When our name came up we were to go to the front of the collective and "pitch" our story to the EP.

This process went on for a couple of weeks. A number of interesting things happened.

Jeffery Smith-Gurney wrote a fantastic synopsis that involved Martians solving our pollution problem. His film was to have culminated in a giant space battle, where half the universe was blown to smithereens. It was a rousing story, delivered with a verve never before seen in the shy Smith-Gurney, although at five pages it was hardly a synopsis any more. The EP agreed. However, in the spirit of encouragement, she recommended that we all vote in its favour, that perhaps one day, in the not-so-distant future, Jeffery's story would finally be told. But in the meantime, though, she suggested that Jeffery might want to pare things down a little, and only blow up those parts of the universe that were "wholly resistant to pollution solutions."

When Nettie Smart pitched her story everybody looked puzzled. It didn't seem to jive at all, sounding more like a poem than a story. "What Nettie seems to be doing," said the EP, "is a little more experimental, a little less narrative than what we find in a traditional story." Nettie said her favourite film ever was *2001: A Space Odyssey*, and that she'd seen it three times. She said she wanted to make a film just like that one. The EP agreed that *2001* was an excellent film, but that it might be a little too ambitious for our purposes. The EP went on to say that Stanley Kubrick made a half-dozen films before making *2001*, and that he had to prove he could make a traditional narrative film before taking on something less conventional — much like Picasso, who began as a realist before venturing into abstraction. But Nettie, sensing that she was going to lose the EP's endorsement, appealed to the collective directly. Her poem passed by a slim margin. The EP seemed pleased with the results. "Let us see, then, what democracy produces," she said, before reaching back in the box.

The weirdest moment, though, came after Alistar Chen's presentation. The EP said she couldn't remember ever seeing a movie about a day in the life of a family-run grocery store. Alistar beamed. He gave Ms. Singleton a quick proud nod. Moreover, the EP continued, getting up from her desk, she could count on one hand the number of times she'd seen a Chinese person speak in a Hollywood movie. But then she asked, very carefully, if Alistar thought anyone would want to go see a movie about a Chinese family-run grocery store. Alistar looked down at his shoes and said no. The EP then asked why she should endorse a film that nobody would want to see, a film that in real life would surely lose money. Alistar continued to stare at his shoes. The room was very quiet all of a sudden. I remember the hum of the overhead fluorescents. A moment passed. It was starting to get very uncomfortable. "Alistar," said the EP, moving slowly towards the budding documentarian, "the reason why I've never seen anything about a day in the life of a Chinese family-run grocery store is because the people who decide what goes into our theatres and onto our TVs aren't interested in showing such a film." The EP took Alistar under her arm. Many of us squirmed when Alistar hid his face in her waist and began to cry. The EP held Alistar for a moment. Then she turned to address the collective. "They aren't interested in showing such a film because they don't think anybody's interested. They think that way because they think everybody who goes to the movies is white and middle class; that every father drives off to work each morning; that every mother stays home and bakes pies; and that all the children run home from school each day to watch reruns of 'Leave It to Beaver,'" said the EP, before recommending to the collective that we vote overwhelmingly in favour of *A Day in the Life of C.B.S. Chen Grocery.*

3.13

— Were you one of the squirmers?

— At first. But Nettie leaned over and told me it was just a trick. She said Ms. Singleton was only trying to make us listen. She said she'd seen something like this once before on "Gunsmoke."

3.14

As it turned out, my name came up last. This was a good thing, because I was certainly benefiting from all the discussion. Every day that week I'd come home from school and touch up my synopsis. I'd spend hours on it, going over every little detail. But the funny thing was, the version I pitched to the EP wasn't that different from the one I'd originally submitted. I'd kinda worked full circle. I told all this to Bobby and he asked me if I felt stupid for wasting all that time on something that ended up the same as when I'd started. And

I told him no, that I didn't, that I actually felt like I'd worked through something, that I'd learned something, that my instincts were right, and that I now had proof that they were right. But he didn't believe me. He still thought I was stupid.

The name of my story was *Joe and Barbie*. It was about a married couple who fought all the time and were struck by tragedy. When the time came for me to pitch it, I really took my time because I knew it was good and I wanted the collective to hang on every word. Which they did. The EP seemed to like it, too. She said that I demonstrated a good understanding of the format, and that I had all the elements necessary for a good film: story, plot, character, conflict. But that's all she said. After a very favourable vote from the collective, the EP suggested we spend our last few minutes on the next stage of development — the treatment.

I think the EP sensed my disappointment. For during those few remaining minutes, she seemed to glance my way a little more than usual. I remember feeling extremely disappointed — no, crushed — that we didn't spend more time talking about my synopsis, like we did with some of the others. There was all this stuff I wanted to get to, stuff that wouldn't fit on the one page. I guess I wanted her to ask me about my dialogue, which I had already started to write. Or what techniques I was going to use to tell my story in film. And I guess I wanted some kind of feedback from the collective, too, because I'd spent a lot of time anticipating the kinds of questions they might ask. And I had some real snappy answers prepared, some real funny stuff I wanted to lay on them. But whatever. I was well on my way to self-pity when the EP turned to me and began explaining how some of us may have already gotten a jump on this treatment stage, how some of us more advanced types might even have some dialogue on hand. Then she said my name in that questioning way, and I just sorta shrugged and said yeah, like it was no big deal or nothing.

Amazing. I felt amazing. The lunch buzzer went and I floated out of my desk all set to tear into my sandwich when the EP asked me if we could have a quick word together. Even better! "Sure," I shrugged, then shuffled my way towards the front of the class. "This story of yours," the EP began, waiting for the room to empty, "what inspired you to write it?" I didn't quite know what to say. "What do you mean?" I replied. The EP looked concerned. She started again. "Do you mind me asking you a personal question?" she said, attaching my name very carefully at the end. I shrugged another *sure*. The EP asked me how things were going at home and I told her they were going fine. Then she asked if my parents were getting along okay. I told her they got along a lot better since my mom kicked my dad out, but that they still didn't really get along, no. And then she asked me if I felt safe. And I told her yes. "Can you show me some more of your story after we meet again on Monday?" she asked. All of a sudden I didn't feel so amazing any more. But I said yes anyway.

3.15

The Synopsis for *Joe and Barbie*

> *Joe and Barbie* is about an unhappily married couple named Joe and Barbie. His name is Joe. Her name is Barbie. The story begins with Joe and Barbie having a fight. Barbie is telling Joe that he's never home any more, that he's always off fighting in some war. Joe responds by telling Barbie that she's never around either, that she's always off somewhere in her camper. Joe also wants to know who this Ken guy is. Barbie says that Ken's just an old friend from high school. Ken walks in during the fight and Joe beats him up. Barbie then kicks Joe out. Barbie nurses Ken back to health. Once Ken is well again, Barbie takes him for a ride in her camper. They bump into Joe at a café. He's sitting with Barbie's younger sister, Skipper. Barbie gets really mad at Skipper. Skipper runs out of the café crying. Ken chases after her. Skipper gets into Barbie's camper, starts it up (because she has the extra set of keys), and drives off. Ken then jumps on the back of the camper and begins calling out Skipper's name. When Skipper finally hears Ken she looks around to see where the voice is coming from. At that moment she loses control of the camper and smashes into a tree. The last thing you see is Joe and Barbie crying at Skipper's funeral.

3.16

— How close was the *Joe and Barbie* story to your own?

— Not very.

— But it was similar enough, right?

— Similar enough to what was on TV at the time.

— What happened when you and Ms. Singleton met after class the following Monday?

— Nothing. We just talked about TV shows.

— Weren't you two going to talk about your project?

— Well, that's what I thought was going to happen. I mean, we'd spent a few minutes on it, and I told her how I was gonna make the film and this and that. But then it was just more interesting to talk about other stuff — anything that came to mind, really. She was just like that.

3.17

Monday's meeting of the Language Arts Film Collective was devoted entirely to the concept of treatment. The EP told us a treatment is similar to a synopsis except fleshier. Our assignment, then, was to expand our synopsis to include an outline of the events that made up our story. We were also asked to include some dialogue and some character sketches as well. In the case of certain projects, like Nettie's, where there wasn't a narrative or a story or characters or speaking parts, the EP was asking for something called "detailed descriptions."

The EP wanted to see some technical notations, too. With that, she gave us some handout sheets full of definitions and guidelines she said would ease us into the screenplay stage. Margie's hand went up almost immediately: "How long is this treatment supposed to be?" The EP told us no more than three pages, double-spaced. "And how are we supposed to write this when we don't even know how to use a camera yet?" Smith-Gurney added. "We're going to start that tomorrow," said the EP, "when Mr. McKinney comes in for his demonstration."

None of us knew that Ms. Singleton and Mr. McKinney were married. Had we known, I think we would have been so distracted by how different they were from each other that we might not have learned anything at all about how to use a camera. For instance: Ms. Singleton was tall and slim, well groomed, spoke proper English, and was black; Mr. McKinney, on the other hand, was short and stubby, unkempt, a pasty redhead who spoke Mancunian English. But despite their immediate differences, they both had one thing in common: together, they were very, very funny — with Ms. Singleton playing the straight man to Mr. McKinney's buffoon.

"Sowallofsyawannabefilmmakahs, then, eh?" said McKinney, bursting into the classroom, unannounced, dragging a cardboard box behind him. "Sowallofsyawannabethenext Stanley Kewwwbrick? Ormaybethenext Raw-but Alt-mun?" he jived. Without missing a beat, the EP reminded the collective that Raw-but Altmun made *A Cold Day in the Park* in Vancouver a few years back, before telling Mr. McKinney that if he ever charged into her classroom like that again, she would toss him out on his ear. Mr. McKinney then crouched into something mock-humble and crept towards an empty desk, apologizing profusely. With her left foot, and without looking, the EP gently pushed Mr. McKinney's cardboard box aside and finished defining the term "insert." When she officially turned our attention towards Mr. McKinney, he had taken up the empty desk, his hands clasped together, his face a confusion of fear and earnestness.

The EP's introduction was as funny as it was solemn. She introduced Mr. McKinney entirely in the past tense, like a minister would at a funeral. "And so, after graduating from the University of Edinburgh, the penniless McKinney finally found peace in the Americas, where his body now rests in the desk before you," she intoned, her head bowed, pointing to the collapsed McKinney. "Ladies and gentlemen of the Church of the Language Arts Film Collective, I would like you to join me now in a moment of silence while the ghost of the Great McKinney takes my position at the head of the collective and demonstrates the power and glory of the Nikon super-8 film camera," she said, as the collective, agiggle with anticipation, applauded the rising McKinney.

For the next half-hour McKinney had us in stitches. He was so funny — completely over the top. He began his demonstration in mime, pretending to take the camera from the box, then pretending to load the film, then pretending to film the class. He stalked the room, directing us to stand up or put our arms around the person next to us or lie down or whatever he felt was germane to his demonstration. During this time the EP would narrate, in a voice so deadpan, so sarcastic, you could butter toast with it. Then McKinney went back to the front of the class and did the whole thing over again for real. But this time, it was the EP who'd be getting all the laughs. She'd demo the camera like an airline stewardess would an oxygen mask. Everything was a gag. But we were learning. When it finally came time to explain the f-stop function, Mr. McKinney stopped halfway through and asked the EP what the *f* stood for. To which the EP replied: "For finish. You've gone on long enough."

By the time the lunch buzzer went, we were all in love with Mr. McKinney. Not only that, we also knew how to load and unload a camera. We also knew about f-stops, filters, lighting, sound, zoom and telescopic lenses. We could hardly wait to make our films now, which was great because most of us were getting a little bored with the writing stage. By the end of the week, everybody had their treatments finished and handed in. The EP said she would be reading them over the weekend, and that if everything went well, we could actually begin filming before the Christmas holidays.

3.18

Treatment: Scene Breakdown for *Joe and Barbie*

1. EXT. CAMPGROUND. DAY

WIDE ANGLE

Joe (early 30s) is sitting on a rock. He is dressed in his camouflage uniform and black knee-high boots. He has brown lifelike hair and beard. Beside him is an AK-47 rifle. Behind him is a camper. A woman's voice (late 20s) calls out to Joe, but he doesn't answer.

Barbie is sitting at the wheel of her camper. She honks the horn. She calls out for Joe again. Her voice sounds tired. Joe answers this time. He says, "All right, all right." His voice sounds angry. Barbie starts the camper.

2. INT. CAMPER. DAY

Joe and Barbie are sitting in the front seat. They are arguing. Barbie is complaining that Joe is never home any more. Joe says there's a war going on. Barbie asks which one is he fighting in this week. Joe says Vietnam. Barbie says she thought Joe quit Vietnam. Joe says he went back there 'cause they gave him a raise. Barbie gets mad at Joe for not telling her, but Joe changes the subject. He asks Barbie where she goes in her camper every day. Barbie says, "Out." Joe asks Barbie to describe "out." Barbie says, "To work, then sometimes the mall." Joe asks Barbie who Ken is. Barbie says Ken is someone from work, but that she knew him from high school, too.

3. EXT. OUTDOOR CAFÉ. DAY

Joe and Barbie are sitting at a table with an umbrella over it. They continue their fight. Joe says he doesn't want Barbie to talk to Ken any more. Barbie says she can't stop talking to Ken because she has to work with him. Joe tells her to quit her job then. Joe says he doesn't like her working in the first place.

A man (late 20s) walks up to the table. He is wearing a tan panatella jacket and white pants. His shoes are white also. He says hi to Barbie. Barbie says, "Hi, Ken." Joe gets up and starts punching Ken. Barbie screams for Joe to stop.

4. INT. BEDROOM

CLOSE ON KEN

Ken is lying in a bed. His whole head is covered in gauze.

ZOOM OUT

Barbie is sitting beside him. She puts a cup to his
mouth. He drinks from it. Through the gauze. She asks
Ken if he is feeling better. Ken says yes. She tells Ken
that it's over with Joe. Ken says, "Good." Barbie bends
over and kisses the gauze.

5. INT. CAMPER. DAY

Ken and Barbie are in the front seat of the camper.
They are wearing their bathing suits. They are singing
"Sweet City Woman" by the Stampeders. The gauze is
off Ken's face.

6. EXT. OUTDOOR CAFÉ. DAY

Joe and another woman (late teens) are sitting at a table
with an umbrella over it. (Actually, she is sitting on
Joe's lap.) She is wearing Joe's denim navy shirt —
nothing else. She says she's always had a crush on Joe.
Joe says he's noticed. The girl says she's never done it
before. Joe says, "Oh?"

Ken and Barbie walk up to the table. Barbie says,
"Skipper, how could you?" Joe tells Barbie to mind her
own bloody business. Ken tells Joe that it is her business,
that Skipper's Barbie's sister. Skipper gets upset and runs
off. Ken chases after Skipper. We track her as she gets
into Barbie's camper. The engine starts. Ken jumps on
the back of the camper. The camper drives off. We hear
the voices of Joe and Barbie shouting for them to stop.

7. EXT. FOREST. DAY

Skipper is driving (dangerously) down a gravel road. She is crying. She keeps saying, "What have I done? What have I done?" We hear the faint voice of Ken calling. He is still clinging to the back of the camper. He calls out loudly. Skipper hears him this time. She turns around. The camper smashes into a tree.

8. EXT. CEMETERY. DAY

CLOSE ON JOE AND BARBIE

They look sad.

ZOOM OUT

Two coffins are being lowered into the ground. Joe and Barbie are dressed in black. Barbie is wearing a black dress. Joe has on his scuba suit because those are the only black clothes I have for him. They begin to cry. They keep saying, "What have we done? What have we done?"

3.19

As it turned out, things didn't go very well. The EP was so upset with our treatments that she began to question whether or not we should just ditch the whole project and go back to the Grade Seven reader. It was heavy. For the entire period the EP went around the room and told each of us exactly what she thought of our projects. Jeffery Smith-Gurney's *Space Polluters* was "indulgent and gratuitous." The EP even went so far as to suggest that Jeffery didn't really care about our pollution problem at all, that *Space Polluters* was nothing more than a "vehicle for violence." Nettie's *Mud and Flowers* didn't fare much better. "A bunch of lilies in a mud puddle with the Guess Who singing 'These Eyes' does not a good film make. The song and the image, at the very least, Nettie, have to suggest some kind of a relationship. You might get away with this once you've become a famous filmmaker, but, in the meantime, as I've already told you, you have to prove to your audience that you have an understanding of the medium before you can start playing with its conventions," said the EP, before turning to Margie Stott's "cheerless documentary" on her spoon collection, then Alistar Chen's "boring advertisement" for his family's grocery store, and, finally, my "pitiful male fantasy."

We were devastated. And even though we could only understand half of what the EP was saying, we knew that what we didn't understand could only be that much worse. There were tears, of course. Margie Stott was crying, which wasn't that out of the ordinary given her high-strung nature. And Nettie, who was always happy-go-lucky, she was crying a bit, too. Even the guys were a bit pink. But I think that's what the EP wanted. She wanted to scare us. She wanted us to go home that night and rethink our stories. When she handed us back our treatments, all of them were covered in red ink and all of them had extra pages attached, with suggestions about how we could make our treatments into good screenplays. "Now I know I'm being hard on you," she began, "but I'm only being hard on you because, as the EP, that's my job. Every one of you has produced work that has great potential. And rather than have you rewrite these treatments, I'm giving you the opportunity to incorporate these suggestions into your screenplays. It's a huge leap of faith, so please don't disappoint me again." When the EP finished, Margie's hand went up. "So what you're saying is — " she began. "Is that I expect you to consider my suggestions," said the EP, wearily, as if all of us had somehow turned into Stinsons.

3.20

— It sounds like the EP was losing faith in the collective.

— Well, yeah, I suppose she was. I mean, part of it was a ploy. But she really was pissed about our treatments.

— Did you feel hurt by this?

— Of course. We all did. We loved her. We wanted to please her.

— Because she was amazing?

— Because we wanted her to love us as much as we loved her.

After school that day I walked home with Nettie. We were still upset with the way the EP ripped apart our treatments, but agreed that it was only a tactic, a way to get us to work harder. Then Nettie said a funny thing. She said, "What do you think Mr. Gingell would have done in a situation like this?" I didn't know. But I told her I still spent a lot of time thinking about him, not so much about what he did to Timmy Waite but what he would have been like to have as a Grade Seven teacher. Nettie agreed. In fact, we both agreed that as much as we loved Ms. Singleton, we still loved Mr. Gingell. Then Nettie told me she thought about Mr. Gingell every day: whether he might be in jail or maybe even teaching in another school. I told her that it was doubtful that he would be teaching in another school given what had happened last summer. Then she said, "I think if Mr. Gingell didn't like our treatments, he would have made us do them over again." And I agreed. He was pretty straight that way. "I can't ever remember Mr. Gingell getting mad at us the way Ms. Singleton does," she said. "I think if Mr. Gingell got mad at us, he might stay mad at us, kinda like the way Mr. Stinson is with Ms. Singleton." And I agreed. He was pretty consistent that way. But how did she know Stinson was still mad at Ms. Singleton? So I asked her. Nettie told me she'd overheard her mom and Miss Murray talking. Oh. We walked on in silence before Nettie turned to me and said, "We should do everything we can to make our screenplays excellent — for Mr. Gingell!" And I agreed. Wherever he may be.

3.22

— Describe Nettie.

— What for? You know what she looks like.

— Just describe her. Think of it like a character sketch for one of your treatments.

— Well, for her whole life Nettie's always been about average height, light brown hair, high cheekbones. Not slim, but not robust either. I would never describe her as good-looking, but she had a fluid way of doing things that made her attractive. I'd notice people picking up on that fact. Plus she was funny, insightful, kind — a good friend. And what else? I don't know. Her mind always seemed to work differently from what was going on around her, though she was pretty good at math. She was always reading, too. Brainiac stuff. She had some health problems — a bad heart. A murmur, I think. She caught cold a lot. A bit of a loner, too, I guess.

— Like you?

— Sure.

— What about Bobby?

— Galt's most prominent feature was his jaw. It jutted. When I first met him, back in kindergarten, I assumed it was a birth defect. Only later did I realize it was an affectation, a point of departure for whatever bullshit he was laying on you at the time. So yeah, you could say that everything about Galt centred around that jaw of his. The guy had an opinion on everything — of which he was always misinformed. But he was convincing, I'll give him that. He fooled a lot of people. I'd seen bigger, tougher, smarter guys back off because of what they thought was going on behind that jaw. And what else? He had blond hair, blue eyes, little pink hands with bitten-down nails. He also had large perfect teeth. And when he smiled, it looked like the grill of an oncoming truck. He was a good athlete, but he didn't play well without the ball. "Useless when not in possession," I believe, was the scouting report on Robert "Redford" Galt. It bothered me that people thought of him as my best friend.

— Margie Stott?

— The best way to describe Margie Stott would be to direct whoever gives a shit to the comics section of the newspaper. She's Margaret in *Dennis the Menace*.

— Jeffery Smith-Gurney?

— A long, thin piece of stick. A praying-mantis kind of guy: no shoulders, an overbite, tiny eyes that were always so far ahead of what was going on he seemed out of it.

— Alistar Chen?

— He always seemed to be wearing a mauve cardigan. His whole family wore cardigans. He was from one of Vancouver's oldest families. His great-great-grandfather was the third Chinese person ever to come to Vancouver, after it became known as Vancouver. He was quiet like Smith-Gurney, but for different reasons. What I mean by that is he wasn't necessarily shy — just nobody bothered with him. He followed sports and sometimes we talked hockey. I think a lot of people felt uncomfortable being seen with him. Mostly the Bobby Galts of the world.

— Do you think a lot about Nettie Smart?

— You know I do.

— Do you know where she is right now?

— No.

— Do you want to know?

— Of course I do.

— Then continue.

3.23

It was a week before Christmas holidays and the very day the EP was going to hand us back our screenplays. Needless to say, we were all very nervous. By now the EP had quite a reputation for unpredictability. What game might she play this time? We were about to find out. The EP clapped her hands and announced that Social Studies was over and that it was now time for our next meeting of the collective. The room was abuzz with speculation.

Right off the bat the EP told us our screenplays were all acceptable and that at the end of class she'd be assigning each of us a camera and three rolls of film. What? No lecture? No freak-out? All eyes were on Margie. "Aren't you going to tell us why our screenplays are acceptable, Miss Singleton?" Margie asked, her hand cowering at chin level. The EP told us that everything she had to say was laid out in the margins.

The remainder of our meeting time was spent on the topic of the shooting script. The EP told us that the shooting of a film — particularly one that involves numerous outdoor locations — can be a logistical nightmare. "Remember: Anything that can go wrong, will go wrong," she kept repeating, as if we were doomed already. The EP then held up a small, mimeographed booklet which she'd obviously made herself. She said that each of us would be given one of these booklets, and that they would prove helpful when it came time to plan our shoot. She went on to explain that each page in the first section was divided into categories like "scene number," "date," "time," and "place." We were then instructed to divide our screenplay up in a manner that would make the most sense when it came time to shoot film. For example, all outdoor scenes could be done one day, while all indoor scenes could be done another day; rather than jump back and forth trying to shoot the film in the order it appears in the screenplay. The next section of the booklet was called "Pick-up Shots." This section was for things that we might forget to film or for things we had to postpone because of stuff like bad weather. The final section was a single page called "Telephone Numbers," with each of our names followed by more blank space. And it was here that the EP seemed to place the most emphasis, suggesting that the first thing we should do is exchange numbers with each other because, at some point, we were going to need each other's help, that filmmaking requires many energies working together, and that — just like life itself — it was something one couldn't go alone.

Once the lunch buzzer sounded, the EP called us all up to the front to collect our screenplays, cameras, film, and booklets. This seemed odd because the EP always handed stuff out to us individually. In fact, she seemed to really enjoy handing stuff out to us that way, and often took those moments to speak with us one-to-one, in a casual sort of way that made us feel connected. And I know she knew this. So it seemed strange to me that she no longer wanted to acknowledge the connection.

I guess that's why I lagged behind. I wanted to ask her if she was okay. I mean, she had been a bit lacklustre the past couple of days, not her usual active self. I reached over to grab the last package off the table, then snuck a look her way. She was crying. Not balling-her-head-off crying, but she was definitely choking up. "Is everything okay at home, Ms. Singleton?" And she chuckled at that. "Yes, everything's okay at home," she said, reaching into her purse for a Kleenex. "I suppose I'm just a little homesick for England, for my family," she added, her face brave. Then I asked her where she was going to be spending Christmas, and she told me that she would be staying in town with her husband and that they would be celebrating Christmas at the Sylvia Hotel. A hotel? That's not a good place to spend Christmas. "It's been very difficult finding a place here," she said, dabbing at her eyes.

3.24

— So you spent the weekend shooting your film?

— Yeah. It was a lot of fun. And it was pretty easy, too. The EP had us really well prepped.

— The EP had suggested the collective exchange phone numbers, yet nobody bothered to do so. Why?

— I don't know. But I know she was pissed that we didn't. I think part of what this project was all about was getting people working together. I didn't exchange numbers because I wasn't going to need any people in my movie. My actors were all dolls. And besides, nobody asked me for my number either.

3.25

Monday morning. Perfect attendance. Everybody at their desks, smiling, our film and cameras in neat shapes before us. The EP made her way around the room, collecting. You could almost see her thinking. "No problems, horror stories ...?" she inquired. We shook our collective heads. "Did any of you *not* finish?" she added. More head-shakes. Then the EP began singling people out, asking each of us about our respective shoots.

Jeffery Smith-Gurney told us how he shot *Space Polluters* entirely in his bedroom, using an animation technique called pixilation. "Naturally you used a tripod," said the EP. "Well, not really," said Smith-Gurney, who went on to describe what is known as an animation stand, a device used in stop-motion photography, whereby the camera is mounted overtop the field of action. "So you had some help, then?" smiled the EP, looking around the room. "Well, no — not really. I mean — my father kept trying to butt in, so I had to keep getting my mom to find him something else to do," he replied uneasily, perhaps embarrassed that by mentioning his parents he had to involve his family after all. The EP seemed to wilt a bit.

"Nettie?" said the EP desperately. "And how did things work out with *Mud and Flowers?*" "Great," said Nettie, "I think the images I got turned out even better than I thought they would. And I changed the soundtrack, too. I substituted 'These Eyes' with a song from my parents' record collection: 'The White Cliffs of Dover' by Vera Lynn. My parents thought it was a bad idea, though. They thought it was too, um, iron-ick. Is that the word? *Iron-ick?*" The EP nodded, then repronounced the word *ironic*, explaining to us its meaning.

I was getting the feeling that the EP was a little disappointed with our successes. She seemed disheartened when Margie Stott described how the sun shone perfectly off her spoon collection, and positively crushed when Alistar Chen explained how his shoot went off without a hitch, how he seemed to have chosen the busiest day to make his documentary, and how he even managed to film an argument between his father and a customer. "And not one of you called on each other for help?" said the EP, almost pleading. "Not one of you needed each other to act or hold the camera or assist with the lighting? Nobody had any problems with the f-stop?" The collective was quiet. "Well, I did have a bit of a problem with the auto-zoom," I lied. The EP's face lit up. "And?" she said, raising her eyebrows, begging me to continue. "So I just did all my adjustments manually," I replied, as if disappointed with my ingenuity. "Oh. Well. Good for you, then," the EP smiled, weakly, as she set the box of spent film down on her desk.

The remainder of the week was dedicated to editing. Ms. Singleton brought in some editing blocks and a big box of blacked-out super-8 film rushes for us to practise on. Despite the fact that super-8 film stock is temperamental stuff and tends to break easily, we all managed to get the hang of editing pretty quick. We tried telling this to the EP, that we were bored with editing, and that maybe we could watch some more film or something, but she insisted we keep at it, that we can never get enough practice "on the block." Naturally, being kids, our minds began to wander. That's when Nettie came over to my desk and told me she wanted to show me something after school, that maybe we should walk home together. I said sure.

As we turned the corner down Cypress, Nettie pulled a rush from her pocket. "Look what I've got," she said. "Oh God, that's the last thing I want to see — more film," I said. "No. Not just *more film*. Here, look — I figured out a way to get the black stuff off," she said, spitting on the emulsion, rubbing it between her fingers. "It's just felt pen." I took the rush and held it up to the sun. "I can't make out what's happening here," I told her. "No, not like that. Here — use this," she said, handing me a pocket-size magnifying glass. It was Ms. Singleton and Mr. McKinney standing in front of an old grey building. "It's London, England. Piccadilly Circus! I was standing in exactly the same spot with my mom last summer," said Nettie. I had no reason to doubt her, because I knew the Smarts were always going back and forth to Britain. "And look at this one," Nettie giggled. "In this one they're necking." They were, too!

Nettie and I spent the last half-hour of light sitting on the train tracks, going through the rushes. She had a pocketful. She had tons of rushes. And she kept licking her finger, rubbing the stuff off until her tongue and thumb had gone totally black. I kept telling her that the ink was probably toxic, that she should just use snow instead; but she kept at it, ignoring me, intent on uncovering what was underneath. Then she stopped. "Oh, wow. Look at this one," she said, handing me a nine-frame rush. I held the strip up to the sun and focused in with the magnifying glass. The first eight frames looked hot and exotic: there were palm trees, some turquoise water, and a couple in the foreground — Ms. Singleton and Mr. McKinney. And Ms. Singleton was pregnant! The last frame, however, was nowhere near as sunny. The inside of a church and a very small coffin. The death of a child. "Do you think this is the funeral of Ms. Singleton and Mr. McKinney's baby?" I said. Nettie nodded, her expression glum. "Sad," I said. "Yeah," said Nettie.

We got up to leave once we lost the light. By the time we got to Nettie's house, we'd decided that if Ms. Singleton and Mr. McKinney weren't married, then they were most definitely a couple. We'd also decided that they travelled a lot, liked outdoor music festivals, and trusted others to operate their camera. Then, just as I was about to leave, just as I was beginning to feel both the satisfaction and the shame that comes with peering into somebody's private life, Nettie reminded me of something — something Ms. Singleton talked about just before we'd watched *The Battleship Potemkin*.

"You know, we only saw that part of the Russian Revolution that Eisenstein wanted us to see. And I think you could apply that to Ms. Singleton and Mr. McKinney as well because we only saw that part of their lives that they chose to film. And the fact that they chose to throw that part of their lives away when they blacked out those rushes, well, that should tell us something, right? So I guess what I'm saying is we shouldn't feel so bad for looking into their lives like that. We should only feel bad if we draw conclusions from it. If we judge them," she said.

I think I understood what Nettie was saying that day. And I gave it a lot of thought before telling her that it would be impossible for us to not draw conclusions, that if their baby died, then it wouldn't be unfair of us to think that they felt grief. But then Nettie reminded me that we were still not absolutely sure the baby in the coffin was their baby. And I agreed. It was a good point. It was good enough to make me feel a little less certain, but no less shameful.

The streetlights flicked on as I came up the back steps. I could see my mother in the kitchen, still in her lab coat, stirring what looked like a curry. Just beyond that I could see my sister down the hall, in the den, jumping up and down on the gold sofa. The "Dark Shadows" theme was blaring and I could hear it all the way outside. "Could you please turn that thing down!" my mother called out. "Face down?" my sister shouted back as I opened the door, laughing, charmed for the first time by my literal sister.

"Oh, you're home. I was beginning to worry. It's almost five, you know" — kiss, kiss — "Where've you been?" my mother said, returning to the curry. I told her I was with Nettie. "You two going steady?" The volume dropped. "No, we were just talking about our Language Arts projects," I replied, my whisper defensive. "Okay, okay," my mom said, backing off. I opened the fridge, withdrew a carrot, bit off the tip, then asked her if what she just did was called "drawing a conclusion." "You mean because I asked if you two were going steady?" I told her that's what I meant, yeah. Then she said, "No, that's not drawing a conclusion. That's just ... *teasing*." Oh. Was my mom trying to be funny? Then I asked her if what she just did was funny. "Nope. Just evasive," she said with a wink. I hated when she did stuff like that. Then I asked her what "evasive" meant, and she laughed. "Go look it up."

I went into the den, where my sister handed me the dictionary. "You shouldn't eavesdrop, you know," I told her, as I proceeded to flip through the *E*'s. When I found it I laughed — not that the meaning was funny or anything. Then my mother came into the room and we laughed together. Then my sister laughed at us for laughing. And for a brief second we were all laughing.

3.26

— Tell us about the house you lived in?

— Our house was part of an oddly shaped block where each side was a different length. The length of our end of the block, which ran along Thirty-third Avenue, was the smallest, enough for three houses. We were in the middle. To the west was a huge Dutch Colonial where the Billingtons lived — white with green shutters. They had something to do with lumber, the Billingtons. To the east was another huge house, a black-and-white Tudor. I remember there was a sign above the door, written in gold calligraphy, that read LEWELLYN, even though the people living there were named O'Farrell. They were really old; I think they'd been there since Confederation. But whatever. Our house was a lot smaller than the others. I had no idea what "style" it was either, whether it had a name like our neighbours'. And I didn't much care until Mrs. Smart pointed out to me that the other two houses were representative of their respective styles. So I went to the library to look it up, but couldn't find anything. It was just a white stucco house with red steps and cedars all around it. I think it was built during the Depression.

— And your mother?

— My mother grew up in Kerrisdale, a mercantile neighbourhood just west of Shaughnessy. Kerrisdale was originally conceived of as a place where all the classes could live together. That's what Ms. Singleton told us once when Margie asked her what a utopia was. And Kerrisdale was where a lot of people in Shaughnessy shopped because Shaughnessy was just a place to dwell, if you know what I mean. But whatever. My mother was about average height. She wore her hair streaked and was partial to the colour blue. Her eyes were green, like mine. Whenever I was in Kerrisdale, people would always stop and ask me if I was my mother's son. They'd always smile when I said I was. I took that to mean they liked her; but later on I realized that there are people in this world who are happy just to be right about something. I think my mother was known as a "bad girl" when she was younger. But only because her father died when she was ten. What I mean by that is there was an assumption back then that the absence of a man around the house meant trouble. And I think my mother was always fighting that. She didn't want people thinking that about us. I think that's why she went on all those dates. She was a good mom.

3.27

The following day was our final meeting of the Language Arts Film Collective before the Christmas holidays. Because we had a school assembly that morning, and because the last day was always a half-day, all our class times were reduced. This only left the collective with a few minutes — just enough time for the EP to tell us what good students we were and how we all worked really hard and how proud she was of each and every one of us. To great applause, the EP then told us that our films had been sent to Kodak for developing and that we should be getting them back around the first week of February.

Just before dismissing us, the EP asked us if there were any questions. Margie Stott: "Will you be coming back in January?" Ms. Singleton was taken aback. "Well, as far as I know, Margie. Unless, of course, you know otherwise," replied the EP, her head at the inquisitive tilt. Margie shrugged her shoulders. Silence. The hum of the overhead lights. There was a tension in the room reminiscent of the Alistar Chen synopsis pitch. It was as if we were all frozen, staring at a picture of ourselves staring at a picture of ourselves frozen.

Not a good note to break on. "Okay, then," said the EP, after a single handclap, a clap just dismissive enough to bring us back to the matter at hand. "Happy holidays." As we struggled with our coats, the EP reminded us that Christmas was a time of sharing and that it was not about who got the most presents — blah blah blah — before once again wishing all of us a happy holiday, and that all of us — with the exception of Nettie and myself — were excused.

Nettie and I looked at each other. We were in shit and we knew it. And we knew it had something to do with the film rushes.

It seemed to take ages for the classroom to empty. And Margie Stott, never one to miss an opportunity, took a particulary long time, wrapping and rewrapping that tartan scarf of hers before finally being ushered out by the EP so she, too, could take her time futzing about the room, torturing us with one of those silences that's always such a big part of getting in shit. "I was gathering up the practice film yesterday when I noticed that roughly one-third of the rushes were missing," said the EP, her back to us as she began to erase, in long vertical strokes, the huge purple HAPPY HOLIDAYS she'd written on the blackboard. "I don't suppose either of you would happen to know what became of it, would you?"

Nettie was in shock. It was obvious she'd never been in trouble before. So this was totally new to her. But I was in shock, too. Not because I'd never been in shit but because I was feeling so protective of her. The EP adjusted her strokes to the horizontal plane. I stared into the blackboard's wispy grid, searching for something good to say, something that would, at the very least, get Nettie off the hook. Nettie cleared her throat, as if she, too, was searching. The EP finished with the chalk brush, then picked up the chamois. She began again, this time in tight circular motions. "Well?" she asked, as her chamois scalloped the purple haze. "Uh ... I took it," I lied. "Now why would you do that?" said the EP, her back still to us, her voice labouring under the weight of her circling. "I wanted to practise at home," I lied again. "Weren't you one of the people complaining to me a couple of days back that you were sick of practising?" the EP shot back. "Yes," I said, "but I guess I was lying." The EP threw me a quick look as she folded the chamois, putting it to bed on the chalkboard ledge. Then she dismissed Nettie.

"I don't know whether to punish you for lying or to punish you for theft," she said, back at her desk, looking through a folder.

For a brief second I considered which would be worse — still frightened by the prospect of either. "Maybe I should punish you for both." Then I realized only both would be worse. "What's the punishment for lying?" I asked, only to speed things up. "It's twice as painful as the punishment for theft," said the EP, slipping the folder into her bag. "Then I guess I'll take the punishment for theft," I said. Then the EP said, "But you didn't steal anything. Nettie stole the practice film." I wondered if Nettie had left the building yet. "I know Nettie stole the film because I saw her sneak it into her coat. And I suspect you're complicit in this because right after she pocketed the film she went over to whisper something in your ear," said the EP, leaning back, resting her hands behind her head, stretching. "And I know from the black stuff under her fingernails," she persisted, "that she was looking at the contents of that film." I was terrified. Run, Nettie, run! "And as for you — I suspect that you, too, now know the contents of that film," she said, her voice breaking into unfamiliar territory.

I didn't know what to say any more. I wanted to protect Nettie, but I also wanted to get the hell out of this detention. I had nothing left to confess, other than the fact that I'd lied about stealing the rushes — although stealing, it seemed, was no longer the issue. So: "Okay, I lied about stealing the film. And I apologize for that. And yes, I did see what was on it. And I'm sorry for that, too." There, I said it. Now what? The EP opened her desk drawer, felt around for something, then slammed it shut. Something missing from there as well? The EP rubbed her eyes. Again, the hum of the overhead lights. Finally: "Okay, so you no longer qualify for theft. It's just lying now." And the EP's punishment for lying? "Fortunately for you I'm too tired to devise an adequate penance right now," she sighed, leaning forward on her elbows. "But in the meantime, I think an honest description of what you saw on the film will suffice." She was right. This was gonna be painful. I couldn't think of a worse punishment than having to describe to somebody a part of their life that they so obviously chose to forget.

I described to her the locations: the palm trees, the white sands, the turquoise water. I described the music festival: the musicians in their brightly coloured outfits — the greens, golds, and reds — and their strange assortment of instruments, the decorations, people dancing. I described Mr. McKinney: his many hats, his changing facial hair, his tire-soled sandals. And I described Ms. Singleton: her tie-dyed dresses, her big sunglasses, her smiling face. I described everything just as I remembered it. Honestly. Everything except the funeral. And that's all I did. Just described. And at the end of it I thought I did a pretty good job. In fact, I was feeling so confident about my descriptive abilities I felt empowered enough to change the topic altogether. So I asked the EP why she blacked out all that film in the first place, because the images were so beautifully shot, and that even though she might not want those images around right now, she may change her mind later, that maybe her children might one day want to see them, too.

I don't think Ms. Singleton took too kindly to my sudden interest in her life. "I find your questions a little patronizing, given the seriousness of your crimes," she said curtly, reaching for her purse. "Perhaps we should add invasion of privacy to your list of offences." Now I felt nauseous, confused — no longer merely condemned. For something larger was looming. And when she asked me to come up to the front of the room — that she wanted to show me something — I was reeling.

Ms. Singleton opened her purse and took from it a small wallet. From the wallet she withdrew a tiny photograph. "This is my family," she said, handing it over. "This is who I'll be spending Christmas with." It was a picture of her and Mr. McKinney — and a baby. I stared at the photo far longer than I needed to, clutching it tightly with both hands, as if it was the steadiest thing in the world. Because it was the only thing in the world that could keep me from looking at her. Because I knew she was crying and I needed time to think about what to do, what to say, once I handed it back. And when I did, I said it. This is exactly what I said: "But your baby — isn't your baby dead?" And Ms. Singelton nodded. And then she smiled, wiping the tears away with her thumb. "Yes, I know," she said, replacing the photo, thanking me for finally owning up to what I did, for finally telling the truth.

3.28

— That was an amazing piece of bullshit. You really had us going there.

— Thank you.

— Looking through our records, roughly half of what you've told us can be corroborated. But many of your thoughts seem really inconsistent with what we have on file. It seems you've presented a much different version of yourself in certain instances —

— Which?

— Nice try.

— Hey — it's all I can do! I mean —

— But in other instances there remain certain ambiguities —

— Look, it was a really confusing time in my life. My mother saying one thing, my teacher something else.

— Yes, but we know you knew better. You learned something from all this.

— Of course. It all comes down to property.

— Penny Singleton gave you something.

— She certainly did.

— A lesson?

— More like an insight.

4.1

Bobby Galt was right. Ms. Singleton wasn't coming back after Christmas. She was fired in the school parking lot on the last day of classes. By Mr. Dickson. I didn't see it though. But apparently Margie Stott did.

Margie told us that Ms. Singleton did not take the news well at all. She told us how Ms. Singleton laid into Mr. Dickson real hard, and how Mr. Dickson — whom Margie kept referring to as "too polite a man" — kept backing up and backing up until he was just about to hit his heels against the curb when Ms. Singleton reached out to steady him, which startled Dickson so much he fell anyway. Right into a laurel bush. Margie said they were both so rattled by what happened that "they froze like robots." Then they lunged towards each other, apologizing. Then Ms. Singleton started to cry. That's when Mr. Dickson regained his composure and helped Ms. Singleton to her car.

But Bobby had a different version. Bobby said that Ms. Singleton "went ape shit" and pushed Mr. Dickson into the laurel after Mr. Dickson called her a nigger. Only he didn't call her a nigger, according to Bobby. Instead, Bobby said, Mr. Dickson called her a "niggler," and that he — Bobby — was willing to "testify in a court of law" that Ms. Singleton is a liar if she tells anybody that Mr. Dickson called her a nigger.

Nettie called Bobby a knob when he told us this at lunch. She accused Bobby of making the whole thing up, because he was nowhere near the school parking lot when all this was supposed to have happened; that, in fact, she saw him after school that same day, booting a soccer ball across the south field; and that there would be no testifying in a court of law because none of this would ever go to trial. And besides, all this didn't make Ms. Singleton a liar because none of it happened in the first place. Then Nettie pushed Bobby into a quince.

The school board version came from Stinson. Stinson told us that Ms. Singleton wasn't coming back for health reasons, and that he would be filling in for the remainder of the year. A fill-in for a substitute. I couldn't believe it. The class was stunned. Much more so, I reckoned, than when we first heard the news of Mr. Gingell way back in September. "Although it's nothing serious," Stinson began, his voice thinning over the din, "it *is* enough to keep Miss Singleton from teaching." Margie Stott's hand. "Does this mean that Miss Singleton has the same illness as Mr. Gingell?" Stinson smiled. "No, my dear — I'm afraid it's a bit more serious than that."

4.2

— Three different versions of one event! Which one did you believe?

— None of them, of course.

51

— So what did happen to Ms. Singleton?

4.3

About a month later Nettie showed up at my door and asked me to guess who she saw at the Safeway. Mr. Gingell? Nope. Then she told me: Ms. Singleton and Mr. McKinney. "No way," I said. "Oh yes," said Nettie.

Apparently Ms. Singleton had been real friendly to Nettie and told her that she and John had just bought a house in Kitsilano. But the good news was our films were back from Kodak. Then she gave Nettie their phone number and told her to tell the rest of the class that we could continue the Language Arts Film Collective at their new house, and that there was no reason why we couldn't just because it didn't have anything to do with school. Great, I told her. I'm game. But when Nettie went around to the other students the reaction was pretty much the opposite. Nobody could understand why we would want to continue with a project that didn't count for grades — especially Margie Stott, who had taken it upon herself to run a counter-campaign based on the current paranoia attending strangers' houses. Only Alistar Chen seemed interested, but he couldn't commit because he had to work at the store when he wasn't involved with school stuff.

So it was just me and Nettie. Which turned out to be fine, because I don't know if I could stand any more of Margie Stott's suckhole behaviours. I mean, it had gotten to the point where her and Stinson were carrying on like a couple of newlyweds or something. It was all so *Ryan's Daughter*. Totally gross. But whatever. Every Saturday Nettie and I would tell our mothers we were going over to Kerrisdale to watch soccer, although what we were really doing was going up to the tracks where we'd meet John McKinney. Then McKinney'd drive us to his place so we could work on our films with Penny. And this went on for quite some time.

4.4

— Why didn't you tell your mothers?

— We were afraid they'd say no.

— Why would they have said no?

— I don't know. I guess Nettie's mom might've said no. It was Nettie's idea that we keep it a secret. She had to keep all sorts of secrets from her mom.

4.5

It was a blast hanging out with John and Penny. Just like that day Penny brought John to class. A real team, those two. Always joking around. Just like me and Nettie.

But it wasn't just the joking around that made them great. No, it was the way they treated us, like we were adults, you know, just like them. They seemed really interested in what we thought about things and they urged us to talk at length about stuff that neither one of us were ever encouraged to talk about at home. And they were the same with us. That is, we could ask them just about anything and they would tell us as much as we wanted to know.

Now I admit, in the beginning, it was a bit much. Usually I'd back off at a certain point. But Nettie was such a prober. One time, when Nettie was asking them about birth control, I felt myself blush up. I kept wanting to cover my ears. A very strange sensation. I told John and Penny about this and they said it was a natural reaction, that hearing things we weren't comfortable with sometimes brings about impulses that manifest in equally unusual responses. But that it was okay. It was nothing to be ashamed of. It was all part of society's conditioning process. The key was to explore those feelings, break them down, try to isolate exactly what it was that makes us not want to know. Or something like that. At any rate, I'd always feel better after hearing what they had to say. And after a while I could listen comfortably to all of Nettie's questions. And it made answering John's and Penny's questions just that much easier.

We told them everything. I can't remember all the stuff we talked about, but a lot of it had to do with school — the other students, teachers, what we were supposed to be reading, writing. We also told them a lot about our home lives as well. Our relationships with our parents. My younger sister, Nettie's older brother. How sometimes we fought with them. How one time Nettie's brother punched her for snooping in his room. And we talked a lot about sex, too. That's how the topic of Mr. Gingell came up.

It was the third or fourth Saturday after we'd started at John and Penny's, and Nettie and I were just finishing up our edits. During lunch — John had made a shepherd's pie — Penny ran some double-eight footage of a trip they'd taken to Greece. Penny was right in the middle of telling us about Attic vase painting when Nettie interrupted and turned the subject to Mr. Gingell and Timmy Waite. It was a super-heavy moment: because John and Penny did not tolerate interruptions. That was probably the only hard rule they had. And they were quite strict about this. In fact, it was the only time they ever got mad at us. But this time Penny turned off the projector and listened. John came out of the kitchen and leaned against the door. He seemed just as intent on what Nettie had to say as Penny. Once Nettie said what she had to say, Penny looked over at John. And John — who would often make jokes over silences such as these — just shrugged it back to Penny.

Penny took a breath. Then she told us why Mr. Gingell was fired, just as she said she would that first day in class. She told us the "official" reason.

Penny told us that Mr. Gingell was fired because he wasn't following curriculum. It was as simple as that. And that's basically all she said, because she quickly switched back into questioning mode. She seemed intent on finding out exactly what Nettie and I knew about these allegations that Mr. Gingell was a child molester. She made us tell her everything. And I mean everything — every little bit of gossip, every little speculation, opinion, consequence — you name it. So we did. And when it was all over we asked her why. "Because I don't want the same thing happening to me," she said. "But nobody's going to accuse you of child molestation," I said, incredulous that a woman could be accused of such a thing. "Why not?" said John. For a moment I didn't know what to say. But John and Penny were patient. For patience was one of the many lessons those two taught us during our education in their house. "I just didn't think women did such things," I said finally. "Only when they never happen in the first place," said Nettie, in a tone reminiscent of the one she used on Bobby the day she pushed him into the quince.

— And you believed Ms. Singleton? That Mr. Gingell was fired for not following curriculum?

— Why wouldn't I?

— What evidence did she have? How do you know she wasn't just making it all up?

— I don't know. Faith, I guess.

— And why do you think Penny was fired? Did she give you a reason?

— No. We just assumed it was for the same reason Mr. Gingell was fired. For not following curriculum. But, looking back, I think it all came down to the colour of her skin.

4.7

John and Penny told us to keep the Mr. Gingell story a secret. They told us that as much as we wanted to tell people what really happened to Mr. Gingell, as much as we wanted to set the record straight, we would ultimately hurt ourselves if we got caught up in what John and Penny kept referring to as "these kinds of politics," and that if we did get caught up in "these kinds of politics," then we'd for sure get kicked out of school. I was fine with this. I could see the logic in it. But Nettie really needed coaxing. It took her a long time to calm down. And when she did, it was time to go.

Nettie said nothing the whole ride back. She just sat there, arms crossed, staring out the window. I think this was making John and Penny nervous because they were trying a little too hard to appeal to those things that usually made Nettie laugh. In fact, it was a bit pathetic. Me, I didn't think it was that big a deal. I mean, what was the problem with us knowing the "official" reason Mr. Gingell was kicked out? Especially when it *wasn't* for child molestation! And didn't Penny once promise the entire class — on Day One of her teaching career! — that she was going to help us find out what had happened to Mr. Gingell anyway? So what had happened to change all that? Now I was confused. But whatever. John and Penny were panicked. I think they were concerned Nettie might tell her dad, maybe urge him to get involved. I know how much Nettie cared about Mr. Gingell and certain kinds of justice.

Usually when John dropped us off he would just pull over and leave the motor running. But this time he put the car in park and shut off the engine. He turned around. "Now, Nettie, you have to promise us that you won't tell anyone about what Penny told you." Nettie ignored him. She didn't budge from the window. "You know it's really important that we keep this between the four of us, Nettie," said Penny. "If word gets out, a lot of innocent people — including yourselves — could get hurt." Nettie shrugged: "Well, what about Mr. Gingell? Everybody thinks he's a child molester. I think we have a responsibility to do something about that, don't you? I think we have to do everything we can to clear his name, *don't you?*" John and Penny looked at each other, then they looked at me. They looked scared, helpless. I think they wanted me to help them out. But I was beginning to see Nettie's point. Plus I had my own questions: How is it that Penny — who was at one time so willing to tell us what had happened to Mr. Gingell — had suddenly changed her mind? Was she worried that a scandal might affect her future employment? Is that what she meant by "these kinds of politics"? Questions, questions, questions. I didn't know where to start. In the meantime, I thought the best thing for me to do would be to keep my mouth shut. Maybe I'd take it up with them later, when I had a better idea of what the fuck was going on.

4.8

— Do you think Mr. Gingell was fired because he was a homosexual?

— Probably.

4.9

It took ages before Nettie gave her word that she would keep Mr. Gingell's story a secret. But it didn't come easy. Nettie was a tough negotiator. She made Penny promise that she would help us get in touch with Mr. Gingell. But not only that, she also made Penny promise that she would one day help erase Mr. Gingell's tarnished reputation. I could tell Penny was reluctant to agree, even though she was very relieved to finally get Nettie's word. I'll never forget the moment we waved them goodbye: John leaning over the wheel like he'd just taken a bullet; Penny in the passenger seat like she'd been dead for a week.

4.10

— So did Penny keep up her end of the —

— Just a sec — this is important.

4.11

The railroad tracks ran through the west side of the city in pretty much a straight line. There were exceptions, of course. One of which was the half-mile length of track that ran through our neighbour-hood, just north of the school, a winding S shape that curved along a bluff overlooking a lane, a row of rooftops, then the northwest portion of Vancouver proper. The first major bend was where the blackberry bushes were at their thickest, fifty yards west of the Cypress crossing where we said our hellos and goodbyes to John McKinney.

We were just about to cross when Nettie motioned for me to stop. "Look!" she said. "Isn't that Billington's car?" Indeed. About a hundred yards down the tracks, idling in the lane, was Billington's white Rolls-Royce. And climbing up from the lane, carrying a white plastic Safeway bag, was my next-door neighbour — Billington. "Hide," said Nettie, and the two of us ducked into a ditch. Nettie poked her head up and gave the play-by-play: "I see the toupee ... the tweed coat, the tan slacks ... he's looking right, he's looking left ... he's taking a couple more steps ... he's stepping over the tracks ... he's looking around again ... he's swinging the bag once, twice ... he's let go! Billington has let go of the bag! It's in the air, folks. It's falling into the blackberries. He's looking around again. He's turning back. He's going down. Down, down, down. He's gone! Mr. Billington has left the building!" Nettie settled back into her crouch and giggled. "What's so funny?" I asked. "Mr. Billington's a space polluter," she said, cracking up. I got the reference. It was total Smith-Gurney. We shared the joke: Billington as alien. His door opened and shut. Billington drove slowly past, oblivious. Nettie turned to me: "Race you there. On three. One, two — "

Nettie cheated, of course. Bolting on the two-count. Why she did stuff like that I'll never know. She was, by a mile, the fastest Grade Seven I'd ever met. Boy or girl. "So what's the deal?" I shouted after her. "It's only a bag of fuckin' garbage." But Nettie didn't answer. She ran hard till she hit the bushes, where she picked up a switch and hacked her way into the tangle.

I was really impressed with the way she went at it. The way her face tightened up, intensified, her little mouth puckering above her dimpled chin, her strokes swift and decisive. Obviously she had the same determination for bushwhacking as she had for baseball. But of course this was different. There was no field, no arena — no ball or bat. I began to feel a tingle for Nettie, a new sensation. As she whipped her way deeper into the brambles I began to notice, with each swipe, the jiggle of her ass — and that she had an ass — and how that ass was a little bigger, proportionately, than the rest of her body, and how she might one day have an ass like her mother's, which looked good in a swimsuit the one time I saw it. Nettie called out, but I didn't catch what she said. Too caught up in this new sensation.

Nettie turned around. Her face was flush, her stick limp and ragged. "Why are you just standing there, shit-for-brains? I told you to get a bigger stick. We can't reach this thing until we get *a bigger stick*," she said, tossing the spent switch. I shook off my thoughts and went looking. When I returned — I'd found an old car antenna — Nettie was on her stomach, beating up the bush, just her feet sticking out. "I've almost got it," she said, her voice strained and creepy. I was about to ask her for a second time why we were going through all this effort over a lousy bag of garbage, when I realized it didn't matter. Sometimes it was enough just to be around Nettie's enthusiasm. She always had a way of making something out of nothing. But she answered me anyway, as if she knew what I was thinking. "If ... it was only ... a bag of garbage ... why wouldn't he ... throw it ... into ... his ... own ... garbage can?" I stretched the rusty antenna as far as it would go and crawled in beside her, passing up the tool.

Nettie was on fire. Her body writhing, jerking, banging

against me. At one point she had herself turned in such a way that her ass was rubbing right up against my groin. But the weird thing was, it had nothing to do with retrieving the bag. In fact, from where I could see, Nettie wasn't making a very good attempt at snagging the bag at all. She certainly had enough antenna to work with. Yet her arm was only half-extended. I looked down at Nettie's ass as it arched into me — grinding, clenching, retracting, withdrawing. Then she'd roll over on her stomach, take a few swipes, then repeat the whole thing all over again. Clearly, a pattern was emerging.

I decided to test my theory. The next time Nettie rolled over onto her stomach I'd inch away and wait.

Nettie's back arched, thrusting her butt into nothing. She froze for a moment. I was about to laugh, but then she startled me with a loud grunt, lunging forward, announcing for the tenth time that she'd "just about got it." I looked up. I could see through the brambles that the antenna was now waving back and forth over Billington's bag. Nettie let out another grunt, before pushing her ass towards me, into me, hard this time, winding me. She did a quick little shimmy, then lunged forth for yet another lame swipe.

I could feel the heat off her body now. And this heat seemed infectious, shooting down my thighs and up under my arms, a gyro, convincing me of my own heat. Again, she ground into me. But this time when she clenched her ass I could feel the squeeze of each cheek tighten. I'm not clear on what happened next. I think it went like this: I reached between her legs, dug in my heels, and slid her deeper into the bush, where she rolled onto her stomach, pushed her pelvis into the ground, and thrust the antenna forward. At that point, of course, she could've grabbed the bag with her teeth.

Nettie collapsed, exhausted. She was breathing quite heavily now. And this worried me. Her mother was always going on about how Nettie was born with a heart murmur, and how she disapproved of Nettie's tomboy behaviours if only, she claimed, because of the strain sports put on her delicate condition. Not that you'd notice, given what she was capable of on the playing field. But still. "Nettie? Are you okay?" A breathy yes. I reached up and pulled the bag between us. I was about to open it, then changed my mind.

What did I want with a bag of garbage? Besides, it wasn't about that anyway. So I touched her shoulder instead. "Do you wanna look inside?" I said. Nettie shivered. I watched her ass slowly unclench, relax over the mud we'd made. We lay there for quite some time, just breathing.

It was getting dark. The cold air was making plastic of our sweat. Nettie rolled over and started fiddling with the twist-tie. I'd kinda forgotten about the garbage. "Whoa!" she said, quickly closing the bag. "What?" She opened the bag again. I tried to peek in, but she closed it tight against her chest. Her face a strange shape, that place where horror meets delight. "C'mon, lemme see," I said, gesturing towards the bag. But Nettie rolled away. She kept going, "Whoa, whoa, whoa — this is unreal." I reached over and grabbed her shoulder, pulling her towards me, playfully. Nettie rolled over on her own strength, opening the bag in my face. I was speechless.

4.11a

The Contents of Mr. Billington's Garbage

 1 copy of *Garçons de Maroc* magazine

 1 copy of *Big Boys on Bikes Illustrated*

 1 copy of *Hot Rod Hunks* magazine

 1 8-oz. jar of Vaseline petroleum jelly

 1 roll of Scott toilet paper

 3 or 4 crumpled tissues, shit-streaked with flecks of blood

 1 condom wrapper

 1 condom, fully extended over ...

 1 Schneider's beer sausage

— Why is this so important?

— It's important because it's something that happened right after John and Penny dropped us off.

— Yes, but what does it have to do with John and Penny?

— I don't know. I mean, it might make sense later on — but you're just gonna have to trust me. I've already figured out that this line of questioning is, for the most part, not so much to do with what I think is important but why I think it's important. Am I right?

— Continue.

— Not until you tell me what you were going to ask me.

— What if we told you that we weren't going to ask you anything, that we're finished with you?

— Then you'd be lying.

— Well, in that case, we were going to ask you if Nettie ever told anyone about what happened to Mr. Gingell.

— She didn't.

— And did Penny keep up her end of the bargain?

— I don't know. The Gingell affair never came up again. Besides, Nettie had moved onto other causes.

— One more thing.

— Sure.

— Do you think John and Penny had something to hide?

— No. I just think they were worried about us stirring up trouble. They were applying for citizenship, so that might've had something to do with it.

5.1

Nettie and I finished our films the following Saturday. Although John and Penny were really pleased with the results, I must admit I was getting a little bored with the project by then. Nettie, on the other hand, was super-excited — and once again it was Nettie's enthusiasm that brought me back to the moment: the first screening of our brand new films. John made a big bowl of popcorn and Penny closed the drapes. We watched Nettie's film first, since it was what Penny kept referring to as a "lyrical work." John thought it would make more sense to end with a narrative.

After the films were over — we watched them twice — John gave us his critique. He told Nettie he liked her film a lot — even more the second time — especially after Penny suggested we view it without the Vera Lynn. John particulary liked the metric montage sequence in the middle of the film. He thought that the relationship Nettie established between the ninety-six frames of rain falling on the aluminium watering can, intercut with the stillness of the sunlit mud puddle, at forty-eight frames, was an "effective rotation." He also remarked that the reflection of the watering can in the muddy puddle was a "nice opposition." The weak link, however, lay in the flowers. John felt that the flowers, which inexplicably appeared near the end of the film, seemed unnecessary, gratuitous even. He suggested Nettie either rethink that section or just cut the flowers altogether and go with the out-of-focus clouds she used in her intro. Penny added that a looping effect would keep the film open-ended, cyclical. Nettie agreed. The three of them looked at me with such determination that I had no choice but to go along.

The first thing John said to me was that he liked my film a lot more than what was originally scripted. I smiled when he said that, but a second later felt a twinge of hurt. A backhanded compliment? Penny was quick to ask John what he didn't like about the writing. John pursed his lips. "Well, I felt it was a little too TV," he said — to Penny. Nettie agreed. Traitor. I was beginning to feel ganged up on. "But that was the point," I blurted, not quite sure what I meant yet. John raised an eyebrow. "I wanted to make fun of TV. I wanted to do something that would remind people of TV, but then twist it into something unexpected, something you wouldn't see on prime-time." John's eyes lit up. Penny's, too. "You mean by having Joe and Ken run off together?" she said excitedly. Exactly, I guessed. And then Nettie made this face.

After watching *Joe and Barbie* a third time, John and Penny seemed won over to my ad-lib way of thinking. "I must say, I had no idea you put so much thought into this," John said. And Penny agreed. "Yes, now I know why you opened with Joe sitting before a cluster of lilies," she said, before turning back to John, "long a symbol of male homosexuality." I looked to Nettie and smiled, well aware that the misplaced symbolism in her film involved those very same lilies. Nettie was so pissed off. She didn't have to say anything. The raves continued to pour in. "And that scene in the end, where Barbie alludes to Joe's abandoned weapon collection, as if those discarded guns and bazookas were symbols of Joe's violent past, and how violence was just a symptom of Joe's repressed sexuality; and then cutting to the very last scene where Joe and Ken walk into the lavender together — brilliant!" John said, before turning it back to Penny, who liked the fact that "the relationship between Barbie and Skipper was no longer sororal but sexually ambiguous as well," before turning it over to Nettie, who said that we should probably get going soon because soccer ended an hour ago.

We were at the exact same spot on the tracks where Nettie told me to stop the week before when she told me, this time, that I was nothing but a bullshitter. "You didn't intend to do any of what you talked about during the critique, did you?" she said, her head down, kicking a rock against the clang of track. All I could do was shrug. "Then it's not fair," she said, stepping onto the rail, steadying herself. "What's not fair?" I asked, as if it were no biggy. Nettie ignored me in an effort to balance. The silent treatment. "A lot of my shots didn't turn out so I had to improvise," I said. "A lot of the writing came in the edit." Nettie took a couple of shaky steps. "I guess I stumbled onto something," I said, almost ashamed, as Nettie lost her balance and jumped off. "It's interesting, though, isn't it?" she said, remounting. "It's interesting how sometimes we set out to do things one way, but then once they're done they often take on a completely different meaning." I agreed, then reminded Nettie of that day in class when

Penny used the example of *Reefer Madness*, how it was originally intended to be an anti-marijuana film, but how, over the years, it became a cult film frequented by marijuana smokers. "That wasn't the example she used," Nettie said, rebalancing. "That was the example she used for irony." Nettie took three steps on the rail and told me the example Penny used for intent was *Triumph of the Will*.

5.2

— How did you and Nettie discuss the contents of Mr. Billington's garbage?

— I didn't think you were interested in talking about that.

— Why?

— I don't know. I sensed you were trying to get at something and —

— So you changed the topic in order to find out if we would try to get you to go back to it later?

— That's right.

— Just like you're doing right now.

— Right.

— Well, then?

— Well, I suppose I *could* tell you about what we talked about regarding Mr. Billington's garbage. But I don't see the point. We were able to figure out what he was up to just from what was in the bag. And sure, we talked about it. We were curious. We had imaginations. But it didn't change our lives or anything. In fact, it quickly became a segue into something else: Nettie wanted me to come over to her house because she wanted to show me something related to Billington's garbage, something that would really blow my mind. I mean, I could tell you how she made me guess what that might be. I could tell you how she refused to tell me, and how I got bored guessing. I could also tell you about seeing Mr. and Mrs. Billington out walking their poodles after we crawled out of the bush and how Nettie said extra loud how she was glad they replaced the teeter-totters at the park because the old ones made her *bum hurt* and would I like to come over for lunch tomorrow for *beer sausage* sandwiches and — *ouch* — her lips crack if she forgets to put *Vaseline* on them when reading *Garçons de Maroc* in her room overlooking *the lane* and how that was infinitely more interesting than our reactions to a complex bag of garbage. So why don't I just tell you about what happened after that.

— Continue.

5.3

We walked down Cypress from the tracks, turning left at Quilchena Crescent, the street where Nettie lived, just around the corner from me. All of a sudden Nettie bolts towards the Galts' driveway. She saw it first: Bobby and his older cousins, Mitch and Donal, had a pissed-off Timmy Waite up and out of his wheelchair. They were leading him towards the giant bear trap that usually hung from the ceiling of the Galts' garage but which was now spread open in the middle of the lawn. Totally bizarre. I couldn't believe my eyes. To this day a very strong image, much stronger than the contents of Billington's garbage: the three Galts laughing their heads off, barely able to contain themselves, Timmy spazzing out in all directions, and looming six feet away, this rusty trap, it's steel jaws yawning, everyone oblivious to the full-tilt Nettie.

She arrived swinging, corking Donal, the biggest of the three, right on the side of the head, knocking him out. Then she went for Mitch, grabbing his shoulder, swinging him around, ripping the sleeve clean off his Edgar Winter T-shirt. Bobby, meanwhile, took off down the side of the house. He kept screaming, "No way, no way am I gonna hit a girl." Nettie followed. Within seconds you could hear Bobby's laugh, then his plea, his cries of "Uncle, uncle, uncle ..."

5.4

— Stop.

— Why?

— You're lying. This never happened.

— Sure it did. It just didn't happen that day. This was something that happened years before. See, I'm just trying to get a handle on the way you're set up to recall the facts of my life.

— So you can continue your lying ways?

— Naturally.

— And what would be the point of that?

— To protect myself.

— From what?

— From whatever's coming next.

6.1

I awoke to my name, my mother's voice calling up from the kitchen. "It's Nettie!" I shut my eyes and took a deep breath, all set to let go with something just as loud, something about my being asleep. But of course I was too late: the shush of Mom's slippers, the receiver rocking gently on the sideboard, Nettie's mouth pressing on the other end. And as for all that air? My big inhalation? I yawned instead. Then I put on some gaunch and stumbled down to say hi.

That's what it was like when I was a kid. Whenever the phone was for me — and if I was around, and if I wasn't sick or grounded — my mother always made me answer. Never made excuses, never took a message. No help that way at all. And what a piss-off, too! I used to love sleeping in. All those warm thoughts. And to this day I hate waking. I remember calling her on it once. But she played tough: Why should I be your social secretary? Why should I lie for you? I mean, in a way she was right. After all, I was the man of the house now. I had to be responsible. But whatever. Nettie always called early on a Sunday. And my mother was always glad to see me up. She liked Nettie for that reason. My mother always had stuff for me to do after she kicked my dad out.

Nettie wanted me to come over to her place — which was

new, because usually we'd just meet in the park and do something sporty depending on the season. "Well, for what?" I asked her. "Whaddaya wanna do?" There was a pause. Somewhere in the background James Taylor and Carly Simon were singing "Mockingbird."

"I have an idea for a new film," she said. And then she went on to say that she'd done up some storyboards and had written a voice-over and she was really excited about it and she wanted to know what I thought. I reminded her that she'd just finished a film, and that maybe she should take a break before launching into a new one. "Asshole!" she said, sounding more dejected than menacing. Still, I felt menaced enough to tell her that I'd come over in a couple of hours, and that she shouldn't get her hopes up because, to be quite honest, I was sick of anything to do with film. But really, though, I just hated to see Nettie dejected. And I guess I felt a bit guilty, too. I think she was still pissed off over how I wrangled genius out of *Joe and Barbie*. So I guess I owed her.

There were no cars in the Smarts' driveway — which was odd, because usually at least one of her folks was home when I was over. I think that was a rule. Also, I began to sense that what Nettie and I were about to do was wrong, especially since she'd told me to come around the basement way. But whatever. I walked down the back steps and was just about to knock when suddenly the door swings open, sucking me into the rec room. "Good. You're here," said Nettie, grabbing my hand, leading me towards a paper-strewn table. "These are some of the boards I've done up. I'm working with the title *A Bird and a Worm*," she said, carefully arranging the pages in numerical order. I checked out the drawings, most of which consisted of stiffly drawn robins. Only the worms had any life to them. "Well, whaddaya think?" she said, hands on hips, a gesture she'd picked up from her mom. "Well," I began, "it looks like the story of a bird catching a worm." Nettie gave me a hard nod. She was very serious. "Or," I continued, "it could also be the story of a worm being caught by a bird." Nettie smiled. "Exactly," she said. "It's from the worm's point of view."

Nettie sat down at the table and opened a brand new notebook, entitled: NETTIE SMART: FILM IDEAS: MARCH 15, 1975. She pushed a chair towards me, then began flipping, stopping on a page, making a mental note, then flipping back to something else, then flipping forward a couple more. I remarked on how her jagged writing looked like fish hooks, but the comment went unnoticed. "I've written some narration and I want you to help me with it," she said, slowing down on her flipping, then looking up for an answer. I think I made a discouraging face because Nettie responded as if I'd said no. "It'll be really easy if we work on this together," she said, going back to her flipping, before stopping on a neatly printed page. "Here," she said. "This is how I'd like it to start."

> The lowly worm. It crawls through the dirt on a daily basis, tilling the soil for whatever the people are growing. Tomatoes, roses, lilies, trees.
> Up in the cedars the robins chirp. They watch for a wriggle in the people's compost. They watch for the worms that crave the bright light. The robins swoop down and pull the worms from the ground.
> The worms are carried in the beaks of the birds. They are fed to the robins' squeaky children. They die in the darkness of the robins' young tummies.

"That's all I've got so far. What I need is some help on the edit," she said, sliding the notebook over to me.

I reread the text. In my head. I even pretended to read it twice. Because I needed time. I needed to think of something to say. I didn't want to tell her that worms don't crave the sun, and that they're actually digested by adult robins who then regurgitate them back to their chicks. No point in telling her all that. And besides, I sort of knew what Nettie was getting at: narration, this time, as opposed to a wash of images, what Penny would call "the lyrical." "Well, I think the story's fine. Maybe drop a word or two. But other than that, it's fine. Great even!" I said, looking up from the notebook. But Nettie had stopped listening. She was drawing a thought bubble above a "lowly worm." In the bubble she wrote the word *help*.

So was that it? Was that all she wanted to show me? Not likely. I was about to ask her if I could go, but thought otherwise just as quick. I knew better. Something was on her mind. And I knew my leaving would only piss her off. What we needed was a change. Nettie was acting really hyper, super-fidgety, like she needed to burn something off. So I suggested we go to the park and kick field goals.

Nettie scrunched her face, shook her head no. Now she was being a baby. What was her fucking problem? Why was she being so ... *evasive*. That's when I noticed the heat.

"Have you got the thermostat cranked or something?" I said, taking off my sweater. "Nope," said Nettie, shading the underside of her worm. I went over to the window and pulled back the curtains. The driveway lay in wait. "Where're your parents?" I asked her. "Mom's in Seattle shopping and my dad's giving a speech at some lawyer thing," she replied. Oh. "And my brother's with my mom," she added. "He's getting an electric guitar. They're cheaper in the States, y'know." Thank you, Nettie. I did not know that. "Besides," she continued, "he didn't want me watching him rock out in the music store, so" — Nettie's chair creaked; I refocused on the window and caught her reflection, her approach — "so I guess that just leaves the two of us."

I could feel the heat off her body, just like the day before, in the brambles. But this time was different. This time something was going to be acknowledged. I could tell. I brought my arms up to rest on the sill, let my breath smudge the pane. Nettie came to rest beside me, and her breath did the same — but her smudge was huge. "Know what I found in my dad's study?" she said, fingering a bird shape into her section of the vapoured pane. "What?" I said, happy to break the silence. "Some pictures," she said, making a worm shape with her nail. "Oh yeah? Pictures of what?" I said quickly, hoping she'd get to the point. "Pictures that Mr. Billington might like," she replied matter-of-factly, dotting a sight line between the bird's eye and the worm. So that's what this was all about. "Yeah, they were in a folder under some of his court notes," she added. "That seems like a pretty funny place to put them," I said, not knowing what else to say, wondering whether all men that age shared something that I, a boy of twelve, knew nothing about. Nettie smiled. I could feel her staring at me, studying me for some kind of reaction. "I bet your mom would flip out if she found them, huh?" I said, hoping to get her talking again. "Nope. She'd know they were just evidence in some case," she replied, unfazed. I laughed like it was funny or something. Nettie made a strange face, said nothing. I watched the corner of her mouth curl. "So let's go look at them," she said, pushing off from the sill. "Unless, of course, you're chicken."

Judge Smart's study was dark and sinister and smelled like a pipe. I'd never actually been inside before, having only walked past it twice in my life. Once to use the washroom; another time when I helped Nettie and her mom carry up a carpet. Both times the door had been ajar, and all I could make out was the back of the judge's silver head, the emerald-green desk lamp that glowed like a lantern.

Nettie flicked on the lamp, deepening the grain in the woody room. "You've never been inside here before, have you?" she said, knowing full well that I hadn't. "Duh?" I said, just for something to say, just to be cool. Nettie went up on her tiptoes and withdrew a binder from one of the judge's mighty shelves. Her bum flexed as she did this. "We'll start with the white one first," she said, plopping the binder down over the judge's leather blotter.

The binder had a title: CROWN VS. WHITLOCK, STOKES, AND MARSHALL. "This doesn't feel right," I said, frightened by the detail in the provincial court logo. "Aren't you interested in what my dad does for a living?" she said, flipping open the binder to reveal an eight-by-ten glossy of a freckle-faced boy sitting on a tree stump, naked but for a pair of oversized gumboots. "This isn't what he does for living," I said to the boy in the photo. "This is just evidence in a case."

Nettie turned the photo over to reveal another photo. Once again, the freckle-faced boy. But this time he had his legs spread, and crouched before him was a girl, also about our age, looking over her shoulder at the camera. She had big dark eyes and loopy brown curls and her little mouth was smooched towards whoever was taking the picture. Between the thumb and forefinger of the girl's right hand was the boy's penis. She was pulling it towards her, stretching it into something thin, like an elastic band. The boy had a surprised look on his face, like Alfalfa from *Little Rascals*. Nettie turned the photo over. This time the boy was standing sideways, and the girl, who was still crouched before him, still pulling on his penis, had her tongue extended so that it was just touching the underside of the boy's scrotum. Nettie turned the photo over to reveal yet another photo: a close-up of the little girl's mouth stretched over an adult penis. The strain in the little girl's face made me weak. "There's tons like this," Nettie said, fishing for something near the back.

Nettie removed a folder marked STOKES. She opened it over

70

the binder. The first photo was of a playground. Children on swings, climbing monkey bars, teeter-totters. "These belong to a different series, so we can't get them mixed up," she said, turning the photo over. The next photo was a medium-shot of three boys, maybe fourteen or fifteen, sitting in front of a tree. The boys were all wearing cut-offs and one of them, a bigger boy with a faint moustache, was shirtless. "I like his chest," Nettie said of the young moustache. I agreed. I wanted pecs like that, too. Nettie flipped through the pile and withdrew two photos. The first photo showed the three boys in what looked like an old garage. They were huddled together, naked, mugging for the camera, each one holding rulers up to the other's erections. "Do you think his penis is bigger because he's older?" Nettie said, pointing to the young moustache. I didn't know, so I just said maybe. "Well, is your penis that big yet?" she said. "I don't know. It's hard to say," I said, suprised by her candour. Nettie nodded. "Yes," she agreed. "There's nothing in the photo to give a sense of scale. I mean, the numbers on the rulers are totally out of focus." Nettie lingered for a moment, then showed me another.

6.2

— Mr. Billington?

— Either Billington or someone who looked just like him.

— So you weren't sure?

— No, but that's the first thing I thought.

— Did Nettie say it was Billington?

— Not really. I mean, I think she knew that I might think it was him. I think she was waiting for me to ask.

— Continue.

— What for?

— We need a description.

— You have the photo.

— Yes, but we need your description.

6.3

I guess Nettie already had her mind-blowing moment. So I guess that's why she was more interested in getting my reaction than she was in revisiting the photo. And she certainly must have gotten what she was looking for, because I just couldn't believe what I was seeing. *I could not believe it!* There before me were the three teenagers, all in various stages of sexual activity. And who should they be working on? Who should be lying there — on his back, legs in the air, his face and chest covered in ejaculate — but Billington! Or someone who looked a hell of a lot like him. So yeah — I couldn't believe it. It was super-heavy — way heavier, of course, than what we'd found in the guy's garbage the day before. In fact, now that I think about it, I remember the moment so well if only because of the way the photo seemed to animate that garbage, how each item — the Vaseline, the beer sausage, the tissues, the magazines — came to life, leapt from the page, how they danced about my neighbour like something from *Fantasia*. That was really the moment: Billington twirling like a rotisserie pig, the condom jumping out of its wrapper, opening wide, receiving the sausage, then dipping itself in the Vaseline, before going to work on Billington's ass, while the mothy tissues dabbed at his spunk and the magazines hovered like birds in a gale. Total Disney. I could not believe it!

Nettie nudged me. "Ironic, huh?" I agreed. Then I asked her if that's why she was so eager to chase the bag down in the first place. "Duh?" she said, careful to replace the photo in the exact same spot she took it from. "Do you want to see more?" she said. "One more," I said. "You won't like it," she said. "It couldn't be any more fucked than the last one," I told her.

The next folder we looked at was the one marked MARSHALL. Nettie opened it up, lay it before me. A woman, about forty, stared back. She looked like somebody's mother. "This is the woman who took those first pictures, the ones with that kid in the gumboots," Nettie said, pushing the photo aside to reveal another photo of the same woman. But this time she was being accompanied by a man.

They looked like some average middle-aged couple stepping out of a McDonald's. "That man she's with — he's the boy's legal guardian," she said, handing me the photo. I took the photo and examined it closely. There was nothing out of the ordinary. But then again, what was I looking for anyway? I guess that's what made this photo the creepiest one of all. "They look so normal," I said. "Exactly!" said Nettie. "That's why it took so long for the cops to catch up to them." Nettie went on to say that the man and the woman were part of a ring.

Nettie shelved the binder, then plunked herself down on the judge's chair. She tested the swivel with her hips, her feet firmly planted. Her top half seemed relaxed, but her knees were knocking wildly. She stared at me kinda weird, like she was trying to be sly or something. "I don't know," I said, scratching my head. "I mean, I don't know how I feel about all this. Do you look at your dad's stuff often?" Nettie smiled. "All the time," she replied. "But I figure it's okay as long as I don't tell anyone." Hmm. "Well, you kinda told me by showing me, didn't you?" I said. Nettie spun a three-sixty. "Yeah, so?" she said, slamming her feet down. I was confused. I decided to go on the offensive. "Does this stuff do anything for you?" I asked her. Nettie laughed out loud. "Yeah, it does. *Sometimes*," she said, almost giggly. "Some of it makes me feel kinda ... *sexy*." Nettie cocked her eyebrow, effectively turning the question around. I shrugged. Nettie's smile gave way to a scowl. She looked away. "But some of it does the opposite," she added, spinning again, this time stopping with her back to me. "Some of it," she began, "makes me feel sorta ... *sad*." And with that, Nettie jumped from the chair and returned to the shelf. She removed the binder a second time.

A car was slowing. I glanced at the window. "Our brakes don't squeak," Nettie said, miles ahead. Once again, she opened the binder over the judge's desk. "Why do these photos make you feel sexy?" I asked, curious about Nettie's mixed feelings. She gave me a puzzled look, which scared me, took me back. For now I had to account for my own feelings. And the only thing I was feeling at that moment was the fear of being caught. "Well, what I mean is — these little kids are being used, right?" I said, aware of the quiver in my voice, but happy just to get something out. Nettie gave me a withering look. "You are *so* repressed," she said. I wasn't sure what she meant by that. But it was too late to ask. She was leading up to something. I could tell. "What if I told you that the boy and the girl liked each other — *a lot*," she said, her tone too serious, almost defensive. I shrugged. Maybe she was right. I guess you'd really have to like someone in order to do what those two were doing — especially with people taking pictures and stuff. "I mean, what if I told you those adults never went to jail, that the Crown had no case, and that the whole thing never even made it to court?" she continued. I shrugged again. I wasn't sure what we were talking about any more. "And what if I told you that in the eyes of the law none of these people have done anything wrong, and how that therefore makes none of these photos illegal?" she said, flipping to the back, stopping on a section of text, tapping it with her finger for emphasis. "I mean, that's basically what it says in the report."

I adjusted the desk lamp. I was all set to start reading when Nettie flipped back to the beginning. "I like this one the best," she said, removing a five-by-seven colour snap, a low-angle shot of the boy in the gumboots and the girl with the big eyes. They were both on their sides, in the sixty-nine position, over a fuzzy pumpkin-coloured rug. The boy had his finger in the girl's anus, while the girl's kissy lips pressed against his testicles. The photo did nothing for me. "What's so great about this one?" I asked, leaning a hand on the desk, steadying myself. "I just think it's beautiful. They both look so happy. I think they love each other a lot, don't you?" Nettie said, picking up the photo, holding it out between us. "Is that what it says in the report?" I asked. "I haven't read everything yet," she replied, absently, as she set the photo down.

I felt Nettie's hand brush the small of my back, the twist of her thumb in my belt loop. I was still concentrating on the photo. "Looks like they used a wide-angle lens," I said, my voice dry. Nettie ignored me, tugging gently on the loop, pulling herself closer. I could feel the heat off her body, her coloured scent curling up and under my nose. Nettie tilted her head into the flesh of my shoulder. From the corner of my eye I could see that she was no longer interested in the photo. She seemed to be looking off, towards the black hole of the judge's waste-paper basket. I wasn't sure where this was going, so I continued my critique: "The POV is odd, though. Don'tcha think? I mean, the person taking this photo had to be lying on their stomach. Pretty weird, huh? With all that going on?"

Nettie responded by pushing closer. I could feel the calf of her leg squish against my shin. Her breath seemed to hiccup. I lifted my arm over hers and let it slide down her back, to where the heel of my hand came to rest on her ass. I wasn't sure why I did this, but I did. "The lighting's a bit bad, too. I don't think they should've used a filter," I said, stuttering on the *f* in "filter." Nettie began to sway — slowly, gently. I lowered my eyes. I could see where the corner of the desk met her groin. Then the leg I was sharing with Nettie suddenly began to shake. I shifted my weight. Nettie moved with me. Now *that* leg was shaking. Again, she pulled on my belt loop. It felt like she was trying to turn me. So I let her. I opened my mouth. Our teeth clicked. Our tongues met. We were kissing. It was my first wet kiss. Not like those other dry puckers I'd known in the past. And it felt great, too. But it wasn't what I wanted. Not like this. Not with Nettie.

It was as if something exploded between us. Nettie jumped back. Her face went wide. "It's my dad!" Somewhere in the distance: an emergency brake engaging. "Don't just stand there," she said, all frantic. "Go down to the basement." I tore out of the study, ran down the stairs, through the kitchen, then down the short flight to the rec room. I leaned against the door and quietly caught my breath. I could hear the tinkle of keys, the crunch of the opening door. Nettie's faint "Daddy!" Then the judge's low cough, his grumble. I scanned the room for hiding spots. The house shook with footsteps. I listened as they went from carpet to hardwood, finally coming to rest on the kitchen tile, just above my head. The rec room was cold now. I grabbed my sweater and strained to listen. All I could make out was the chirp of Nettie's high notes. My heart was beating like a bass drum. A couple of footsteps, then the shuffle of the judge's slow retreat, the tamp of his feet up the stairs. Nettie's descent seemed in counterpoint. She walked in spinning a football.

6.4

— Your descriptions could do with a touch more lyricism.

— Your approach to my life could be a lot less linear.

— Continue.

75

— To the end of the day?

— To the end of that day.

6.5

The park looked different. Everything looked different after what had just happened at Nettie's. The trees looked bigger, the grass seemed greener, the goalposts glowed like a precious metal. "Let's kick field goals," Nettie said, jamming her heel into the frozen ground. "We'll need a tee," I said, looking around for a twig, something I could improv a tee from. Nettie tried standing the ball up in the little divot, but it kept rolling over. "Fuck!" she shouted, giving up, booting the ball anyway. The thing spun off like a hit dog. I walked into the end zone, picked it up, and tossed her back a decent spiral. Nettie caught it, turned around, and punted it towards a stand of yews. I walked towards the yews, resigned to Nettie's mood, wondering how the hell I was going to get out of this one. Just as I was reaching down to pick up the ball, Nettie tackled me. I landed with the ball under my stomach, winded. Nettie wrapped her arms around my neck. She was making grunting sounds. I was beginning to get a little freaked out, trying to catch my breath and reason with her at the same time. I wanted her off me. And I told her so. I said: "Get the fuck off me, you psycho." And then she did. And we lay there. We lay there for a long, long time.

I thought of nothing but the grey clouds above. Nettie broke the silence: "You don't like me, do you?" she said, staring up at the sky. "Yes, I do. You're my friend," I said easily. A moment passed. "You don't like me as a girlfriend, though," she said, fishing. Another moment. "I've never thought about you that way," I said. Nettie grrred, all pissed off. "You're just like the Bobby Galts! You think I'm a lez. You guys think that ditz Cindy Carruthers is the girlfriend type, don't you?" she said, rolling away. "I don't think you're a lez. And Cindy Carruthers — she's just a rumour," I said, propping myself up on an elbow, happy with the truth. "Yeah, but you're still just like the Bobby Galts," she said, her back turned. I wasn't like the Bobby Galts, but I wasn't sure why. Nettie rolled back. She looked scared. That's when I told her that maybe we should get up and go, that it was cold.

Neither of us spoke on the walk home. I began to feel shittier and shittier about the whole afternoon, how my friendship with Nettie was all fucked up now, and how I couldn't get it out of my head that it was her fault, even if it was just a big misunderstanding. I thought: How can a friendship get so fucked up over one person liking the other too much?

We turned the corner towards Nettie's. There were two cars in the driveway now. Relief. As we got closer it became apparent that Nettie's brother got his electric guitar. "Can you come in for a minute?" Nettie asked, just like her old self. "Yeah, sure," I said. "We'll have to go in the front this time," she said, grinning. I laughed, happy that things were back on track. Then Nettie laughed. "I'm sorry about what happened," she said. "Don't worry about it," I said quickly, hoping she wouldn't elaborate. And I think my quickness worked because Nettie threw me another grin. "I'm just gonna get you those storyboards. Maybe you'll look over the script again, too," she said. A smiling Mrs. Smart greeted us at the door, the sound of a guitar distorting in the background.

Later, when I got home, my mother asked me what was in the bag. "Just some storyboards." I said, tossing the bag onto the kitchen counter. "Storyboards?" she said, taking delight in the fact that I'd used a word she wasn't familiar with. "Sure," I said. "Have a look — Nettie did them." Just then the phone rang. I was closest, so I answered. "Hello?" It was Mrs. Smart. Her voice was firm: "Your mother, please." Fuck! Now what? Do I hand the phone over? Or do I take a message? Either way I was fucked. Because I knew the call had something to do with me.

I called for my mom and felt instantly betrayed by the sound of my voice, all broken and fearful. "Hey — your voice's cracking!" my mom proclaimed, loud enough to share with Mrs. Smart. I passed her the phone and watched as she listened, the way her brow knit, the way her eyes squinted up like slits in a mask. I listened through the long series of "uh-huhs" — the first couple in the lower register, the rest progressively higher — before she threw me the first of her pissed-off looks, the stock one she keeps when shit like this happens. One more "uh-huh" before she passed back the phone. I was terrified. But I couldn't let it show. Maybe it was nothing. So, just to show her how cool I was, I asked her to take a message. She wasn't amused.

Mrs. Smart wasted no time. "What the dickens did you two get up to today?" I took a breath. "Nettie showed me some drawings. Then we went to the park to kick field goals," I said, like it was no big deal. "Drawings of what?" she snapped. "Movie drawings." I said. "Storyboards." Mrs. Smart paused. "You know you shouldn't be over here when there's no one around to supervise." I agreed, told her she was absolutely right.

After that Mrs. Smart stuck to statements. "Nettie is up in her room crying right now." I couldn't say anything more than "oh." "She's up in her room crying and she won't tell me why," she continued, sounding a little more on the downside of upset. "Well, all we did was look at her storyboards — which were great, by the way — and then we went to the park and kicked field goals — that's all," I said, refusing to budge. Mrs. Smart sighed hard. A resigning sigh. We were almost done. Mrs. Smart was in retreat. But what had she told my mom?

I went back to the kitchen. My mother was at the sink scrubbing beets. She had her back to me, the water going full blast. The bag with the storyboards had gone from the counter to the table, where my sister sat colouring. My sister noticed me looking at the bag, so she reached for it. I grabbed it from her. I didn't want her opinion. And I told her so. She complained, of course. My mother brought down the water volume. "You two go upstairs and wash up. Dinner's almost ready," she said, banging the scrubber twice on the sink, not turning around. It was hard to get a read on my mom. My sister raced past me as I made my way out. I wondered whether I was in trouble or not. I hated this feeling. It was just like the old days, when my dad was around.

I sat down at my desk and stared out at the park, waiting for my sister to finish in the bathroom. It was almost dark. I could barely make out the goalposts. The bushes were black, without definition. I felt bad for Nettie. Maybe looking at the storyboards might cheer me up. Maybe I'd have some ideas about the text. I decided then and there that I would accept her offer to help. So I reached into the bag and pulled out the storyboards, the text, and — *the photo!* The photo of those kids on the pumpkin rug! Could this be the reason for Mrs. Smart's phone call? Had the judge noticed the photo missing? Or was I being paranoid? I looked out at the park. The bushes were gone. The goalposts, too. Everything outside was black.

The bathroom taps squeaked off. I slid the photo into my desk drawer. I had to struggle to shut it. Then it slammed. A little too loudly. "Whaddaya doing?" my sister said, peering in, staring at the drawer. "Nothing," I said, opening the drawer, pulling out an eraser, pretending to erase something. "Whaddaya erasing?" she said, stepping forward. "Here," I said, holding up a very detailed drawing of a worm, "I just erased the 'me' in 'help me.'" My sister looked around the room instead. She was sniffing. I shook the picture a bit, trying to get her attention. "See?" I said. She ignored me, took a step closer. "You never let me in your room," she said, her eyes going back to the drawer.

Mom called up: "Dinner." Neither of us budged. "Get out," I said quietly. I said it again, and this time I stood. My sister took a step back. "Get out of my room," I said, stepping towards her, because it was my room and I didn't want her in it. "You've got something in there, don't you?" she said, walking backwards, her eyes still fixed on the drawer. "You didn't erase anything on that drawing, *did you?* That was just a trick, *wasn't it?*" I smiled blankly. I knew she'd make a big deal out of this at dinner. But I also knew it could work in my favour, that it might detract from my mother pursuing whatever Mrs. Smart might have said earlier. My mother always backed off when she felt her and my sister might be ganging up on me. And I also knew that my sister hadn't cottoned onto this yet, which made her even less of a threat. I closed the door slowly, aware that she was standing firm on the threshold. It was a game we played. My sister would stand as close to the door as possible, daring me to bump her in the nose. Which I did this time, very lightly. She screamed like I'd hit her with a brick. I locked the door, then slid the photo under my mattress. I could hear my mother charging up the stairs. Good, I thought. Now we'd have something else to talk about at dinner.

I cruised into the kitchen and took my place at the table. I was cocky with confidence, so I decided to go on the offensive. "Nettie's a little depressed," I said, waiting for my mom to look up. "Yeah, I just told her the truth: that her drawings weren't very good, but that as storyboards they were just fine, that I could see what she was getting at." My mother nodded, dropping a couple of pork chops onto my plate. My sister came down hard on a carrot stick. "You have to be careful with the truth sometimes," my mother said, to both of us, extending the lesson. "Yeah," I said, helping myself to the potatoes. "I guess I went a bit too far. I guess I was a little bit mad that she phoned so early this morning." I looked at my sister and shrugged. She gave me a shitty face, as if Mom's comment on the truth was a hard lesson to accept. But she wasn't fooled, my sister. She knew how clever I was. And as for my mom — she just smiled. I think she was happy to have imparted something with such little effort. She pushed the beets towards me, suggesting that I help myself. And I did, knowing full well that the judge's photo was not going to be an issue.

After dinner the three of us went into the den to watch TV. What I really wanted to do, though, was go upstairs and find a better hiding spot for that photo. I looked over at my sister, fading fast on the couch. "C'mon now, dear, time for bed," my mother said, placing her hand on my sister's shoulder. "C'mon now." My mother reached under my sister's back, carefully lifting her off the couch. My sister looked at me. Her hair tangled, eyes puffy, her face imprinted with the embroidery of the throw pillow. "I'm not tired yet," she creaked, rubbing at the red flower stamped into her cheek. "I know you're not," my mother said, trying to humour her, "but it's well past your bedtime." My sister looked away. "Say goodnight to your brother," Mom said, presenting my sister to me. I looked at my mom smiling down on my sister. I watched as she fussed a knot out of her tousled hair. Then my sister rolled her sleepy head towards me once more. Her eyes were shut. Her mouth was small and smoochy. Just like the girl under my mattress — but not quite.

To be on the safe side, I let an hour pass before telling my mother that I was going upstairs to bed. My sister would be fast asleep by then. "Oh," she said, "*Lawrence of Arabia* is on at eight." Shit! I loved that movie. And Mom knew it, too. Now it's gonna look weird if I don't change my mind. So I yawned, stretching it out until I could come up with a plausible excuse. Mom gave me a puzzled look, which only served to stall my excuse-making process. "Are you okay?" she said. "Yeah, yeah," I said, deciding to go with what was easiest. "I'm just a bit tired, that's all." But Mom wasn't convinced. "You're not coming down with something, are you?" she said, reaching for my forehead. "No," I said, pushing her hand away. "I just feel a bit tired, that's all. I guess it's been a long day, getting up so early and all." My mother nodded, still not convinced.

"Everything okay between you and Nettie?" she said. "We had a fight," I lied. "But we'll make up tomorrow." My mother smiled like I'd said what she'd wanted to hear. Then I kissed her goodnight and stole away like I'd done something terribly wrong.

6.6

— You masturbated to the photo.

— That's correct.

— But weren't you disturbed by it when Nettie first showed it to you?

— Sorta.

— What changed your mind?

— Once I stopped associating it with the judge's study it turned into something else.

— What was that?

— Whatever I wanted it to be at the time.

7.1

June 10, 1975

Mr. Dickson, please ...
    Where I go to school, the last day of Grade Seven is also the last day of elementary school. What I mean by that is this: when we return to school in September we will be attending a new school, a secondary school (or a high school as it is commonly known). Once there, we will begin the long wait (five whole years!) before finally getting our next opportunity to take part in something we should be given the right to partake in right now. I am speaking, of course, of a graduation ceremony. As it stands, I can only imagine.

During the last month of Grade Twelve we will drift apart from the lower grades. We will become oblivious to them. Yet, to them, we will take on the glow of those about to go through something massive. We will also begin to gravitate towards our fellow classmates and form a bond based on nothing more than the arithmetics of being born at the same time, the demographics of finding ourselves in exactly the same place.

During the second-to-last weekend of Grade Twelve we will be declared insane by our parents and teachers. We will be encouraged, with love, to do all the things that they are allowed to do. And we will be encouraged to do those things to excess — like drinking too much and staying up all night. There will be chauffeurs and limousines to take us to fancy hotels. There will be gigantic stereo systems to propel us across those fancy dance floors until we're ready to visit those brass-handled toilets and vomit on the floor before them. The next morning we will reconsider our commitment to instantaneous eroto-violent activities brought about through inexplicable anxieties towards things left undone — like the perfection of the ultimate act of vandalism or the loss of one's virginity. The emotional range will be huge.

These are things I can only look forward to.

But because we are still in elementary school, and because our elementary school has no such graduation policy, I can only imagine. And I don't think that's fair, do you? Why can't Grade Sevens have their own ceremony, just like the Grade Twelves get in high school?

Signed,
Nettie Smart

I gave the letter back to Nettie. "It's excellent," I said, meaning it. "Thanks," she said. "I took some of it from magazines — *National Lampoon* and *Time* both had articles on the graduation ritual." Nettie folded the letter and tucked it into her pants' pocket. "Are you gonna get people to sign it?" I asked. "No point," she said. "I've already shown it to Dickson. He said even if I got everyone in the city to sign, he still won't let us have a grad." *The Dickson!*

It was a hot and sunny Friday evening. Nettie and I were sitting in the shade of the Smarts' front steps, our baseball mitts in our laps, taking in the spectacle.

A moment passed. We let it.

Nettie nudged me. "I feel sorry for him," she said, gesturing towards her stoned brother, Dunc, who, along with his grad partner, the uptight *Aw-nuh* Hirsh, was being paraded around the Smarts' front lawn while relatives snapped photographs and neighbours stopped to watch. "I mean, this isn't his trip at all. He's only doing it for my mom, you know," she added, retying a shoelace just for something to do. "Well, I won't hold it against him," I said, before asking Nettie if she thought those powder-blue tuxedos would still be the rage by the time we finally graduated. To which Nettie laughed a no. I was going to ask her what she thought of *Aw-nuh*'s dress, but thought otherwise just as quick. Nettie hated dresses. But would she still feel that way in five years? Maybe that was a question. But whatever.

Another moment passed. We let it. Then we left for the park with our mitts.

Nettie pitched and I caught. I always found this relaxing: Nettie working on her curve, while I took the time to problem-solve. Today's problem: Nettie's letter. I know I told her it was excellent, but to be honest I had no idea what the fuck she was on about, other than the fact that she was right to complain about us not getting a grad. "Nettie, why didn't you just write down some of the stuff Grade Sevens might do on a grad night instead of spending so much time talking about what the Grade Twelves get up to?" Nettie responded with a rocket, high and inside. "Because it's a ritual and we don't have one," she added, kicking at the mound. I lobbed her the ball, then adjusted my squat, shaking the sting from my catching hand. "Yeah, I know. But don't you think all that stuff about puking and limos is just gonna work against us?" Nettie ignored me. She was preparing a knuckler, the most impossible pitch of all. "Don't, Nettie! You'll just wreck your arm!" I shouted, standing up, ready to run to wherever this weird pitch was gonna take me.

Back in February we told John and Penny about our school's no-grad policy. They weren't at all surprised. John told us the reason there was no graduation was because the powers that be thought we weren't old enough to appreciate what we were leaving behind. That's when Penny suggested we try once more to activate the collective, bring them all over to their place for a party. John agreed, said we deserved to be fêted, what with the up and down year we'd all had. Both Nettie and I exchanged sidelongs. Although we appreciated John and Penny's offer, we knew the collective was long past reviving, and that any attempt to do so would only make our graduation ritual an even bigger dud than it was already becoming. I think we both wanted to say something, but couldn't. We'd only insult them. And they'd been so nice to us. Fortunately John sensed our discomfort, because he quickly turned to Penny and said, "Aw, what the fuck — let's just make it a foursome." And Penny agreed.

So: it was the Sunday after Dunc's graduation and the beginning of our second-to-last week of elementary. Nettie and I rode our bikes over to Kerrisdale where we could phone John and Penny from the Big Scoop. Because that was the plan: we were to phone John and Penny two weeks before and confirm that we'd be coming. I'd sorta forgotten this, because it had been my experience that adults often make promises they sometimes didn't mean. But Nettie hadn't forgotten. She phoned me first thing that morning.

I was halfway through dialling when I hung up. "What did you do that for?" Nettie asked, grabbing the receiver. "Are you chicken or something? Do you want me to do it?" I grabbed back the receiver. I told her to hang on a minute, that I had some concerns.

I told Nettie that too much time had passed since we last saw John and Penny. I told her that they'd probably gotten on with their lives, and that this call might embarrass them to the point where they'd feel obliged to do something they'd long forgotten. "Bullshitter," Nettie said, grabbing back the phone, fishing a dime out of her pocket. "They like us. They like having us around."

But Nettie was wrong. I wasn't bullshitting. I really was worried that John and Penny had forgotten us. And I just couldn't stand the disappointment. So I came at it from another angle. I said: "Yeah, you're right. I was bullshitting you." This time it was

Nettie who hung up halfway. "All right," she said, "something's bugging you, let's have it." So I told her. I told her the biggest lie I could think of. I said, "Well, I guess what's really bugging me is that I don't trust adults much since we looked at the stuff in your dad's study. And, I mean, it's been bothering me so much I'm beginning to wonder if Mr. Gingell's a child molester after all." Nettie shook her head. She couldn't believe what I was saying. I tried to rephrase, but only got a few words in before she lost it on me. "You're totally fucked in the head, you know that?" And that was just the beginning of what she had to say before the manager told us to take it outside.

7.3

— So you told a lie to cover up how you really felt.

— That's right.

— Because you thought Nettie wouldn't believe you.

— Well, she didn't, did she?

— What made you think she'd believe you in the first place?

— Because it was such a huge lie.

— But she seemed even less convinced.

— True. I guess what I was trying to do was two things. The first part had to do with getting out of visiting John and Penny; and the second part, I guess, had to do with coming up with an explanation for my coolness towards her that day in the park, after we looked at the judge's photos.

— But you were honest with her in the park. You told her you liked her as a friend.

— Yeah, and look what that got me: if my mother ever found what Nettie snuck in with those storyboards, I'd be dead right now.

Nettie was doing her best to contain herself, keep it from bursting, but I knew she was going to explode again once we got in the alley. She'd been really hot-headed lately. And this pretend-honesty kick I'd been on wasn't helping matters much at all. "What the hell's happened to you? You're beginning to sound like Margie fuckin' Stott," Nettie said, hands on hips. "I'm sorry," I said. "It's just the way I feel — I can't help it." Nettie threw her hands in the air and began storming around, stomping out these figure eights, suddenly stopping, half-attempting to say something, then just giving up, grunting, winding her way into new shapes. It was a classic temper tantrum, just like the ones Margie used to pull back in Grade Two. Not a very relaxing atmosphere. Especially now that I had a lie to uphold.

There was a paper shack at the end of the alley. I sat down on the shady side and bit into a long blade of grass. Nettie joined me a couple of minutes later. I waited for her breathing to slow before continuing my untruths.

I elaborated on my confusion over the judge's photographs. I said, "Look, Nettie, I'm really sorry but it's just the way I feel. Those photos totally creeped me out. I mean, what if we went over to John and Penny's and they made us take all our clothes off. For all we know they could be in cahoots with Mr. Gingell, maybe even part of that ring you were telling me about." Nettie scoffed. "That's the most stupidest thing I have ever heard in my life. You are so fucking paranoid. I can't believe you think like that," she said, getting up and booting a rock for emphasis. Nettie was right. I wasn't very convincing. So I tried another tack. "Okay, I'll be honest with you. I guess what's really bothering me is whether those kids really wanted to be involved in all that nudie stuff. Because I think they were forced into it. And if they were, then that's abusive and exploitive and I'm against it. So that's why I'm boycotting adults from now on," I said, happy with my defence. Nettie picked up a bottle cap and threw it at a garbage can, missing it, hitting a hubcap instead. I thought this would fire her up even more, but no. She let her shoulders slump, then sat back down beside me.

A moment passed. We let it.

I was about to suggest we leave when Nettie turned to me. "You know, you didn't seem to feel too badly for those boys in Billington's magazines. I mean, if you had your way, we'd still be sitting up there on the tracks looking through them right now." Nettie was going somewhere with this. And wherever it ended up, I knew it was only meant to hurt. I suggested we split, but Nettie wasn't listening. "So what are we to make of that, huh?" she continued. "I mean, is it okay for Moroccan boys to be in those magazines but not okay if they're Canadians? Is that what you're saying? Because if it is, then you're just as much a racist as that pig, Mr. Dickson. And if that's the case, then that would bother me a helluva lot more than how those kids ended up in those photos in the first place." I thought about this for a moment while Nettie went back inside to use the phone. I wondered if this was something I could ask John and Penny. But no way — I'd be so embarrassed.

7.5

We were invited to John and Penny's the following Saturday. Soccer had long since ended, so we told our moms we were going shopping instead. Nettie came up with the excuse: the two of us had been entrusted by the class to get a present for Mr. Stinson. I laughed hard when Nettie told me this. She was turning out to be a pretty good liar, too.

John and Penny had gone all out. They'd decorated their house with streamers and balloons, and John had done up a huge poster that said CON-GRADUATIONS TO 2/31STS OF PENNY'S CLASS OF '75. The dining-room table was covered with cookies and candies and two big pitchers of Kool-Aid — one lime green and one strawberry. In the centre was a huge chocolate cake, decorated in a film theme, frosted to look like film stock. Beside the cake were two gift-wrapped boxes. And on top of each box was an envelope. One envelope had Nettie's name on it. The other, mine.

Nettie grabbed her envelope and asked John and Penny the obvious. "Is this for me?" John and Penny smiled. Nettie ripped into the envelope. "Aren't you going to open yours?" Penny asked, adding my name affectionately at the end. "Yes," John said. "Open yours." All of a sudden I felt very sad. I felt a mood coming on. Nettie opened her card. She was just about to read the sentiment when she stopped. "Why are you crying?" Nettie asked me. I shrugged. I didn't know. Penny touched my shoulder. "What's wrong, dear?" Now I was balling my eyes out. "Goodness! And we haven't even started into all this sugar yet," John joked. And I laughed at that, remembering John's rant against dextrose a couple of months before. But whatever. The laughter relaxed me. I looked at Nettie. She was smiling. I told her to go ahead and read her card. Which she did, with flare.

7.6

— So what was troubling you?

— I don't know. I think I felt ashamed of myself.

— John and Penny gave you presents.

— Well, sort of.

— What do you mean?

— Well, I was never sure whether they were presents or —

— Awards.

— Or maybe even something else.

— Like what?

— Like ... I don't quite know. I mean, in a way we were told we'd won these things. But they were presented to us like gifts, right? Or maybe they were bribes to keep us from bringing up the Gingell affair. I honestly don't know. I mean, I was at a point in my life where I was desperate for certainty, if that makes any sense. And what John and Penny presented to us that day had more to do with confusion than anything else.

— Did Mr. Gingell's name come up?

— No.

Nettie tore open her box. "All right!" she said, pulling out a Nikon super-8 movie camera. "Those are brand new, Nettie," John said. "They just came out last month." Penny turned to me and smiled. "Aren't you going to open yours?" I smiled weakly, then started picking at the gift wrap. I remember thinking: These cameras are expensive. What did we do to deserve stuff like this? That's when things got fuzzy. Everything seemed really far away, and I could barely make out the conversation. It took a few tries before I clued in that John was talking about some university conference. I only caught the last bit.

"So all these people from education departments from all over the world came to town last month and we showed them the films you guys did and we decided that your two films were the best." Nettie looked confused. "But only Nettie and I finished our films," I said, totally pissed off. "Yeah, and who's we?" said Nettie. Penny shrugged. "John, me — a couple of people in his department," she said, slightly startled by our tone. Nettie began to say something, but I cut her off. "Wait a minute," I said. "You mean you showed the rest of the collective's films even though they weren't edited." John swallowed what he was eating. "Yes," he said, like we were making something out of nothing. "Well, I don't think that's right," I said. "I don't think it's fair that we were judged against work that wasn't finished. It's not fair. I don't think we can accept these awards." I looked over at Nettie. I could tell she was with me. John's laugh was all nerves. "Okay, then," he said. "Don't think of them as awards, then. Think of them as graduation presents." He then raised his glass and toasted 2/31sts of Penny's class of '75. I looked over at Penny. She knew us too well. She looked like she did when she came back from her fight with Stinson. That's when I got up and left.

— Those cameras —

— Right.

— How did you two explain them to your parents?

— I didn't have to. I left mine behind.

— What about Nettie?

— She just told her mom the truth. She said she won an award at school for best film and they gave her a camera.

7.9

On the second-to-last day of elementary I had my final meeting with the district guidance counsellor, Mrs. Leggie. For some reason — we weren't going alphabetically — mine was the last meeting. After her standard good-luck speech, Mrs. Leggie took from her desk the results of my aptitude test. "You were the one who was most confused over Mr. Gingell's departure, weren't you?" she said, opening my folder. "Yes," I said. "Well, I'm glad to see you've gotten over it," she said. "Now, would you like me to tell you about the three occupations the computer feels you're most suited to?" I nodded. "Okay, then," she said. "In order of success: florist, mortician, military."

7.10

Our last walk home from elementary. Nettie and I hardly said a peep. What Nettie did have to say, however, was that she was proud of me for what I had to say at John and Penny's, and that I was right to say it. But she had already told me this twice by then, so I didn't say much back. Old news. And that was that for talking. Yeah, I suppose we were both in the same mood, just taking in what was around us — the houses, the trees, the cars, the pets — all those details we'd passed by on the eight years we'd walked to and from elementary. I remember thinking how little thought I'd given to all these things, how I'd just sloughed them off as familiar landmarks, little things that measured time and distance. And I remember contradicting myself right after, because as kids we thought of everything. Only nothing much seemed to happen. Everything got familiar real fast. Or at least that's how I was remembering my life at the time.

8.1

Grade Eight. You are on the bottom. Like every boot-camp movie I've ever seen. The bottom. You are green, you are small, you are hairless from the lashes down. Your metabolism, childlike. I am speaking, of course, of the boys. Of which I was one. The contrast is greatest for boys. Most of the girls, by then, are young women. And if they're not yet young women, they're protected by a young woman's indifference. Most of the boys are sexless, generic children. There are young men and there are young women — and there were a good many boys in Grade Eight.

It was survival. The unexpected mattered. Humiliations. You submitted to losers. You lost to losers. And by losers here I mean those bitter twisted fucks who got beat on so much when they were our age that all they had left was to beat on those newer versions of themselves. But for people like me and Galt, it was okay. The school knew we were coming. We were privileged athletes and we would help our school win prizes. And in doing so we would perpetuate another kind of authority: that of the male student-athlete. And by that I mean *hero*. So those who had a stake in that looked after us — those older versions of ourselves. That was implicit. And the losers knew it. They wouldn't fuck with us because they knew we were protected, that any insult laid upon us would be avenged. Besides, they had their own cycle of violence to maintain, their own unconscious search for new recruits. So it was the Alistar Chens and the Jeffrey Smith-Gurneys who would pay the price. They were the ones who would experience the towel snaps, the inside of locked lockers, the indignity that comes with having the shit kicked out of you in front of the very people you'd grown up with all your life, the very people who you thought were your friends.

But even with all that protection you still had to play it cool. There was a code. The right clothes helped. You couldn't look too goofy. You couldn't draw too much attention to yourself. Mostly you were judged by your actions. You behaved in a way that spoke of your willingness to be protected. And a lot of this had to do with the things you didn't do. So you didn't go out of your way to associate with the people the losers chose as targets. That would just create too much confusion. The same applied to your association with the opposite sex. You made it clear that your affections were towards the very best-looking, if only to let those protecting you know that you were just like them.

So Nettie Smart had to go.

8.2

— Was this difficult?

— No. Everyone was very understanding. It was like walking into a given. It was no different than religion, rock, fashion, capitalism — the big issues of the day.

— Nettie was a what you'd call a "dog."

— Not a dog, per se. Just someone you didn't need to be seen with.

— The opposite of Cindy Carruthers?

— Yes.

8.3

Cindy Carruthers. The legendary Cindy Carruthers. What can I say about Cindy Carruthers?

We had been aware of Cindy Carruthers since Grade Five. Word had trickled in from Churchill Elementary — the feeder school to Hamber — that there was this beautiful girl named Cindy Carruthers who was so impossibly hot it was unlikely she could even exist. Descriptions varied, which only added to her value. Adding to our intrigue, however, was the rumour that Cindy would be attending our soon-to-be high school — Point Grey — because of its winning tradition in basketball and, most importantly, its number-one ranking as the cheerleading capital of B.C. So there was a vested interest, shared by both the sexes, in knowing as much as possible about this Cindy Carruthers.

Churchill was located at the southeast end of Shaughnessy. Oakridge, actually. The area was predominately a Jewish neighbourhood, and it was the Jewish kids at our school who first introduced us to this someone named Cindy. Not that they'd ever seen her. And they would have had little reason to: Cindy wasn't Jewish, and the Jewish kids at our school only knew the Jewish kids at Churchill. So any information the rest of us had was merely second-hand. Or third-hand when it was just the rest of us sitting around talking about what the Jews said of Cindy.

It was like that, then. You must understand: our world was very small.

But what we knew was this: Cindy was a fox. A Nordic beauty. Long blonde hair, blue eyes, tall and thin. She drew comparisons to everyone from Farrah to Suzi Quattro. She also had an older sister, Colleen, who was supposed to be even more beautiful, a model with the Marnie Ross Agency. Naturally this worked in Cindy's favour, because there was now proof that Cindy would undoubtedly grow up to be at least as good-looking as her sister. As for the rest of the family: Cindy's father was Chuck Carruthers — as in the brokerage house of Anton, Carruthers, and Mead. Bobby was sure it was the same Chuck Carruthers who once held the B.C. high school record for triple jump. Cindy's mother, Connie, we also learned from Bobby, was related to the guy who invented Clorets and, in her own right, a former Miss Vancouver. Like the Billingtons, they lived in a Dutch Colonial.

Cindy's hobby was riding. Rumour had it she kept a horse down in Southlands, a small patch of farmland off the south end of Kerrisdale, on the north bank of the Fraser River. I suppose it was only fitting that Cindy kept a horse down there because Southlands, too, was just a rumour. None of us had ever been there. So before long Southlands became as mythical a place as Cindy was a person. All of which got to Bobby big time. Although not known for his imagination, Bobby had managed to create a whole world around Cindy, an exportable world that, by Grade Six, had a large number of followers. I remember it well: Bobby, who, by that time, had become absolutely obsessed with the idea of Cindy, began planning an expedition down to Southlands, where he and his commandos hoped to catch a glimpse of this Cindy — or, at the very least, her horse. Anything that would bring him just that much closer. Talk went on for months. It was impossible to be around. It was as if Cindy was a princess, her horse a unicorn, Southlands' Camelot. It was all so fairy tale. Eventually a group of them set out, only to turn back at Maple Grove Park where a Josh Peter sighting scared the gang home.

It's hard to believe that during all that time we never saw Cindy Carruthers. Every time our soccer or floor hockey teams travelled to Churchill to play their soccer or floor hockey teams, whether we won or not we always lost out on our chance to see Cindy. When we asked the Jewish kids if they could get us a picture of Cindy — like a class photo or something — they would promise to do everything they possibly could, only to report back empty-handed. About two months after Ms. Singleton was canned, right around the time Nettie and I began editing our films, Bobby, in a fit of frustration, turned on the Jews, accusing them of making all this up, that there was no Cindy Carruthers, that these Jewish kids were part of some global conspiracy. Things got so bad that Bobby threatened to throw a salted pork through Hyman Goldie's window. It took a series of meetings between Bobby, his parents, and Mr. Dickson — and then a painfully long assembly, featuring a two-hour Holocaust slide show narrated by the late Rabbi Yosef Kuhn — before Bobby finally apologized to the Jewish people of Vancouver. But by then it didn't matter. Bobby had refocused.

8.4

A couple of weeks after Nettie and I found the Billington garbage, this new guy showed up at school. He was immediately debriefed by Margie Stott. And Margie, never one to savour information, was quick to issue her report. The new guy's name was Randy Cobb. He had just transferred in from Churchill.

That night I got a call from Bobby. He did not mince words. "What do you know about this Randy Cobb?" he said. "Oh, so you've heard?" I said, thinking hard about what I might say next, something to set him off. "Well, very little, Bob. I mean — he went to Churchill. And I think he, uh — " But Bobby was impatient. "How come the Jews haven't heard of him?" he demanded. I didn't know what to say. I was hit with the image of poor Hyman Goldie, bound to the tether pole, Bobby circling him, his slow interrogation. "Don't you remember anything about what Rabbi Kuhn — " I began. "To hell with Rabbi Kuhn!" Bobby shouted. "Who the hell is Randy Cobb?" I'd had enough. "How the hell do I know, Bob? I haven't even seen him yet. I mean — he's no more real to me than Cindy Carruthers."

Later on Randy would tell us he was only at Churchill a week before he got kicked out for drinking a bottle of beer at a soccer game, even though he insisted it was just a Tab. But he retracted the story a short time later, admitting that he only told us that just to see how we'd react. Then he told us the real reason they'd kicked him out was because he was just plain different. Randy was a bit of a hippie kid.

So: Randy Cobb. A long, tall stretch of gangle with California hair who could sink baskets from centre court and stop anything kicked, flicked, or hit his way. He was amazing, this guy. Fluent in all sports. Quite the charmer, too. For the first week or so, all the girls had crushes on him — Nettie included — until a rumour started going around — which was probably started by Bobby, and which Randy didn't deny — that Randy Cobb had a sixteen-year-old girlfriend in Malibu. Nettie suspected that the reason Bobby started the rumour was to put a cap on Randy's popularity — and to keep Randy for himself. Once all the crushes were crushed Nettie announced that she, too, was over Randy, that Randy's appeal had soured once he became the property of Bobby Galt.

Although reluctant to play sports, Randy was a natural. This made him very cool. I liked his attitude. I liked the way he would casually remind us — right in the middle of a game — of the competitive nature of sport, how the emphasis on sport and young people was no coincidence, how it was meant to condition us, turn us into greedy businessmen when we got older. Then he would do something wild like sink a hook shot or tuck a puck just under the crossbar for no other reason than to emphasize his point. But more than anything I loved what it did to Bobby, how it would turn him inside out, how Randy's contempt for the very thing he was so good at went right in the face of everything Bobby believed in. And I wasn't the only one who felt this way. We'd all peek at Bobby before resuming play, while Bobby just stood there and tried to remind anyone who'd listen that Randy's abilities owed more to the fact that he was a year older than us 'cause he failed Grade Five. Anyway, Randy, like Bobby, was in Mr. Tomlinson's class. And despite Bobby's pettiness, the two became fast friends. They quickly became known as "the Odd Couple," a tag Bobby hated because he feared a passing resemblance to Tony Randall, whom most of us assumed was a faggot.

It was about a month after Nettie and I found Billington's garbage. I remember it well. The first reasonably warm day of the year, a Sunday. And we knew it was coming, too. The weather was way more accurate back then. So Randy suggested that the three of us — him, me, and Bobby — plan that day to go on a "wildlife adventure." He said there were all these trails around the University Endowment Lands and that we should be exploring them. Randy said he'd even heard rumours about the place being a last refuge for wild horses, and that this time of year would be a perfect time to go because "like, wow, man, these horses — they're gonna be fucking." Bobby made a kind of turned-up face when Randy mentioned the fucking horses, but feigned excitement anyway. I knew there weren't any wild horses in the Endowment Lands, but I didn't want to pass up a trip on Randy's imagination.

The fact that Randy's father was going to be driving made the trip just that much easier to sell to our moms. However, when Randy's long-haired dad pulled up in his VW microbus and hopped out wearing cut-offs and tie-dye, I quickly yelled goodbye to my mom and shot out the front door. "Hey, man, how's it hangin'? Name's Ray," Ray drawled, reeling me in for a hug that seemed to go on a beat too long. At which point Randy slid open the side door and provided the narration: "All right." Obviously he thought our hug was cool. I could hardly wait till we pulled up to Bobby's.

We were blocks from Shaughnessy and Bobby still hadn't said a peep. It was a beautiful thing watching Bobby stew in the back of Ray Cobb's microbus. I mean, the guy had so much to be pissed off about, too. Ray Cobb walking up to Mr. Galt like that, right in front of their house, giving him the big hug. And then Mrs. Galt stepping outside that very instance, the terror on her face — Who is this hippie with his arms around my husband? — then her jumping back inside, like a rabbit down a hole. And then Bobby coming down the side of the house, freezing in his tracks, not sure whether to obey his father's glare or get in the car with me and the hippies. I will never forget that for as long as I live. And I must say, as much as Bobby drove me nuts, I think it was pretty brave of him to do what he did that day.

Ray Cobb hit the highway flying. The wind gusted in through the open windows, whipping at Ray's hair till it lifted, swarmed about him, Ray cranked the stereo and turned to shout: "The brand new Tull! Fucking amazing!" Bobby winced. The song: "Pig Me and the Whore." Bobby knew he'd have to explain all this to his father. Every last detail. Because there was definitely going to be an exorcism at the Galts' when Bobby got home.

We turned off the highway and drove down a service road towards the Foreshores cliffs, pulling up outside the School of Social

Work. "We're here," Ray said, turning down the Tull. Bobby looked around, confused. "The Endowment Lands are back that way," he said, pointing over his shoulder. Ray made a what-can-I-say? face. "You're right, Bob. But I can't let you guys go in there." I felt a twinge of panic. Was all this a set-up? Were we gonna end up in a photograph on Judge Smart's desk? "Whaddaya mean we can't go in there?" Bobby snapped. I stifled a laugh, a very nervous one. "Bobs, I can't let you guys go in there, I'm sorry. There's this dude on the loose and he's been layin' some real bad trips on boys your age," Ray said, finishing up with a glum smile. I looked over at Randy. He seemed to have known all along. "So I thought I could drop you dudes here, pick ya up around four," Ray said, flipping the tape. "You'll be a helluva lot safer here, hangin' out on these cliffs. That's for sure."

Bobby shook his head as he watched Ray drive off. "Come on, Bobby," Randy called back, as the two of us made our way towards the edge.

It was a beautiful day. The summer's heat and the bloom of spring. That's what Randy said as we pushed against the warm wind and took in the tankers off English Bay. "The summer heat and ..." I looked back to see Bobby collapse his shoulders in resignation. But when he turned around to look for us he stiffened: we were here and he was there. The time was now. So Bobby ran towards us, not wanting to miss a second. Man, he really had it bad for Randy.

Randy had been here before. He knew his way around. I could tell. Because I'd been here, too. With my dad. "I know a trail that leads down to the beach," said Randy. "It's really cool. There's even an old gun tower we can check out." And with that, he was off. We followed, weaving through the yellowing broom, down a narrow crack in the sand cliffs to where it opened onto a small ledge hidden from above. "That's the real drop — *there*," Randy said, pointing over the lip. Sure enough, a twenty-foot drop to a fan of sand, a fringe of bush, then the beach. But what was going on down there? Was I seeing right? Were those people naked? "That's the unofficial border between Wreck Beach and Foreshores," Randy said. "But it looks to me like the Wreck Beachers are takin' over. Pretty cool, huh." Bobby glared down at the nudes. He disapproved.

Randy took off his Tretorns, tied the laces together, and threw them off the cliff. "The sand below's super soft. It feels really cool on the toes when you hit," Randy said, rubbing his hands together, all set to jump. I looked at Randy's feet. They were tough and leathery, like they'd spent most of their life outdoors. "I'll jump first just to show you how it's done. Watch me now," he said stepping back, closing his eyes, taking a breath. I couldn't believe what he was about to do. The next thing I know Randy bolts. We watched astounded as he hovered in the air, then fell to earth like Apollo, exploding the fan into little black patches of wet, tumbling forward and stopping before a whooping horseshoe of dinks and boobs.

Bobby was freaked, scared shitless. But I was loving it. Not so much because of the adventure — meeting Randy's dad, driving around listening to Jethro Tull, hanging out on these groovy cliffs — but for seeing it all refracted back through Bobby. The day was beginning to shape up like no other. I mean, when I was little my dad and I would have tons of adventures like these. He would take me to weird places, where we'd eat weird food, talk to weird people. And he was forever bringing people like Ray Cobb around the house, if only to rattle my mom. But this time was different. It was different because now I had the background. And Bobby didn't. And Randy did. But Bobby didn't.

So now it was my turn. I took off my Pumas, tied them together, and threw them towards the sun, just like Randy. My runners twirled like birds. Randy was now at sea level, waving okay, calling out, "The coast is clear." I took a step back, took a breath. "You're not!" said Bobby, horrified. "I am!" I said, though still not a hundred per cent sure. Bobby grabbed my arm. He was desperate. "I swear — if you jump, I will never be your friend again." Now I was certain.

And it was easy. Randy was right, the sand was super-soft. I would've done it again if it wasn't such a steep climb back.

By the time I retrieved my shoes Randy had given up encouraging Bobby. Now he was calling out instructions. Bobby was to climb back up the narrow crack, walk around to the bowed fir, climb down through the exposed roots, and bum slide from there. All this took Bobby about half an hour.

In the meantime, Randy and I picked a log and settled in. Bobby was still a speck in the distance, jogging towards us. From the way he was moving I could tell he was steamed. But the closer he got, the slower he got. His walk was so self-conscious. "How do we get back up?" Bobby called out, as if it were already time to leave. Randy chuckled, turning to me. It was a strange look, but I liked it. It seemed to say something about *us*, just him and me. And not Bobby. It seemed to say that he knew I knew my way around these parts, that riding out here in his dad's VW was fun but not unusual. That I'd been to places where people didn't wear clothes, that I wasn't afraid to jump off stuff, that I could appreciate how weird all this was for Bobby, and that maybe it was okay to dick with his pain. I chuckled something back, something like: "My father used to take me here as a kid you know." Randy nodded, looked away. There was nothing more to say.

"What's so funny?" Bobby demanded, out of breath. "Nothing, really," Randy said. "It's just that when you were running these nude joggers came out of a trail behind you and for a second it looked like you were trying to get away from them." Bobby spun around. "I don't see any fuckin' nude joggers." Randy let out a big laugh. I joined him. Bobby plunked himself down and stared at the tankers. Randy and I nudged each other. Then Bobby took off his shoes, placed them nicely beside him. A couple walked by. They were nude, gay, and beautiful. The sun had just gotten hotter.

Randy stood up and announced that he was going to "get nekkid." Bobby looked repulsed. "What the hell for?" Randy shrugged. "It's boiling," he replied, pulling off his T-shirt, revealing a body smooth and beautiful. I took it in: the way his muscles rippled under his olive skin, the thick brown hairs that sprung from his pits, his nipples plump and purple. He gave his shirt a couple of shakes, then tossed it over the log. He was moving quickly. I could tell he'd done this before. I realized I would have to move quickly, too, if I wanted to keep pace with Randy. So I stood up. Bobby looked at me — You're not? I pulled off my shirt and laid it down. I took off my shorts and underwear together, adding them to the length of my shirt. Randy saw what I was doing and seemed to think it was a good idea. He made a blanket out of his clothes, too.

It all happened so fast. And I'm glad it did. Because it would have been really uncomfortable any other way. Like sipping castor oil, or taking a long hard look at the sun. The next thing I knew I was lying on my stomach, the sun spreading out over the small of my back, the light breeze tickling the soles of my feet. I wondered what I could say next to Bobby, but nothing came to mind. He was no more than three feet away, yet it seemed like he didn't exist. I would have to turn my whole body to see him. And right now that would require too much effort on my part. Like walking to the airport, or swimming to Seattle. Bobby would have to come to me now.

I looked over at Randy, on his haunches, fiddling with the knot that bound his shoes. What a profile, I thought. And what an amazing body. His skin a perfect fit. The lines his muscles made, how they worked so well with his bones. And in the shade he made beneath his squat: his genitals full and flaccid, hanging there, batlike, the hairs of his balls frizzing off, in silhouette. Randy the man, I thought, closing my eyes. Which was cool. He was, after all, a year older than us, having failed Grade Five.

I could hear Bobby struggling with his clothes. I'd never seen him naked before, nor him me. I wondered: Would he look like Randy or would he look like me? Man or boy? So I rolled over. Bobby had his back to us. He was all hunched over, down to his Stanfields. He looked back at me and I saw the face of his father, that angry Galt face you'd see at Sports Day, screaming at poor Bobby to run faster, faster. Then Bobby, with one leg out, all caught up and self-conscious, leaning away from his face, hopping on that one clothed leg, hoping to find his balance. The gaunch came off, but Bobby fell. I could see how he looked like me. Still a boy. Randy laughed, but it wasn't so funny.

So there we were, the three of us, naked, lying on our stomachs, when Randy, who was in the middle, turned over on his back and asked us if we wanted to hear about Cindy Carruthers. "You told us you didn't even know who she was!" Bobby said, arms at his side, afraid to move. "I know I did," Randy said. "But I only told you that because I didn't want you guys to be my friend just because of what Cindy and I *did* together." Bobby leaned up on his elbows. "Whaddaya mean what you guys *did* together? You said you were only at Churchill a week." Randy held onto the moment, flicking some non-existent sand off his abs. "Four days, actually. I was enrolled on the Wednesday and expelled on the Monday. But I got there just in time to go to a party. Which was where I met Cindy." he said, flicking at some more non-existences. His cock jiggled as he did this.

8.5

— Your memory of Randy's story is very cinematic.

— Yeah. When he told us the story I kept picturing it as a movie. So I guess that had some bearing on the way I remembered it.

— Was this after you finished your films at John and Penny's?

— Yeah.

— And before their graduation party?

— About a month before.

8.6

INT. ELEMENTARY SCHOOL LUNCHROOM. DAY

It is 1975.

A boy (13) is seated alone at a retractable formica table. He is tall, blond, and blue-eyed. Very mature for his age. Before him is a wrinkled brown paper bag. He is eating an apple, reading a comic. He is oblivious to the noise and activity around him. Behind him, in the distance, a group of girls (12). The are looking his way, giggling. Then one of the girls gets up and walks towards the boy, stopping directly behind him, tapping him on the shoulder.

The boy is slow to respond. After a beat he turns around, looks up.

The girl is, by Sears catalogue standards, attractive. She is tall and slim, blonde and blue-eyed. Her skin is unblemished. She seems to have a good start on a set of breasts. She is also without expression. And she seems to be waiting for the boy to say something. Which he doesn't, turning back to his comic instead.

GIRL
(judgementally)
You're new, aren't you?

101

BOY

Nope. I've been around about thirteen years now.

GIRL

(slightly pissed off)

Oh, I bet you think that's funny?

BOY

(turning a page)

Nope. Just true.

GIRL

My name's Cindy Carruthers and I'm having a party this Saturday.

She tosses an invitation onto the boy's comic.

CLOSE ON INVITATION: YOU'RE INVITED

You can come if you want.

The girl storms off. The boy picks up the card. He reads it, smiles, puts it in his breast pocket. He returns to his comic.

BOY

(to himself)

And my name's Randy Cobb.

"Why were you being such a goof to her?" Bobby demanded. Randy shrugged. "I didn't know who she was?" he replied, scratching at his pubic hair. Bobby scoffed. He couldn't believe it. So he let Randy know: "She's just the most beautiful girl in Vancouver!" Randy shrugged again. He was playing Bobby perfectly. "Yeah, but you don't know that yet, do you, Bobby? I mean, you don't even know what she looks like," he said, scratching at his pubic hair once more. I looked around for sand fleas, but of course there weren't any.

EXT. A LARGE DUTCH COLONIAL. NIGHT

Warm, yellow light in the windows. Lots of movement inside. A party. The muffled voice of Elton John announcing to the revellers that the "Bitch Is Back."

INT. HALLWAY

HIGH ANGLE

A uniformed caterer walks past the front door carrying a platter of Rice Krispie squares. Going the other way is a snappily dressed girl (12) and, just behind her, an equally snappy boy (12). He seems to be pleading with her. She ignores him.

Once the hall is clear the doorbell rings.

Footsteps. Somebody is coming downstairs. A man (50), conservatively dressed in a light blue cardigan and grey slacks, a pipe in hand, enters the frame and opens the door.

REVERSE

The man is taken aback.

REVERSE

Randy is standing on the porch, decked out in a tight black vest, white flared jeans, and platforms. He is holding some daisies and Zappa's *Hot Rats* LP.

> RANDY
>
> Hey.

> CINDY
> (off)
>
> Who is it, Daddy?

Daddy shuts the door.

                                FATHER
                    (off, his voice trailing away)
        One of the Allman Brothers — how the hell should
        I know?

The door opens.

                                CINDY
                        (happy, then stern)
        Oh. It's you.

                                RANDY
                    (handing Cindy the flowers)
        I brought you these.

Cindy makes a hard smile. She accepts the flowers.

                                CINDY
                            (shyly)
        Thank you.

Bobby was squirming around on his stomach, full of guffaws as he
listened to Randy's story. He was loving it. "Oh my God! Why
didn't you just jump on her right there?" he shrieked. Randy
chuckled. "Not yet," he said, sitting up, opening his legs so that
his cock and testicles dropped between them. "I was just playing it
cool. I still wasn't sure if I wanted to get involved." Bobby
collapsed in disbelief. Randy was still playing it cool. And it was
too funny.

EXT. BACKYARD. NIGHT

Patio lanterns. A shimmering kidney-shaped pool. Kids mingling, a
few of them dancing to Brownsville Station. A buffet table. And a
pool house.

Randy is standing by the buffet table. He picks up an hors d'oeuvre,
examines it, sniffs it, puts it in his mouth.

Cindy is sitting with her war party — three other girls of similarly attractive dispositions. They are staring in Randy's direction.

Randy picks up a Rice Krispie square, examines it, then puts it back on the tray.

> CINDY
> (looking over at one of the girls, crossly)
> Forget it, Trish. You already told me you were going after Tom Dean.

Trish sighs.

> CINDY
> Randy Cobb is mine.

DISSOLVE

Poolside. A group of six or seven couples are doing an awkward slow dance to the Beach Boys' "Little Surfer Girl." The caterers are cleaning up. It feels like the last dance of the night.

> ADULT WOMAN'S VOICE
> (off)
> Susie Wolf and Tommy Hanson — one foot apart, please. I don't want to have to tell you two again.

A girl (12) and a boy (12) suddenly jump back from each other and assume the position — one foot apart.

Randy and Cindy are dancing "properly." His arms fully extended, hands above her hip bones; her arms fully extended, hands on his shoulders. They rock side-to-side, slowly. It's called "snowballing."

> CINDY
> (keenly)
> So your mom's from California and your dad's from here.

> RANDY

Right.

> CINDY

Wow. So you're, like, half Californian?

> RANDY

Right. But now I'm gonna be a full-time Canadian 'cause the courts awarded me to my dad.

> CINDY

But if I tell people you're from California, then that wouldn't be a lie, right?

> RANDY

Nope. I was born in Bakersfield.

> ADULT VOICE
> (off)

Okay, Susie and Tommy. That's enough.

Susie and Tommy are locked in a necking embrace.

All right, everybody. I think that's enough for tonight.

The record is scratched to a stop. Exterior lights go up.

> CINDY
> (urgently)

Do you live near here?

> RANDY

We're living at my aunt's. It's about three blocks —

> CINDY
> (quickly)

Can you meet me later? There's a hole in the hedge behind the pool house. You can get through it from the lane. I'll leave the door in the pool house open.

                         RANDY
                    (a bit surprised)
Well ...

                         CINDY
                    (desperately)
    Can you or can't you?

                         RANDY

What time?

                         CINDY

    Midnight?

                         RANDY
                     (smiling)

Okay.

                         CINDY
                     (beaming)

Okay.

Cindy runs off towards the house. Randy looks around, notices
everyone else is gone. He makes his way towards the hedge.

TRACKING RANDY

He steps through the hole in the hedge.

EXT. ALLEY. NIGHT

Randy emerges from the hedge. He dusts himself off. He walks
towards the camera and stops.

                         RANDY
                    (to the camera)
    So I went back at midnight and burned down their
    house.

8.7

— That's when Bobby lost it.

— Right. He told Randy to go fuck himself, told him he didn't like being bullshitted. Then he put on his clothes and stormed off down the beach. He'd told us he was going home, but he ended up about ten logs down, on the clothed side of Foreshores, chucking rocks at the gun tower.

— Did you try and stop him?

— No, we were laughing too hard. Besides, he wasn't going any-where; he didn't know where the hell he was. We reckoned he'd just sit there and wait for us once it was time to go.

— What did you two do in the meantime?

— Randy told me what really happened.

— How did you know what he told you was real?

— I don't know — was it? You tell me.

8.8

It was the Friday after Randy started at Churchill. He was on his way home from school when he decided to split from his usual route and take the alleyway. Three houses in, he heard somebody call his name. It was a girl's voice. Randy stopped, looked around. Nothing. He took a step forward, then heard it again — this time with gig-gles. The voice was coming from a hole in a hedge. Randy poked his head through and saw Cindy Carruthers and another girl crouched behind a pool house, each of them holding pint glasses. They were drinking something orange. And they were drunk.

"Hello, big boy," said Cindy's friend, cracking up. Randy shook his head and turned to leave. "No, don't go!" Cindy shouted after him. Randy heard footsteps. The next thing he knew the girls were on him, their fingers hooked through his belt loops, pulling him backwards towards the hedge. "No, no, no, no, no," Cindy slurred. "You can't go yet. You have to sit with us. We're having a tea party." So Randy thought, Why not? They crawled through the hole and sat down behind the pool house, in the shape of a triangle.

Cindy's friend was a darker, more robust version of Cindy. As it turns out, she was Cindy's neighbour, Jenny Wolf. Although two years older than Cindy, Jenny was Cindy's best friend. A lot of what Cindy learned from life must have come from Jenny. Or that's what I gathered from what Randy had to say.

The girls watched Randy, Randy watched the girls. He was bemused by the way they'd turn to each other, giggle, then go back to sipping. Jenny handed Randy her glass. "Here," she said. Randy took a sip. "A Harvey Wallbanger," he said, handing it back. Cindy just sat there, her eyes glazed, grinning. "Maybe he's the one," Jenny said, nudging Cindy. More giggles. Then Randy said to Jenny, "The one for what?" Jenny nudged Cindy again. "Ask him," Jenny said. "I dare you." Then Cindy nodded. Going from cross-legs to all fours, Cindy crawled over to Randy, where she knelt before him and stuck out her chest. "Put your hands up my top — *new guy.*"

So he did. He reached under Cindy's T-shirt and explored. Cindy's soft breasts filled his hands. Water balloons, he kept thinking. Nothing like the siliconed breasts of his mother's friend, the woman who had first introduced Randy to the female form. Cindy closed her eyes and began a slow rotation, pressing her breasts against Randy's open palms. Jenny, in the meantime, had crawled over to join them. But instead of asking for Randy's hands, she just lifted her top up and let her breasts plunge forth. They looked like crescent moons, Randy thought. He liked their curve, the way the nipples pointed up and out. He'd heard somewhere that the French had breasts like that.

Now they were all pressed together. Everybody's shirt was untucked and the breathing was heavy. Cindy sucked on Randy's neck, while Jenny rubbed his crotch. Randy reached down and squeezed Cindy's bum. Then he reached down and squeezed Jenny's bum. Although both bums felt the same, Randy was sure that Jenny's bum was bigger. It was certainly less bony. Jenny pushed her crotch into Randy's hip and struggled with his button and fly. Randy reached between both girls' legs and squeezed gently. Jenny moaned. Then Cindy moaned, too. A strange harmonic interval,

Randy thought. How both moans made an overtone. How it sounded so much like music from a movie.

Randy felt the cool air on his cock. He watched as Jenny pulled on it, letting it fall out of her pudgy hand, then grabbing it again, repeating the motion. Randy's cock grew longer, harder. But now what was Cindy up to? Now she was kissing her way across Randy's face, totally wrecking his view of Jenny's hand. Not a problem, though. For Randy knew he could just as easily go the other way on Cindy. Which is what he did. Kissing. So now Randy was sucking on Cindy's neck, where he could watch as both Jenny's hands tugged down his Levi's. Then Jenny did something that turned Randy on so much he almost shot off right then and there. Jenny took Cindy's hand and wrapped it as far as it would go around Randy's erection, giving it a quick lesson in grips. Randy was so turned on. He loved it that these two girls could have that kind of friendship.

Her lesson imparted, Jenny sat back and supervised. Randy watched Jenny watching. He thought, This is so cool. He liked it that Jenny was so professional, as if Cindy were being graded on her technique, as if there was a chance Cindy might blow this thing and have to be shown up by an expert. Randy also liked it that Jenny would occasionally reach over and squeeze his balls, jiggling them, if only to demo something for Cindy to pick up on, something she could do with her other hand once she felt comfortable with this first assignment. But as this went on, Randy felt troubled by the way Jenny became more and more detached from his pleasure, that her petting was really more for Cindy's benefit rather than his own — just as Cindy's hand-job wasn't really for him so much as it was for her instructor, Jenny. This is where Randy began to lose it. He sensed a softening. Which, of course, would only reflect poorly on Cindy.

As Randy's cock shrank, Cindy became more and more desperate. For now she was trying stuff she wasn't sure would work. Of course, Randy found this out the hard way: at one point he jumped back, convinced that Cindy had cut him with one of her nails. Cindy threw Jenny a pleading look, and Jenny decided it was time for her to step back in. Randy thought this was an even worse idea. They were only doing this for each other; it had nothing to do with him. So now he wanted out. He was all set to hike his pants up when Jenny introduced something new. Because now she was using her mouth. And Jenny's mouth felt warm and right over Randy's cock. So now it was the combined efforts of hand and mouth that were bringing Randy around: the way they worked together, pumping and sucking ...

Randy felt he was ready to come. And Jenny sensed this, which turned on Randy even more. Now Jenny was motioning for Cindy to join her. And Cindy was into it. Jenny took Randy's cock out of her mouth and pushed it into Cindy's. Randy couldn't believe this. He was reeling. But what was that? Did somebody say something? It was Jenny! She was giving Cindy oral instruction! "Don't suck — blow," she whispered, her hand on the back of Cindy's bobbing head, as if to keep the beat. "Good. Now grab his nuts." And sure enough Cindy's free hand came up and lifted Randy's testicles, rolling them between her fingers, pulling them. The next time Randy looked over at Jenny she was smiling at him. She seemed really pleased that Randy was getting off, as if she were blowing him herself.

Jenny continued her supervision. But this time she didn't look so concerned. Her pupil was passing, and the only thing that seemed to be worrying Jenny was what to do with Randy's come. At least that's what Randy was thinking. Because Randy began to feel lightheaded, and all kinds of thoughts were going through his mind. Jenny seemed experienced enough to know this. Something about the way she looked at him just before he shut his eyes.

One of the last things Randy noticed: Jenny's hand was underneath Cindy's ass, and it was active. This was all he needed. Everything after that was strobic. He felt something sharp pierce the dull hum in his body. Jenny looked up, quickly grabbed Randy's cock out of Cindy's mouth; she pumped it hard, pointing it earthwards. Cindy let go of Randy's testicles, took in the show. Jenny was going a million miles per hour. The foreskin blurred. Randy let go with a moan as he fired his first shot, a dribble. Then a quick little spurt. Then a big one. Then one so big it caused Cindy to jump. Three or four shorter spurts followed. Then they stopped altogether. The three of them fell back on the grass. Cindy's dog came around the corner and sniffed the sperm. Someone was home. Randy had to go. Fast. Like a house on fire.

8.9

— You had plans to make that into a film. *Poolside Attraction.*

— Yeah, I thought that might be our first feature. Did up a shooting script and everything.

— What happened?

— Well, I'd be lying if I told you we were even close.

8.10

If Randy's story gave me an erection, the epilogue took it away. The combined effect was that I now had to pee. So I got up and went to the bushes. It took a while to find a good spot. As I was making my way around I began to replay not only Randy's story but Randy lying there telling it. My mind lit up: the shine off his shoulders, his thick nipples, his bumpy abs. I closed my eyes and peed. I thought of him just as he was, lying there in the sun, the head of his cock peeking out of his foreskin, the sweat beading up on his balls. I thought of the shadowed depressions in the sides of his buttocks, and how they clenched when he moved. Then I imagined him with girls. All sorts of girls. Girls from movies, TV, the Sears catalogue. I saw hands tug on his shoulders, breasts pressing against his chest, pink tongues flicking at his nipples, the rise of an ass. But those images were fleeting. The sun had mushed my brain, so once they flashed off they were hard to replay. Plus Randy himself kept getting in the way. Because the only thing I knew for sure was Randy. He was so real. And I still wasn't convinced Cindy Carruthers was anything more than a rumour. I stopped pissing just as Randy came, in my mind, a second time.

8.11

— What do you mean when you say that Randy kept "getting in the way"?

— Well, I guess what I was doing was using Randy to imagine what it might be like to be with other girls. But all I could concentrate on was Randy.

— Why didn't you imagine yourself with these girls?

— Because I'd done that. I'd been doing that for ages. This just seemed more exciting.

— Because you wanted to be Randy?

— No, because I wanted to be with Randy.

— As one of these girls.

— No, as myself.

— Did you ever entertain the idea of being with Nettie as Randy?

— Sure.

— Was this more exciting than being yourself with Nettie?

— Sometimes.

— So what happened after you urinated?

8.12

When I came out of the bush, Randy was gone. What I mean by that is he wasn't at the log any more. So I went looking for him. I started down the beach towards the gun tower, then turned back because I didn't want to deal with Bobby. On my way back I saw Randy playing Frisbee. So I started jogging towards him. I was all set to call out, when who should pop up from behind a log but Penny Singleton. And she's stark naked! So I ducked behind a rock and watched as Randy made his way over to Penny. Turns out the guy Randy was playing Frisbee with was John. So now it's just the three of them sitting there. And what? Were they waiting for me to join them? Were the four of us gonna sit around in the buff and *talk?* That's when I snuck over to our log, scooped up my clothes, and hightailed it down the beach towards Bobby, stopping ever fifty feet or so to put on another article. Somehow the two of us found our way home.

— Are you sure it was John and Penny you saw on the beach that day?

— Of course, I'm sure.

— Just like you weren't sure it was Mr. Billington you saw in Judge Smart's study?

— I'm pretty sure it was Billington.

— Did seeing John and Penny on the beach that day have any bearing on why you didn't want to go over to their house for your graduation party?

— Sort of.

— Then why didn't you mention that when you were telling us about how you lied to Nettie at the Big Scoop?

— I don't know. It didn't seem important.

— So even in the retelling of a lie you were lying?

— No, I wasn't lying. I really thought they'd forgotten us. Besides, I just didn't think it was that big a deal. I think it had more to do with not wanting to know them without their clothes on.

— But hadn't you already seen them "naked," so to speak, when you rubbed the felt pen off their film rushes? And didn't they "bare" themselves to you regarding what happened to Mr. Gingell?

— I suppose.

— Then why would you have a problem being naked with them? You've already told us that you didn't have a problem with your body, being naked around other people.

— I don't know. I mean, if I were to guess, I would say that sitting around naked with John and Penny would kinda work against the fact that they'd always made me feel like an adult in their company. And if they had forgotten us, I would have at least wanted them to remember us as adults — and not appear in their life, out of the blue, as a child. Does that make any sense?

— What happened at school on Monday, the next time you saw Randy?

— He told me about these cool people he met on the beach.

— Was he mad you abandoned him?

— Not really. I mean, I told him some lie about how I went looking for Bobby and that I got lost. But he didn't care. He seemed to be used to people coming and going in his life.

— Did you see much of Randy after that?

— Oh yeah. He was around. For a while. He went back to California about a month later. I only found this out because I went over to his place to return his Eagles records and his aunt said I might as well just keep them because Randy wasn't coming back. Yeah, he didn't even phone or nothin'. It was like — *poof!*

9.1a

June 18, 1978

Dear Nettie,
How are you? I'm fine. I miss you. Everyone misses you. When will you be coming

9.1b

June 18, 1978

Dear Nettie,
How are you feeling? Okay? I hope so. Bobby called yesterday to say that [his sister] Amy is the editor

115

of this year's annual (which comes out tomorrow) and she told him that one of your poems (I don't know which one) got its own page. I can tell you this because you have a good sense of humour: even though everyone agrees it's a good poem, Bobby said the only reason his sister published it was because all of us thought you were going to die. (You know what he's like.) Anyway, I told him that you weren't in the clear yet, that you still had a few more hospital meals left in you. Ha-ha-ha.

Your mother was over yesterday and she

9.1c

June 18, 1978

Dear Nettie,

Your mother was over at our house yesterday and she told us you were up and talking. Phew! She said if I sent you a letter, you'd probably be able to read it, but that you still weren't well enough for visitors. I asked her if I could come by the hospital and deliver the letter to you personally (I assured her that I wouldn't do anything other than sit there and watch you read it), but she said no. She thought you might find visitors too stressful. I told her that you and I used to do all kinds of stuff like that in elementary [pass notes] and that you seemed to get a real kick out of it (the opposite of stress, I suppose), but your mom still said no. Then she told me she was glad I was speaking in the past tense because she didn't want to hear any more about us fucking around with notes (okay, she didn't use the word "fucking") and that you've missed too much school already and that you'll need all your strength to catch up. I told her that you were a brain (which is true) and that missing a month of school wouldn't affect you like it would the rest of us; but your mom said the stress of getting caught [fucking around] might cause your heart further trauma and the last thing we all needed was a relapse. Yeah, right. As if we ever got caught [fucking around].

There was a rumour going around school today that Bobby Galt and I tied for Grade Ten Male Athlete of the Year. No big deal — until Bobby caught wind of it. I was on my way home when up struts Galt. He asks me if I heard the rumour and I make the mistake of saying yeah. Then he tells me that if the rumour's true, he's going to appeal because it isn't fair that there could be two winners. (Obviously he wants the award all to himself, right?) So I tease him a little, egg him on, tell him that he may have sunk a couple more baskets than I did but my defensive game was miles better. But other than that we were dead even when it came to rugby and track. That really got him going. So he tells me that star athletes are always those players with the best offensive production — that it's a proven fact! (What a great attitude for a team captain to have, eh?) So I just shrug my shoulders and give up; the guy is so lost. But then he starts gassing on about how there's not enough room on the nameplate for the both of us and that if they try to put two names up there, there's no way you'll be able to read them because the names will be too small and the trophy case has such shitty lighting. So I tell him that maybe his cheap-ass dad might spring for a new bulb. That's when the goof goes ballistic! He tells me how he's going to sue the PE Department if both our names are called out at the awards ceremony, that it's in the best interest of sport that we refuse to accept a tie, and that I should begin preparing myself for the inevitable letdown that comes with not winning. I told him he'd better act fast, that the awards ceremony is only three days away. Then he calms down a bit, starts to "think." After a while he tells me in this real nice voice — and you'll love this — that once he wins he expects me to be big about it, take it like a man, that there's no reason why the two of us can't still be friends, that we are, after all, the heart of the team, and how, "like anybody sharing a heart, we have to beat as one." Those were his exact words! Can you believe it! So I told him he could take the award and shove it up his ass for all I care. I told him

9.1d

June 18, 1978

Dear Nettie,
    I don't know what to say. I'm really sorry. Not just for your illness, but for everything that's happened (or hasn't happened) since

9.2

— You started four letters and you didn't finish one.

— That's right. And by the way, I didn't start using semicolons until I was seventeen.

— We did a line edit.

— Which accounts for the square brackets?

— Correct.

— Okay, then. Answer me this: If you know so much about my life, why the need for square brackets?

— We have some of the best editors at our disposal. We have to keep them busy.

— Oh.

— So you never did see Nettie, did you?

— No.

— And that third letter — you made all that up, didn't you? You made up reasons for not going to see her?

— Yes.

— Because you felt guilty.

— That's correct.

— Then say it.

— Okay. Because I felt guilty.

9.3

A week before Nettie was due back from hospital, Mrs. Smart phoned up a bunch of Nettie's "friends" and invited us over for a party. She said she wanted to do something special for Nettie, something fun, a surprise because Nettie loved surprises. My first reaction was: Since when does Nettie love surprises? But I couldn't tell Mrs. Smart that. She'd already made up her mind.

Nettie was discharged from VGH on a Saturday afternoon. The plan was to gather at the Smarts' an hour beforehand for a briefing. Once all the guests arrived — I was shocked at how few friends Nettie seemed to have — Mrs. Smart told us everything we needed to know about Nettie's condition, what had happened, how we were to deal with it. The whole nine yards. Much of what Mrs. Smart told us appeared in a story she'd published in *B.C. Housewife* fifteen years before — though, according to my mom, Mrs. Smart had originally intended it for *Reader's Digest* and never quite got over the disappointment of having it serialized in a local magazine. I came across it once while snooping through my mother's drawers. I can't imagine why she saved it. It was so self-centred, so badly written.

9.3a

B.C. Housewife Magazine, April, 1962

When the nurse told me I had given birth to a daughter I was the happiest woman in the world. For there I was: twenty-five years old, with a successful husband, a beautiful home, and now a beautiful daughter to go with a handsome son of five years. What more could a married woman ask of life? Everything was perfect. I could hardly wait for the pictures.

However, as I was being wheeled back to my

private room — which my attentive husband insisted I have — a young internist named Dr. Max Wright [Ed. note: Later the husband of our society columnist Pamela Moss] came running down the hall to tell me that there was a complication with my daughter Annette. He said I would need to consent to emergency surgery. My heart broke. And just like that it appeared my perfect life — only minutes old — was over. I signed the release. Then I cried like a baby. I cried like the baby I was told I might lose.

I never did get to hold my daughter in the hospital. I never did get that photo of the two of us. Now I can only imagine: sitting up in bed, exhausted, smiling wearily for the camera, my daughter at my breast, the gold metal frame propped up on my make-up table ... That's when the tears start rolling down my cheeks. It never fails to happen. Oh my, I'm crying right now. As I write this, I'm crying. If only I'd had a photo to cling to. If only my husband and I weren't so alone with our remembrances of that terrible day.

A week later I was sent home, without my baby. And without a photo. Annette and I were off to a very bad start.

(See next month's issue: "Changing the Bandages")

9.4

I don't remember when *exactly* I tuned out of Mrs. Smart's story, but I do remember reflecting on the faces gathered at the Smarts'. I wondered whether these people were actually Nettie's friends or whether they were just the friends her mother wanted her to have. Then I thought of my own status, how I'd been invited even though I sensed I was clearly not wanted.

So could any of these people really be friends of Nettie's? Did she even have any friends? Or were these people just names and numbers plucked from her address book? Names and numbers as described in her diary? And if that was the case, was there anything in her diary about me? Anything nasty?

Sitting beside Mrs. Smart was the girl who ran the Lost and Found. I remembered her from elementary. Her name was Shawna Kowalchuk and she was forever knitting sweaters. She was also horribly disfigured — *acne vulgaris* — and had this bum leg that required a heavy boot-and-brace contraption that clanked when she walked.

I remember once, in Grade Eight Phys Ed, Mr. Longley gave us a lecture on hygiene. Part of the lecture dealt with acne. Halfway through Longley's ramble, Bobby Galt raised his hand and asked — in that fake earnest way of his — if what Shawna Kowalchuk had all over her face was acne vulgaris. The idiot Longley, who was lecturing without the use of visual aids, lit up. "Yes, Bobby! Very good," he said, all proud of his future biddy-ball star. "Shawna Kowalchuk is a living example of acne vulgaris." So from that day on Shawna Kowalchuk became commonly known as "The Living Example."

To Shawna's right was Cheryl Parks. Originally from Winnipeg, Cheryl transferred to our high school in Grade Nine. When she first arrived Cheryl turned a few heads. Though not particulary foxy, she had an asset that most guys were going in for at the time: that pleasant face/nice butt/funny girl combo. After a couple of parties, I could see that Cheryl was closing in on the Cindy crowd and had attracted the eye of the increasingly popular Mark Irwin, another Grade Nine transferee who came to us from Montreal. It seemed a match made in heaven, and we were eager to welcome this couple into our power circle. Then something happened.

New Year's Eve at Cindy Carruthers'. The last night of 1976. It was about eleven o'clock and all of us were sitting around the rec room getting buzzed on grass and Baby Duck. There was some necking going on, but nothing major. Cindy seemed particularly pleased that Mark and Cheryl were "consummating" — which, for all intents and purposes, was the assent those two would need for induction into our group. I think it was a rule of Cindy's that new kids had to enter her circle in pairs. But whatever. It was getting near time for her dad's nightly visit. So when we heard the stairs creak, we knew what to do.

Although by no means a liberal man, Chuck Carruthers knew exactly what we got up to in the basement of his house. And he was forever making a point of telling us how tolerant he was, if only to tell us, at the same time, how much he disapproved. He was often heard to say stuff like: "Although I don't condone how you kids behave these days, there's not a helluva lot I can do about it — just so long as you don't shove it in my face." Or something like that. So, out of deference to Chuck, we'd open a window and turn down the music. Then we'd sit up straight like the nice kids we weren't and wait for his pre-emptive knock. When Mr. Carruthers entered he'd always flicked on and off the overhead lights. And this, I think, was what triggered Cheryl.

After Chuck's look around, Cindy would fake mortification and skulk her way over to the light switch, turn off the overheads, and apologize for her nerdy dad. But this time was different. Because just as Cindy was making her way across the room, Mark Irwin screamed, "Holy shit, man!" and we all turned around to find Cheryl Parks flopping on the floor, her eyes rolling back in her head, her mouth making the strangest sounds this side of *The Exorcist*. It was very Linda Blair. And we had no idea what was happening — even though it was obvious she was having an epileptic seizure. So what did we do? Nothing. We just stood there, like idiots, while Cheryl bit through her lip and gurgled blood all over the Carruthers' white shag. When it was over we thought she was dead.

The ambulance showed up at the stroke of midnight, just as everybody in the neighbourhood was spilling out to bang their pots and pans. The combined effect was bizarre: the swirl of the ambulance cherry and all that clang. Then Cheryl's parents pulling up in their battered Valiant. I'll never forget the look on Cindy's face when she first saw the Parkses. It was total judgement. Pure disgust. The same face she made when Cheryl seizured.

They seemed like nice people, the Parkses. And naturally they were concerned over their daughter's health. But I think it was the way they expressed their concern that bothered Cindy so much. Because Mrs. Parks was hysterical. Absolutely out of her mind. And this hysteria was made even more profound by her appearance: her gigantic curlers, her ratty housecoat, her matted slippers. Mr. Parks, on the other hand, was very calm — a Milquetoast kind of calm. He didn't seem to have a problem letting his wife take charge of the situation. So while Mrs. Parks attended to her daughter, Mr. Parks just stood there and cried.

The pots-and-pans crowd gathered as Cheryl was loaded into the ambulance, her face all bloodied as though she'd been punched. I overheard one of the neighbours comment, rather loudly, that it appeared Cindy's temper had finally caught up with her, and that he was glad something like this had happened because now Cindy was going to get what was coming. I wasn't quite sure what he meant by this until another neighbour pointed out that from the condition of the Parkses' car there would no doubt be a lawsuit. I was pretty sure Cindy heard this, because she was standing right beside me when it happened. All of which was too bad for Cheryl, because now she would no doubt be banished from Cindy's circle. Not that she stood any chance of redemption after what she did to upstage Cindy's party. So I suppose that might explain, then, how Cheryl ended up at Nettie's.

There were a couple of other girls at the Smarts' as well. One of which was Lydia, the girl who delivered the morning paper. Lydia told me she'd never even met Nettie, and that the only reason she was there was because Mrs. Smart had given her a really decent tip at Christmas. But it was the other girl in attendance who provided the ultimate shockeroo — Margie Stott. Just what Margie was doing there was beyond me. But anything was possible back in those days. I mean, I never would have thought, that Nettie and I would have drifted as far apart as we did.

Oh, and Alistar Chen — he was there, too. He brought a big basket of raspberries. The first I'd seen all year.

9.5

Nettie looked awful. So small and gaunt. I felt bad for her. So bad. The judge carrying her in like that, standing her up in the foyer like a doll, then peeling off her coat to reveal some dowdy jumpsuit her mother had no doubt found, something the Nettie I knew never would have stood for.

So: poor Nettie. Her back to us, by the coat rack, oblivious. And all of us just sitting there, paper plates in our laps, frozen, watching, afraid to say anything, let alone "Surprise!" Then Nettie turning around, her faint hello. And all of us, at once, gushing back with Hellos! How are yas! Welcome back, Netties! I felt something well up inside me. More an anger than a sympathy, really. Not that I was mad at her, or that I didn't feel bad. I mean, I just thought it was so unfair that she had to go through all that surgery. And her voice — so cracked and scratchy.

Margie Stott was the first one up. She made a big deal about it, too. Throwing her arms around Nettie, bursting into tears. This seemed funny to me, and I tried not to laugh. So much of what Margie was doing was about Margie. I mean, she didn't give a shit about Nettie. Those two were mortal enemies. But whatever. Mrs. Smart was getting the rest of us to form a proper welcoming line. But I just sat there, still unsure. Nettie's mom seemed pleased with the affection being accorded her daughter, so I guess I was happy for her.

Eventually I did stand up, taking my place behind Alistar. I was pretty nervous. I wasn't sure how Nettie would react. I mean, if she punched me in the face, I would have totally understood. I'd completely ignored her the past couple of years and she had every right to let me have it. So when it came time for Alistar to greet Nettie, I sorta peeked out from behind him and smiled. Nettie was just brushing aside her hair. But we made contact. I could tell. Because she did something with her mouth that spoke volumes: that the party was a dumb idea; that she didn't even know half the people in the room; and that when we got alone she was definitely going to let me have it. That's when I knew we were back.

9.6

— You two renewed your friendship.

— Well, it was more like we renegotiated it. It had been a long time since we'd really spoken and Nettie had a lot to say.

— Were you surprised?

— No. In fact, most of what we talked about was outlined in her letter.

— Which letter?

— You don't know?

— She wrote many letters to you in that time.

— Yes, but they all came at once. The one I'm referring to is the last one, which, as you already know, contained the first ten or so. And the last one was the one she wrote around the time her mom came by to tell us she wasn't yet ready for visitors.

— The "Dear Asshole" series?

— That's correct.

9.6a

June 18, 1978
Vancouver General Hospital

Dear Asshole,

I am sending you a letter that began in my diary two years ago. I fully intended to send it before my operation, but changed my mind at the last minute because I thought if I survived the surgery, I might have a change of heart (pun intended). So now I'm sending it to you anyway just because I feel it might do you some good and because life's too short and I just don't care about certain things any more like I used to. But also because I still care about you no matter what happens and that I'd like you to know that.

As I said before: I began writing this in my diary, so that's why the pages are torn and the lines are pink and not blue foolscap. I thought if anything should happen to me, it would be better for you to know about my feelings towards you, because these pages were addressed to you and not my diary. Plus I didn't want my mom getting ahold of it. These are some of the things I wrote:

September 17, 1975

You are such an asshole. Not you, Diary. I mean YOU, ASSHOLE. YOU whose name I'll never mention again. ASSHOLE. You are such an asshole for what you've done to me. For ignoring me. For avoiding me. For dropping me like that. I thought you were different. I thought you weren't like the Bobby Galts of the world. I thought we were friends.

September 18, 1975

Sell-out fucking loser asshole. I should have known. I did know. I'd heard about what happens when people go to high school. Dunc told me. Dunc said that things get splintered into cliques. So I should have known. I should have asked you what your intentions were, if you were going to go in for all that cliquey shit — ASSHOLE. And that's the hard part. That's the part that hurts me the most. Not what you did, but that I never thought you'd do it. You make me feel stupid and I hate you.

September 19, 1975

All the girls are being encouraged to try out for grass hockey, but I thought, Fuck that! I'm gonna come out for rugby! I'm gonna come out for rugby so I can bust your butt, you scrawny piece of shit! So watch out, ASSHOLE. Rugby starts tomorrow.

October 20, 1975

Saw you today. You and Bobby and your new friends. You're such a pretty bunch. You all look so good together. You and your fashions. Your floppy wide-legs. And you told me in Grade Seven you'd never wear flares! Liar. All of you. Deep down — so scared.

November 21, 1975

I hear you're going to ask Julie Kyle if she wants to go around with you. I heard that from the horse's mouth — HER. I was getting changed for Phys Ed and I overheard them talking. Julie said she heard from Nevermind that Nevermind overheard you tell

Nevermind that you were going to ask her at the dance to go around. Oh, and she was so happy about that, too! She heard that you were such a good kisser. She told the other scrags that she'd heard from Cindy Carruthers that you two necked with each other once just to see who knew more about necking. So I guess you two will be official next week. I guess you two will be GOING AROUND. I know that would make stupid Julie happy. As if I care. But I doubt you two will ever get very far. I truly doubt you'll ever get to see that ugly birthmark on her butt (even though I hope you do). Yeah, and I hope those little black hairs sticking out make you sick just so you'll know what a knob you really are.

January 2, 1976

Sorry I haven't written lately. I've been busy with other things. While you've been in the bushes with your wife, Julie, I've been seeing this guy named Nathan who works at the Aquatic Centre and who's seventeen and hot. I thought you'd like to know that the two of us get together on Sundays and go to his apartment downtown where I let him feel me up. He's got a nice body, too. He tells me he likes my mind and he thinks I'm cute and the last time we got together I held his boner in my hand while he fingered me, then put his tongue down there, and it felt fucking great! The next time I write you I will probably not be a virgin any more. By the way, have you seen Julie's birthmark yet?

February 5, 1976

Saw you at the Elton John concert. What were you doing way up in the blue seats? It was festival seating, you idiot. You could stand anywhere. So why were you hiding up in the rafters? All the action was in front of the stage. That's where me and Nathan were. Maybe you saw us dancing to "Island Girl"? That was me in the burgundy top. By the way, I'm not a virgin any more. Thought you should know.

February 5, 1978

Saw you hanging out in the McDonald's parking lot last weekend. I was driving by with Nathan. I have my learner's permit now, and Nathan is teaching me how to parallel park. Has it really been two years since I'd forgotten you?

March 11, 1978

Ha! Ha-ha-ha-ha! So the talk all over school is that Julie Kyle broke up with you. SUCKER! I heard she broke up with you to go out with Brian Archer in Grade Twelve. Seems that's what all the other pop girls in Grade Ten are doing. Seems that Cindy Carruthers started something when she snagged that hunky Derek Lane. Seems like your tight little circle's turned into a horseshoe of boys now, doesn't it? I guess little boys like you will have to wait another couple of years before you get some action again. Unless you start dating those little airheads in Grade Eight. Either way, I hope you'll figure out what to do with a girl by the time you get there. Not that I give two shits.

June 16, 1978

My mother's throwing me a welcome home party. I suppose you'll be feeling guilty enough to come. She's invited a bunch of people that I really don't care to see, so don't get all smug about them being my friends.

9.7

— Was there any truth to Nettie's letters?

— What's the truth? I think her feelings speak for themselves.

— How does that make you feel?

— Fine.

— What if you'd read those letters at the time they were being written?

— God only knows.

10.1

We met at the Big Scoop. It was a good place, the Scoop. Never full. The only people who went there any more were crumblies, and they would just sit there, half-dead, sipping tea by the windows. So we ordered some coffee and fries and took a booth in the back. Nettie, who looked good and rested considering all the shit she'd been through, didn't waste much time. She asked me what I thought of the letters.

She said, "So tell me, asshole, did you notice how much better my writing got since Grade Eight?" And I came right back with something just as sarcastic. I told her how relieved I was that she finally stopped dotting her *i*'s with those stupid little circles. Nettie laughed at that. "What about those block letters? Did you miss those, too?" she said. And I said yeah, I did. But this time I didn't turn it into a joke. This time we just looked at each other, said nothing. It had been ages since I'd looked into Nettie's face. It was great. Time passed. And we let it.

Nettie lit a cigarette. "Hey, d'ya know what my mom told me?" she said, all excited. "That she hates my guts?" I said. "No, no — c'mon, she loves you! But d'ya know what she told me?" I shrugged. "What then?" Nettie looked over her shoulder, leaned forward, and whispered: "That the Billingtons are moving." Man, the Smarts knew everything! "And you know what else?" I didn't. Nettie went right up to my ear this time. "Now we're gonna have to find somebody else's garbage to pick through." Ha-ha-ha. Just like old times. That Nettie!

So yeah — time passed. Between the two of us we probably drank about three pots of Bun-O-Matic coffee, smoked a whole pack of Player's. Near the end of our summit Nettie began telling me how much I looked like Hero, the sailor on the Player's package. "Nettie, I look nothing like Hero," I told her. "I mean, c'mon — the guy's in his fifties!" Nettie reached over to the next booth, picked up an empty package of Export A's. "Okay, what about me?" she said, sticking the package in my face. "Do I or do I not look like the MacDonald Lassie?" I took the package and studied it. The MacDonald Lassie was cute, but not beautiful. A total girl-next-door type. I pulled a pen from my coat pocket and drew a stick-body underneath her cameo face. "There," I said, handing it back. "Now you look just like the MacDonald Lassie." Nettie smiled. She took the Player's package and aligned the head of Hero with that of the Lassie, kissing them together. "Those two were made for each other," I said. Nettie snickered as she squished. Her eyes flashed quick between the packages and me.

10.2

We walked home like we did in elementary, down Cypress to the crossing. It was summer now, and all along the tracks the foliage was green and cool. We didn't say much once we got to the crossing. We knew what we were doing.

Down the tracks, just before the blackberries, was a sunken area protected by tall grasses. When Bobby and I were kids we used to play war in there. But that was ages ago.

We climbed in, got down on our knees. Nettie began unbuttoning her shirt. I looked around, not totally convinced we couldn't be seen. Nettie told me not to worry, so I didn't. The sky above was white and blue. It was all you could see.

"This could be anywhere," I said. Nettie smiled, opening her shirt just enough to expose her scar, a pink line that ran from sternum to belly button. On either side of the scar were two red circles. "That's where the tubes went," she said, touching one, then the other. I noticed one of the circles had a slight discharge. I don't know why, but I leaned over and kissed it. Salty, I thought. Then I looked up at Nettie. "What about the other one?" she said, her voice high and childlike. I leaned over to kiss that one, too. Nettie took my head in her hands and pressed it against her. I kissed my way up from her stomach. When I was between her breasts, she steered me right, then left. She did this a few times.

130

A jet rumbled overhead. We sat back from each other and took in its vapour trail. I closed my eyes for a second, heard a bird chirp ...

The rattle of Nettie's belt buckle brought me back. She had her back turned and was pushing down her pants. So I did the same. I barely had my gaunch off when Nettie was on me, pulling my T-shirt up over my arms, her breasts squishing against my back, turning me, grabbing at my cock and balls.

We were on our knees now, facing each other, kissing. Nettie was rubbing my cock in the wet between her legs, while I played with her ass and nipples. And it felt great. I could've done this all day. Just this. "I like it that you don't rush things," she said, reaching down to cup my balls, squeezing them. "I didn't think you were so experienced," I said, slipping a finger inside her vagina. Nettie shut her eyes and lifted her hips. I just held my finger there and she fucked it. This felt good, too. "Put it in me now," she said, her voice one big breath. And I did.

10.3

— You made up.

— We made up at the Big Scoop, we had sex on the tracks.

— And what happened after you put it in?

— I pulled it out.

— Then what?

— I put it back in again.

— Then?

— Then I pulled it out, then I put it in, then I pulled it out — et cetera. It's called fucking. C'mon! Do you want a stroke count or something! Jesus Christ! What kind of —

— Okay, okay. Calm down. This is very important. You need to concentrate here because, yes, we need to know exactly how many times you put your penis in and out of Nettie's —

— Oh God, I don't believe this! How the fuck am I to remember how many times I ... Well, I'll tell you right now I'll never remember, so you might as well —

— Right, okay. Well, we have you down for twenty strokes —

— Whatever. You're probably right. It was my very first time and it felt great and —

— Okay, that's enough now. But what happened as you began to orgasm?

— What kind of a question is that?

— It's a question like any other. We want you to think about what was going on in your head.

— I don't think I can put it into words.

— We didn't ask you to. We just want you to think. Just like in the beginning, when we asked you how old you were when you saw your first pornographic movie.

— But I wasn't thinking then, I was still gapping out.

10.4

Putting it back into thoughts. *Hmmm.* Nettie's architecture. Her rhythm.
    As it happens. Her back arched, her weight spread. Over heels and elbows. She's rocking. The grass beneath us ... matting. Pushes into pulls. I look down at her ass. Hanging there. Jiggling. The lag and snap. Our bodies slapping. She keeps *doing* this. My cock floats hot, at times detached. The friction's in the middle at its fattest. I am being moved. Scrotum stuck to buttocks, how it peels off, like a sticker. Thrust. It's good. Unh. And when it happens —unh, unh — it will be excellent. Kiss. Though not so good for her, I guess. Thrust. And thus: bad for both of us. Uh-huh. So: less than perfect will always mean mixed for me. Unh. She seems to know this ...

thrust ... She's so fucking understanding ... uh-huh ... She's so much more experienced than me ...

I follow her scar to slow us down. I see the suture marks and the tracks beside us and those little circles for the tubes and that just sends me back to where I am right now being fucked before I start back fucking ... thrust ... Her hurry to get to where I'm about to. I know she's racing me; she knows I'm no good for holding. Not yet anyway. So she knows she has to do it just ... like ... this .... That's *why*. I remember her film: the flowers she cut for her final edit. It's just how it's done. Making it better ... thrust ... thrust ... thrust ... Look at her tits whip up and down like that. Ooops! Her heel slips. She digs back in, reaches down to touch herself. Her middle fingers bow and tamp. I smell the dirt unearthing.

Such a talker. Not words but round sounds. Something between a *wow* and an *oh*, but not a *whoa*. "Oh-ah-ho." I try to read her lips and am caught up with the sweat dots below her nose ... thrust ... The little wet hairs ... thrust ... Her teeth bare ... thrust ... Her eyes blink. I look between her legs. She is rubbing herself into something. I've had to stop inside her. She keeps rubbing. I feel this twitch. Something's up. She rubs and tamps but mostly rubs. I think of the genie in the lamp. Nettie's rub is *wa-ha-oh*. I look down between her legs ... thrust ... The hair there ... thrust ... thicker than her head ... thrust ... but brown all the same. And curly. Smells. Down there. I've been with four women up until today. Half-naked. All in the dark. I replay them as Nettie rubs. Sheila Bonner, Julie Kyle, Nancy Goldie, Dana Ferris. "Oh-wow-oh." I'm out. Her eyes open. Oh-no-no-no. I splash. She goes. We're both on our own. It's two as both, though we're each upon it slow.

So where did I go? That place between a dream and waking? No, this was better. Fresher. Better than the first time I buzzed on pot. I could just do this from now on. Nettie, relaxed, my cum on her scar. I squeeze the last drops. Nettie cups. The things I've missed. Elided. I was inventing something. In the spaces. Between things. Yes. You will have to ask me about this.

10.5

— The Bullshit Detector.

— That's right. I guess it was the prototype. It was a while yet before I could articulate it.

— You invented the Bullshit Detector during intercourse.

— Between that and Nettie's scar, yes.

10.6

The Bullshit Detector was a feel-out piece of abstraction that found its way into a diagram, something that started with Nettie's scar and became something else after we'd fucked. I was tracing my finger over her chest when — boom! — it hit me, even though it was months before I could finally put it into words. So yeah, the Bullshit Detector. I'd write it into books, draw it on walls, recite it to myself every time I came up on something suspicious. It was the first real thing we made together — me and Nettie. And I'd completely forgotten about it. When it was first written it looked like this:

Where do you want to go?

What will you
do to get there?   ○ │ ○   What have you done
to get where you are?

Where are you coming from?

10.7

We mopped Nettie off. "You shoot a lot," she said, tossing the cummy grass over her shoulder. "Been saving up or something?" I didn't know what to say. "I mean, don't you ever jerk off?" she asked. I shrugged. "Sometimes," I told her, pulling on my T-shirt, watching her watch me, okay with that. Nettie scratched her cheek. She was thinking. I could tell. "You're not as long as Nathan," she began, "but you do have a nice cock." Huh? "A thick one," she added. I thanked her for that, not sure whether I was being complimented or merely appraised. Either way, it didn't really matter. I mean, if she was trying to embarrass me, then it was just as well. I'd been such a prick to her.

Nettie did up her top. "I was with this guy once — he had a long one. But it was so ugly. Had this creepy foreskin, this dark wrinkly thing that looked like the finger of an old golf glove. Hated it," she said. "He wanted me to go down on him and I thought I was gonna puke. Don't like foreskins one bit. Don't ever get one." I laughed, then told her Galt had a foreskin up until last year. "That's why he missed the first biddy-ball game. Had to get it cut off at Christmas because it started bleeding every time he got a boner," I said, hoping the mere mention of Galt would change the topic altogether. Nettie bent down to tie her laces. "Shoulda cut the whole thing off," she said to her shoe.

Nettie pulled out her smokes, tossed me one, then took one for herself. "Do you see much of Bobby?" she asked. "Not much," I told her. Nettie blew a smoke ring, a good one. "Have you been with many guys?" I asked. "A few," she said, stretching, grinning. "I mentioned some of them in my letter, remember?" I nodded, though I only recalled her friend Nathan. "By the way, I heard what you did at the awards. That was great," she said. "You mean declining Grade Ten Male Athlete of the Year?" I asked, knowing full well that's what she meant. "What else would I mean?" she said. I shrugged, then leaned against the opposite side of the depression. Nettie stared at me. Her face was hard. She was thinking. "Don't ever bullshit me again," she said. "Okay," I said.

A car was coming down the lane. I poked my head up and thought I saw the Stotts' Impala. "Probably just the Galts," Nettie said, butting her cigarette. Then it stopped. A door opened, slammed. A voice cleared. Nettie straightened. "What?" I asked. "Shh — " said Nettie, sinking down, motioning for me to do the same. We listened. Footsteps over earth. A huffing and puffing. The crunch of gravel. Nettie smiled, put a finger to her lips. The ripple of wind over weighted plastic just as it's being released ... Crash! Then more gravel, the shaking earth. Nettie doubled over, laughing against the grass.

I peeked over to see the back of Billington's head. Nettie scrambled out and ran towards the blackberries. I followed fast, pulling even the moment she stopped. "You can see it!" she said, cracking up. Billington was getting careless. His toss was pathetic. The bag hung from the brambles like a decoration, the sausage wet against it. "Any kid could reach that," I said to Nettie, concerned

135

about the damage it could do if it got into the wrong hands. Nettie cracked up even more. But I didn't think it was *that* funny. Still, it was fun watching Nettie laugh. It had been so long. So I started laughing, too. "I guess Billington's lost some strength over the years," I said. Nettie shook her head. "Nope. That's not it at all," she said, turning to me. "It's just that we've gotten bigger."

10.8

Nettie and I parted, just like we did when we were kids. We'd be talking about something, then, when it came time for her to turn off onto Quilchena and for me to keep going, we'd just cut it off right there ... "See ya tomorrow," one of us would say. "See ya, then," the other would reply. And that would be that. No need to sum up, no need for closure. We'd just start up again where we last left off. So I suppose the next time I saw Nettie she'd finish telling me more about why the Billingtons were moving, since that's what we'd been talking about when we parted.

Sure enough, as I made my way down Aspen, I saw the FOR SALE sign on the Billingtons' front lawn. Mrs. Billington was waiting near the side gate; Mr. Billington was locking the garage door. When the poodles saw me they started yapping. It was time for their four o'clock walk. I couldn't resist.

So I call out: "Hey, where you guys movin' to?" Mrs. Billington bristled, gave me one of her please-keep-the-noise-down faces. "Goin' south?" I said, over the poodle yaps. "As a matter of fact, yes," she said, passing a leash to her husband. "We've purchased land in the desert."

The Billingtons weren't budging. The just stood there, annoyed, waiting for me to skip off. But I chose not to. I knew what I was doing. I was enjoying the tension too much, thought maybe I'd stick around a while, rub it in a little. "So how much are you asking?" I asked, taking in their Colonial. "That's none of your business," Mr. B. called back. "Two hundred thousand?" I said, bending down to tie my shoe. "More," said Mrs. B., taking the bait.

Billington had had enough. He turned towards the gate, opened it, then motioned for his wife to go first. I watched as they cut diagonally across the driveway, away from me. "Well, if you're throwing anything out and you need a hand ..." I yelled after them. "We'll be hiring a professional," Mrs. B. shot back. They took a couple more steps before Billington looked over his shoulder. And he looked scared. Because he knew what I was on about. I mouthed the words "chicken shit," and immediately felt bad.

I was coming up the back steps when my mother poked her head out the door. She seemed excited, like she had something to tell me. She put her finger to her lips: "Shh." What? "Your sister has some company," she whispered. I could hear Mary Hartman's creaky voice rerunning from the den. "Who?" I whispered back. "A boy." Oh. "Here, let's sit outside," she said. "I have something to ask you."

We sat on the lawn chairs under the poplars, facing the lilies. I asked my mom who the boy was and she told me. I didn't know him. I wanted to know more, but she said she wanted to talk about something else. I knew it was going to be important because she kept up the whisper. "Did you know the Billingtons are moving?" she said. I told her I just saw the sign. Mom looked over her shoulder, towards the Billingtons'. "They're out with their poodles," I said. "You don't need to whisper." But she kept it up anyway. "Mrs. Smart was over yesterday and she said that Mr. Billington was in some trouble and that charges had been laid." I nodded. "Now I have to ask you something," she said, looking back over her shoulder again. "It's very important." I nodded. She lowered her voice even more, took my hand in hers. I didn't like the way she was behaving. It was difficult to read. She was being super-serious, yet I knew it had nothing to do with being in shit. "Did Mr. Billington ever touch you?" I shook my head. "Are you sure?" I nodded. "I won't be mad if he did, but you have to tell me the truth," she said, putting her hand on my shoulder. "I'm sure," I said impatiently, eager to find out more about this boy my sister was dating.

11.1

The Billington house sold about three days after the sign went up. On Canada Day, as I recall. July 1, 1978. I remember this because the country was now exactly 111 years old, and Canada's oldest living human being, who also shared this birthday, died the day before at 110. Within the week, the Billingtons would be gone. A few weeks after that, I'd be sixteen. Just like Nettie.

I awoke one morning to find an Atlas moving van idling out front, a team of movers milling around, sipping coffee, smoking and joking. Mom said the Billingtons were moving to the Interior, even though Mrs. Billington had already told me they were taking it Stateside. When I mentioned this to my mom, she said she'd heard that news, too — but that according to Mrs. Smart, it was all just a ruse, that the Billingtons didn't want anyone knowing where they were going, and that they couldn't leave the country anyway because Mr. Billington had a court case coming up. Besides, she added, the two of them wanted to get a fresh start.

A fresh start? You'd think their marriage would be over after what Mr. Billington had pulled. I mentioned this to my mom, but she quickly changed the subject. Wrecked marriages weren't her topic. They upset her. So I was sorry. But whatever. In a couple of hours we'd all be out on the lawn — just like the other hypocrites in the neighbourhood — waving the Billingtons off, wishing them the best of luck, even though we all knew in our heads that in a year's time Billington would be mopping floors in Okalla while a mysterious woman in sunglasses walked her poodles along some dead-end stretch of Lake Okanagan.

11.2

— So did Nettie ever finish telling you why the Billingtons were moving?

— I just assumed Mr. Billington got busted for child molesting or possession of pornography or — I don't know — littering? I never gave it much thought.

— So you're not sure.

— No.

— And did Nettie ever bring it up again?

— No. She ended up going to the hospital for a few days after we got back from the tracks. An infection or something. By the time she got out, the Billingtons were old news.

— Tell us about your new neighbours?

The night the Billington house sold I was in the den watching *Dr. Zhivago* when all of a sudden there's a knock at the door. Mom answers, and I can tell from the high heels it's Mrs. Smart. "Blah blah blah ... Kai Ragnarsson — he's an heir to a teak fortune!" I lowered the volume and listened as Mrs. Smart told my mom how she'd heard from the agent who sold the Billington house that the purchaser was none other than Kai Ragnarsson, son of Bengt Ragnarsson, the guy who started Great Dane Interiors on Fourth Avenue. "So of course the kid's loaded," Mrs. Smart continued, over her shoulder to my mother in tow, as the two of them clacked their way down the hall to where I had my feet up on what Mrs. Smart was convinced was Classic Early-Ragnarsson. "Hey! Feet off!" she barked, all bossy with purpose, as if the beat-up coffee table we once thought of chucking no longer belonged to us but to her and her buddy Bengt.

Mom grabbed the magazines, I lifted the ashtray, Mrs. Smart did the flip. She examined the underside like the forensic expert she wasn't. Nowhere did it say what it was. It just lay there, legs up, nameless. She ran her hand over the unfinished wood, as if that might expose what was clearly never there. I sat back on the couch, happy in my head that the table's origins were inconclusive, that it didn't belong to anything — *that it was just a coffee table, for fucksakes!* But that didn't stop Mrs. Smart. Oh no. She got mean. She turned on the table. "Obviously it's a fake," she declared, getting up, as if there was nothing more she could do to save this worthless piece of shit.

My poor mom. I could tell she was hurt by this. Which hurt me, too. But what bugged me the most was the way people can get so excited about being right only to turn into assholes once they realize they're not. So I decided, right then and there, that when the time came for me to leave I would most certainly take this table with me. Whether or not I had any use for it was beside the point. If nothing else, it would stand as a monument to the pretence I'd be leaving behind.

A couple of days after the Billingtons fled, Nettie and I were coming down Thirty-third on our ten-speeds when we saw yet another moving van parked out front. We stopped to watch. "Know anything about the Ragnarssons?" Nettie asked. I told her what I knew: that for about twenty seconds her mother had us convinced we owned one of their tables. "Just as well," she said. "Teak's out." Nettie went on to say that the Ragnarssons, too, were out — out of the design business. "There was an article in yesterday's *Sun* — said the Ragnarssons sold to a chain."

Since Nettie knew everything, I asked her what Kai Ragnarsson was going to do now that there was no longer a family business to inherit. She scoffed at this, looked at me like I was the biggest goof in the world. "Kai Ragnarsson never worked for his family. God, don't you know *anything?*" I hated it when her voice did that, curling up and snapping just like her mom's. But I think Nettie sensed this, because after that she softened her tone. "Yeah, there's talk that Kai Ragnarsson's a big-time drug dealer," she said, flexing her break grips, spinning a pedal, "so I suppose we'll be seeing a lot more ghost cars cruising the neighbourhood from now on, eh?" Hmm. As if there weren't enough cops out already, what with all the death threats Judge Smart had been getting of late. After chasing the pornographers out of Shaughnessy, the good judge had taken a keen interest in the drug trade. But I wasn't supposed to know that, even though his bias was all over town.

We shifted to the cool of my front steps, where we popped Cokes and took in the move. The Ragnarssons definitely had some wild stuff, way wilder than the Billingtons' staid Victoriana. Lots of chrome, glass, white plastic — quite the contrast to the Billingtons' old-world charm, their dark and woody feel. And whereas the Billingtons had tons of plants — big palms, figs, violets, ferns — the Ragnarssons didn't have anything that couldn't look after itself. The only living thing we could see was this huge green parrot sitting up in the van's cab, its great beak wrestling with the bars of its cage. A strange-looking thing. "D'ya think the parrot talks?" Nettie asked. "Probably," I told her. We had all day to find out.

I was just about to go inside and get my mitt when a shiny white 2002 skidded to a stop in front of the van. The driver poked his head from the sunroof. He looked loose but tough. Bleached hair and sunglasses, a California type. Nettie guessed it was Kai. Was she ever wrong? Getting out of the passenger seat was a very attractive woman. "That'll be Dottie Ragnarsson," Nettie said, as if reading off a program. "You've heard of her, right? She used to be on TV. Used to be a model, then had this cheesy lifestyles show called 'Inside

Vancouver.' Totally stupid, of course." Of course. Not that I remembered the show. But I had no doubt Dottie was a model. She really was a very attractive woman. An intriguing mix: the Sarah Miles chin, the Shelly Duvall gait, bits of Suzi Quattro, Nettie, Cheryl Parks. A look I was going in for at the time.

There was something appealing about Kai and Dottie. Sure, once upon a time they were probably full-tilt hippies — both had the jangle of the over-jewelled; both wore sandals with every toe open. But there was also something very fresh about these two, especially when compared to the rest of the neighbourhood, where most of the adults carried on like they were living in some fifties Disney dreamland.

Nettie pointed out that Kai and Dottie reminded her of one of those rock 'n' roll couples you'd see in record-store promos. I had to agree. Not that we thought that was something to aspire to — but, again, compared to the world we were living in. So: think Paul and Linda McCartney, James Taylor and Carly Simon, Buckingham/Nicks. Imagine the deep tans, the wind-blown hair, the look of a couple who just flew in from somewhere important, somewhere that mattered, somewhere sexy. Yeah, I could tell just by the way these people moved — that strange ride of soft and jerky — that not only did they think differently than everyone else in the neighbourhood, but that they were probably going to behave differently, too. Factor in Kai's drug dealing and who knows what kind of colour they'd attract? But whatever. We were most impressed with the Ragnarssons.

11.4

— How did you become acquainted with Kai and Dottie?

— Nettie and I were walking by their house one day when Dottie was unloading groceries from her Rover. She looked like she was having a hard time of it, too. So we offered to help. Turns out she was pissed drunk.

— How did she treat you?

— She was very nice. Dottie was what you call a happy drunk. Fun to goof around with. She invited us for drinks later that day.

— So she treated you like adults?

— Yeah, but I think she treated everyone the same.

— How's that?

— Like children.

— Why did you introduce yourselves as Sonny and Cher?

— That was Nettie's idea. I asked her later and she said she just wanted to see how out of it Dottie really was.

11.5

We lied and told our moms we were going to a late-night screening of *Saturday Night Fever*. Of course, what we were really doing was going over to Kai and Dottie's. But it wasn't gonna be easy. We'd have to sneak through the back way, otherwise my mom would see us for sure. Plus there were all these ghost cars floating around, not to mention my sister's watchful eye. Fortunately my mom was going out on one of those crummy dates of hers, and my sister was babysitting in Kerrisdale. Besides, I was pretty certain I'd figured out the cops' surveillance schedule by then. Still, we went around back. Just to be on the safe side.

Knock, knock, knock. The howl of a dog, the slap of bare feet. The parrot squawked "Fuck" and the back door opened. "Alll riiiiight!" drawled the drunken Dot. "It's Sonny and Cher!" Growling at Dottie's feet was an enormous Great Dane. I recall making my hello particularly friendly, if only to appease the dog. Dottie responded with a head jiggle, a gesture she'd often return to. Right on, she seemed to be saying, as if the information we'd given her was just *way* too much. There was a pause while we waited for her reorbit. "Uhhh ... *so yeah!* This is Bengt Jr.," she said, clueing-in to the fact that she was holding back a 120-pound animal. Dottie let the dog loose so it could better sniff Nettie's crotch. "Yeah — Bengt Jr. just flew in. All the way from Frisco." The dog's huge tongue sopped a wet patch onto Nettie's tan cords.

Dottie stumbled into the hall and called upstairs. "Kaiiiii ... " A long and winding call, it had many of the notes you'd find in the air-raid siren scale, before busting up into something rough and glottal. Nettie continued to struggle with the dog, then finally gave in. Bengt just kept on licking. I grabbed his collar, and it took all my strength to haul him off. Dottie turned to me: "Can you believe he's still a pup?" I told her no, my voice tight under the strain. Then she turned to Nettie: "Would you agree, Cher, that Bengt Jr. has the biggest nuts you've ever seen?" Nettie wavered like she wasn't sure.

It had been years since I'd been in the Billington house. Maybe a Hallowe'en ten years ago. Or maybe the time I went over to tell them their poodles were loose. I wasn't sure. But what I did remember of the inside was a lot of dark wood and all this gold-embossed wallpaper, how the main-floor rooms were huge and ordered even though they were super-cluttered, and how the foyer stunk of Lemon Pledge. And something about the basement, too. Not that I could remember why I was down there. But that was then. Now there were drop sheets everywhere, big buckets of paint, ladders, the dumbing odour of oil-based enamel. I'd known something was up from all the trade-van action out front.

"You'll have to excuse the mess," Dottie slurred, knife in hand, as she came down hard on a lime. "I mean, as you can see we're in the middle of a reno." The parrot called out, "Hello, Dottie!" And Dottie stopped, put the knife down. She turned to the blender and said: "I think the paint fumes are getting me high, don't you?" When it was clear the blender wasn't going to respond, Dottie dumped the limes into a Kool-Aid pitcher and began stirring with a wooden spoon, which seemed to have spaghetti sauce stuck to it. "You twos wanna sangria?" she said. Nettie giggled. I helped Dottie pour. Something was thundering down the stairs. Bengt Jr. growled. "Too perfect!" said Kai. "It's Sonny and Cher."

Now, when I was that age, I couldn't give two shits about interior design. A house was just a house, right? But I couldn't believe how anybody could paint over all that natural wood. It almost seemed illegal. "Hey, after spending the better part of my life … in the teak trade … you get pretty sick … and tired … of staring at wood grain all day — believe me!" Kai stuttered, before blowing out his toke. "This is beautiful pot," Dottie said dreamily, holding up the joint, examining it like a glass of wine. "So fuck it! I don't care if it's Philippine mahogany, bird's-eye maple — whatever," Kai said, as if to justify why he painted the wainscoting gun-metal grey. "My aesthetic, now, is Bauhaus. Know what I'm saying? *Bow-house.*" I had no idea what Kai was on about; but Nettie seemed to. She was the expert on this kind of stuff. "So what are you doing in Dutch Colonial then?" she said. But Kai basically ignored her, although he did mumble something about a "deconstruction project" before continuing on with his rant. "I mean — fuck this hippie shit," he said. "The days of peace and love are over. I'm gonna turn this place into a warehouse — a laboratory or something." Dottie nodded along, careful to emphasize those nods when Kai looked her way. "I don't know," said Kai, winding down, taking a sip of sangria. "I'm just so fucking sick of exposed wood."

Nettie took the joint from Dottie, wet her finger, then rubbed a little gob near the heater, putting a damper on the run. "So what kind of experiments are you two planning?" Nettie asked matter-of-factly. "Experiments in *love*," Dottie replied, exaggerating the "uh" sound in "love" — as in "The Love Boat." Nettie turned to me, gave me the Face. It was something she'd picked up from Penny. Because whenever something funny happened, Penny would look over at John and give him the Face, too. So I laughed. I laughed just like John would laugh. "Hey, she's not kidding," Kai said, pulling out another rollie. "Dottie's a genuine sexual scientist." We looked over at Dottie. She smiled back sheepishly. "What can I say?" she said. "I just love to fuck." Once again, it was the way she said "love."

We were ripped out of our minds. But it was nothing we couldn't handle. As part of our reconciliation, Nettie and I had been spending the past couple of weeks getting loaded, so we'd built up a pretty good tolerance to the woozy part of booze and drugs. Unfortunately the same couldn't be said for Kai and Dottie, who were now teetering on the edge of consciousness. But hey — they were older. And their age, no doubt, was beginning to work against them. I mean, we couldn't believe they were only thirty-two years old. They seemed like they'd been around a long, long time.

It was approximately 9:30 P.M. when Kai and Dottie left the waking world. I wanted to split, catch this party in Kits, but Nettie insisted we snoop. "Let's just see what else the Ragnarssons have gotten up to," she said, lifting the needle off Kraftwerk, then replacing it with side one of Bowie's *Low.*

So we went down to the basement. Not much reno going on down there, it seemed. Just the concrete foundation and some exposed wooden beams. Something about its mustiness, though, got me mildly excited. But I wasn't sure why. There was an air-hockey game in what was probably the wine cellar. So we played a few games — Nettie was really good — before heading back upstairs to check on our hosts. I was sure the racket would've woken them — but nope, still zoned. Bengt Jr. cruised by and threw us a strange raised-eyebrow look. We watched as he made his way up the winding staircase, those gigantic nuts of his wagging away as if self-propelled, as if something were trapped inside, beckoning, trying to get out. "Do you get the feeling he wants us to follow him?" I asked Nettie. "Yeah," she replied. Halfway up the stairs, I whispered, "Hey, maybe we should do it on their bed?" Nettie smiled: "How experimental." We were, after all, in a laboratory.

I was checking out a room in the upstairs front of the house, a room I'd always imagined to be Billington's study. Most of the room was taken up with milk-crated records. Steeleye Span, Steely Dan, Styx ... I reckoned Kai would be tossing these out soon, rebuilding his collection with more stuff like Kraftwerk, bands that seemed consistent with his description of Bauhaus. Neil Young, Frank Zappa, Warren Zevon ... I was familiar enough with these artists to imagine Kai listening to them, sunken into some overstuffed chesterfield, stoned. I wondered whether he thought of Dottie as the Cinnamon Girl Neil Young used to yearn for. I recited the lyrics to myself, letting them swirl around an image of the young Dot, transforming her into something mildly exotic. I was in mid space-out, having just stumbled over what it might mean to be "chasing the moonlight," when Nettie whispered loudly from down the hall, calling me to come — quick! — to the bedroom.

It was too weird. The entire master bedroom had been painted silver. The only furnishing was a huge circular bed. Suspended above, a huge metal contraption that looked like a stripped-down canopy. I took a closer look. Nettie adjusted the rheostat. Could this be one of those S & M hitching posts? Like the one in that book of Nettie's — *The Concise de Sade*. Chrome handcuffs fastened to the head- and footboards. Whips gripped the crossbars like jungle snakes. A miniature mace hanging from its own little hook. I looked up and saw myself. The biggest mirror I'd ever seen. Covered the whole ceiling.

Nettie nudged me. "I'm gonna show you something — ya

ready?" I nodded. Then I noticed she was hiding something behind her back. I tried to peek, but Nettie swung the other way. "Look," she said, dangling before me a pink dildo attached to a black leather belt. "It's a strap-on," she said, giving it a little swing. I watched it swing. It was pretty big. Then Nettie did something bold: she stuck the dildo in her mouth as far as it would go. "Hey! You don't know where that's been!" I said, concerned that she might catch something. Then she made a gag face and tossed the unit onto the bed. I flipped out, told her to put it back where she found it. Nettie agreed. She reached down and moved the dildo a foot to the left. "There," she said. "That's where I found it. Right where Bengt dropped it." I didn't feel so bad now.

We agreed to can the idea of having sex and go downstairs instead, maybe sneak some dope, play some more air hockey, and maybe then we could go to the party. I agreed. I took a final look around and was just about to hit the lights when I noticed, of all things, my mother. I could see her through the cedars, right into her bedroom. She was home, taking off her earrings. My first thought: What if she saw us? But once I'd turned out the lights I became more concerned about whether or not she'd had a good time. Because she deserved it, my mom. She never had much fun on those stupid dates of hers.

I was on the verge of a 0–4 record. Nettie was getting better and better with each game. Yet with each game she seemed to be trying less and less. Five years before this would have made me crazy. But now, for some reason, it didn't matter; it was only air hockey. So I told her this. Nettie figured I'd lost my competitive spirit. That's what she said. She said I was now free to experience a whole other side of life, and that because I'd lost my competitiveness I was now twice as receptive to new things, no longer resistant to what I'd once found threatening. Something like that. Anyway, I asked her where she got this theory from and she said in some psych book — Jung or something. She didn't know. Wasn't sure. But it didn't matter. I thanked her for telling me. And then she told me that totally turned her on — that I thanked her — which, in turn, totally turned me on — that she was so receptive to being thanked. It wasn't unusual we were talking this way. Our conversations had been getting pretty decent lately.

The basement floor was concrete. Fortunately, Nettie found

some carpet samples for us to kneel on. We opened our pants and played with each other. It wasn't long before I was hard and Nettie was wet. I tried to ease her onto her back, but she told me she wanted to try it from behind this time, since she'd never really had it like that before. I thought, How odd. What about all the boasting she'd done in her letter? All that talk of her excellent love life? And what did she mean by "never really"? So I guess in my hesitation I gave the impression I wasn't open to the idea of fucking from behind. Then Nettie responded like I needed convincing: she reminded me, once again, of the evening's experimental theme. And she did this in a very casual way, as if we were kicking field goals or sitting in the Big Scoop smoking. Something about the tone she used turned me on even more. I wish I could describe it. One of the few times I could've come without touching.

Nettie turned around and slid down her pants and panties. Then she leaned forward, put her weight on both elbows, and stuck that big ass of hers in the air. I remember the way her back arched as she did this, the way her T-shirt fell from her waist, exposing her tailbone; the way each buttock seemed to rise and spread like dough loaves, time-lapsed, the faint brown seam of her crack and the dark little hairs that patrolled it. And, of course, her asshole. How it puckered. The colours of licorice, nutmeg, cinnamon. And at its centre, this tiny black dot from which emitted the faintest whiff of shit — with just enough pussy, powder, and sweat mixed in. I loved it.

She watched from over her shoulder. Watched as I pressed my cock against her crack, pushing it up and down, taking her buttocks in my hands, rubbing them with my thumbs. And then she smiled, closed her eyes, and turned away, very slowly, like an old tortoise I'd once seen on TV. "Mmmm," she said, "don't tease me." I didn't know that's what I was doing, but nodded anyway. In fact, I wasn't sure what the fuck I was doing. It didn't seem right just sticking it in. Not without doing it face to face first. Not without kissing. So I did something I'd always wanted to do. Something that, at the time, seemed so *experimental*. I got down a little lower and started kissing Nettie's crack. Up and down. Pussy to asshole, hole to hole. Before long, my mouth went from kisses to licks. And that's when Nettie started to rock. That's when she arched her back so hard I thought it would either snap or her scar would pop open. *"Oh, fuck. Put it in me now*," she said, her voice all strained and creepy, like she was pissed off or something.

Once again, I pressed myself against her crack, squeezing her buttocks together as far as they would go, and I fucked her like this. I wanted to keep at it, but Nettie's hand was now flickering between my legs, grabbing for my cock, trying to reposition it towards her pussy. So I let go and knelt back, letting my cock bob forth. I was really getting off on this, too: watching how each frantic finger seemed to be informing the other as to my whereabouts. How each time they closed in on a grip, I would flex my cock so it jumped from her hand. And each time I did this Nettie would grunt, arch her back a little more, flare that big ass of hers. But then something happened: I went from enjoying this little game to feeling super-shitty. Not because I was pissing her off — teasing her — but because ... I don't know ... I felt like I was betraying something. Because now I cared for her. So this wasn't a game any more. This wasn't like that day in the brambles. Even if we *were* gonna do it for the first time without kissing.

The moment, I thought, called for slow strokes. But right away Nettie kept calling for me to fuck her hard. Which kinda suprised me. Nevertheless, I complied. My hands on her shoulders, pulling her quick towards me, my balls bouncing back off her panty elastic. I felt ready to come, and I told her so. And this was weird: because I'd never spoken during something like this before. But whatever. Nettie said it was okay. So we did it slow. This time I reached underneath to play with her pussy, and for the first time was fairly certain I was touching her clitoris. And I only knew it was her clitoris because she would jump when I touched it. Then it was her turn to stop. So I gave myself over. I let her take my hand, part the fingers in the middle. I let her mould it to the precise spot where she said it felt best. And I felt complimented when she finally took her hand away, left me alone with what she'd taught me. So another lesson learned. We could have gone on like this forever, I thought. Until we came, together.

We were coming up the basement stairs when Nettie cautioned for me to stop. She'd heard voices. We listened. Turns out it was just Dottie muttering something in her sleep. We stepped quietly into the living room. Dottie was curled up on the sofa, Bengt Jr. licking the soles of her feet. Beautiful. It was a very beautiful sight.

But where was Kai? All of a sudden Bengt Jr. goes rigid. Outside, a car gears down. Brakes creak. Bengt Jr. bolts past us, upstairs. We go to the kitchen, peek out the window. Kai's 2002 is idling in the driveway, a Mac's Milk bag bunched up on the dash. "Do you wanna stay?" Nettie asked. Before I could answer, Bengt Jr. was on his way back downstairs. We turned around just in time to see the dog skid across the hardwood, the strap-on dangling from his mouth. "Oh, is your mommy home now?" Dottie mumbled, half-asleep. I tried hard not to laugh. Nettie grabbed a bottle of Mateus and we snuck out the front door, not giving two shits if anyone saw us or not.

11.6

— Did you see much of Kai and Dottie after that?

— A little. But we never partied together like we had that first night.

— How did they get on with the rest of the neighbourhood?

— People kept their distance. They were way too weird for Shaughnessy.

— They might have been more at home in Kits.

— Oh yeah. They would've fit right in.

11.7

Kits stood for Kitsilano. And when I say that someone went to Kits, what I really mean is they went to Kitsilano Secondary. And when I say we were going to a Kits party, what I really mean is we were going to catch the Arbutus bus to Broadway, then cut left four blocks to Larch. Hardly out of the way for a couple of heads like us.

Unlike some of the other west-side schools — the old-money schools like Magee, the nouveaux-riches schools like Prince of Wales, or the middle-class schools like Point Grey — Kits was a mix. There were some wealthy people, some middle-class people, but a lot of working-class people. And because Kits was the centre for all that sixties hippie shit, there was also a lot of "outside" types there, too. It was way more tolerant on all accounts. Especially if you weren't a honky. But even the white people in Kits looked different, because most of them were Greek. This led to a lot of innuendo about Kits being a place where you went to get your ass fucked, which, I suppose, was what you'd expect from anal-retentive schools like Magee, Prince of Wales, or Point Grey.

So I liked Kits. I liked Kits because the people who went there didn't give a shit about the material things that hung up my school. Kits people had their own slow language, their own way of making nonsense of the world. No judgement, no cliques, no pretence. Plus the girls were super-ballsy and the guys always had good weed. So yeah, Kits people had their own way of doing things, with none of the bullshit you'd find at the south end of Arbutus. Everybody there reminded me of Nettie. But even better, nobody reminded me of Bobby Galt. Kits was the last place in the world you'd expect to find a goof like Bobby. And probably the best place in the world to take someone like Nettie. Kits, for me, was the beginning of the real world.

The girl having the party was typically Kits. Her name was Dana Ferris, and I met her through Robin Locke, who, incidentally, was the first person I ever met who wasn't from Shaughnessy or Kerrisdale. In fact, now that I think about it, there were a lot of firsts where Robin and I were concerned.

Robin Locke lived in his parents' basement behind the Broadway Dairy Queen. We'd met a couple of years before when he worked at A&A Records on Granville. Robin was kind of a cool guy back then, a drop-out with a few more years' experience than me, and I always gave him the time of day when it came to suggestions about how to goof-proof my record collection. And it was Robin who sold me my first album: *Transformer* by Lou Reed — a musician to whom Robin bore a soft resemblance. But whatever. Robin was the first dealer I'd come across who sold nothing but hash, which I thought was rather cool because it told me something about how committed people could be to a single cause. Also, I had reason to believe Robin was gay, which I also thought cool because the only gay person I'd known up till then was Billington — and Billington was more a pedophile than a real homosexual anyway. Those were just some of the firsts I'd experienced with Robin Locke.

But Dana, though.

Dana Ferris was smart, funny, and had these nice high tits

that were super-sensitive. And it just so happened that every time I was over at Robin's, Dana would be there, too. We clicked right away. I remember the first time we met she was sitting at Robin's window, reading *Siddhartha*. I was drawn to her immediately. Not because she was hot or anything, but because I'd been carrying around a copy of *Steppenwolf* in my Adidas bag. I pulled it out and showed her. Dana said, "Oh, wow, that's the one Hermann Hesse book I haven't been able to find." And I said, "Well, once you finish *Siddhartha*, then maybe we can switch." Then I told her *Siddhartha* was the one book of Hesse's that I hadn't been able to find either — a lie I immediately regretted. For as every Hesse fan knows: *Siddhartha* is the book you read first, the one that reels you in.

Anyway, it was Dana Ferris who turned me onto these Kits parties in the first place. I'd been to about three of them so far, and every time I went Dana would be there and we'd get it on. And she was good, too. An amazingly good kisser. She was also one of the few girls I'd ever been with who showed any initiative. What I mean by that is she was really good with her hands. I just loved the way she held my cock. And when it came to what Dana wanted, she was totally motivated, although, for some reason, she never once asked me to put my hand down her pants. Dana said she preferred the "friction method," where you rub yourself against somebody to come. So getting it on with Dana usually looked like this: both of us lying on our side — pants on, shirts open — while Dana humped my leg and I played with her tits. After that she would jerk me off. So yeah, as much as Dana was into letting you know what she liked, she was also into telling you what she didn't, which I thought was pretty honest.

But it was a casual thing. It wasn't like we were calling each other all the time, confessing our love and shit. No way. Dana Ferris was like a lot of people at Kits. There was no dumb-ass talk about bad reps or making commitments. Anyway, I thought Dana and Nettie would make good friends because they seemed to have a lot in common. In fact, it was Nettie who introduced me to Herman Hesse in the first place.

I told all this to Nettie once we got off the bus. She seemed really interested and wanted to know more about Dana's body. Again, I told her that Dana always kept her pants on, and that all I'd seen of her body thus far were her tits. "Well, what did they look like? Were they bigger than mine?" So I told her the truth, that in fact they were smaller. Nettie seemed to like that. But then I added that although they were smaller, her nipples were bigger and darker. I thought this would piss her off, but no — she just got more turned on. Because now she was asking me to go into detail. She asked whether Dana's breasts stuck out or hung down, whether or not they were veiny, whether the nipples were inverted or did they stick out like pencil erasers — quizzing me, I suppose, to make sure I wasn't shitting her. And when she was finally convinced I was telling the truth, she suggested that maybe one day we could try out this "friction method" ourselves. I immediately thought of that time in the brambles, when we were kids, but told her yeah anyway.

We made our way round back. A small group of shadows huddled by a door. Fortunately a couple of these shapes made sense to me, people I'd seen at Robin's. I introed Nettie to those I knew; and they, in that very laid-back Kits way, introed us to those we didn't. Somebody lit a joint. I noticed in the spark-light a couple of guys checking out Nettie's ass. And I noticed Nettie notice. She was diggin' it. I liked it that Nettie was getting some attention. So I dropped a couple of hints about how Nettie and I were just good friends. And I did this by asking where I might find Dana. One of the unfamiliar shapes told me she was upstairs with her boyfriend, Bob what's-his-name. I nodded knowingly. Because I knew they were referring to Robin. And I also knew how Robin was very particular about his first name, and how sometimes, in order to get Robin's attention, Dana would jokingly call him Bob. So that was cool. Nettie could meet Dana and Robin at the same time. I told all this to Nettie as we entered.

INT. REC ROOM. NIGHT

Summer, 1978. The room is hazy with the smoke of dope. You can barely make out the panelled walls. A lamp shines klieg-like from behind a steamer trunk, illuminating the poster for the movie *Tommy*. Bodies pack a lime-green couch, some sit cross-legged on an orange rug. There's some necking, but not enough to make those not necking uncomfortable. Pink Floyd is spinning, "Wishing You Were Here."

Nettie and I enter, pull up a couple of milk crates. We lean against a staircase.

NETTIE
(uneasy)

Do you wanna go?

ME

Why? We just got here.

I accept a joint from an anonymous hand, take a toke, then pass it to Nettie. Nettie takes a toke and passes it off-screen.

Footsteps. I look behind me. Coming down the stairs: a pair of brown leather clogs, olive painter pants, a burgundy T-shirt ...

CLOSE ON ME

Hey, Dana!

CAMERA POV

Dana Ferris (16) approaches, smiling. She is attractive, of average height, brunette, freckles over the bridge of her nose. She has a serious look about her, a confidence. Her face is damp from dancing.

DANA
(suprised)

Hey!

CLOSE ON NETTIE

Her eyes dart up and down.

I introduce Nettie to Dana.

A beat.

DANA
(turning to me)

So yeah. Why don't you two come upstairs? Meet my boyfriend.

(to Nettie)
I think you know him. You guys all go to the same
school.

Dana motions for us to follow. Nettie throws me a quick look. I
ignore it.

CLOSE ON NETTIE

She looks concerned.

We follow Dana up the stairs. At the top of the stairs, a door is ajar.
From behind it we see a bright band of light. We also hear laughter.
A familiar voice is holding court, a familiar story is being told.

REVERSE

The door opens.

ZOOM BACK

A fairly modern kitchen. Flourescent lights burn white. Leaning
against the counters, on both sides of the room, a group of
teenagers. They are watching us. Dana enters first, then Nettie, then
me. I stop. I look startled.

ZOOM IN ON ME

Still startled, shaking my head slowly from side to side.

                    ME
            (voice-over, softly)
        No way.

REVERSE

The teenagers on either side. And at the far end, in the centre,
Bobby Galt.

Dana takes her place at Bobby's side. The two of them share smiles and Bobby kisses the top of her head. Then he turns his attention to me. He raises his jaw slightly and ...

                              BOBBY
        I was just telling everyone about you and Randy Cobb.
        Remember? That day at Wreck Beach?

All eyes are on me.

        So what exactly *did* you guys get up to anyway?

I look over at Dana, see the tilt of her head, her puzzled expression. She looks like she's already heard something, but now she wants to hear it from me.

Galt's smile widens, his jaw juts even further, his eyes dart about the room as if to show off his audience.

CLOSE ON BOBBY

        Well?

CLOSE ON ME

Shaking.

11.8

— Continue.

— With what?

— Your response to Bobby?

— I can't.

— You have to.

— No, really — I can't. And you should know why.

— Well, we know that you made up the kitchen scene at Dana's. But we'd still like to know your response to Bobby — even if it was a lie.

— But I wasn't.

— You're doing it again.

— What? *Lying?* I'm not lying.

— Of course you are. You're lying because we have no record of this event ever taking place. All we have is you and Nettie going to the Ragnarssons', then the two of you leaving at 10:05 P.M. to catch the Arbutus bus. You both arrived at Dana Ferris's party, walked in the basement door, then turned around because the police were coming down the stairs to break things up.

— Go on.

— You arrived back at your place at 11:19 P.M., where you performed oral sex on Nettie in a tree fort you and Bobby built when you were ten. Then you went inside and caught the last half of an NBC special report on punk rock. Nettie went home just after midnight, and you fell asleep on the gold sofa.

— Then what happened?

— Then you woke up at 5:52 A.M. and went into the kitchen and drank a glass of water. You smoked a cigarette, watched the sunrise, then went upstairs to bed, where you masturbated into a tube sock. The next time you woke it was 9:40 A.M. The phone was ringing and it was for you. It was Nettie.

— So what are you saying?

— We're saying that you're lying. That there was a party at Dana Ferris's house, but you barely even got in the door.

— But I'm not lying. I mean — this did happen. Just as I'm not disputing the fact that Nettie and I left the Ragnarssons' at 10:05 P.M., that we went to Dana's, saw that it was being busted, went back to my place, et cetera. I'm not disputing any of that. Don't you get what I'm saying?

— No.

— Well, then you've answered my question.

— What's that?

— That you have no authority when it comes to dreams.

— Dreams don't count.

— Why not?

— They're fictions.

— But they have consequences. And that's what all this seems to be about, right? Isn't that what you're getting at with this stupid Q & A?

— Continue.

— With what?

— With your response to Bobby Galt.

— But it was a dream, a fiction. What does it matter?

— Let's just say it matters.

— But you know what happens next. You already told me. At 5:52 A.M. I woke up and had a glass of water. I mean, my only response to Bobby was waking up.

— Continue.

— And if, in future, I feel the need to relate a dream I had?

— Then we'll take it under consideration. But you must tell us first.

— Or what?

— Just continue.

12.1

The dream was important. It woke me up. Got me thinking. There's no other way to explain it. I'd come to the conclusion that the first fifteen years of my life were not my own, that my life thus far hadn't belonged to me so much as the people I'd grown up with: my family, my teachers, my classmates and friends. All of which pissed me off. Not because I expected these people to get the fuck out of my way. That wasn't realistic. No, it was more like I wanted to break free from their influence. I mean, you can't alter the fact that you're somebody's son or pupil or peer, right? Those things are fixed. So the onus was on me to find a new loop, a new circle of friends, a new set of experiences. Because I was sick and tired of being judged by stuff that I'd done when I was younger, when I didn't know any better. So yeah — what I really wanted more than anything else was to start fresh, keep my changes to myself. I wanted a private life. Something that would belong only to me. Something I could control. And the best way to do that, I thought, was to withdraw from the Teen Age, begin my self-imposed exile from high school.

The following morning Nettie and I met at the Scoop for coffee. I told her about the dream and what I thought it meant. I also told her about the conclusions I'd drawn from it. And as if to prevent any misunderstanding between Nettie and myself — and perhaps get her support — I repeatedly pointed out that she was the exception when it came to my withdrawal strategy, that she was someone I was counting on as an ally in my quest for a new life. When I was finished I listened. Because I knew Nettie would have something to say. Something, no doubt, agreeable. Something that would make my exile not so much self-imposed but — what? — co-imposed? Is that a word? *Co-imposed?*

At first she was empathetic. She knew something was bugging me. She said she'd noticed that I was brooding a lot, not so quick to jump into things. Not like we were as kids. She said at first she put it down to hormones, but then she started going on about this so-called burden I'd been carrying, how the dream was the first instance where it all began to surface. "Your subconscious is stuffed," she said. "Things are bubbling up." I agreed. Because that's exactly what it felt like. But then she sort of abandoned me. She started coming at me from a completely different angle. She told me that withdrawing into myself was not the answer, that I had to face up to what was confronting me, draw strength from what has happened, what was happening. She said I had to deal with my childhood before I could get any sense of who I was and where I was going. And she hardly let up. It got kinda awful. On a couple of occasions I actually pinched myself in the hope that I might wake up from what was becoming yet another crummy dream.

Finally I'd had enough. And I let her have it. I said, "Fuck off, Nettie. Who gives you the right to take apart my life like that?" But what I really meant to say was, Hey, I thought you'd be with me on this. Then a funny thing happened. Instead of coming back with Fuck you, too, she smiled, took my hand. She told me that anger is not necessarily a bad thing, that expressing my rage was the first step towards dealing with my so-called burden. I couldn't believe she said that — though I did feel better for telling her where to go. So I asked her where she'd heard all this stuff about anger and she told me she'd been reading a lot about dreams lately — why we have them, what they mean. Jung, Freud — there were others. And then she said something which scared the piss out of me. She said if I didn't start dealing with my repression soon, then I'd probably go insane. She used Lizzie Borden as an example — the woman with the axe. There's a poem about her, I think. How she chopped up her parents.

12.1a

Excerpt from *The Journals of Nettie Smart*, **vol. 10, pp. 96–99, 1978**

August 20

I don't know how many times I've gone back to the beginning with this guy. Back to when we were kids, running around the neighbourhood — me, him, Bobby, Margie — all of us best friends, looking out for each other. And then when his dad left, how he changed, how he went from being the happiest kid in the world to this sullen little shit who wouldn't do anything unless you begged him. Of course Bobby and Margie turned into their own scary monsters. But he was the first.

So now he wants to change all that. Now he's had this weird dream about something that happened years ago, something at the beach with Randy Cobb and Bobby. Obviously the guy's repressed. He's never actually apologized for what he did to me back in Grade Eight, dropping me like that. I mean, fuck, I had to have open-heart surgery before he would talk to me again! Still, he did make an effort. And I know he's sorry. I made sure of that! So now what?

Yeah, now what? There's still a lot of work to be done. I mean, the guy's so outside of himself it's hard to tell if he even knows when he's telling the truth any more. I still can't figure out why he didn't want to go to John and Penny's for our Grade Seven graduation. And why he seemed so disinterested every time I brought up poor Mr. Gingell. I did feel bad for showing him those photos, though. I should've known he was too immature for that. Maybe that fucked him up? Maybe he's gay? Who knows?

I don't know. I still keep thinking back to that day when John and Penny gave us those cameras. I thought he was pretty right on to give them shit for showing the rest of the collective's unfinished films, then trying to pass off those cameras as awards. That was totally cool, although I think he should look in the mirror next time he calls somebody a hypocrite. Maybe that's the key? Maybe it's guilt he's feeling. I don't know. I'm tired of writing about him.

I think it's sad that he's learning this now, the hard way, all backwards, with everybody watching. It's all so ironic. And yet there's another part of me — the cruellest part — that finds it fascinating. He was such a prick to me when we started high school. He has no idea how much he hurt me. No idea.

It's going to be very painful for him when he

goes back to school, because he'll have to answer to those idiots — the Bobbys, the Cindys — each and every one of them, over and over. And so he should. He's got to deal with this stuff head-on. I just hope he can find the strength, because I'm not going to be around to help him. I keep trying to tell him this, but I can't. I don't have the heart.

12.2

— Do you agree with Nettie's assessment?

— Well, she wrote that when she was what — sixteen years old?

— But is there any truth to it?

— I don't know. Looking back I think it was all about power. I hate the idea of people exerting power over each other. What else have you got written on me?

— Everything. We have an excellent clipping service.

— Show me some more.

— If you're good, we'll show you everything. But we have to finish this first.

— C'mon, just one more. Show me what Nettie wrote the next day.

— Okay. This is from a couple of days later. Your sixteenth birthday.

12.2a

Excerpt from *The Journals of Nettie Smart*, vol. 10, p. 101, 1978

August 23

He's gotten a lot taller since this time last year. But he's still way too skinny. Plus all that facial hair. (I guess he's trying to show off.) He definitely looks more like a man these days, although in his head I think there's a part of him that's still a child. He's gotten a little hot-headed, too. But I can understand that. I was the same way once. Like that time I sent him that letter, all those diary entries. I could never do that now — not just because I'd be totally embarrassed but because it would probably be too much for him emotionally. He's so fucking fragile. Still, it would be interesting to see how he'd react. As adults, we complicate things too much.

He's gotten a lot better at sex, too. And by that I don't mean he's gotten better at getting me off — he's always been okay at that. What I mean is that he's gotten a lot better at getting himself off. I think he's beginning to come to terms with what he wants. I asked him what he'd like for his birthday and he surprised me by saying that he wanted to have anal sex. I told him I'd be willing to try it, but he'd have to convince me he knew what he was doing first. He's a bit thick. He could hurt me.

Time to go see the birthday boy. I'll finish today tomorrow.

12.3

— Let me see the rest.

— We can't. We have to move on.

— C'mon!

— Did you two have anal sex?

— Not really.

— How can you *not really* have anal sex?

— Well, the closest we got was me sticking a finger up her bum.

— So you didn't have anal sex the way you thought you might — with your penis. .

— We tried to, but it didn't work out. I kinda botched it.

— You rushed it.

— Yeah. I was feeling a bit anxious. I started losing my erection, so I panicked and pushed too hard.

— Did she get mad at you?

— No, she was really nice about it. I think she understood. She said that my problem was all in my head. She said she still wanted to try it, but that I had to learn a bit more about myself before we could try something like that again.

— How did she propose you do that?

— She said I should relax, think about my motivations. She also said I should go see a porno movie. She said she'd read somewhere that *The Devil in Miss Jones* had a really good anal scene, and that I might learn something from it. She said it was playing down in Blaine, Washington, where it had been double-billed with *Behind the Green Door* every night for the past five years. It was always being advertised in the *The Province* sports section, in a tiny box near the bottom.

— Why don't you tell us more about your exile from high school.

12.4

Like I said, the dream had a lot to do with my withdrawal from teenage life. The real catalyst, of course, was Nettie. It always has been.

For my birthday, Nettie took me on a picnic. It was a really hot day and the two of us drove over to the North Shore mountains. Nettie had turned sixteen back in January, so she'd been driving for a while by then. Her mom let us borrow their station wagon. Anyway, we found this remote spot near the Lynn Canyon headwaters. The idea was to have a bit of lunch before trying this anal-sex thing.

It was a pretty spot, hidden from the trails by this gigantic fir stump, with just enough light filtering in to keep it from being too dank. Ferns, the soft forest floor, huckleberry bushes. Nice. Nettie had packed a picnic basket: cheese sandwiches, bananas, cans of

163

cream soda — some of my favourite things. I spread out the blanket. We sat down and started in with the sandwiches.

A couple of bites later Nettie tells me, very casually, that she's going away. "Whaddaya mean you're going away?" I ask. "To school," she says. "In England." I was stunned. I asked her when and she tells me in a week. Why hadn't she told me this sooner? So I asked her that. Nettie shrugged. "My mom decided that I'd been through a lot the last little while and that I needed a change." I pressed on: "And you always do what your mother tells you?" Nettie swallowed. "I happen to agree it's a good idea," she said, a tad defensive. "I mean, it's a good school. And it's in a part of England I've never been to before. It'll be an adventure." We chewed on, in silence.

I gathered by then that Nettie had prepared this moment well. I think her plan was to dump all this on me at the last minute, then leave it to me to ask the questions, force my hand, make me commit to something. It was like I was being tested.

"So how long have you known about this?" I asked her. "About a year," she said. "It's sort of an elite school so you have to apply way in advance." A year! I was so pissed off I could hardly speak. Then Nettie distracts me: she reaches into the basket and pulls out a box of K-Y Jelly, emptying the contents in her lap. She unfolds the literature and starts reading. "But I thought you hated elites?" I said, knowing full well that she'd never said anything of the sort — but convinced, all the same, that she would've had the opportunity arisen. "I'm not looking at it that way," she said, still reading. "I'm looking at it as a way out, a place devoid of Bobbys and Cindys." That seemed reasonable. I could relate to that. Hadn't I staked out a similar position a couple of weeks before, over coffee at the Big Scoop? But then again, was it not Nettie who said withdrawal is not the answer? Of course, Nettie had an answer for that, too. "I'm not withdrawing. I made this decision ages ago, long before I decided to let you back into my life." Ouch. "And besides," she continued, "I've already decided I want to go to an English university once I'm done. I was thinking I might study art. Goldsmith's, the Slade — I'm not sure yet. I wanna be an artist." I couldn't argue with that either. Despite the fact that Nettie was good at everything, becoming an artist seemed to make the most sense.

Indeed, I couldn't argue with any of what Nettie was telling me that day because I had no idea what to say. She was definitely baiting me — trying to get me to react, open up, show her something of myself. What this was exactly was still beyond me. I mean, I was totally impressed that she had such a strong sense of what she wanted to do with her life. And I definitely wanted some of that for myself. Because I had absolutely no idea. I really didn't. And now that Nettie was leaving, I'd be on my own. Maybe that was it. Maybe it had to do with me being alone. Or maybe she wanted me to argue a case for her staying. But what was the point in that? She'd be leaving either way. That I knew for sure.

So, in desperation: "Well, what about us, then?" Nettie looked up. "What about us?" she said. "Well ..." I began. "Well, what?" she snapped. "Well, we'll still be friends, right?" I said, then immediately felt stupid for not offering up something more substantial. "Of course," she said, going back to the literature, patting my hand. "Because we care about each other, right?" I said, giving her hand a squeeze. Nettie smiled without looking. Now I wanted to tell her everything. But I spun out instead. "Do you love me?" I said, hoping that she did. Nettie's smile widened. "I'm letting you fuck me in the ass, aren't I?"

She left the following week. We said our goodbyes along the tracks, where we walked past the Cypress crossing, the blackberries, our old elementary — everything. On the way back we stopped at an overgrown spot not far from Billington's drop site, and necked. Just necked. As we were making our way back down Cypress, Nettie asked me if I could stop by her place. She said she had a gift for me. I was a little flushed because I didn't think to get her anything; but she told me that was okay because it wasn't really coming from her anyway. I wasn't quite sure what she meant by that, and I definitely wasn't going to ask her. Because if Nettie's parting gift was intended to be a surprise, then my asking would only wreck it.

Nettie ran upstairs while I waited on the stoop. When she returned she was carrying this big plastic bag from Le Chateau. Oh God — did she get me a sweater? Nettie opened the bag and took out a box all done up in hand-drawn gift wrap. The paper looked familiar. Where had I seen stick-birds and worms before? And all those little words, each letter like a gnarly fish hook. The present seemed so beside the point. I put it back in the bag and we kissed goodbye, on her doorstep, in plain view of the neighbours. A ghost car drove past. She told me she'd see me at Christmas. Then she told me she loved me.

12.5

— A movie camera?

— That's right. It was the same camera John and Penny gave me back in Grade Seven. Nettie'd had it all along.

— Continue.

13.1

Labour Day weekend. I was to begin Grade Eleven the following Tuesday. My mom gave me a hundred dollars to buy some new school clothes. Usually we'd go shopping together, but I guess that year she'd decided I was old enough to shop on my own. But what did I need new clothes for? I was perfectly happy with what I had going. And I told her so. "But don't you want to make a good impression? Don't you want to be in fashion? You used to have such good taste," she said. I told her no, absolutely not, because I didn't care what people thought of me any more. I told her I just wanted to be anonymous. "But all you ever wear are work pants and plaid shirts," she said. "And besides, the best way to be anonymous is to wear what everyone else is wearing, right?" I told her I wear what's comfortable, that maybe I might get some new socks and underwear, but other than that I was perfectly happy picking up stuff when and where I felt like it, and not at the beginning of the school year when everybody else is in the malls doing exactly the same thing. Later on I heard her talking to Mrs. Smart on the phone. I gathered from my mother's end of the conversation that Mrs. Smart was trying to convince her that I was just going through a phase.

But it wasn't a phase. After Nettie left I devised a plan. I was calling it a survival plan, a way to get through the next two years of high school without going nuts. So I decided I'd just show up for class, do what I had to do, then fuck off home. No teams, clubs, dances, parties. No fooling around. Nothing. It was strictly business between me and Point Grey Secondary. I would devote whatever time remained to the advancement of my private life. And whether that meant withdrawing from the Teen Age or not, who cares. Fuck Nettie. Her advice was meaningless now that she'd left me in this state.

13.2

— That's when you perfected the Bullshit Detector?

— Correct. The Bullshit Detector served as a way to negotiate my way through the world. It was a way to read people.

— Did you ever apply it to yourself?

— On occasion.

13.2a

Bullshit Detector Model (with diamond centre)

Where do you want to go?

What will you do
to get there?

What have you done
to get where you are?

Where are you coming from?

13.3

So my days looked like this. I would get up, go to school, go to my classes. Then I'd come home at noon, eat lunch, maybe jerk off. Just before returning I'd put on a record to psych myself up for the afternoon. The Ramones were good for that. Iggy Pop, too. All stuff I got turned onto by my dealer, Robin Locke.

Same thing after school. I'd come home, have a snack, then go down to the basement, where I'd smoke some hash and practise guitar. Sometimes I'd read, sometimes I'd draw in this old ledger I'd picked up at a garage sale. Sometimes I'd just sit there stoned and listen to the stereo I got for my birthday. Sometimes I'd even jerk off again. But mostly I'd think.

Every now and then my sister would come downstairs and bug me. This pissed me off because I'd made it clear to her that the basement was mine, and that as soon as I'd gotten over my fear of spiders I'd be moving down there permanently, so she better start thinking about the basement as *my room*. I told this to my mom, and she told me she'd tell my sister. When she finally did I was fortunate enough to overhear their conversation. I heard my mom say that because I was sixteen I needed more space than I did when I was little. Not that this made any sense to my sister. She was twelve now and wanted to know all the details.

Other times I would come home from school, smoke a joint, jerk off, then get into housework. My mother was always exhausted when she got back from the clinic, so I realized the best way to unexhaust her was to show her how willing I was to pitch in. It didn't matter what it was. Pulling weeds, vacuuming — even something as small as puffing up the throw pillows. The main thing was to make sure my mom saw me engaged in some kind of activity that indicated to her my interest in the upkeep and maintenance of our family home. So after a while it became ingrained. And once it was, I knew I could now use this performance to my advantage, like if I needed some money or permission to do something she'd never heard of before. It was a leverage thing.

I also got a part-time job. A fish and chips shop in Kerrisdale had just opened up. The gig was two evenings a week. Tuesdays and Thursdays. The job was ideal because I got to work alone. I was quick enough to do both the cooking and the cash myself. Mostly it was people phoning in orders, then coming by to pick them up. An anonymous blur of hellos, thank yous, here-you-goes, and goodbyes. And I rarely saw my boss. Perfect for where I was at, at the time.

13.4

— John and Penny used to come in on Tuesdays.

— That's correct.

— They would sit at the table closest to the counter. But then after a few weeks they'd just get take-out. And then by Christmas they stopped coming altogether.

— Right.

— You were very rude to them.

— I wasn't rude, I was busy.

— You hardly talked to them.

— I only said what was necessary. I was running a business.

— But surely you must have realized you were hurting them.

— Sure.

— Is that what you wanted then? To hurt these people?

— I didn't care. They'd become just like everybody else. Very mid-dleclass. They were completely different from the couple I knew back in Grade Seven.

13.5

On the evenings I wasn't working I'd do my homework and read. I hardly ever watched TV any more, although for a while there I was getting into reruns of "Mary Hartman, Mary Hartman." I'd go to bed at eleven every weeknight, and I'd always jerk off because it was the only thing that could get me to sleep.

13.6

— And how did you sleep?

— Like a baby.

— Any more bad dreams?

— None that I could remember. It would be years before I had any-thing like the Bobby dream again.

13.7

Saturdays I'd go downtown. Usually I'd go to A&A and buy a record. Sometimes I'd buy an eight-track tape because my mom had a player in her Falcon. Not that we had similar tastes in music. But there was one tape we both seemed to agree on, and that was by Joan Armatrading. Mom really liked the song "Love and Affection."

After A&A, I'd walk over to Robson Strasse, grab a schnitzel, then mull over catching a matinee. The Cinémathèque had just opened and they were showing all kinds of European films, which I liked because most of them featured nudity. I kinda got addicted to those for a while. And I got pretty good at telling which ones had nude scenes and which ones didn't. I even came up with a system, this weird calculus based on what language the film was in, what the movie poster looked like, when it was made, and who was in it. But if you were to ask me which movies I saw or what they were about — forget it. Most of these films made little or no sense to me at the time. And I don't think it had to do with me forgetting to read the subtitles every time a naked body appeared on screen. No, these movies were weird. They didn't have conventional story lines like Hollywood movies. And even if you thought they did — that is, if you began to recognize something that resembled a story line — then, just as quick, the film would veer off in another direction, almost like it was making fun of you for even trying. In fact, a lot of these movies were similar to the films Penny used to bring into the collective, films that intentionally worked away from what she called "stock narrative." After a while, I got bored with the nude scenes. They never showed that much anyway.

My decision to catch a film was always based on my current supply of hash. If I was out, then I'd go over to Robin's. He'd just moved into an apartment on Davie Street, after his parents came to the conclusion that it wasn't the neighbourhood pets who were trampling their garden but Robin's clientele.

One time I went over to Robin's with some honey oil I got from Kai. I asked him if he wanted to smoke up and the guy gets all weepy, like he's about to cry. I asked him what's wrong and he tells me that nobody's ever done that before — come over with their own drugs and offered to smoke with him. I didn't know what to say, so I just did up a joint. After we got high, Robin told me how he now considered me a friend, and not just a customer. I thought that was a nice thing to say until he wrecked it by telling me something stupid like "friendship has its privileges," and that in future I could expect to get a discount. I told all this to Nettie, in a letter, and she wrote back that Robin had some confidence problems.

13.8

— You saw a lot of Robin Locke.

— Yeah.

— In fact, our records indicate that from April 1978 to June 1980 you visited Robin's apartment 137 times.

— Maybe.

— But you only purchased drugs from him on thirty-eight occasions.

— So?

— So there was something else attracting you besides the hashish.

— Maybe.

13.9

Robin had a huge collection of skin magazines. Mostly gay stuff. And he was forever leaving them lying around. They were impossible to avoid. I think he did this on purpose. He was always creating situations were he could catch me looking. His favourite set-up was when he'd go into his kitchen to make coffee. He'd tell me to relax, smoke some hash, whatever. Then he'd disappear. It didn't take long before I clued in that the mirror he'd hung in his hallway provided him with an indirect view of the living room. So as soon as I picked up a magazine he'd come back real fast like he'd forgotten something, then quickly try and get me talking about whatever it was I was looking at. This used to bother me because it felt so obvious. But I got over it. After a while I didn't mind talking about what was going on in these magazines. Plus I was curious about what it was like to be with another guy.

One time I let him catch me. "Oh, *Garçons de Maroc?*" he said, running back into the room, rummaging around for something. "I just got that last week — you seen my rollies? — check out the centrefold." I held up the magazine, letting the colour-spread fall onto my lap. An elderly German held his semi-hard against the cheek of a young Arab boy. The boy had his hand cupped under the German's testicles. The look on the boy's face was supposed to be awe. But I wasn't that impressed.

I refolded the centrefold, then put the magazine back on the table. Robin picked it up, reopened it, and began: "A friend of mine — Henke — Do you know him? He's a curator — yeah, doesn't matter — anyway, yeah — Henke says he can't get turned on by this photo because it's too colonial. Does that make any sense to you? That it's *too colonial?*" I shrugged. I had a vague sense of what Henke meant. Robin continued: "I mean, sure — colonialism. It's bad right? But whatever. I just happen to think that it's a really sexy photo. I mean, I would love to be this little boy, wouldn't you? I'd give anything to suck on a dick like that. And I don't care who it belongs to or what colour it is or how much money's behind it — y'know what I'm saying?" I shrugged. Then I told him no, that I didn't know what he was saying, because I'd never sucked a cock before. "Never?" said Robin, insincere with disbelief. I shook my head, knowing full well what I was getting into. "Well, have you ever had your cock sucked?" he said, sitting down beside me, tossing the magazine back on the table. "Yes," I said, curious to see where this was leading. "But by a man?" he said. Again, I shook my head. "Then you haven't really had your cock sucked before, have you?" he said, all giggly. I stared at him. He stared back. I looked over at the centrefold, spread open on the table. I remembered the time Nettie and I were trying to retrieve Billington's garbage, the way she bumped against me. I felt my cock twitch. Robin's hand was on my knee now. I felt it travel up the inside of my leg. I waited till his head was on my lap before looking at anything else.

I was surprised by how hard I was. I didn't find Robin particularly attractive, but after a while it didn't matter. A mouth was a mouth was a mouth. He undid my belt, then the button, then the zipper. I lifted my ass as he pulled down my jeans, watched as he positioned himself between my legs, parting them at the knees with the heels of his hands. I felt the itch of the couch against my testicles, Robin's warm hand tightening at the base of my cock, pulling it towards him, dabbing it against his rough tongue. With his other hand he took my balls, tugged them gently. I could feel my bag harden, the pull of each nut tight towards my body. It was a good feeling. I flexed the muscles around my ass and my cock pulsed. Robin looked up at me. Just his eyes, smiling. I closed mine. He asked me to do that again. Close my eyes? "No," he whispered, "what you did with your cock." So I did it again. "Oooh, I just love that," he said, his voice soft and lispy. Then he put his mouth around me, pushing down as far as it would go. I felt my knob press against the back of his throat. He pushed down a little further. He kept doing this. He was that good.

I could've come, but I decided not to. Something was telling me to hold off, save it for later. I mean, maybe there was something more to this than just getting sucked. Maybe I was supposed to fuck him in the ass. Or maybe not. Nettie told me once that there were some gay men who didn't do that kinda shit. She described them as "tops." So maybe Robin's a top? And if he's a top, what's he doing with my cock in his mouth? Because, according to Nettie, tops don't suck either.

Robin took his mouth off my cock, gave it a squeeze, a couple of quick pumps. Then he let go. "I just love your cock," he said, his voice above me now, all scratchy. I opened my eyes. Robin stood there, his shirt out. He began to unbutton. From the top down. I looked up at his face, as he watched his hands unbutton. He looked different now. He didn't look like Robin at all. He didn't look like anything. He gestured towards my cock. "It's nice, you know. The shape of it. Thick." I shrugged. Then he asked me if I wanted to lie down. I was gonna tell him I wasn't tired yet, but I knew that a joke would only wreck the mood.

I'd never seen Robin naked before. All I'd ever seen of his body were his hands, which were pale and densely haired. Would he have a pale, hairy body, too? Probably. And what about his cock? What would that look like? I thought back to his hands, his long thin fingers. Then I remembered the time I came across my mom's copy of *The Happy Hooker*, where I'd read how the size of a man's penis was relative to the shape of his hands, and how I looked at my own hand and thought: Xaviera Hollander's a fucking genius.

Robin asked me to follow him. At first my steps were small, because my pants were down around my ankles. I remember thinking how stupid this looked, like I was escaping from a chain gang or something. But whatever. I stopped to take off my shoes and pants.

Robin took the time to remove his shirt, tossing it over my pants when he was done. I looked back at the clothes heap: it looked like the remains of a man whose body dissolved.

The blinds were drawn, the bedroom was dark. We stripped to the sound of the dump truck braking. I only had my shirt to take off, which made me naked first. So now what? I looked over at Robin. He had his back to me. Even in darkness I could tell that he had a hairy body. Then he opened the blinds. The room filled with light. Outside, English Bay — clouds, windsurfers, boats. Robin turned around. More evidence of Xaviera's genius: although only half-hard, Robin's long, thin fingers added up to a long, thin cock.

"Lie down," he said. And I did. Robin knelt on the other side of the bed. "Come closer," he whispered. And I did that, too. He leaned over and ran his hand across my chest, brushing over my nipples, erecting them. It was a neat trick. So now what? Maybe it was my turn to do something. I reached up and squeezed the base of his cock. I could feel the blood coursing through it. It was like my whole hand was throbbing. I knew when I let go it would jump. And sure enough it did. Robin's cock hovered at forty-five degrees. I was determined to make it stand upright. Nettie once told me about this guy she was with whose cock got so hard it stood flat against his stomach. So I reached for him again, but Robin took my hand and placed it over my own cock. "Show me how you play with yourself," he said.

So I did. And Robin, still on his knees, the sweat from his brow falling onto my chest — he played with himself, too. When my cock was good and hard I looked up at him. "Don't stop," he said. I closed my eyes and kept at it. Then Robin leaned over and stuck his tongue in my mouth. Which was unexpected. Totally unpleasant. The blood flooded from my cock like a dam burst. Fortunately Robin didn't push the kissing much further. He swung his leg overtop, turning himself so we could sixty-nine. His balls came to rest on the bridge of my nose. I took his cock and played with it, my thumb brushing the underside of the head, paying close attention to those areas that always worked best for me. Then I put him in my mouth and thought some more.

Apart from the fact that Robin's cock was shaped just as Xaviera said it would be, I couldn't get over how different it looked from the rest of him. Although Robin was short and doughy, his cock was long and lean, as if it belonged to someone taller, someone fit. Also, its colour. Robin had a pasty complexion, but his cock was a tan brown. And his foreskin was even darker. But the weirdest part of all was the head. I took Robin's cock out of my mouth and pulled back the foreskin. The head of it shone a lavender blue. Such a strange colour, I thought. Like a gem. Then Robin reached underneath and pushed it back in my mouth. "Do what you were doing," he said. So I went back to blowing.

The sun had burned through the clouds, shifting the light from white to yellow. Robin's testicles hung above me like rude fruit. His scrotum, thin and red, stretched to the max by the weight of his balls. I remember thinking how much his bag looked like a tiny little ass, maybe the ass of a tiny old man. I took his cock out of my mouth and lifted my head to where I could lick him. His balls tasted like salt, smelled like the batter I made fish with. I took one in my mouth and felt it jump. Once again, Robin returned his cock to my mouth.

Unfortunately, Robin's ass was not so appealing. I didn't like it that his skin was so white and his hairs so dark. The contrast was way too harsh. But it was his asshole that really grossed me out. It was far too black to be healthy. I was reminded of something Nettie once told me about hoboes: how hoboes always have black assholes from wiping themselves with newspaper. So I went back to his balls to get my mind off his asshole.

We were hard as rocks. I was nearing the point where I was before, where I was wondering what we'd do next. Finally, I asked him. "Do you want me to come now?" And with that, Robin jumped off the bed and skittered out of the room. Very femmy. I got up on my knees and kept myself hard. In no time he was back with a tube of K-Y. He squirted some into his hand and blew on it. "This is how you warm it up," he said. I followed suit, squirting then blowing. "Now rub it on your cock," he said. And I did. Then Robin reached between his legs and applied the K-Y. "Put it in my bum, okay?" he said, turning around on all fours, sticking his hairy ass at me.

I pressed my cock against his crack, moving it up and down. Robin's hairs were coarse and plentiful. Not at all like Nettie's smooth rump. So to get my mind off Robin's rough butt, I closed my eyes and thought of Nettie. Not about my failed attempt at

Lynn Canyon, so much as what we got up to in the Ragnarssons' basement. Now Robin's ass didn't feel so bad after all. I reached underneath and took his cock, pressing it flat against him, rubbing it into his belly. And then a funny thing happened: just like that, Robin, who I'd turned into Nettie, had now become Randy. All of a sudden I was back on Wreck Beach. And when Robin reached underneath to steady me, ready me for his asshole, I thought for sure it was Randy I was about to be fucking. I took my cock from Robin, gave it a squeeze, and pushed against him. When his ass closed tight, I'd pull back; when it opened, I'd push forward again. It wasn't long before I had most of it in. I did everything I could to not open my eyes.

His ass felt great, a little tighter than Nettie's pussy but not by much. I guess the plan was for me to come, then go down on him again. Unless he was going to come from me fucking him, which didn't seem likely, because the more I fucked him the softer he got. He seemed to be preoccupied with just getting fucked. His breathing was heavy. And I wasn't totally convinced he was pain-free. I had to take most of it out before he could get his erection back. And when he did he just wanted me to fuck him again. Even harder this time.

Robin asked me if I was about to come, and I told him yeah, I was. So he tells me to hold off, stop. He reaches underneath and pulls me out slow. Then he swings around, taking my cock in his hand, pumping it, pulling it towards his open mouth. I narrowed my eyes and thought of Randy, while Robin went cross-eyed watching me come on his tongue.

After I'd shot off, Robin told me to lie down on my back. So I did. Then he straddles my chest and starts jerking, swinging his balls over my mouth, back and forth, like one of those perpetual motion machines you'd see in people's offices. "Lick my bag," he said, all breathy, speeding up on his cock. So I did that, too. I lifted my head up and sucked one of his balls into my mouth, letting gravity steal it from me as I fell back towards the bed. I did this until his bag went tight again. After that, I just flicked them with my tongue. "Watch me come," Robin said, his voice jerky. So I opened my eyes and watched his face tighten, contorting into this stunning grimace. Not a very attractive sight. "I'm coming," he said, a drop of sweat falling into my eye, stinging it shut, returning me to Randy.

I could feel the shake in Robin's legs. I reached up and squeezed his ass, felt him bucking at the hips. He grabbed my hand and pushed it against his chest. "Squeeze my nipple," he said. So I did that, too. "I'm coming! I'm coming!" he said. "Watch me come!" I leaned up on my elbows, opened my eyes, my mouth, stuck out my tongue. Robin was pumping super-fast. I reached underneath and held his bag, giving it a slow pull, as his cock tapped at my tongue. I really wanted to close my eyes now. I looked up at Robin and gathered that he wasn't seeing anything right now other than what was going on in his head. So I shut my eyes, closed my throat, and waited for Randy to cum.

And there was lots. Once he pulled out, I swallowed. Then I opened my eyes and saw Robin staring at me, putting the last few strokes into his still-hard cock. He was smiling like he'd had a pretty good time. So I smiled back. I took his cock and rolled it over my lips. He let out a sigh, leaned his head back, closed his eyes. Then he shivered like a sissy.

13.10

— Did this incident happen before or after your visit to the Venus Theatre?

— Just after.

— Were you aroused by what you saw that night at the Venus? The detective?

— I think it was the total experience.

— Why didn't you and Robin have sex again?

— I told him I just wanted to be friends.

— What did he say to that?

— He was a bit hurt.

— But what did he say?

— I forget exactly.

— Didn't he say something about you denying your homosexuality?

— Yeah, he said the reason I didn't want to have sex with him again was because I couldn't handle being gay. He said I was in denial.

— To which you said?

— Something like, just because I didn't want to have sex with him again didn't mean I was denying anything.

— And you weren't, were you?

— Right. To be honest, the reason I didn't want to have sex with Robin again was because I didn't like his ass. It was as simple as that. I mean, the first time was fine. But never again. And it had nothing to do with denying my sexuality. In fact, I think it was just the opposite. I think I'd be in denial if I was to sleep with him again. Because, as I said, I found his ass ugly. So once again, it had nothing to do with denying my sexuality. I mean, I don't know what it is about certain people who identify themselves as gay. I don't know why, for example, when you say you don't want to sleep with someone, the last thing to cross their mind is the fact that you just don't find them attractive. I'll never understand how some people will go to such absurd lengths to provide reasons for things that have nothing to do with what you've been trying to tell them all along.

— Continue.

13.11

It didn't take long before the other kids at school came to the conclusion that I was putting out a loner vibe, and that maybe I should be left alone. I thank them for that. I really do. Because that was the easy part. The tough part, though, turned out to be the coaches. None of them could understand why I wasn't coming out for teams. And many of them took it personally. One of them, in particular, got quite nasty.

178

It was the last day of September, the last hot day of the year. I was coming out the smoke doors, on my way home for lunch, when Mr. Longley, my former basketball coach, came around the corner and called out my name, giving it the sissy twist. I pretended not to hear him, kept on walking. Longley called out again — a little louder, even more sissified — this time getting the attention of my so-called peers. I thought of the faces I'd seen on my way out: how most of them were my ex-teammates, girls I used to kiss with. I'm sure Longley was aware of this, because Longley was the type of guy who couldn't do anything unless there were people in the bleachers. Pretty obvious where this guy stood when it came to trees falling in the forest, right? At least that's what I thought as I kept on walking.

"Hey, faggot." This time I had to turn around. "Made you look," he said. The crowd laughed. Longley laughed with them. Relieved it was over, I laughed, too. Then I turned around and stepped towards the hill. I was almost there when I heard Longley jogging up behind me. He was a big guy and his big Nikes made big noises. I felt the crowd stir. Feet followed. So I turned around, thinking I could face down whatever was coming. Longley slowed, but kept at it. He walked right up to me, just like he used to do at the end of a game, where he'd give me one of those "well done" hugs. But this time was different. Already I was looking at him differently. He wasn't my coach any more, he was just some loser in a tracksuit. A goof who drove a Camaro and drank at the King's Head.

"So we hear you're too good for rugby, and now we hear you're too good for basketball," he said, slamming a chummy hand down on my shoulder. I shrugged, and only one shoulder went up. The crowd laughed. It must've looked weird, the one shoulder. Longley leaned over and whispered in my ear, "What's the matter, faggot? Worried you're gonna get a hard-on in the showers?" I tried pulling away, gave it a real good effort, but Longley tightened his grip, still grinning. The crowd swelled. People were actually running to watch this.

I saw Cheryl Parks in the distance. She was watching, too. Just standing there, watching.

His hand still on my shoulder, Longley turned to address his followers: "Your former Grade Ten Male Athlete of the Year tells me he'd rather write poetry than represent his school." The predictable boos and hisses. Longley definitely knew how to work a crowd. I made a better effort to pull away, but Longley threw another hand over my shoulder. "So what do you think we should do with him?" he shouted, right into my face, still grinning. An assortment of suggestions: "Cut off his balls," "Kick his head in," "Fail him" ... I applied the Bullshit Detector. Longley's score went through the roof. And to think I used to like this guy? Then — quickly, and totally unexpected — he brought his fists together and boxed my ears. It happened so fast I'm sure no one saw it. Not that I didn't feel it. My ears were ringing like a fire alarm. But at least it was over. Longley gave me a wink, whispered "faggot," and walked away. Just like that the crowd inverted, began their analysis, constructed the narrative. I turned around and walked home, pretended it was nothing.

I went up to my room and sat at my desk. It took me a while to block out the noise. The cars rushing past, the constant hammering that had been coming from Kai and Dottie's new addition, the echo of Longley's voice. I listened for the sixty-cycle hum, the warm buzz that electrocutes our house, all houses. I tuned into that for a while. Then I thought about whether or not it was time to move my bedroom down to the basement. Had I overcome my fear of spiders? No. But I had to make some kind of move. So I embraced the change. On Sunday, I said to myself. On Sunday I'll move.

And I thought about Cheryl Parks, too. I thought about her standing there watching me, the look on her face. She almost seemed happy. And why shouldn't she be? She probably associated me with that night at Cindy's, when she had her seizure. She probably thought I was still one of them. She probably thought I had all this coming. Hey, maybe my public humiliation was good for her? But who could tell with Cheryl. She'd never been the same since that night at Cindy's. Then I wondered what the fuck I was doing sitting at my desk like this, like a kid in trouble. I hadn't done anything wrong. That's when I started to cry. I did that for a while.

After deciding that I wouldn't go back to school that afternoon, I went downstairs and made myself some sandwiches. Then I went down to the basement and put on a record. I smoked a joint, tuned my guitar, then caught up to the chorus of "Psycho Killer." I finished the song feeling better. I picked up my Pushkin and randomly selected a poem. But I couldn't focus. All I was getting were words. I was still too distracted by what had happened at school. Longley's face, the crowds, the burn in my ears. And I couldn't stop thinking about Cheryl. The only thing left was to jerk off.

I had a *Hustler* hidden in my guitar case, so I pulled that out and began flipping. I especially liked those little ads at the end. Because of all the dirty magazines that carried ads such as these, *Hustler* made the lamest effort at placing black dots over the raunch. So if you held the magazine up to the light, you could see what was going on underneath. Sometimes it was semen, sometimes penetration. And sometimes it was nothing. Sometimes they just put a dot there to suggest something was happening. But I got bored with that, too. I tossed the magazine aside and let myself go limp. Then I remembered something.

I went into my mother's room, opened the bottom drawer of her night table, lifted up her tax assessments, and pulled out her *Playgirls*. I'd found them during one of my cleaning frenzies, but was too embarrassed to look at them. But now I felt okay about it. And that made me feel good. I lay down on her bed and checked out August.

The men were mostly young. Nobody recognizable. Some of the guys looked vaguely familiar, like the people you'd see in the movies or on TV, look-a-like's — a Burt Reynolds type, a Clint Eastwood type, a Jan-Michael Vincent type. None of them did that much for me. These phonies were only as sexy as their look-a-like's worst role. But there was one guy near the back who definitely caught my eye, an anonymous Mediterranean standing at the wheel of a clipper ship, buck naked, selling musk. The sky around him was overcast, and the whole scene had a cold and stormy feel. He looked like an Argonaut. His body was hard, his cock blowing off to one side. I worked with this guy for a while, before deciding I needed something sunny to finish off with. I found a blond guy, about twenty, bending over his motorcycle. His skin was smooth, and I think it was the contrast at the tan line that did it for me. I flipped back and forth, careful not to spill on Mom's bed.

When I was done I lay there for a while, still replaying the events at lunch hour. I decided it was no big deal, that it might even be the lift I needed. The only thing that bothered me was Cheryl. I really had to know what she was thinking. I devised a couple of plans where I could get close enough to talk to her, but then abandoned them just as quick. She was no friend of mine. And she never would be. I decided to go back downstairs and take on a chore, maybe polish the silver. I tried to get up, but changed my mind again. I was enjoying the silence too much, just lazing about. There was a lull in the traffic and the workers next door had stopped pounding.

That's when I heard Dottie's voice. It sounded close, as if she were just outside the window. I parted the drapes and there she was, no more than thirty feet away, framed between two cedar boughs, naked. She was stepping onto their latest project: a balcony off the bedroom. Dottie placed her hands onto the two-by-four safety rail, went up on her tiptoes, and leaned forward, her long breasts drooping forward, detaching from her tummy, hanging there. She looked up, I ducked down. She told Kai to hurry, get with the program. I made a smaller slit to look through.

Dottie had her back to me, her head tilted to one side. The effect was something. "It's beautiful out here, Kai. I love the privacy," she said, looking around. I could see shadows through their bedroom window, a shadow tossing off its shadowy clothes. Then the shadows disappeared, reappearing on the balcony as Kai, naked, a bottle of wine and two glasses in hand. "You know what that Mrs. Smart bitch told me?" Dottie said, taking a glass from her husband. Kai shook his head as he worked the corkscrew. "She said we were ruining our house's heritage." Kai popped the cork. "How does she know that?" said Kai, pouring. "You can't even see back here for all the fuckin' trees." Then Dottie said, "She says she knows the guy who owns the lumber store — he told her." Kai laughed at that. "Christ, had I known the neighbours were this nosey, I never would've let you talk me into this house in the first place," he said. Then Dottie pulled her husband towards her, rubbing his shoulders. She said something, but I could only make sense of it from Kai's response. "Well," said Kai, "the next time somebody sticks their nose in our business, I'll just shoot it off." Then he stroked the back of Dottie's hair, letting his hand fall across her back, curling just under a buttock.

At first, it was just necking. Then they got serious. Kai began squeezing Dottie's ass, while Dottie brought her hands up to twiddle Kai's nipples. I couldn't believe it. I thought for sure they were going to take it inside, but no. Kai started kissing his way down Dottie's chest, stopping at her breasts. Between Dottie's legs I could see Kai playing with his cock. Although nothing spectacular, his cock looked good poking out of his hand like that. Then he turned Dottie around, leaning her against the rail. Dottie was playing with her tits now as Kai kissed his way lower. Kai had a nice ass. Not a hair on it. I could feel myself getting hard again. If only I were closer.

Then I remembered: I had a pair of binoculars in my bedroom closet. I was certain they were in my bedroom closet, because the last time I used them was at the Kiss concert the year before and that's where I put them when I got home. But when I got to my closet they were gone. However, in their place was the Le Chateau bag. And inside was my gift from Nettie. I'd never even looked at it. But I do remember John telling us that the zoom on this model was out of this world.

So I ran back to the window, removed the box from the bag, the camera from the box, and pressed Zoom. Nothing happened. I checked the lens cap. It was off. I checked the batteries. None. I needed batteries. So I ran downstairs to the kitchen, opened the drawer where we kept that shit, and grabbed a handful of double-A's. Then I ran back upstairs and loaded the camera. Kai and Dottie were now providing me with a side view. And Kai was still eating Dottie, lapping at her pussy like a dog. I stuffed the batteries into the camera, making sure the positives and negatives all lined up. I pressed Zoom and saw where Dottie stiffened, her back arched over the rail. It looked amazing, her nipples up like that, her knuckles white, her mouth smiling, the lines around her eyes tight with concentration.

And that's how it happened. I was adjusting my squat when I felt something underfoot. I looked down to see that there was more to the bag than just the camera. Three rolls of Ektochrome film. An additional gift from my producer-friend Nettie.

The film in, I took aim.

EXT. A BALCONY. DAY

CLOSE ON WOMAN'S FACE

A woman (30s) is leaning against a railing, her head tilted back, in profile. Although smiling, she seems to be straining, as if concentrating on the action below. Surrounding her, green flora, thick with textures.

PANNING DOWN

The woman is topless, her nipples stiff. There is a slight shake to her breasts, as if she is being jiggled. As we continue down, we find a man (30s) squatting before her, performing cunnilingus.

PANNING UP

We stop on the woman's face. Her eyes are closed, and she is biting at her bottom lip.

ZOOM OUT

A woman and a man on a balcony overlooking a back garden. The woman continues to receive cunnilingus.

ZOOM IN ON MAN

He is kissing his way up the woman's body, stopping at the breasts. He takes one of the woman's breasts in his mouth. The woman runs her hands through his hair.

ZOOM OUT

The man kisses his way up to the woman's mouth. She pushes him away, lightly. We see that the man has an erection. The woman takes the erection in her hand and strokes it.

ZOOM IN ON ERECTION

The woman fondles the man's genitals with both hands.

ZOOM OUT

The woman bends down and takes the man's erection in her mouth. She alternates between oral and manual stimulation.

ZOOM IN ON MAN'S FACE

His eyes are closed. He is concentrating hard.

A Great Dane appears carrying a strap-on dildo. The woman takes the strap-on from the dog, pets him, then fastens the device around her waist. The man turns around, leans against the railing, sticks his ass out. The woman disappears into the house, then returns seconds later with a tube of K-Y Jelly. She squirts the jelly onto her hand, massaging it onto the dildo.

ZOOM IN

The woman pushes the dildo into the man's anus. At first, she precedes slowly. However, after a few strokes, she picks up speed. Soon she is working at a frenzied pace.

ZOOM OUT

The woman continues fucking the man's ass. The dog re-enters the frame and mounts the woman.

ZOOM IN ON DOG'S TESTICLES

THE END

13.12

— Your second film.

— That's right. Another "Kodak moment."

— More like another stolen moment.

— It wasn't stolen. It was found.

— Just like you found wetting a finger is a good way to get felt pen off a film rush.

— That was different.

— So how on earth did you get it developed?

— I just sent it in. It all goes to the Kodak lab in New Jersey and they just run it through a machine.

— Weren't you worried the police might be the ones returning it to you?

— Not at all. Penny told me that nobody looks at the footage. They just feed it in the machine and press a button.

14.1

I was engaged in a thinking project. "The reflective life," as Nettie put it. She'd been taking a Classics course at school and she phoned me from England one Sunday to tell me all about Plato, Sophocles, *The Thebian Plays*. She was always giving me advice, always sending me these aphoristic postcards. GET REFLECTIVE, one said. And then a week later: KNOW THYSELF.

So I wrote back and told her all about my invention — the Bullshit Detector. I even included a diagram. Nettie showed it to one of her teachers and they told her it was a "critical tool." And she agreed, although I'm sure she had to ask them what they meant by that — just as I had to ask the same question of her. But whatever. I'd been spending a lot of time with the Bullshit Detector and was getting excellent results. Not only was it the perfect gizmo for self-assessment, it also came in handy on those around me. After a while I devised a scoring system, a feel-out thing that's impossible to explain. The idea, though, was that the highest ratings went to the biggest losers. So Bobby Galt, for example, would top off at .97; while Nettie would never go over .08.

The Bullshit Detector was my compass. It kept me true. I applied it daily, much like you would a toothbrush. I grew to trust it, love it. I even thought about giving it a new name, something a little more respectful. At one point I referred to it as the Versifier, since it sat there on the page like one of those concrete poems I'd come across in Ms. Abbott's English class. But Nettie disagreed. She didn't like the new name at all. So I ended up sticking with the Bullshit Detector. My Bullshit Detector.

14.2

Letter from Nettie Smart

October 11, 1978
Manchester, England

Oi!

The Versifier? What a poofy name. Call a spade a spade, mate. This is a malevolent thing; you just can't take it for granted; it could swing back and hurt you. Besides, it's got nothing in common with poetry! Poems are living things. They get in your head and fuck you up — forever! What you're describing on the page is way too static to be just a poem. More like a tattoo than anything else. You should know better ...

Hey, gotta go. In an hour we leave on a field trip — London! — and I want to send this before I forget. By the way, ditch the Hesse. You're starting to come off like a hippie.

Cheers,
Nettie

14.3

So: thinking was going well. And I had lots to think about, too. The minutiae of my life. Working through it kept me sharp. I was rethinking everything. I'd weaned myself off Hermann Hesse — once I'd decided I was neither Narcissus nor Goldmund — then I took off in a million new directions. I was now straddling a broad range of topics. I'd worked my way from Plato to Descartes. Then I abandoned all that for Nietzsche. I liked what he had to say about the end of the Enlightenment — whatever that was. But I liked his *Maxims* the best. They reminded me of the little notes Nettie used to scribble in her textbooks back in Grade Seven. "Notes for poems," she would say, whenever I asked her. "Lines," she said, "that worked."

14.4

Letter from Nettie Smart

October 25, 1978
Manchester, England

Hey!

See you got my reading list. Got to the part in
Plato yet, where the poet gets banished? You should be
so lucky, what with your lot back home. But I suppose
you're making the best of it. Kicking against the pricks
and all.

Yeah, Descartes. We're ripping him to bits right
now. All that talk of rational science. Bollocks!
Everybody here's a Luddite, an anarchist. And whereas
your classmates are all trying to outdo each other for
Mr. and Mrs. Grade Twelve hero, we're fighting it out
for Antichrist of the Year. Oh yeah, it's a lively bunch,
all right!

Hope you're not too down in the dumps these
days. Remember, keep your chin up. And get out in the
world a bit more. Explore!

Cheers,
Nettie

14.5

Eventually I abandoned philosophy and returned to literature.
Charles Olson in particular. For a while there I actually considered
myself an honorary resident of Gloucester. And when I told all this
to Nettie she wrote back and insisted I start reading Pound. Once I'd
finished with his *Cantos*, I wrote Nettie a thank you and she sent me
back a congratulatory gift: Stein's *Tender Buttons*. What a great book
that was. Then she sent me a list of English writers. Contemporary
stuff. People like Angela Carter, whom I liked the best. I mean, I just
loved *Love*. So I had lots of shit to think about, all of it stuff I wasn't
getting in school.

Postcard from Nettie Smart

November 11, 1978
Manchester, England

Hey!
      Good talking on the telephone the other day.
Glad you liked the new reading list. Don't go too existential on me now! Things getting busy at school, what
with papers and all. I guess that's why I'm keeping it
short this time. Do you like the postcard? One of the
members of the Art and Language group came to our
school yesterday and gave a talk, so that's where the
card comes from. How conceptual!

Cheers,
Nettie

14.7

And I was talking less. I mean, there was no one around to talk to.
After Kai finally got busted, Dottie went psycho and hid behind the
blinds all day. So that took care of them. Dana Ferris, meanwhile,
had met this guy who hated her hash habit, and together they found
God on Sunset Beach. And even Cheryl Parks — who I avidly pur-
sued — she wouldn't have anything to do with me, having made up
her mind that, despite the humiliation I received at the hands of
Longley, I was forever one of the Cindy set. So that just left Robin.
Not that the guy didn't have anything to say. I mean, I considered
him a friend and everything. But he was no Nettie.

But it was more than that. More than all that thinking — all
the not talking. Something weird was happening. I'd come to the
conclusion that I didn't give a shit any more. Because nothing
bugged me. Because nothing mattered. I was perfectly happy within
my own mind. It was a totally liberating experience. At least as far as
school was concerned.

I remember when it hit me. I was sitting in Ms. Abbott's
English class. It was a Friday — a half-day — and all classes had

been shortened to fifteen minutes. Mrs. Abbott was handing back our essays. Anyway, mine was the last to be returned. That's because Ms. Abbott wanted to share it with the class.

The assignment was to write a short essay on a poem from our Canadian Literature anthology. I'd chosen this Margaret Atwood poem — I forget the name of it — and, I dunno, I just looked it over a couple of times and wrote down my thoughts. It was nothing. But Ms. Abbott didn't think so. She loved it. When she read it out that day, all the guys just looked at me and laughed. And even Cheryl Parks — who hated those guys — she got into it, too. Just to see me squirm. Not that I did or anything. Because, like I said, I'd stopped caring.

Once she'd read the essay, Ms. Abbott announced that she was now going to share with us her comments. All of a sudden the class was responding like she was reciting this love letter. Everybody was making these *woo-woo* noises. I mean, it was so lame. Then, just as she'd finished with the comments, the buzzer went. So I bolted. Left her standing there with the assignment in her hands. Didn't even look at her. That shut the class up. But I didn't care. I mean, it was nothing. It meant absolutely nothing to me.

14.7a

Ms. Abbott's Comments

> You have a beautiful lyric voice. You write like I feel when I can't express myself in words. Where did you learn to do this? Is someone in your family a writer? Did they help you?
>
> In terms of form, this essay is extremely well organized. And your insights and analysis are uncanny. I would consider this work on Atwood's poem almost a companion piece, a response, something that would not seem out of place beside "They are hostile nations." Are you familiar with the book from which this poem came? *Power Politics?* If not, I would gladly lend you my copy.

14.8

— And what happened when you got home from school that day?

— I found a little parcel propped against the door. From Kodak.

14.9

Like many small-time smoke dealers, Robin was a terrible business-man. Over half his transactions involved payment-in-kind. So his apartment was stuffed with all kinds of useless crap. Broken appliances, smudged-up toys, bad jewellery, paintings — all stuff he'd taken in exchange for those shiny little foils of fantastic hash. I remember the first time I saw one of his "swaps" go down.

Robin gave this native couple a gram of Black Affi for a giant stuffed panda. Something they'd won at the PNE. A very bizarre negotiation. But Robin loved their story: how the panda spoke to them, how they had to have it, how they'd dropped almost thirty bucks — twice the price of the hash! — before finally sinking one of those overinflated basketballs through one of those too-small hoops. After they left I told Robin that these people were probably just making the whole thing up, that they were bullshitting the hash right out of his hands. I said, "Robin, if you're ever going to survive in this business, you gotta be tough." But then Robin surprised me. He told me that even though their story was a crock it still made him laugh, that he hadn't laughed that hard in a long time, and that this was the first time he'd seen me laugh since we'd met. He said that made it priceless. And the panda, as dumb as it was, would for-ever remind him of that. And Robin was right: we both turned to the panda and laughed. We laughed and laughed and laughed. We were that stoned. I reapplied the Bullshit Detector and Robin dropped from a .30 to a .10. Two points away from Nettie.

Robin's "swaps" began finding their way into our conversation. Whether or not this happened consciously I'll never know. But the next time I was over I was telling him about Nietzsche when all of a sudden Robin darts into the kitchen and comes back with this leather-bound copy of *Ecce Homo*. "Tad and Andy ripped this off from Duthie's. Gave it to me in exchange for smoking them up. So here. Keep it. It's yours." Another time we were hot-knifing in the kitchen and I was telling Robin how I'd moved my bedroom to the basement, how I'd redecorated — painted the walls gun-metal grey, put up some posters — how I positioned my chair so I could look out the little window and see the stars above. Robin smiled, then went to the hall closet, rummaged around, and came back with a telescope. "Got this for an ounce of Red Leb," he said. "Here. Keep it. It's yours."

The third time Robin gave me something was the day after I got my package from Kodak. We were sitting around the apartment, sucking on the bong, listening to his latest T. Rex bootleg. It was one of Marc Bolan's last concerts and you could tell the guy was completely fucked up. "Light of Love" sounded like a cry for help. "I never got to see him," Robin said sadly. I tried to console him. "I heard his last shows were bad," I said, uneasy with my tone. Robin scoffed. "I'd take a bad concert over no concert at all." Then I remembered there was talk of a documentary, something I'd read about in *Hit Parader*. So I told him about it. I told him in this really animated way, too. Thought maybe I could cheer him up. But Robin shrugged. "It's not the same. You have to be there."

The record ended with Bolan alone. It was amazing how his a cappella wail passed so easily from the "Light of Love" chorus into a rant against the audience. I imagine the guy making the bootleg chose to fade his tape where he did because it seemed that Marc was now addressing him directly. You could barely hear it. But if you listened close, you could hear him scream: "... and get that wanker with the microphone out of my ..."

Robin got up, changed records. He put on the Who's *Tommy*. "Did you see the movie?" he asked. "No," I told him. Robin lowered the needle, then he turned to me. He looked me right in the eye and said, "It's playing again. Do you wanna go?" Robin and I had never done anything outside his apartment before. And I was very aware of this. So I guess my awareness, coupled with Robin's invitation, made me extra self-conscious. "Not really," I said, averting my eyes, reaching for my smokes. Robin returned to the couch and sat down beside me. The "Overture" kicked in. He stared out the window, humming along, his pitch flat.

I got up, went to the bathroom. I didn't have to, but I did anyway. Something always comes out. I applied the Bullshit Detector to myself and I didn't like my score. I came back from the bathroom and sat down on the couch.

"I'd like to make movies," Robin said, chopping up a gram —

"rock 'n' roll movies." I lit an Eddy and held it so the flame burned big. Robin nodded. I waved the match over the bowl. He inhaled. The water bubbled. I took the hose and began a slow toke. The hash burned out. "I mean — I can't play worth shit," he said, grabbing an Eddy, striking twice, "so the next best thing, I think, would be to make movies about people playing." Robin applied the match. I inhaled. "What about you? Do you ever think about how cool it would be to make a movie?" I laughed, choking on the smoke. "I guess it's time to clean that thing," he said, passing me a cup of cold coffee. I took a sip, then told him no, still laughing. I told him, between sips, that it was okay ... it was just me ... I was laughing at something else. Robin smiled. I loved it when stuff like this happened — coincidences. I reached inside my pea-coat and took out the reels. "You wanna see my movie?" I said, stacking them on the coffee table. Robin was up in a flash. I could hear him crashing around his bedroom. He came back with a GAF super-8 projector. "You won't believe how I got this," he said, setting it down over the latest issue of *Garçons de Maroc*.

14.10

— You watched the film.

— Oh yes.

— Robin loved it.

— Yes, he did. And he had some very smart things to say about it, too.

— He had a plan.

— That's right. He was going to be my agent. And I must say, he turned out to be a much better agent than he was a drug dealer.

14.11

I was pretty high after I left Robin's. Not so much on the hash, but on Robin's analysis, his big plans. He said he knew this guy named Max who threw parties at a warehouse in False Creek, and that Max was always on the lookout for new stuff to show in his club. Robin was convinced that we could make some serious dough if we premiered what he was now calling *The Family Dog* at Max's. "This is a cult film," he said. "We show it at Max's — everybody will be talking about it. I guarantee you this: After the premier, we'll be able to charge whatever we want. Just trust me."

We watched the film. Then we watched it again. And again and again. With each viewing Robin got more and more excited. "This is amazing," he kept saying. "Amazing." And yes, it was amazing. But there were a lot of things wrong with it. The first reel was okay; however, the second reel was way too shaky. "But it works," Robin said. "It matches the action. You can tell the woman's about to come. It's as if the camera's coming with her." He had a point. But what about the third reel? It kept going in and out of focus. "Yes!" Robin said, "but that works, too. We know the guy's getting a blow job, right? So when it goes out of focus, it's like he's fantasizing about something else. What he really wants is to get fucked in the ass." Maybe. But what about the dog? The dog just appears out of nowhere. And you don't know it's a dog until the camera zooms out. Up until then, it just looks like a woman struggling to get her coat on. So I told him all this. Robin thought for a minute. Then the light bulb went up. "Well," he said, "I guess that's what makes it an art film."

14.12

Robin's Notes on How to Proceed with *The Family Dog*

1. If we agree to work together, we split everything fifty-fifty.

2. I get the gigs, you show the film.

3. We have to be cool. By that I mean we have to look cool and act cool. When you come over next time I will show you some books about what cool looks like these days. In the meantime, go to the library and read everything you can about Andy Warhol. There's some big photo books about the Factory, all the people Warhol hung out with. I'm thinking of going in for a Nico look myself — even though I do look a lot like Lou Reed. Ironic, huh? However, you should pay close attention

to the Joe Dallesandro look. We have to look like these people. Presence is everything.

4. Max is a weird guy. He might try to pick you up, but you can't sleep with him. You can't because we have to present ourselves as a couple. Max is kinky and he might hurt you and I know you're not into that.

5. I'll deal with Max. If he tries to talk to you, just pretend you're from Russia or something. Learn some Russian words. Also, learn how to say "I don't speak English" with a Russian accent. From now on you will speak English as a second language.

14.13

I took my driver's test on the Monday, and passed. To celebrate, Mom offered to take me and my sister out for dinner. She said there was this "nifty" Italian restaurant near Main and Hastings, just off Chinatown. A place called Puccini's. Yeah. She said she'd been there on a date and had a great time. Somehow that took the shine off. So I shrugged. Sure. Whatever. But my sister — who's always lacked my insight, my tact — said, "Can't we go somewhere where you *haven't* gone on a date?" Jerk! How hurtful. So I went to Mom's aid. I told my sister that it was my party we're talking about here — not hers. But this seemed to hurt Mom even more. "No, that's not it at all — it's about the three of us going out and having fun," she said, exasperated, reconfirming my belief that she did indeed have a hidden agenda.

Most of my driver training had been confined to residential streets, so I was pretty nervous about driving downtown. Plus I'd never driven at night before. But Mom was patient. She did her best. She suggested a route, then attempted passive navigation. I took Thirty-third to Granville, then turned left and headed north. No problem. I crossed the Granville Street Bridge, then took the Seymour Street exit. No problem there, either. The light was changing at Drake and I stepped on the brakes — hard. Through a clenched smile Mom told me that a caution didn't necessarily mean a stop. Then my sister jumped in: "Yeah — now the car stinks of rubber."

I was all set to lay into her, remind my sister that it was me who was gonna be driving her to Brownies every Tuesday for the next few years, when who should be crossing but two of Robin's hustler friends, the same two responsible for my copy of *Ecce Homo* — Tad and Andy. And they were looking right at us, making these blow-job gestures, laughing. I was mortified. Did they recognize me? Were they gonna come over and say something? Fuck me up for good? "You know what those two will be doing tonight, don't you?" Mom whispered. Duh? But I had to say something. I felt a blush coming on. "Uh — brushing their teeth?" I said. A moment's silence. Then we all laughed. And this made Mom very happy.

"There — " Mom said, "beside the Venus." I executed a perfect parallel park. "A PPP" as Mom used to call it. We exchanged low-fives. Then Mom turned around in effort to include my sister in this parking triumph. But she was already out the door. We caught up with her under the Venus marquee, where she gleefully recited the hype: "Direct from Denmark ... *The Blue Balloon* ... a sex-ellent film adventure ..." I thought Mom was gonna freak, but no. She just laughed. Man, was she having a good time or what! I mean, it was so obvious she had something heavy to tell us.

And she did, as soon as we sat down. "I'm seeing a man," she said, "and it's serious." She asked us if we'd like to meet him, and right away we said yes. Not because we wanted to, but because we could tell our mother wasn't totally comfortable in this situation — and because, of course, we knew it would make her happy if we showed some interest. Which turned out to be true: Mom was very happy to have gotten that first part out of the way.

"I want you both to know that my feelings towards Carl won't in any way diminish the way I feel about you two," she said, fidgeting with her napkin. We nodded. "In fact," she added, in a moment of uncalled-for desperation, "right now I think I love you two more than ever." Huh? I looked at my sister. I could see her mind at work; she wasn't buying it either. Then I looked at my mom. She was nibbling at her lip, no doubt regretting her choice of words. And rightly so. I mean, how could she say that? How could she love us more if she was so in love with someone else? After all, aren't we — as human beings — only capable of so much love? I wanted to tell her that, but I couldn't. I didn't have the heart. She knew she'd said something stupid, so why rub it in. She didn't mean it. My poor mom. I mean, what made her think she had to try so hard anyway?

Over dinner, Mom's new-man pitch evolved into a mini-tribute to my sister and me. A cavalcade of compliments, really. She went on and on. Told us what great kids we were, how she could trust us with adult matters. And how with this trust comes rewards, freedoms. But with these freedoms come responsibilities, I kept thinking. There had to be a catch. I think my mom was aware of my skepticism, too, because she shifted her focus, began addressing me directly. She knew I was a tough nut to crack. But I was miles ahead of her. I was already thinking about how I could turn this around, use it to my advantage.

"This exile from high school business," she began, "I think I can understand it. I know you're bored. But please don't shut the world out." I nodded like the advice was good, like I needed it. Then I looked over at my sister. She rolled her eyes. She'd seen me play this game before. So after excusing herself to the washroom, Mom poured on the positives. "I'm very proud of what your English teacher wrote in your report card." More nodding. "You'll show me that Margaret Atwood essay, right? I'd really like to read it," she said. "When we get home," I said, taking her hand.

But she wasn't finished. She told me how happy she was with all the work I'd done around the house recently, what a big help I'd been, how she couldn't have done it without me. And I was loving it, of course. Playing it up. So I told her it was nothing, that I appreciated a clean house just as much as the next person. Man, did she ever fall for that one! Because now she was crying. And that's when I knew I'd struck gold. I was all set to renegotiate my curfew, but Mom had beaten me to it, totally caught me offguard. It was as if she'd read my mind. "You're a good boy, you know that, don't you?" What could I say? "You've always been independent." Yes, Mother. "And you've become such a responsible young man." Indeed. "So when we get home tonight, we can talk more about allowances and things like that. I think you've proven to me that you're capable of setting your own rules now." Which was exactly what I wanted to hear, particularly since Robin said there'd be some late nights ahead.

When it was over I sat back, lit a cigarette, and savoured the moment. I tried my best to avoid eye contact with my sister. I could see that she was totally pissed off. Pissed off, of course, because she knew what a suckhole I'd been. But pissed off, especially, because she smoked, too — except Mom didn't know that yet. So I blew a smoke ring her way, just to rub it in. But she got her revenge. In that big voice of hers, she told everyone in the restaurant how she was glad I'd learned how to set fire to something other than our family photos.

Mom brought up the photos on the drive back. Which totally pissed me off, because I knew she wouldn't have said anything had my sister not been so attention-starved. "You've come a long way since then, haven't you?" Mom said, nudging me, as if I didn't know that green meant go. "Yes, I think I have," I said, stepping on the gas, pretending like it was no big deal. "You've dealt with all that now, right? You're fine now, right?" she added. "Oh yes," I said, turning south on Howe. There was silence. I looked in the rear-view. My sister looked just like Nettie did the day John and Penny drove us back to the tracks. I wondered whatever happened to those two — John and Penny. "Stop!" my mother shouted. I hit the brakes. The car skidded. I'd run a red light. Worse yet — I'd almost hit somebody. An old man. My mother rolled down the window. "Are you okay, sir?" she asked. Mr. Gingell's face flashed before us. He smiled, told us he was fine, thanked us anyway.

14.14

— You went back there four days later.

— Yes, I did. My second drive downtown. To the Venus. I saw my first porno. Pornos, really ...

— After you were escorted out, you found your window broken.

— Yeah, they took the Joan Armatrading tape.

— Did you report it?

— Of course not! What would I tell my mom? *Oh, by the way — I was in the worst part of town yesterday — watching pornos, of course — and somebody had the nerve to break in and steal the Joan Armatrading?* I don't think so.

— So how did you explain the broken window?

— I told her I'd locked myself out and left the car running.

— And what did you say when she asked you why you didn't phone BCAA?

— I told her I was afraid to leave the car. I said there were some dubious people hanging out by the library, and they were watching. She believed me, of course. She said I probably did the right thing.

— How did you explain the lost Joan Armatrading?

— I told her the tape deck ate it.

— And when she gave you money to buy a new one?

— I told her I looked everywhere, but they were out.

— What did she say to that?

— She said maybe there was something else out there we both might like.

— Did you find something new then?

— No, I took a screwdriver to the tape deck, broke the thing.

— Did you give her back the money?

— No, I put the money towards an editing block. I still had to put the film together.

14.15

Robin was right. *The Family Dog* was a hit. People were blown away. One guy — this West Van art collector — he offered to buy it off us for a thousand dollars. Right on the spot. One thousand dollars! It was amazing. He said he wanted to show it at the Vancouver Art Gallery, wig-out the blue hairs. Yeah. He even said he could make me a star, told me I'd be the next big thing, wanted to know what part of Russia I was from. I laughed and laughed and laughed. But Robin played it cool. He knew stuff like this would happen. That's what he told me before we left the apartment. "And if anybody offers you money, just laugh at them. Laugh and laugh and laugh." So after a quick negotiation, Robin arranged for me to show the film at the collector's house the following week — for three hundred dollars! Yeah. And that was just one of the many deals he cut that night at Max's.

And it was a long night, too. I'd never been to one of these things before. I had no idea what to expect. But Robin had me prepped. That afternoon he took me to Ruby's and bought me a silver lamé shirt. Fuckin' thing was an itch-fest. But Robin said that was cool: all that itching would make me look like a junkie. And these people loved to watch junkies. Then we went down the street to this woman's apartment. Real weird, this chick. She had green hair and dressed head-to-toe in leather. I think her name was Gemma. Anyway, Robin paid her ten bucks to make me a skinny tie. A pink one. Then we went to this little shop on Granville and he bought me some patent-leather boots. After that we went back to the apartment. Robin got me into these tight white pants that seemed designed to advertise the head of my cock. Then he did my hair, bouffed it up so I looked like one of the fags in Blondie. We looked in the mirror together. And I flipped. "I can't go out like this," I told him, meaning it. "Yes, you can," he said, putting the final touches on my forelocks. "You have to. You can't afford to look too normal. Not with this crowd. If you look too normal, it just won't work."

Nothing Robin said could have prepared me for what happened that night. I mean, this place was weird. Way different from anything I'd experienced before. But you'd never know it from the outside. For Max's was just another dirty warehouse on the north side of False Creek. But whatever. It's about 9:00 P.M. when we arrive by taxi. We walk up to this orange door and Robin buzzes. A voice comes on, barks "What?" Robin barks back: "The Family Dog." The door opens and standing there is this huge bald guy — and I mean football-player huge — and all he's got on is this diaper. A cloth one. The size of a twin duvet. And holding it together is this bayonet-like safety pin. Too weird. I was already feeling wigged out from the hash oil we'd smoked at dress up. And speaking of which, did I mention that Robin — for some reason we'd never discussed — was wearing a nurse's uniform? So now all I can think of is Robin assisting in the delivery of this three-hundred-pound baby-man. But from what, though? I mean, what could this guy's mother look like? It was too weird. That hash we'd smoked was totally expansive.

We followed the baby down this dingy hallway, then turned left and climbed up a long flight of stairs. At the top of the stairs the baby opens a metal door. Inside is this massive silver room. And I mean massive, like a ballroom or something. Tables and chairs, huge dance floor. At the far end, a cinema-sized movie screen. Far too big for super-8 projection, I thought. No doubt expectations were high. But no matter. We'd make it work somehow.

A crew fiddled with a lighting rack. The same woman who made my tie was tweaking the PA. Somebody — somewhere — was screaming their head off about a lack of ice. The voice reminded me a lot of Marc Bolan's "Light of Love" reprise. Then the punk seamstress/DJ puts on this song by the New York Dolls. I cringe because I can't stand David Johansen. But she takes it off just as quick, replacing it with something unfamiliar, cranking it. We're told by the baby to wait.

We stood and listened to a song about a baby on fire. I'm not kidding. So, of course, all I can think about is our doorman in flames, Nurse Robin throwing a blanket over his burning flesh. I look over at Robin, watch him groove to the music. His movements reminded me of Dottie's — all hip and sway. I wondered about Dottie, how she was doing. Then I wondered about Kai, how he was adjusting to prison life ... A cacophonic interlude as the DJ/seamstress mixes into something else — Robin's idol: Lou Reed. The song: "How Do You Think It Feels?" Robin snapped out of his sway and took up the Lou stance. It all happened so fast. So fast, in fact, I wasn't sure it happened at all. Weird though, huh?

The baby returns and takes us to a sparsely furnished office behind the bar. A desk, a chair, and an adding machine. On the wall, a clock that ran fifteen minutes fast. The baby tells us to hang, that Max is on his way. Then he leaves, closing the door behind him. "Have you met this Max?" I ask Robin. Robin shakes his head. He tells me he's only talked to him on the phone. I ask Robin if the voice we'd heard earlier belonged to Max and he gives me an absent nod. I light a cigarette. Robin takes the cigarette out of my mouth, butts it on the sole of his shoe, and tucks it into his purse. I look at him and he just stares straight ahead. Clearly, his mind was elsewhere.

The voice was approaching. It stopped just outside the door. It told the door that it was not in the mood to hear about an ice shortage. It then reminded the door that lowballs would be served with two cubes, not one. The door said nothing when the voice asked if it understood the reasoning behind two cubes, not one. The voice then educated the door, telling it that the club's liquor profit is derived from a displacement ratio that can only be provided through the inclusion of a second cube. Then the voice got angry, as if the door was too stupid to comprehend the lesson. The voice then called the door so many names it finally gave way and in walked Max. He was wearing a red satin evening gown.

"I'll have you know that I'm the biggest bitch you'll ever work for," he said, pointing a nail-bitten finger an inch from my nose. "I'm ten times meaner than Joan Crawford. A hundred times tougher than John fuckin' Wayne." I figured this Max was just trying to rattle me, so in my best Russian accent, I give it right back to him: "And this Joan Crawford — who the fuck is she anyway?" Max does a double take. He hikes up his dress, reaches between his legs, and pinch-pulls his cock, holding it there like a bad outcome. A twisted little thing, black hairs kinking off in all directions, the balls bound tight like a dead lemon. "That, my sweet prince, is Joan Crawford." Gross.

After the introductions, Max went over the program. We were to be given a room — Room Four — where we were to screen our film continuously from 10:00 P.M. to 2:00 A.M., non-stop. Under no circumstances were we to leave the room. "So if you have to piss, piss now. And if you have to shit — tough." Moreover, we were not to talk to anybody unless we were asked a question. Also, we were not to do anything that involved a monetary exchange. Nor were we allowed to have any physical contact with the patrons. Then Max asked us to repeat back what he'd just told us. We couldn't. We were petrified. So he did the whole thing over again — but twice as bitchy. This time we did fine. Max seemed satisfied. He sat down on the desk, took a couple of drags off his cigarette before butting it on the rug. Then he turned to me. His face seemed almost kind. He put his hand on my shoulder, gave it a tender squeeze, and said, "We usually have a little party at the end of the night. Just friends."

Room Four was actually behind the movie screen. What ended up being projected on the outside, I'll never know. Anyway, there was about a four-foot width between the screen and the wall, and the baby took us there by flashlight. The room itself was small, about sixteen-by-sixteen. The floor was covered in plastic, with three of the four walls painted black. We were to project onto the white wall. We set up the projector, fed the film, then ran it once to make sure everything was okay. Then we waited. We waited and waited and waited.

It was 9:55 when the baby poked his head in. "We're just about to open the doors — you ready?" We nodded. Just as Robin said thanks, the music started. A Giorgio Moroder beat. It was loud. Loud enough that we couldn't hear the door slam. So now it was just me, Robin, and the image of Dottie Ragnarsson.

"Has Max even seen this thing?" I shouted to Robin. "Nope," Robin shouted back. "He's not interested." I found that hard to believe. "He looks like the type who'd be into this kinda stuff," I said, maybe a little hurt that the freak didn't give a shit. "All Max wanted to know was if there were any boys in it. And when I said no, he said, 'Too bad,'" Robin replied. Then, after a beat, he added, "Maybe next time we'll take up that theme." I agreed, if only because I thought it might make Max happy. The guy was such a crank.

The crowds that came through that night were a surprisingly civil bunch. Robin had said that there'd be all kinds of nutcases, but no. These people were extremely normal. Conservatively dressed, polite, a little standoffish. A real disappointment compared to what I'd been psyched for.

I asked the baby about this later, back in the office, over lines. He told me that Max's clientele had changed a lot in the last year. He said that all the groovers had ended up on staff, that it was much easier that way, a much more reliable way of preserving the party atmosphere. I think I understood. The baby cut up another gram of coke. I did a line, then carried the mirror over to Max and Robin. Max took his mouth off Robin's cock and told me that it was just rich fucks who came to the club now, thrill seekers, voyeurs. He figured he had another year before he'd have to change locations, start again. And besides, the cops had been onto him a while now. They told him he'd be busted as soon as things slowed down. Then Robin came all over Max's red dress.

14.16

Excerpt from *The Journals of Nettie Smart*, vol. 11, pp. 12–13, 1978

> Had the strangest phone call today from Our Boy in Vancouver. Apparently he's filmed the Ragnarssons having

sex on their balcony, a three-way with their dog, Bengt Jr. And get this: he sent the film to Kodak — and they dutifully sent it back! Processed! But even weirder: now he's hatched some plan with this Robin fellow, something about showing it around for money. What a loon! Obviously he's spending way too much time in his head.

But as much as I find this hard to believe, as much as I think he's shitting me, half of me believes him. So okay — maybe he's exaggerating a bit. Maybe the Ragnarssons were naked, and maybe they were necking, and maybe they even felt each other up. But a hard-core sex act with a dog? Forget it! No way. Not because I don't think the Ragnarssons are into that kinda stuff — I just don't think he's *that* imaginative. Or is he?

Which reminds me: a group of us went to a lecture the other day at the Whitworth. Angela Carter was giving a talk from a book she's writing on the Marquis de Sade, women, and pornography. A lot of it was over my head, but I did get a couple of things down in my notebook. A very interesting afternoon. I'll make sure to pass these on to Our Boy.

14.16a

Nettie's Notes

"Sexual relations between men and women always render explicit the nature of social relations in the society in which they take place and, if described explicitly, will form a critique of those relations, even if that is not and never has been the intention of the pornographer."

"A male-dominated society produces a pornography of universal female aquiescence."

"When pornography serves ... to reinforce the prevailing system of values and ideas in a given society, it is tolerated; and when it does not, it is banned."

"Once pornography is labelled 'art' or 'literature' it is stamped with the approval of an elitist culture and many ordinary people will avoid it on principle, out of fear of being bored."

"When pornography abandons its quality of existential solitude and moves out of the kitsch area of timeless, placeless fantasy and into the real world, then it loses its function of safety valve. It begins to comment on real relations in the world."

14.17

Robin had bookings well into the new year. And with each booking came more offers, then more bookings. Just like Robin said would happen. One day I screened the film at five different locations. But each screening was really more like five screenings because people kept wanting to see it over and over until they got bored. So you can just imagine how boring it was for me. The only thing keeping my interest was all the money we were making. I reckon in that first month alone Robin and I made about three thousand dollars apiece.

14.18

— What did you do with all that money?

— I hid it away.

— Where?

— In a tin can I kept buried in the ground.

— Where did you bury it?

— Up by the railroad tracks, in a blackberry bush.

— You were operating on the assumption that lightning doesn't strike twice?

— That's correct.

— And what about Robin? What did he do with his share?

— Most of it went up his nose.

Like I said before, our first booking was at this art collector's house. He lived over on the North Shore, in this ritzy neighbourhood known as the British Properties, the West Van equivalent to Shaughnessy.

In celebration of our first paid gig, Robin got me an even tighter pair of pants to wear. And he was really adamant that I pack my genitals on the side this time. "We have to make a statement," he said. "I thought this time we'd go for the *Querelle* look." Then he showed me a way to hang myself so I'd be in a continual state of semi-erection. It was a neat trick.

Robin insisted I wear one of those way-too-small gondolier shirts. "These shirts are tapered in such a way as to accentuate your pecs," he said, stepping back, taking in the look. "More like my veins," I complained, unable to bring my arms down. But Robin ignored me, scrunching up his nose like he wasn't quite sure of something. We compromised on a similar shirt, one size up.

The last thing to attend to was my hair. "I'd like to go short and flat," said Robin, sitting me down on the toilet, reaching for his spray bottle. But I told him no. I told him my mom would be suspicious if I came home at night with a haircut. "How would I explain it?" I said. "She knows my barber closes at five." But Robin insisted. "We need something new to complete the look," he replied, scissors in hand, all set to snip. So we made a deal. Once I got back from the collector's, Robin would provide me with a list of plausible excuses, the ten ways to best explain the new hair. Which, as it turned out, didn't matter because my mom never noticed the difference.

It was snowing when I got there. The collector's house was modest compared to some of the manors I'd passed along the way: a ground-level rancher surrounded by shrubs, one of them cut in the shape of an auger. As I made my way up the walk the collector opened the door, greeted me with a shy smile. He was nowhere near as bubbly as he was that night at Max's. In fact, he seemed a bit distracted, like he was in the middle of something else. As it turned out, he was having a dinner party.

From the entrance I could see into a dining room. About a dozen people gathered around a long table, eating what looked like sherbet, preoccupied by someone talking, holding court. But I only caught a glimpse, because the collector whisked me down the hall to a den, where he told me to make myself comfortable, get set up, and that they'd be in shortly. The collector had cleared some space on the wall to project on, and I thanked him for that. I was trying to appear professional. But instead of acknowledging my professionalism the collector eyed me up and down, told me I looked cute, liked the shirt. This pissed me off. I thought about being a prick to him but thought otherwise just as quick. I would make a statement with my professionalism. Then the kettle blew and off he went.

I set up the projector and waited. It was impossible not to listen in. The voice was slow and emphatic, very proper, a voice that had obviously come from England, an especially low voice that I would have thought belonged to a man had she not been talking when I caught my glimpse. This was part of it:

"... so yes, I believe it was 1963, and it *was* New York, yes, and we had just seen Carolee Schneemann perform *Eye Body*. A beautiful work. And Martin loved those umbrellas — he really did — he just loved them. So Martin said he wanted to buy them up, and I said he couldn't because they were part of Carolee's performance. Now, as everybody knows, performance art is ephemeral and not about the object. So you just can't decide to buy the properties. Because they belong to the performance. But Martin wouldn't have it. He said he would wait until the artist washed off and then he would approach her, offer her a hundred dollars apiece." Laughter. A man's tired groan. Then his protest: "No, Jo-Jo, it wasn't like that at all. I didn't say I was going to — " But Jo-Jo cut him off. "And so Martin turns to me all stuffy and says, 'I'm on the acquisitions committee and — goddamnit — I can do whatever the hell I want.'" Laughter. "So I said, 'Then you'll have to buy the artist, too'" — more laughter — "'because without the artist the work is meaningless, incomplete, of no value whatsoever,' just like that boy in the next room" — pause — "I mean, let's not kid ourselves — there will come a point during the screening of his film where we are going to find ourselves looking over at this young man, wondering just how is it that he has come into our lives, bearing a film that, we've been told, contains a scene where a woman has congress with a dog. Do you see my point? How this young man will be forever linked to our viewing experience?"

There was no reply. I felt a chill. The only sounds coming from the dining room now were the clicks of spoons over glass, the empty sounds of food being finished. So now what? Wasn't somebody going to say something? Change the topic? Move on? Because I couldn't stand the idea of people thinking about me — sitting there thinking about me sitting around waiting — maybe wondering whether I overheard Jo-Jo's comment, maybe happy that they might find *The Family Dog* so offensive that they will be glad that I did overhear Jo-Jo's comment and thus deserve the discomfort I was definitely going through. But then a voice. Finally. The collector's. "Martin, tell me something — did you find Schneemann's umbrellas phallic or yonic?" Martin waited a while before responding. But even when he did, it was impossible to make out what he was saying. All I could gather was that the man's mouth was full of food. Which was confirmed by Jo-Jo, who berated Martin for not swallowing before he spoke.

Five minutes later the group filed in. A well-groomed bunch, all of them had on the grey clothes, the tight smiles, the creaky poise that comes with money. They sat down in pairs. Six couples, not one of them under forty. They filled the chairs and couches and stared at the white wall ahead, cups and saucers balanced in their laps. None of them looked my way. Then the collector asked me if I was ready. I told him I was. He said okay, smiled, then hit the lights. This would be the only occasion where I wasn't asked to show *The Family Dog* more than once.

I got back to Robin's at about 11:00 P.M. I wanted to keep going, go straight home, but Robin insisted on a debriefing. I told him I was tired, but he nagged me. So we sat up and did some lines. It turned out to be a good idea because only through retelling the story was I able to make sense of it. Robin made me describe everything in the most minute detail. Which I did.

So I told him about the collector's modest house, Jo-Jo and the other guests, what I overheard. I told him about the post-screening conversation, how they argued with each other over why *The Family Dog* wasn't art, how stupid and offensive it was, who hated it the most and why. I told Robin how I was completely ignored during this process, how I had to sit there while everybody took turns telling each other how depraved young people are these days, how they have no taste for the finer things. I told Robin about this one guy, Thomas, who started getting all upset because he was active in the SPCA, and how he wasn't sure whether or not he should phone the cops and have the film confiscated. Robin howled at that one. Then I told him about the guy's wife, Doris, and how she started crying because she felt she'd somehow broken the law just by being there, and how if she ever went to jail, she would no doubt be raped with a broom handle on account of her fragile beauty, and how this led to another woman confessing to the group that her daughter had a drug problem, and that if her daughter ever ended up being sentenced to jail, she would surely kill her first rather than have her suffer through the indignity of being a woman in chains.

And that was just the beginning. These people were insane. Absolutely out of their minds. I wanted to leave, but I knew if I got up to go, I would just keep on walking and we'd never get paid and I had no money and didn't know where the fuck I was so I was trapped. Then Robin asked what the collector was doing all this time. I told him how the collector spent most of his time moderating, how he raised questions every time the conversation lagged, milking his guests, getting them to say the wildest things. I told Robin how every now and then Jo-Jo would get up and take a few photographs, jot down some notes, then sit down next to the collector, where they'd whisper stuff in private. Robin asked me if I caught anything of their conversation, but I hadn't. Not a word. And that's when it dawned on me. That's when I realized what was really going on.

It was near the end of the evening, and I'd noticed that Jo-Jo had contributed very little to the discussion. Nothing, in fact. She'd spent the whole night writing, taking pictures, whispering to the collector. Not once did she say anything to the other guests. And I was beginning to wonder why. Because wasn't she the one who'd been so vocal earlier on? Wasn't she the one most likely of an opinion? I thought if I were to say anything at all that night — and Robin and I had already agreed that I wouldn't because it wouldn't be professional — then I would most certainly ask the woman why she was being so mum. So I rehearsed something in my head, and was all set to ask her — all set to break my own rule — when suddenly she turns to me and winks. I'm not kidding! This wink! And then I think back to all that shit she was saying earlier about Carolee Schneemann and performance art and the object. And it was like — bang! Now I get it. How could I have been so stupid? This had nothing to do with *The Family Dog* at all.

I handed Robin the cheque. He looked at it and nodded. The cheque was issued not by the collector but by Jo-Jo herself. That's when Robin told me that I was just one of Carolee Schneemann's umbrellas.

14.20

— You were upset by this revelation.

— I was humiliated. I told Robin I didn't want to show the film any more.

— What did he say?

— He told me that what had happened at the collector's house was unusual, but that nothing like that would ever happen again.

— And you believed him?

— No.

— He was right, though.

— In a way. The rest of the screenings were nowhere near as complex.

— How did Jo-Jo rate on the Bullshit Detector?

— Yeah, that was interesting. I knew where Jo-Jo was coming from, but I had no idea where she was going. So that kinda fucked things up. She was my first big exception.

— Did Robin continue to dress you up for screenings?

— No. I sorta got my own schtick together after that. I just wore black. And the Russian accent was long gone.

— Why didn't Robin accompany you after the premiere?

— He'd gotten too busy. Robin was into coke big time. After the premiere, he started spending most of his nights at Max's.

14.21

The next three screenings were all within a few blocks of Robin's. All three were hosted by people I'd seen at the premiere. Younger people. Artsy types. A musician, a writer, and a visual artist. Funny how similar these screenings were to each other. There was very little variation from one to the next. At least that's how I remember it.

I would show up at an apartment, buzz the number. At the door I'd be greeted by the occupant. It was always a guy. The guy would smile, seem really happy to see me, help me with my gear. There would be loud music playing. The first time it was Iggy Pop. The second time, Modern Lovers. And the third time, Brian Eno.

Then there were the introductions. The occupant would introduce me to his guests, which, in every case, consisted of four guys and two girls. Everybody would be sitting around looking bored, as if they'd been dragged there against their will. Behaviour, I assumed, which was meant to be read as cool. Then one of the guys would light up a joint. Eventually the joint would come my way. And when it did, I'd always refuse it. Not because I didn't want to get high. Because I did. I loved smoking up. It's just that Robin and I agreed that I should do this straight. Which turned out to be a wise idea. Not only was I able to retain my professionalism but, as it turned out, it lent some quirk to my ID as a smut pedlar.

I learned quickly that people found me intriguing when I told them I didn't use drugs. I guess the assumption was that sex and drugs went hand in hand. The artist, in particular, was very curious about this, especially when I told him I didn't like rock 'n' roll either. "So much for the unholy trinity," he said. But whatever. It worked. Everybody thought I was fascinating. A tea-drinking jazz enthusiast who travelled around showing porn. That was my schtick. And thank God I had one. Because as a sixteen-year-old I needed all the leverage I could get.

Once I decided where to project the film, the host would clear a wall. By the time the wall was cleared, I'd have the projector plugged in and threaded. The only thing left would be to turn out the lights and press Play. It was then that I'd give my speech. This would be the speech I wrote after the North Shore screening. I decided to write a speech because I felt it was important to orient the audience, provide some kind of context for what they were about to watch. I guess that was what Nettie was getting at with all those Angela Carter quotations. But whatever. I'd committed the speech to memory and rehearsed it in front of a mirror, so I knew what was I doing. It had to be convincing. And it was. That was part of my schtick, too.

14.21a

The Speech

Contrary to some of the rumours floating around town, the film I am about to show you — which has come to be known in some circles as *The Family Dog* — is not what the British art critic Nettie Smart, in her latest book, *The Bird and the Worm*, refers to as a "found performance." What I'm about to show you is an actual out-take from a film that was made by my father back in the late 1960s, a film called *The Story of This Family — So Far*. Basically, then, this is the story of a man who does unspeakable things to his family, and then, when he goes to bed at night, dreams about what they might do to him. I should also add that at no time during the making of this film was the dog in any way hurt. Like the actors in this production, he, too, is a professional.

Now, some of you may find this document offensive. If you do, then I ask that you please refrain from comment until the screening is finished. I would prefer it if you went to another room and waited. I think that's fair, don't you? (Await the response.) I would also like to emphasize that just because you may see something you don't like doesn't mean you have the right to take away someone else's right to see it.

14.22

— The first part is an outright lie.

— I prefer to think of it as a fiction.

— So they took your introduction seriously?

— For a while there, yeah. At least I thought they did. Because nobody said anything. But now, looking back, I think they were just flabbergasted; I don't think they were expecting a back story. I don't know. Maybe they just thought I was a nutcase, that I was somehow part of the experience. And I suppose, in a way, I was.

— Just like Jo-Jo said.

— Sure.

— And the last part of your speech?

— That was something my mom once said.

— Just checking.

14.23

Of those first three groups, the first two responses were pretty much the same. Once the film ended, there was silence. Then somebody would let out a long sigh. There'd be head-scratches, a couple of coughs, then somebody would say "wow" or "holy shit" or "I can't believe what we just saw." Then the person who had been the quietest up until that point would ask if we could see it again.

The first group I showed this to were mostly musicians. Rock musicians. They were the most obvious. To wit: "Did you see the nuts on that dog?" And: "That chick had the nicest ass." And: "You know, I'd like to put music to that. I know just what I'd do, too. Something heavy, like Crimson's 'Lark's Tongue in Aspic.'" They were also by far the most demonstrative in their comments. They really threw their bodies into what they had to say — even though it wasn't very well thought out.

The second group were mostly writers. Freelancers. But a couple wrote novels. And one of them had just finished a book of poems. They were by far the dullest of the three groups, the slowest off the mark. I mean, it was ages before anyone said something. And when they did, it was tepid. "I found it hard to tell what was going on." And: "I think that woman is sick." And: "I think it would be more interesting with dialogue."

The third group was hosted by a visual artist. This group included sculptors, a photographer, a videographer. It seemed weird that none of them painted. But I liked this group best because, as Nettie put it, "they seemed to be united by ideas rather than by discipline." And they were really quick, too. "Looks like something I saw at the Cinémathèque a couple of years ago. Anyone remember that?" Someone did. "Yeah, Schneemann's *Fuse*." Then someone else piped in: "It's interesting the way the camera behaves during all this — strobing back and forth between gaze and subjectivity." Then another voice: "I'm not sure what you mean?" Then back to the previous voice: "The way the out-of-focus passages suggest a dream-state, the way the jerky parts suggest arousal on the part of the cameraman. I like the way it goes back and forth, in-and-out of the filming and the *being filmed*." There was more. A lot more. These people loved to talk. It was ages before they asked if they could see it again.

I thought Robin would be really happy to hear what this third group had to say. I mean, their commentary seemed similar to Robin's. But no. He didn't give a shit. By that time Robin was no longer interested in the post-screening briefings. Most of his time had been taken up dealing coke at Max's. He'd definitely moved on.

14.24

— Basically you just serviced the bookings you got that night at Max's?

— Yeah, though about a third of them ended up getting cancelled. There were quite a few occasions where I'd show up and knock on a door and nobody would answer.

— But you continued to keep busy with screenings.

— At that point, most of it was happening by word of mouth.

— A different clientele, too.

— Absolutely.

— You dropped the introduction by then.

— Like you said, it was a different clientele.

14.25

The final phase of screenings — the screenings where we made most of our dough — turned out to be stags and frats. In many ways these screenings were the most useful to me in that I learned a lot about the male species. Whereas those first audiences were, for the most, cerebral, these audiences were purely visceral. I guess you could say that these male clusters had a lot of bearing on why I chose to start reading up on human behaviour. Because after having seen the film a million times, I was definitely more interested in the audiences than I was in *The Family Dog*. So next to Plato and Nietzsche, I added Erving Goffman, Desmond Morris, and Lionel Tiger to my shelf.

So yeah, those final screenings were definitely the most debauched. Obviously, a lot of this had to do with alcohol. And I suppose you could say that very little of it had to do with *The Family Dog*. The film was just an excuse for people to go weird. But still, to see a mild-mannered guy transform into a naked wild man over the course of an evening was fascinating. That's what it was like at these kinds of affairs. And of course I took notes. There was this one guy in particular.

14.25a

The Case of Derrick Sweeney

> — the first person in the room as I arrive to set up
> — wears a slightly too-big business suit that might have belonged to his dad
> — is twenty-two years old

— a Catholic

— an American citizen

— holds a commerce degree from the U of Mass.

— holds a treasury position with the Phi Beta Kappa Fraternity Association (I think)

— his father, an accountant, was also Phi Beta Kappa

— has come to town to check on the "locals" (as he calls them)

— is engaged to a woman named Willow

— admits right away that he is "not known as a partier"

— admits "in fact, I'm really quite a relaxed kinda guy"

— has his first beer while I do a quick run-through

— watches the projector while I go to the washroom to write this up

— opens his second beer upon my return

— has removed his tie

— reiterates that he's a Catholic, then insists that once he's married he may continue to "fuck around"

— tells me he thinks my film is sick but it's just the kind of thing they need to boost recruitment

— gets the hiccups

— drinks a third beer upside down in an attempt to squelch those hiccups

— burps, then tells me "Canadian beer is so potent"

— tells me for the second time that I have a good vocabulary — "for a kid"

— goes to the washroom while I write this up

— returns with a "local," drinking a fourth beer

— tells the "local" that their business records are a mess

— accepts the local's apology, but not his excuse

— accepts a fifth beer from the "local"

— greets a group of five that have just entered carrying a keg of beer and a pump

— accepts the first draft of the keg even though it is entirely comprised of foam

— continues to greet "locals" though they've stopped acknowledging him

— goes to the washroom while I write this up

— returns with his sixth and seventh beers
— shouts words of encouragement to the thirty-odd members who have assembled for the screening, and is ignored
— attempts more words of encouragement and is helped to a seat by two "locals"
— staggers back to the projector, tells me he hasn't eaten a thing all day, asks if he can have the rest of my Cheezies
— takes the Cheezies and staggers up to the front of the room, shouting something about an announcement
— the lower half of his face is now Cheezie orange
— someone throws a plastic cup at him; it bounces off his forehead
— takes off his shirt, throws it at the cup-thrower
— Dottie Ragnarsson is projected onto his singlet
— the crowd laughs, and he thinks they're laughing with him
— he notices the image on his body, then takes off his singlet like a man on fire
— shouts of "Take it off — take it all off" begin
— begins a striptease, then falls over trying to get his pants off
— is carried away by two "locals"
— returns five minutes later with an erection and a paper bag over his head
— is led away screaming: "*Post hoc ergo propter hoc*"

15.1

I'd screened *The Family Dog* maybe fifty times before Nettie arrived home for Christmas. By then, everybody who'd heard about the film had seen it. And Robin's phone had definitely stopped ringing. Robin wanted to do a return engagement at Max's, but Max told him he was only interested in our next world premiere. So when he asked us if we'd done anything new — that is, anything with young boys — Robin lied and told him we had something in development.

— What did Nettie think of *The Family Dog?*

— She said it was pretty much what she'd expected.

— Did she like it?

— She said it was okay. She had some criticisms, though. But basically she said it was pretty good for what it was.

— And what was it then?

— Whatever you wanted it to be.

— Was it a product of what Angela Carter meant when she wrote that "a male-dominated society produces a pornography of universal female acquiescence?"

— No, I think it had more to do with something else she said: how pornography, if it's used properly — and by that I mean in the context of the larger world — how it can call into question all the inequalities inherent in the way that world is organized. Or something like that. I think.

— But wasn't your film a good example of "existential solitude" and "timeless, placeless fantasy"?

— That's what the speech was for. An attempt to provide a context.

— And what did Nettie think of your speech?

— She critiqued the shit out of it.

— Did that bother you? Her critique?

— Not at all. John and Penny had taught us that the critique was an important part of the process. Besides, I think Nettie was still trying to get even with me over my defence of *Joe and Barbie.*

— Seems like she was miles ahead of you.

— You're only saying that to bug me.

— Did you two talk about making films together?

— Oh yeah. We were always talking about films. We both knew that's what we'd probably end up doing with our lives. But to answer your question — yeah, we knew we'd make at least one film together.

15.2a

Nettie's Critique

Your speech is so stupid. You could have done so much more, so many more interesting things to set up your film. But, in fact, what you *really* did was just set it back. And do you know how I think you did this? You don't, do you? Well, I'll tell you: I think you did this by allowing the man to have power not only in the real world, the waking world, but in the dream world as well. You only *think* his power is reversed in the dream world because he's getting fucked by his wife, that she prefers getting fucked by their dog over him. But it doesn't read that way at all. Why? Because you are telling the audience that the man *chose* to dream about how his family would act out against him. I mean, how do we know he didn't *like* what was happening to him? Not that that's the point here: because the point here is that this man has complete control over all aspects of the film. I mean, if you wanted to make it really interesting, you could have, at the very least, suggested that the film was the story of a dog that committed unspeakable acts on his family, then curled up at night and dreamt about doing more unspeakable acts. You could have at least told the audience the film was made by your mother.

I'd overheard my mom talking to Mrs. Smart on the phone. Nettie would be arriving the following day, late morning. I could hardly sleep that night. I was that excited.

After breakfast I went up to my old room and sat down where my desk used to be, where my mother's sewing table now stood. It was from there that I waited for the Smarts' car to return from the airport, west down Thirty-third hill. My mom's boyfriend, Carl, had spent the night again and was in the bathroom, showering. He'd been hanging around a lot lately, and I'd grown sick and tired of all his dumb talk about hockey and how much better things were in Alberta. I tried to block out his singing — "Volare!" — because it was totally fucking up my mood.

Carl lumbered in, said hey. I turned around, gave him a polite hi back, hoping he'd fuck off so I wouldn't miss the Lincoln. "I didn't know you sewed," he said, adjusting his towel, showing off what appeared to be a fairly extensive rig. "Maybe I should sew that up for you," I said, immediately regretting it. "What the hell do you mean by that?" he said, all defensive, pissed that I challenged his challenge. I was into it now; there was no turning back. "Mom says you've got a big dick, but you're no good with it," I said, returning to the window, hoping he'd leave, knowing he wouldn't. Carl came up behind me, slamming a hand down on my shoulder. A total Longely. "Look, you little faggot. I'm gonna be around here a lot longer than you are. So the sooner you get used to it, the better. Got that?" Whatever. Then he pushed off and made his way towards the door. But he wasn't finished. "I mean, I'm the one who's gonna be looking after your mom from now on — not you," he said, as if to convince himself. Still, I spun around. I was all set to lay into him, tell him something truly nasty, but thought otherwise. He had his towel clutched so tightly it ate into his waist. And that was enough for me.

The moment I'd been waiting for. Judge Smart's Lincoln. I ran downstairs, got on my bike, then quickly made my way around the block to where I would just happen to be passing just as Nettie was getting out of the car. And my timing was perfect. "Hey, Nettie," I called out. Nettie waved. Then she gave me a funny look. Not that it put me off. I wanted to present myself like the nut she'd remembered, someone who thought nothing of riding their bike through a foot of snow.

Of course Nettie had to spend *some* time with her family. So after dinner I phoned her and she accepted my offer of coffee. I picked her up in the Falcon and the two of us split for Kits.

It didn't take long to see that she'd changed. All that time in England, I suppose. "You have an accent now," I said. "Just like your dad's." Nettie scrunched up her face, gave me a hearty scoff. She'd gotten good at that. Nobody scoffs like the Brits. "I am haw-dly like my faw-thuh," she said, lighting a cigarette. I was beginning to wonder if we had anything left in common. Everything I said seemed to exhaust her. "I loved your last letter," I said, hoping to hear more about her travels. "Hmph," she replied.

We went to this little espresso bar at Fourth and Alma. I thought she'd be impressed with my selection. "This place is so faux," she said, feigning a headache. We took a seat by the window. The waitress came and went. A latte for me, a tea for Nettie. "So what's England like?" I asked, all earnest. Another "hmph." Nettie lit a cigarette, and I noticed how yellow her fingers were. "How many cigarettes do you smoke a day?" I asked her. Yet another "hmph!" This was going nowhere.

It was an hour before Nettie warmed up. I'd gathered by then that her behaviour was really just a way of responding to my equally inane questions. I guess it was the attitude talking. But once we got onto the topic of *The Family Dog*, the accent fell away and Nettie was back to her old self. The only visible difference now was her appearance: her hair short and spiky, a black leather bomber hanging off her skinny frame, a button on the lapel that said ROCK THE BOTHA. But other than that, it was just like old times.

Nettie wanted the details and I told her everything. On the way home we made a date for the following day. She wanted to meet "this Robin."

15.3a

Nettie's Last Letter

> December 10, 1978
> Manchester, England

> Hey!
>   Sorry it's been so long. (Been busy, busy, busy!) Thought I'd make up for it by sending you something more substantial.

Just finished my last paper — "The End of Art As We Know It: The Viennese Actionists and the Music of the Sex Pistols." Now I have to run off and prepare for the performance I'll be doing tomorrow on the set of "Coronation Street." Do you know the program? It's this corny British soap opera that airs three times a week, and everybody in Britain watches it. Anyway, a bunch of us are going to sneak in, and for my performance I'm going to moon the Rover's Return Pub. One of the girls I go to school with knows an assistant editor at Granada TV, this guy who's about to get sacked because he's a punk, and he's gonna videotape it and sneak it into next Monday's episode. Pretty good, eh? My first performance, and everybody in Britain's gonna see it!

What else? Things are going well at school, although the program is very demanding. Remember how hard Penny used to make us work? Well, this is twice as hard as that. And as much as I like being here, as much as our instructors let us do what we want, we're still responsible for shit-loads of work. I'm sure had Penny not been our teacher I never would have lasted this long. Because I had no idea what to expect. But I've learned so much! And we've had all these great artists and writers and musicians drop by. Just last week Martin Amis came through to read from *The Rachel Papers*, and then something from his new book, *Success*, which I'm reading right now. And then the week before Billy Idol from Generation X stopped in to give a talk on attitude. (Just kidding!) Oh yeah, and how's this for a coincidence: the artist Stuart Brisley was here to lecture on Joseph Beuys, Hermann Nitsch and — get this! — that woman you mentioned on the phone that day, Carolee Schneemann. Talk about a small world!

I must say, it's way more fun being over here without my parents, without having to visit relatives. On our last field trip to London, our chaperones just sat in the pub all day and let us do our own thing. So it was great getting out and going to places I'd only seen with my folks before, seeing them in a totally differently light this time. Like Piccadilly Circus. I had no idea there were so many porno shops around. One of the guys in our class bought a couple of Dutch sex mags, and on the bus back he passed them around. Nothing shocking, mind you, but one of our teachers caught us, and so the next day we spent the whole morning sitting in a circle talking about sex, the body, representation. It was really interesting. I learned so much. And remember that lecture Angela Carter gave at the Whitworth? The one I told you about? Well, all that stuff totally came in handy.

The clock on the wall says I'm late. But there's so much more I have to tell you. I guess I'll have to leave it for now, save something for my visit next week. As much as I'm having fun here, I really do miss things in Vancouver. Terribly so. I just wanted to tell you that. Do you think you miss me? Tell me you do. Even if you don't, say that you do. Please. Just for me.

Your friend,
Nettie

15.4

— What happened after you left the Boca Bar?

— Nothing. I took her home. She was tired — jet-lagged.

— You parked the car on Valley Drive. We have you clocked at fifty-seven minutes.

— Yeah? Were you watching, too?

— Can you tell us what you did?

— We necked. Felt each other up.

— Anything unusual happen?

— I suppose.

— What, then?

— She cried.

— Why?

— I don't know.

— Did you say something to her?

— No.

— What happened then?

— I played with her pussy, the way she liked it. Then she came. Then she told me how much she missed me. And that's when she started to cry.

— And what did you do?

— Nothing. I just held her. She was so skinny.

15.5

It took a while for Nettie and Robin to click. I'm sure had they met earlier — before Nettie went to England — the two would have gotten on just fine. But not now. Both, it seemed, had something to prove. Nettie had reactivated her English accent. And Robin — who had been doing a lot of coke lately — was behaving the perfect jerk, both fawning and paranoid at exactly the same time. A very strange mix. But one that favoured Nettie. She'd become an excellent button-pusher.

Things got heated after the screening. Much of what Nettie had to say was similar to Robin's earlier analysis, albeit delivered in a very off-hand and strategically detached manner. And I guess Robin was intimidated by the way Nettie was expressing herself. Once again, it wasn't so much what Nettie was saying but how she was saying it. And I think that's what Robin was reacting to, because he kept challenging Nettie on the very stuff he'd been saying during the first screening. "Wot do you mean the out-of-focus sequence suggests a fantastic transition," he said, mocking Nettie's accent. Nettie winced and hmphed. "You aw puh-thetic, Raw-bun," she kept saying. Which wound Robin up even more.

Eventually things settled down. I'd learned something from the collector about mediation, so I employed those skills. I started introducing questions, found some common ground. An appeal to the intellect, really. And I was pleased with the results. In fact, I was amazed at how much insight I had into these two. I knew them. They were my friends. Pretty soon the three of us were talking about making movies, which had secretly been my hope all along.

15.6

— Your third film.

— That's right. *Rich Kid Gang Bang*.

— Which turned out to be quite a bit different from your original synopsis.

— That was Robin's idea. He didn't think shooting a porno in the North Shore mountains was very practical. Besides, the original synopsis called for about fifteen people.

— What did Nettie think of the revised version?

— She loved it, thought it was great.

— Because she rewrote it?

— Of course.

15.6a

Treatment for *Rich Kid Gang Bang*

EXT. CINDY CARRUTHERS' HOUSE. NIGHT

Muffled sounds. Music playing.

INT. AN L-SHAPED RECROOM

The lighting is low. A boy and a girl (16) are making out on the couch. Both are well-heeled. The boy is wearing a lettered school sweater. Around the corner from them is a wet bar.

The boy's hands are moving fast and furious. On two occasions, the girl pushes him away, tells him to slow down, stop groping. They resume. There's a knock at the door. The boy gets up, answers.

The door opens. We see a woman (30s) dressed in a maid's uniform. Beside her, a man (30s). He is dressed in coveralls, carrying a toolbox. The maid tells the boy that the plumber's here to fix the wet-bar sink. The boy invites them in.

MEDIUM CLOSE ON PLUMBER

He is twisting a wrench around a drainpipe. As he wraps his beefy hand around the drainpipe we return to the maid, who is standing over him, holding a flashlight. She cocks an eyebrow. The man removes the drainpipe, passes it towards the camera. "Hold that, would you?" he says.

CLOSE ON WOMAN'S HAND

It is wrapped around the drainpipe.

COUCH

The boy and girl are making out.

CLOSE ON GIRL'S FACE

Suddenly the girl lets go with a "hey," pushing the boy away.

CUT TO

Indistinguishable skin footage from *The Family Dog*.

226

The boy looks surprised as the girl starts into him. She tells him he's totally insensitive, that he's too rough, that maybe he should go somewhere and "get some fuckin' lessons."

WET BAR

The plumber, still under the sink, and the maid, who is now crouched beside him, listen to the action off-screen. The girl continues to berate the boy. Then the plumber turns to the maid, tells her he's done, that he's just gonna use the washroom before he splits. The woman nods absently, continues to listen.

COUCH

The girl, still pissed off, gets up and tells the boy she's going to the washroom. The boy, convinced he hasn't done anything wrong, remains seated, shaking his head.

BATHROOM

The man is pissing in the toilet when the door bursts open. He looks up. The girl is startled for a second, then her eyes drop, widen. "Boyfriend sounds a bit inexperienced," the man says. The girl, still staring, replies, "Uh, yeah." The man then asks the girl if she knows what experience looks like. The girl nods.

COUCH

The maid is sitting beside the boy. "You have to be more sensitive to people's needs," she says. The boy nods. "Try to imagine yourself in your girlfriend's shoes," she adds.

BATHROOM
CLOSE ON GIRL'S FACE

Her head is tilted back, her eyes are closed, she seems happy.

ZOOM OUT

227

The girl is sitting on the counter, her legs spread. The man is between her legs. He is licking her pussy.

COUCH
CLOSE ON WOMAN'S FACE

She is looking down at something. "A little more gently," she says.

ZOOM OUT

The boy is between the woman's legs. The woman continues to call out instructions.

BATHROOM
CLOSE ON MAN'S FACE

His eyes are closed.

ZOOM OUT

The girl is sucking on the man's cock.

COUCH
CLOSE ON BOY'S FACE

He is lying on the couch, breathing heavy.

ZOOM OUT

The woman is on top of the boy, fucking him.

PANNING LEFT

In front of the couch is the man and the girl. She is lying on one side, facing the camera, while the plumber fucks her from behind.

Sex play continues. Last scene features the girl going down on the woman and the boy going down on the man.

We didn't have much time. Christmas was two days away. And Nettie was leaving a week later. So we made a plan. Robin told us he'd get some people together for a casting session — since people, he kept boasting, were his expertise. Then on Boxing Day Nettie and I would come down and together we'd pick out the talent. We hoped to shoot the whole thing on New Year's Eve, since our *Family Dog* screening that night had been cancelled.

So: we pull up to Robin's around two in the afternoon. A beautiful sunny day. No problem parking. Nettie's carrying with her a tinfoil package — turkey and stuffing and cranberry sauce — which she keeps referring to as a "peace offering," as if she's just discovered the term. I'm a little nervous as we climb the stairs, half expecting to find a casting queue outside the apartment, then half relieved to find the hall empty. As we approach I glance over to Nettie and she's beaming in anticipation. I'm encouraged by this. I remind myself to think positively, but I've got a bad feeling in my stomach and I know something's about to fuck up. And sure enough it does.

Robin looks awful, like he hasn't slept since we last left him. He sits us down on the couch, then makes a lame effort to clear the coffee table. He's wearing a ratty old dressing gown, and every time he leans over it opens so you can see right in. The room reeks of rot and body odour, and there's take-out bags everywhere. I look at Nettie, try to gauge her mood. Her face is hard, her knuckles white as she clutches the tinfoil package to her lap. There will be no peace, I think. And from the looks of things, there'll be no casting session either. Besides Robin, there's nobody in the apartment but us.

"Where is everybody?" I ask. Robin mumbles something unintelligible, then picks up the 1979 *Garçons de Maroc* calendar, still in its shrink-wrap. He uses the calendar to sweep the ash-and-crumb combo off the table. I can feel Nettie's heat. She's gonna blow any minute. I wish Robin would say something. Then the toilet flushes. "Anyone for coffee?" Robin says, disappearing into the kitchen. I had the feeling that whoever walked out of the bathroom was going to be playing our maid.

Her name was Tanya. Tanya Suzanne. I'd seen her around Robin's a couple of times, but was never formally introduced. Robin told me she used to hook the corner of Davie and Comox in the early 1970s, then got beat up so bad she ended up in St. Paul's for a year and hasn't been the same since. According to Robin, Tanya now spends most of her time dealing junk from the washroom of the Mr. Steak across the street, which was basically the domain of Marty Flynn. Everything Robin told me about those two added up to bad news. Rumour had it they killed people.

Tanya looked as bad as Robin. She came out of the bathroom wearing a Ramones T-shirt, her black hair long and stringy just like the band's. Definitely the last person I had in mind to play our maid. "D'ya mind?" she said, pointing at something on the coffee table. I wasn't sure what she was referring to but said yeah anyway. Tanya reached over and withdrew a couple of Nettie's cigarettes, lit one, then put the other behind her ear. She sat down on the floor and crossed her bruised legs. From her ankles you could tell she was a hype.

Robin came back with a tray. A pot of coffee, cups, and a plate of Ding-Dongs still in the foil. His belt had come undone and he was oblivious to the fact that his crotch was on display. Pathetic that he took no notice. I mean, this would have been funny if it wasn't about business. "So Tanya's our maid," said Robin, squatting, handing me a cup. "I thought I'd play the plumber," he added, passing Tanya the Ding-Dongs. "And you, Nettie — I thought you'd play the girlfriend role." Robin set down Nettie's coffee. I looked over at Tanya. She was checking Nettie out. "Yeah, I could do a scene with you," she said, as if Nettie barely passed.

Well, I thought that was it right there. I thought it was all over. Nettie was gonna take the peace offering, throw it in Robin's face, and storm out. But no. Nettie smiles, sips the coffee, then presents the leftovers. "This is for you, Robin — Merry Christmas," she says. Robin takes the package, opens it up, and dips his finger in the cranberry sauce, licking it off. Then, just like he almost did with me that time with Kai's hash oil, he starts to cry.

— That's very touching.

— Yes, it was. Nettie heated up the turkey and stuffing, then sat Robin and Tanya down in the kitchen and sang them Christmas carols. It was bizarre.

— Nettie has a very beautiful voice.

— Like an angel. And that was the first time I'd ever heard her sing.

— But what a strategist!

— Yeah, pretty clever on her part, eh? Things were looking bleak there for a minute. We definitely didn't intend on having Robin and Tanya star in our film. And we knew we didn't want to cast ourselves in the role of young lovers, either. So what does Nettie do? She smothers them with love. After that, they would have agreed to anything. I never would have thought of that.

— Sometimes the best defence is a good offence.

— You sound like Bobby Galt.

— Nettie had a name for this strategy of hers, didn't she?

— Yeah. I had the Bullshit Detector, she had the Love Light.

15.10

We rescheduled casting for the following day. The plan was to meet at Robin's, then Tanya would take us over to Mr. Steak where she'd point to people and we'd say yes or no. If we saw something we liked, Tanya would approach them and ask them if they were interested in making a couple of hundred bucks for being in a short. It was that simple.

Things were going smoothly. I liked the look of these people. They were all so real. A refreshing change from the Shaughnessy set. At one point Nettie leaned over and told me how exciting this was, how we should make a documentary about this one day. I agreed. After *Rich Kid Gang Bang*, we would make a documentary on casting.

Once we had a group together, we all went back to Robin's. Thank God for Tanya. She was a natural.

15.11

INT. A VERY CLEAN CHARACTER'S APARTMENT. DAY

(Scoring note: Side Two of *Led Zeppelin IV*)

Seated on a sofa are four women. They range in age (from 18 to 20). They are all dressed in faded jeans. Two are wearing jean jackets, two are jacketless. The two without jackets look the youngest. They are wearing T-shirts. One of the T-shirts has a cat on it. It reads: HANG IN THERE, BABY. The other T-shirt features a rose. Above the rose, written in silver commercial script: A TOUCH OF CLASS.

On either side of the women, sitting on the arms of the sofa, are two men (mid-20s). Both are wearing faded jeans. One has a lumberjack shirt on, the other a grey kangaroo top.

Seated opposite, in chairs, are me, Nettie, Robin, and Tanya. Nettie is holding a clipboard. She leans forward.

> NETTIE
> Can I have your names, please?
>
> (pointing to the far left)
> Starting with you.

> MAN #1
> Why?

> NETTIE
> So I'll know what to call you.

> MAN #1
> You don't have to call me anything. I just thought we were making a porno.

Everyone laughs.

                              NETTIE
              Okay, I'll just call you Lance.

                         A TOUCH OF CLASS
              That would be appropriate.

More laughter.

                              NETTIE
                            (grinning)
              You well hung or something?

MAN #1 smiles.

Laughter.

                              NETTIE
                     (to A TOUCH OF CLASS)
              What's your name?

                         A TOUCH OF CLASS
              Um ... Tiffany!

Laughter.

Younger woman looks at the woman seated next to her.

The rest sound off.

                         JEAN JACKET #1
              Cherry.

                         JEAN JACKET #2
              Marushka.

Laughter.

Candace.

> MAN #2

Drainpipe.

Loud laughter.

> NETTIE

You're familiar with the treatment then?

Laughter.

Drainpipe grins.

Light laughter.

A beat.

> NETTIE

So all you guys are aware of what we're going to be doing.

The sofa responds with yeses and yeps.

Nettie gets up and hands out a single sheet of paper to each member of the sofa. They take the sheet and begin reading.

> NETTIE

So what you're being given is a film treatment, everything that's going to happen in our film. The film is going to be about twenty-two minutes long. And we intend to shoot it over one day on New Year's Eve. There are parts for two women and two men. You will each be paid two hundred dollars for your work ...

> CHERRY
> (looking up from the treatment)

'Kay — I don't think I want to do a scene with another chick.

CLOSE ON MARUSHKA

She is looking towards Cherry.

> CHERRY
> (VO)
> I just don't do that.

CLOSE ON MARUSHKA

She nods.

> MARUSHKA
> Yeah, me too. I don't want to do a scene with another chick if there's a guy in it.

CUT TO

Tanya at the door. She thanks Cherry and Marushka as they exit.

Tiffany, Candace, Lance, and Drainpipe are sitting on the couch, staring straight ahead. They are expressionless.

REVERSE

Me, Nettie, Robin, and Tanya.

REVERSE

Tiffany, Candace, Lance, and Drainpipe are now standing before the sofa, naked.

JUMP CUT

Lance stands before the two woman, sporting an erection.

JUMP CUT

Tiffany is in the middle, waving a feather duster.

JUMP CUT

Now Candace is in the middle, sticking out her tongue.

JUMP CUT

Drainpipe does a handstand, falls out of frame.

REVERSE

Nettie is scribbling furiously on the clipboard.

REVERSE

Tiffany, Candace, Lance and Drainpipe are seated in their original positions, dressed.

                         NETTIE
                      (looking up)
        Okay, so now we have our cast.

A loud knock.

The sound of someone getting up from a chair, making their way towards the door. The door opens.

                          TANYA
                          (VO)
        About time you got here!

15.12

— Flynn!

— The Mighty Flynn.

He was supposed to be the biggest goof on Davie Street, but I'd never met a cooler guy than Flynn. When he walked into Robin's that day, all I saw was what I wanted to be. I couldn't believe it. He was so sexy. Amazing. Like a full-grown Randy Cobb. And tall! He was so tall. Had the look down, too. Just like Nettie. Same spiky hair, same black leather bomber. And when he slumped down next to her — told her to carry on, forget he was even there — I could've cracked up. How could she ignore a guy like that? Especially when the two of them looked so good together, like they'd been running together since birth. I was so jealous. But I was also madly in love. With both of them. Together. All this before we even knew who he was.

Robin started to mumble something, an introduction. But Flynn jumped in, took over. He was so smooth, this guy. Yet so full of quirk! "Now if my name's Flynn ..." he began, slowly, like an amnesiac just coming to terms with his memory, "then you must be Nettie!" Nettie blushed. Never seen her do that before. Then Flynn turned to me, gave me the same treatment. Even though my pea-coat didn't quite match up like his and Nettie's jackets, Flynn made me feel just as important, just as cool, as if there were more to life than stuff that matched. Then he spun back to Nettie. "Yeah! And if my name is Flynn ..." he said, taking the clipboard out of her hands, turning to the sofa, "then you four must be Man #1, Man #2, A Touch of Class, and Hang In There, Baby." The sofa laughed. "Hello, Flynn," they said in unison. And Flynn's response? Out of nowhere. Like a shy old lady, he creaked, "Why — hello children."

If I was to hazard a guess at Flynn's age, I would say he was probably late-twenties. But like so many things about Flynn, it was impossible to say. You just didn't know what was going on with this guy. And any time you thought you knew, he would totally prove you wrong, as if he saw it all coming, as if he were setting you up just for fun, just for something to do. I mean — I could give you examples. But there were just too many. Suffice it to say, you could never underestimate this Flynn. Everywhere he went he demanded respect. And he got it. Everything that happened on Davie Street he had a piece of. Drugs, hooking, loans, protection — you name it. Flynn was huge.

16.2

— Marty Flynn was branching out.

— That's right. After our casting session, he wanted to have a meeting.

16.3

Flynn gave Tanya a hundred-dollar bill, told her to "take the children for dinner." He did the same with Robin, told him to pick up some Chinese food and "something bubbly." Once they left, Flynn got super-serious. He told me and Nettie to sit down on the sofa, get comfortable. Said he wanted to have a little chat. Said he wanted us to know where he was coming from. Then he pulled back the coffee table, went into the kitchen and came back with a stool. He plunked it down in front of us, sat, crossed a leg, and leaned into this speech:

"Now my name is Marty Flynn. That is my real name. Martin Patrick McDougall Flynn. A lot of people around here don't use their real names because they think they've got something to hide or they're running from something or they want to start fresh or whatever. That's up to them. I use my real name 'cause I'm not like the others. Y'know what I'm saying? I have nothing to hide, I'm staying put, and I see no need to start anything fresh. I want you to know that. I want you to know that I use my real name because I'm proud of what I do. And the best expression of pride that I can think of is honesty, right? Are you with me so far? Honesty. Remember that. Do you have any questions? Good.

"So what is it that I do? Well, let me tell you something right off the bat: Whatever you've heard about me you can cut in half. Got that? Cut it right in half. For example: there's a rumour going around that I'm a pimp, that I live off the avails of prostitution. So let's cut that in half, shall we? True, there's a rumour going around — false that I'm a pimp. I am not a pimp. Let me repeat that: I am not a pimp. In fact, what I do is offer protection to a group of independently minded people — young women, mostly — who refuse to give over the bulk of their income to some dumb-ass goof who's gonna screw them out of what little they have left by hooking them on booze and drugs. Got that? So what I provide, then, is protection. I keep the pimps off their backs. And the guidance I give, I give for free.

"Now what about this rumour regarding my involvement with drugs? I've heard the talk. I've heard people say that Marty Flynn's the guy who supplies all the pimps with coke. Cut that in half. Do I sell drugs? Yes, I do. But I do not sell drugs to pimps. I hate pimps. They are the scourge of the earth. So who do I sell drugs to? I sell drugs to these rich kids who come down here from Shaughnessy and West Vancouver. I sell them drugs because I enjoy the fact that these rich kids are getting all fucked up. And you wanna know something else? I've got a theory about this. I've got it in my head that if I get these rich kids all fucked up on drugs, then I'm doing humanity a service. D'ya know what I'm saying? Do you ever think about what a better world this might be if a whole generation of rich people got so fucked up on drugs they stopped spending all their time being greedy? And do you ever wonder how decent the world might be without all those rich people fucking things up? I mean, maybe we could have a little equality for a change? Whaddaya think of that? Doesn't that sound good? Sounds pretty good to me. The rich are pimps as far as I'm concerned. And you already know my position on pimps.

"And what about this rumour about me being a loan shark? Some cunt who charges unbelievably high interest rates, then beats people up if they can't make their payments? Once again: Cut that in half. Yes, I lend money. In fact, I lend out a lot of money — most of it with the knowledge that I'll never see it again. And if that doesn't sound like I'm giving it away, then let me just say that I do that, too. Last year I gave away over ten thousand dollars to a whole pile of relief agencies who look after all the runaways pouring into this city every day, kids fleeing abusive situations, kids who would rather eat out of a garbage can than have to go home from school and get knocked around by their parents. And as for all this talk about high interest rates and beating people up? Sure, I charge a little more money than the banks. But do I beat people up? No. The only physical contact I've ever had with the people I lend money to is a handshake. Got that? I haven't touched a soul. And unlike those bankers up in Kerrisdale and West Van, I actually give a shit about the people I lend money to. And I mean that from the bottom of my heart.

"Finally — and this is a rumour I find truly despicable — there's been some talk recently that I kill people. People who've betrayed me. Please — and for God's sake! — *cut that in half*. Yes, the true part is that people have betrayed me; the false part is that I am not a murderer. D'ya follow me? I have never killed anyone in my life. And I'm not about to. Okay? I mean, I know I'm not the nicest guy in the world, but I do pride myself on certain principles. Call them Christian principles if you want — I don't give a fuck. Murder is beyond my comprehension, the ultimate sin. I value human life more than anything else in the world. Besides, everyone who's betrayed me atones one way or the other. I mean, eventually they have to answer to something higher, right? Am I making myself clear? Are you with me? Because it's really important that you are. I mean, you can call me a bullshitter about everything else if you have to; but you've got to believe me when I tell you that I have never in my life murdered anyone. Those rumours were started by the pimps, all the assholes who want me off the street so they can screw more profits out of the girls. So I ask you — no, I beg of you — please consider the source. Please look at who stands to gain by discrediting my good name. Because I'm a real soft touch when it comes right down to it. I really am. Trust me. Do you trust me? You do? Then that's good. So I've set the record straight? And you believe me? You do! Then that's good. So let's get down to business. I've got a proposition for you two."

16.4

— We can't believe you fell for that?

— We were young.

— But you seemed like you should've known better.

— There were parts of Flynn that added up to things we found intriguing.

— Like what, for instance?

— His conviction.

— And what about his proposition?

— He wanted to start a film collective, make and distribute pornos. Me, Nettie, Robin, and him.

— Was it a sound proposal?

— He didn't have anything written down. Just some ideas. But he knew a lot of people. And he had some really good insight into the way films travel.

— So did you commit?

— I was ready to. I mean, I was sick and tired of hauling that projector around. But I definitely wanted to keep making films. Nettie, too.

— So what happened?

16.5

Nettie said she wanted to see something written down first, and I backed her up. Flynn grinned. "Good then," he said, hopping off the stool, returning it to the kitchen. Nettie and I exchanged side-longs. They were identical. So if you were to take our sidelongs and cut them in half: the first part meant that Flynn was okay; the second part meant we'd discuss it later. But taken together they were pretty positive. Flynn was smart and dangerous and that's exactly what we were into at the time. We were that taken.

Flynn came back with a carrot and a kabob skewer. "I'm gonna show you guys how to make an edible pipe." Nettie's eyes lit up. "Okay!" In no time Flynn had converted the vegetable to a chillum. He pulled a Thai stick from his jacket pocket, broke off the tip, then loaded the bowl. He passed Nettie a lighter. Flynn held the pipe in a space between his middle fingers, then cupped his hands together and nodded. Nettie lit the carrot and Flynn inhaled from the space between his thumbs. He motioned for Nettie to suck. Which she did, awkwardly, eventually finding position in Flynn's arms. Nettie held her toke, then turned to Flynn. I watched as their eyes locked. Nettie exhaled. Flynn passed me the pipe. I worked it into my hands, no problem. But by the time I was ready to toke, the dope had gone out. I asked for a light. I had to ask twice.

It was amazing how fast those two got rapt. So, to be on the safe side, I applied the Bullshit Detector. Are your intentions honourable, Mr. Flynn? Do you like my friend Nettie? Hmm ... Hard to say. It was still early. I thought, Mr. Flynn, is it possible to penetrate your cool demeanour? Then he looked at me and winked. It was as if he'd heard me. And I liked that. I liked it that we were on the same wave-length. Then I told him I liked what he had to say about the rich, how intoxification seemed like a good strategy. Flynn smiled, thanked me. But what I really wanted to tell him was how much I liked the way he kept saying "Cut that in half," adding a little karate chop to his palm for emphasis. It was such a cool way of putting things. Flynn was full of shit like that. Little sayings. So I made a mental note. I would use the karate chop the next time I had to work something to my advantage.

Nettie wanted to hold the pipe herself. So she did. She got a good toke, too. Then she passed it back to me and I toked. I passed it back to Flynn and he frowned, gave me a don't-bug-me grunt, waved it away. I passed it to Nettie and she did the same. Again, their eyes locked. I felt a million miles away, like I'd have to shout to be heard. And there was so much more I needed to know. I wanted to ask Flynn if he considered us to be like those other rich fucks he sold drugs to. And if not, then why? I needed to know why. But by then he and Nettie had passed into their own little world. So I set the pipe down and went to the can, where I pissed just for something to do.

But I was really there to listen. I found the prospect of Nettie and Flynn together exciting. I shook the piss from my cock, felt it fatten, become something else, something other than just for pissing. Fuck, was I stoned. I'd never smoked Thai weed before. And I was getting a bit paranoid, too. So I turned on the faucet. I put my ear to the door. Nothing. Were they necking already? And if they were, how could I come out without interrupting, create a situation. Everything was happening so fast. Everything was changing. I bent down, peeked through the keyhole. All I could see were their midriffs. Flynn had his hands on Nettie's ass, while Nettie's were presumably around his neck. I continued to play with my cock. I reached down and pulled my balls out, holding my belt buckle still so it wouldn't rattle. I would come on the count of ten. I'd gotten to four when the front door opened. It was Robin. "About time you got here," Flynn said, as if it were his apartment.

16.6

— And it didn't bother you that Flynn was seducing your girlfriend?

— Jesus Christ! Haven't you been listening to anything I've said? Do

I have to go over all this again? Nettie was never my girlfriend, I was not into commitment; and I was intrigued by the prospect of those two together.

— Yes, but didn't you feel a bit hurt?

— The only thing that bothered me was that Flynn gave Nettie a bit more attention than me. But that's only natural, right? They looked so good together. They seemed meant for each other. Can you blame them for wanting to explore that?

16.7

Champagne and Chinese food. And lots of tokes. The four of us had a blast. Got blasted. By the end of the night the carrot was inedible. A limp, wet, leathery thing. Every now and then Robin would hold it up, wave it around, do something goofy like pretend it was a puppet, give it a voice. "Hi. My name's Mr. Carrot. I smoked so much pot when I was a seedling that it turned me into a vegetable." We laughed and laughed and laughed. Then Flynn announced that he had a meeting to go to. And Robin had to split for Max's. So Nettie and I caught the bus back to Shaughnessy. We were so fucking loaded. But it was still early. Barely ten.

Nettie wanted to get out at King Ed and walk along the tracks. Good idea, I thought. All that fresh air. I'd never seen her so giddy. But it had nothing to do with the booze and drugs. No. Nettie was in love. With Flynn. So I asked her about it. I asked her what she thought. This is what she told me:

> "I mean, at first I thought he was just a fake, right? I mean, I just hate that cool shit — hate it. But the thing is: this guy's for real. He's really like that. Y'know what I'm saying? A totally right-on guy. Super-smart, too. D'ya know he went to university? Did a master's degree in Arabic poetry? I just think that is *so cool*. Y'know what I'm saying? That somebody can be, like, a punk — and not be a complete idiot. England is just full of guys who look like that — guys that have the look down but have nothing upstairs. But Flynn's not like that at all. He's the real thing."

On the topic of Honesty:

> "I believe him. I don't believe everything he says, but I do believe that deep down he's a good person. I think it's important to remember that people who live that close to the street have a different way of doing things. And I think that things like truth and honesty, even thought they're different from what we mean when we say truth and honesty, are still, you know, held in high regard. I mean, they just take on a different shape. Maybe they're not as clearly defined as we're used to. I don't know. I just believe him."

On the topic of Production and Distribution:

> "I think if he gave us a proper proposal, and if it looked good, then we should definitely consider working with him. He seems to know a lot of people. And neither one of us knows the first thing about distribution. Besides, if he's gonna pay for everything, how could we go wrong? We get to play and he takes care of the rest, right? But then again, I'd like to learn a bit more about the business side of things, wouldn't you? I mean, this could be a really good opportunity."

We were parallel to the park when Nettie, still on the topic of Flynn, veered off towards the fence. I followed. We climbed over the chain-link and cut through the bushes, eventually coming upon a small clearing surrounded by elms. The air was cool, and we stopped to watch our breath. I could see my house at the south end. The front porch light was on, but everything else was out — including the Falcon. Mom's probably at Carl's, I thought. There'll be a note on the kitchen table. Something like: I'm spending the night at Carl's, Love, Mom.

Nettie turned to me: "You wanna go to your place? Listen to records?" I told her yeah. I was dying to hear more about her thoughts on Flynn.

One of the records Nettie brought back from England was the Clash EP. She cued it up, then jumped on the bed, pulling off her sweater as she sang along in her new British accent. I thought, If she starts unbuttoning, then I'll do the same. Nettie paused for a second, her eyes glazing over the white nothing of my comforter. Nettie's thinking face. Then she scratched her head, came to. "Hey," she said, "do you still have that K-Y?" I told her yeah, then began to unbutton.

I kicked off my clothes and stumbled over to the guitar case, where I'd kept the tube. I thought about how sex with Nettie would be different this time. Because I'm sure when she gapped out like that her mind was filling with Flynn.

As I bent over I caught a glimpse of her body. She was on her side, her back to me, naked. I could tell from her shoulder that she was playing with herself. Then she rolled over. Her tits swelled. Beautiful, I thought. Beautiful because tits look best when they're in action. Round white breasts, making and reshaping, playing with the light, the shadows. Nettie's breasts had gotten bigger since the last time I'd seen them. Maybe because the rest of her had gotten so skinny. Still, I imagined they wouldn't be getting that much bigger. Nettie was an adult now. So of course she'd stopped growing.

I approached her slowly. Nettie's eyes were closed. Imagining Flynn, no doubt. I watched as Flynn lay down beside her, resting his weight on an elbow, his back rippling, the flex of his ass as he shifted into position. It would be their first time together, so there'd be lots of soft talk, kissing. Flynn would kiss his way down her neck, stopping on her tits while she played with his hair. Then he'd kiss a little further, drag his tongue over her tummy, kiss a circle around her pussy, before kissing his way back up, over her clitoris, to her mouth, his cock hard and pressing. More soft talk and kissing. Then Nettie would kiss her way down Flynn, licking his nipples, reaching around to play with his ass, between his legs. She would kiss her way past his belly button, along the fringes of his pubic hair, behind his testicles. Then she'd take his scrotum in her teeth and nibble, tease him. Flynn would say something, tell her to put her mouth around him, blow, play with his balls, something. And Nettie would consider that, put the information into some kind of order, make a sex plan. Then she would act. She would take his cock and kiss it, lick it, put it in her mouth, get her lips tight around it, pull it out, squint, make an assessment, gauge its duration, determine its efficacy. And when Flynn had had enough, he would put his hands under her arms and pull her up, whisper to her, kiss her on the mouth. But he would do something strange, something she wasn't used to. A new position. He would turn her over, fuck her from the side. And Nettie would think: How odd. She would think: Is there something wrong with my face? But she would like the way his cock fit in this position. She would like the slap of his balls against her buttocks, the way his thumb flicked at her nipples, the way he fluffed her clit gently, quickly, just enough for her to come.

I was so turned on. I was so turned on because now I was Flynn. Now I was Flynn and I'd get to fuck Nettie.

So: we began with kisses. Spent a long time kissing. And this was weird. Weird because we'd never done much kissing before. Usually we'd just get to it. Usually we'd get to what we wanted. Or: if we didn't want the other to know how desperate we were for what it was that we wanted, then we'd go to the edge of what we wanted and work our way in. But this time was different. It was different because I was Flynn and that's who Nettie was kissing. It took some getting used to. "What do you think Flynn's cock looks like?" she said, pushing me onto my back, kissing my neck. "Judging from his hands I would guess he has a big one," I said, squeezing a breast, pinching off at the nipple. Nettie shivered. She cleared her throat. She said, "Funny, I thought from his nose it would be long and thin." I thought for a second. "Then maybe it's both," I told her, rolling her over.

We're sixty-nining now. I'd barely touched her, and her pussy was like melted butter. "Don't touch my clit," she said. "I don't want to come yet." So I didn't. I put in a finger, hooked it, felt for the bump and traced a slow circle around it. With my thumb I pushed on her outer lips. Nettie ran her hand up and down my shaft, licked the head of my cock. She had a good grip — a Dana Ferris-type grip — and her tongue was hot. Every tenth stroke or so Nettie would gather up my nuts, give them a squeeze, a kiss. I put my tongue inside her pussy, pushing it in as far as it would go. I did this a few times, fucking her with my tongue. Then I fucked my way out, kissed my way down, blew on her crack till her asshole opened.

And Nettie's was rank. But it was nowhere near as sickly as Robin's. It seemed like ages since the two of us had gotten it on, Robin and I. But now Robin's ass served a purpose, because it was the only thing I could think of to keep from coming. I also thought about how bad Robin had been looking lately, how out of it he'd been since he'd started at Max's. And that made me feel sad. But back to Nettie's ass. Must be all that British food, I thought.

So yeah — that helped, too. For a while. I mean, nothing's so bad once you understand it. But what happened to all those other nice smells she had? That time at the Ragnarssons'? I kept licking. I gave her asshole as much attention as I would her pussy. And Nettie seemed to like that, pushing her ass into my face, telling me to stick my tongue "right up there, as far as it goes." Pretty soon I could smell those old smells again. The pussy, the sweat, the powder. How they all floated into each other, making this new smell. How, after a while, everything smelled the same. How, in the end, all colours make brown. So it only makes sense that smells should do that, too, right? Isn't that just the way it is: How everything, in the end, comes out our ass.

We rolled onto our sides. I pulled the K-Y towards me, warming it with my body.

Nettie said, "Put your cock in me." So I got up on my knees, into position. I rubbed my cock over her clitoris, popping the head in and out of her pussy, pushing it from left to right. She moaned. "What about his balls?" Huh? "What about Flynn's balls?" she said, panting. "They're big," I said, pulling out my cock, raising myself slightly, rubbing my bag against her clit, "Oh fuck, stop!" she said. "Put it in me — now." So I did. All of it. Nice and slow.

I worked on her ass while we fucked. Using pussy fluids and whatever spit I was able to muster, I managed to get two fingers in deep. I was soon alternating cock thrusts with finger fucks. Then I reached over and grabbed the K-Y. I pulled out my fingers, gently, and dabbed my hand with lube. "Do you think Flynn likes ass fucking?" she said, all breathy. I ignored her intentionally. I knew that asking again would only make her hotter. I blew on the lube, then rubbed it into her crack. I returned my fingers to her asshole with ease. She gasped. Then she asked again: "Do you think Flynn likes ass fucking?" But this time my imagination was running loose. I didn't know what I was thinking. I lifted her legs and pointed my cock at her asshole. I was pressing down slow when I told her: "I'll bet Tanya loves having Flynn up her butt, don't you?"

Nettie pushed off, rolled over. She pulled a pillow over her face and screamed. Something was wrong. "You okay?" I asked her. Nettie shook her head. I sat back. I didn't know what to say. Had I hurt her? Was her heart acting up? Would I know what to do if it was? Nettie pulled the pillow away. She was laughing. But I could also tell she was pissed off. It was an exasperated laugh. "Why did you have to mention that woman's name?" she said, sitting up, pulling her knees against her chest. "Tanya?" I said. Nettie *grrred*, shook her head. "I don't know about you," she said, "but that chick gives me the creeps."

16.8

— How did Flynn and Tanya rate on the Bullshit Detector?

— Flynn was around .22. But Tanya varied day-to-day. At one point she was an .86. But after we shot *Rich Kid*, she dropped to a .44.

16.9

In all my time making porn, *Rich Kid Gang Bang* was one of the biggest drags I'd ever been a part of. But the problem had nothing to do with time or budget — that was the easy part. No, the problem with *Rich Kid* had to do with the fact that it was nowhere near the film we'd talked about making. And I blame Flynn for that. Even though it went on to be a hit, *Rich Kid* was a total compromise, a production nightmare that set the tone for all the bullshit that followed.

So what happened? We began filming at 5:00 P.M. and wrapped at nine, shooting all but the titles in sequence. The production was budgeted at twelve rolls of Kodachrome 25, but we quit after ten because we'd gotten what we wanted. Once the film came back from Kodak, I would edit the thirty or so minutes down to twenty-two. Anything longer would've been boring. We shot the titles last, using the letter magnets on Robin's refrigerator. I think the credits tell the tale.

THE LANGUAGE ARTS FILM COLLECTIVE PRESENTS

A BETSY DICK picture

RICH KID GANG BANG

Starring

TIFFANY ROTHCHILD

LOU BOLAN

Introducing TANYA SUZANNE as THE MAID

Executive Producer: MARTIN FLYNN

Written by HENRY Z. MILLER

Directed by BETSY DICK

16.10

— You're not Henry Z. Miller.

— And Nettie isn't Betsy Dick, either.

— Why didn't you use your real names?

— Flynn advised us not to. He said it would look bad if it was found out we were minors.

— But Robin wasn't a minor. Why did he have a fake name?

— Because he wanted one.

— Would you have liked to use your real name?

— I don't think so. This was not something we were particularly proud of.

— Because of Flynn's intervention?

— Exactly. A precedent had been set. In Hollywood they call it "studio interference."

— Is that how Tanya was cast in the role of the Maid?

16.11

We agreed to meet at Robin's apartment at four o'clock, New Year's

Eve. Me and Nettie, Flynn, Robin, and the actors. It was then that one of the girls told us that our plumber Drainpipe had NGU. So Flynn fired him on the spot and somehow convinced Robin to take his place. To make matters worse, our maid had gone AWOL. Nettie was going over the opening sequence when all of a sudden there's a pounding at the door.

Robin gets up to answer, and who should walk in but Tanya — all dudded-up like one of those fifties strippers. You know the look? The big hair, the boa, the fishnet stockings. Anyway, she's wearing what looks like one of those Army and Navy housecoats, this god-awful paisley thing with all the bruise colours in it. And to top it off, she's got the glow going, the junkie strut. It was really sad. Right away I knew what was going on. I threw Nettie a look and she met me.

Tanya walked up to Flynn and said, "I'm ready for my close-up, Mr. De Mille." Of course, I laughed; I'd seen the flick. But it wasn't *that* funny. And Flynn — he definitely wasn't amused. He started laying into Tanya, gave her shit for being high, told her if she ever fucked up again, she'd be dog meat. This went on for quite some time.

From the berating, I gathered that Tanya had been bugging Flynn about a role, to which Flynn had eventually relented. I also gathered that this role was conditional on some kind of sales quota from Tanya's gig at Mr. Steak — a quota she'd failed to reach. Plus she was ripped out of her mind. And Flynn wasn't taking too kindly to the fact that she was doing drugs on the company nickel. So Flynn tells her she's out — out of the picture. "Go on, get out," he said. Told her to fuck off, go home. That's when Tanya started to cry. She slumped down to Flynn's feet and grabbed his ankles, begging his forgiveness. It was awful. Impossible to watch. All eyes were on Flynn. What would he do?

Flynn helps Tanya to her feet, wipes the tears from her eyes. He leans over and whispers something in her ear. Tanya sniffles — says yes. Flynn kisses her cheek. Then he turns to us and says, "Why don't you guys go downstairs, get the exterior shot." Of course, I wanted to tell Flynn that I already got the exterior shot the day before, over in Shaughnessy, but changed my mind. It was obvious Flynn wanted some privacy. We watched as he carried Tanya into the bedroom, hooking the door shut with his foot.

So we went across the street to Mr. Steak. Nettie and the others went over lines, while I did a repair on the camera's manual zoom. When I finished I pointed the camera at Robin's apartment window. At first I thought I had the apartment below, because the people in the window were dancing. But once I zoomed in I realized it wasn't dancers I was spying on but Flynn and Tanya. And they definitely weren't dancing.

The next thing I know I'm tearing out of the restaurant, running across the street, up the stairs to Robin's. I open the door and what do I find? Flynn sitting on the couch reading *Garçons de Maroc*. He looks up for a second, then goes back to the magazine. He says, "Tanya's in the bathroom if you're waiting to go."

16.12

— He was beating her.

— I don't know. It was hard to tell. But I can tell you this: When she came out of the bathroom, she'd redone her make-up.

— She'd changed her outfit, too.

— That's right. Now she was dressed as a nineteenth-century French maid.

— Did your feelings towards Flynn change after what you saw from Mr. Steak?

— Sorta. But what could I do? I had zero evidence. There was no film in the camera.

16.13

So everything's moving along smoothly. We're getting our shots, and the performances are all excellent. We're nearing the end of our sixth cartridge when it's time for the scene between the Maid and the Boyfriend. Even though Tanya only had the one line — "Maybe you should put yourself in your girlfriend's shoes?" — she keeps fucking up. So if she isn't blowing her line, she's mugging for the camera or leaning out of frame or whatever. It's just not happening. Took us a whole roll just to get the line. But that wasn't the worst of it.

We're on our tenth roll. Nettie wasn't totally satisfied with the earlier oral footage we'd shot between Lance and Tanya, so, to be on the safe side, she insisted we do it again. I'm in tight on tongue and pussy when Nettie, who's leaning over my shoulder, calls out a cut. "Thank you," Tanya says, casting a withering eye at Lance. "What do you mean by that?" Lance asks defensively. Tanya ignores him, sits up, lights a cigarette. But Lance is persistent: "C'mon, whaddaya mean?" Tanya shrugs, looks away. Then, under her breath, she says, "You couldn't lick a stamp if your tongue were two foot long." That did it. Lance stands up, starts screaming his head off. He calls Tanya a fuck-up, a shit-head hype, insists she's nowhere near as good at acting as she is at stealing drugs — "And we already know you're the shits at that, too!" Pretty heavy stuff, of course. But that wasn't the best part: because the angrier Lance got, the more his cock would soften. I'd never seen anything like it before in my life, and I could just kick myself for not getting it on film. But whatever. The next scene called for a blow-job scene between these two and I was beginning to have my doubts it would ever happen.

After a brief pep talk, Flynn, Lance, and Tanya emerge from the bedroom. Flynn announces happily that we're once again ready to roll. So Lance lays down on the couch, holds up his erection, while Tanya takes her place between his legs. I move in close for the shot, Nettie whispers "Action," and Tanya leans over, takes the cock in her mouth, and bites it. Lance bolts forward, and the two of them are at it again, only this time they have to be pulled apart. But unlike last time, this time I got it on film. In fact, Flynn thought so highly of the scene that he suggested we try something similar — faked, of course — whereby the Plumber pulls a *Cape Fear* move on the Girlfriend. So we tried it, and of course it didn't work. Still, Flynn insisted I supply him with the alternate ending. He said the market was huge for revenge porn fantasies. I wasn't so sure, but supplied him with it anyway. After all, what did I know? Flynn seemed to know everything about the business. It was his idea we hire a demographer.

16.14

— Did you ever find out what ending was used?

— No. Flynn said he was gonna show it to me when he had it blown up to sixteen. But by then our relationship wasn't so good.

— Did you ever suspect he used the revenge-ending?

— I'm pretty certain he did, but I have no proof. I prefer to think that both versions are out there.

16.15

We'd wrapped. Lance was still pissed off over the biting incident, so he buggered off quick. Tiffany stuck around for a while, drank some champagne. Then Flynn went over and whispered something in her ear. The next thing I knew she had her coat on. Robin was late for Max's, so the two of them left together. That just left the four us. Me and Nettie, Flynn and Tanya.

Flynn and Nettie were in the kitchen doing hot knives, while Tanya and I sat on the couch. I remember we were talking about something Tanya had read in the paper that day, something about the Pope, how there was a rumour going around that he'd been murdered. Then she got all weepy, and I thought it was because she liked this pope, because I'd heard he wasn't such a bad guy, that he was gonna reform the Church or something. But no. Tanya hated the Pope. All popes. In fact, she hated everything to do with the Catholic church. She hated their power, their hypocrisy, the way they ruined people's lives. She was super-emotional about this. And it totally caught me off guard.

Tanya told me the story about her Catholic beginnings, in Nova Scotia. She told me about how she was raised in an orphanage by nuns, and how these nuns were all fucked up, how they used to beat the shit out of her all the time because they thought she was impure. She told me one time they beat her up so bad she pissed blood for a week. And when the nuns found that out they beat her even more. Because now they thought the devil was inside her, and that he was trying to empty her of Christ so he could possess her soul. Which, she said, was how she ended up meeting Flynn. She ran away and came out here. Flynn was the first person she ever met who cared.

She continued: "It was the late sixties and I'd just started turning tricks. I was a little young to be working, but I was tough and I knew it. That's most of it right there — the confidence, right? Most young girls don't have that. And sure, the innocence looks good on them. But once your youth goes there's nothing uglier than a shy old

253

whore. So yeah. I'd been hooking for a week or two, doing well, getting it together, when I get picked up by these four college types and they wanna go to Stanley Park and get blown in the zoo. They showed me the money and I said yeah.

"So off we go to the park and we get out of the car and walk over to where the kangaroos are and they line up around me and I start going to work on them. And I'm thinking, This is pretty fucked up, blowing these guys by the kangaroos. But they've given me the money and they're treating me real nice and I kinda like the look of these guys standing around with their dicks hanging out, eyes shut, shaking. They seemed really vulnerable and I liked that. I felt safe.

"So the one guy I'm blowing is about to come and I start working him real hard when one of the guys behind me — and he's by far the biggest of the four — sorta tugs at my hair, tells me he's coming, too. So I turn around and tell him not to grab my hair like that. And then I see that he's already shooting and I'm afraid he's gonna come all over my clothes, get me dirty, so I put my mouth over him and he just rams his huge dick down my throat and I gag. Then the guy I was blowing earlier — he grabs my hair really hard and yanks me towards him and I fall over, right? And I'm pretty pissed off and I'm coughing and my voice is sounding really scary to me but I tell him anyway, right? I tell him where to go. 'Fuck you!' I say. And then the guy who just came boots me in the ribs. And then this other guy starts coming all over me as I'm trying to get up. And then another guy starts coming on me, too. And then I feel another kick. So I try to move away and then I get kicked again, right in the face. So the next thing I know I'm getting the shit kicked out of me and I'm seeing stars and all this cum dropping on my face and then everything goes black real fast.

"I wake up the next morning across from the monkey cages. I'm lying there covered in dried-up blood and cum and I thank God my head isn't kicked in. I mean, I've got cuts and bruises and my clothes are all torn but my head's okay. So I get up and brush myself off and take a step forward and my heel breaks. I fall flat on my ass. So I get up again and manage to crawl out onto the path and I look up and I see this kid tossing peanuts to the monkeys. He turns around and says hi and then goes back to the monkeys. Except the monkeys are all cowering in the corner, screaming. And I guess it's all those monkey screams that woke me up in the first place, right?

Then the kid turns back to me and says, 'You don't look so good.' And I say, 'No, I don't suppose I do.' And he says, 'Yeah, I guess I'm not the only one who feels that way.' And then he points to the monkeys and one of them just screams like it's his last breath. So you know what I did? I laughed. I don't know how or why but I just did. I just laughed and laughed and laughed. And then this kid laughed, too. He walked right up to me, took off his coat, wrapped it around my shoulders, helped me to a bench. He was so gentle, this kid. Then he says, 'C'mon, I'll take you home.' And he's looked after me ever since. And that's how I came to know Flynn."

Tanya was just finishing up her story when I noticed Flynn and Nettie sneak past, into the bedroom. I think Tanya noticed this, too, because once she finished her story she immediately asked if Nettie and I were friends. So I told her yeah. "Nettie and I grew up together," I said. "But she goes to school in England now." Tanya nodded, took a drag off her cigarette. "You know Flynn likes her," she said, flicking her ash. I nodded, then glanced over at the bedroom door. "He likes you, too," she added, catching my eye. I was about to tell her that I felt the same, but that I was still confused by what I'd seen earlier. I wanted to ask her about that. In fact, I was all set to ask her if Flynn beat her up very much, but thought that would be pointless. Because she wouldn't tell me anyway. So I thought of another way of asking. I said, "Do you like Flynn?" And Tanya said yes, but looked away when she said it.

A short time later we were necking. It wasn't my idea, but Tanya asked me if I'd kiss her and for some reason I did. She seemed different after her story; not that same person who bit Lance earlier in the day. And she was such a hard kisser. Man, I'd never been kissed with such force before, such determination. And I must say, it was a bit of a turn-off. But she was very good with her hands. And she moved them over my body in a way that was different from the other women I'd been with. So when she got to my crotch, I was bulging.

It's funny what happens when a hand gets down there, the way some hands are able to make sense of what's happening in all that bunching, what's cock and what's balls. Tanya seemed to possess such a hand. She was an expert when it came to that. But why wouldn't she be? After all, she'd done this for a living once. But whatever. In what seemed like one continuous motion, Tanya undid my belt, my button, my fly. Then she asked me to sit up a bit. So I did. She took hold of my belt loops and gave my pants a hard yank. My cock slapped back. Tanya took hold of it, squeezed it extra hard. My cock responded. She kept doing this. And it felt great. Very similar to what Dana Ferris used to do, except Dana's hands were nowhere near as rough. Something about the roughness, then.

Tanya was sucking on my neck. This was freaking me out because I didn't want to go home with a hickey. So I pulled away. She gave me a funny look, like I'd hurt her or something. I was about to apologize, when I remembered something Flynn once said: "If you're gonna be wrong, be wrong and strong." So I thought of the cockiest thing I could say, and then I said it. I said, "Show me your tits." And Tanya seemed to like that, coming from a squirt like me. She chuckled as she opened her housecoat and showed them.

Now, I admit — as much as I protested Tanya's role in *Rich Kid*, as much as I resented working with her — I was totally turned on once I'd seen her breasts. They were nothing like the breasts you'd see in *Penthouse* and *Playboy*. And this, I think, was what made them so sexy. So now I had one in my mouth. And I was sucking in as much as I could. I thought back to her performance: the way her breasts drooped off her chest, fell forward; her dark conical nipples, how they pointed down like plumb bobs. I was totally getting off on the replay when Tanya pulled away, told me to stop. She said she wanted to suck on my cock.

Tanya's mouth was hot. The mouth of someone with a very high temperature, a fever. I thought back to a time when Nettie was going down on me, the time she had the Hong Kong flu. I couldn't believe how hot her mouth was. So maybe Tanya had a fever, too? I decided to check. I reached down and felt her forehead. Tanya took her mouth off my cock and told me not to touch her head. So I took my hand away and refocused on her pubic hair, which was big and black and a total turn-on. I thought about my cock going in and out of her pussy, what that might look like. Then Tanya reached underneath and scooped up my balls, jostling them in her hand. I took this as a prompt. Maybe I should put my hand between her legs, too? So I ran my hand up the inside of her thigh. I rolled the tip of my finger around what I thought was her vagina, where I thought she'd be sopping. But no. Tanya was as dry as a bone. "Don't!" she said, her mouth off my cock.

I could hear Nettie in the other room. Her voice was low. There were some other sounds, too. Sounds I was familiar with. Sounds particular to that part of the apartment: the soft knock of the headboard, the way the floor creaked underneath. It was pretty obvious they were fucking, which turned me on even more. I listened to the heavy breathing, the grunts, maybe a squeak of discomfort. Then the stopping of things, whispers. There was a click, which I recognized as the lamp by the bed. I looked down and saw a thin crack of light under the door. I heard shifting, the sifting sounds of clothes being sorted. I felt myself going soft, so I pulled out of Tanya's mouth, zipped up. "What are you doing?" she asked, a little pissed. I didn't know how to say it. "Is there a problem?" she furthered. I told her there was. The bedroom door opened and I knew we'd be leaving immediately.

We flagged a cab on Davie, took it up Burrard, then hopped out at King Ed. We hadn't said much on the ride, other than a couple of things about the production. Nettie was pretty happy with it, although she was now adamant about ditching the revenge-ending. "I just think we should stick with the script," she insisted. I was fine with that. But I was curious as to why she felt so strongly all of a sudden, because earlier she seemed fine with Flynn's suggestion. So I asked her. "I guess I just fell under his spell," she said. "I mean, the guy's so fucking convincing."

16.16

We celebrated New Year's alone on the tracks. It was really just a matter of holding a match to my watch and waiting for the second hand to pass. And when it did, we kissed. Just as friends do. Then we went back to walking, not talking. Nettie asked if she could come over to my place and listen to records. I told her I was okay with that.

We'd just turned off the tracks at Thirty-third when all of a sudden the houses around us erupted. People were coming out onto their doorsteps banging pots and pans, shouting "Happy New Year!" I checked my watch and saw that it was ten minutes fast. Then Nettie grabbed me and gave me this really deep kiss. Everybody saw it, I could tell. Because the pots and pans got that much louder.

257

16.17

— What happened in the bedroom?

— Between Nettie and Flynn?

16.18

The house was empty. My mom and sister were out on Carl's boat.
Part of some flotilla or something. There was a note. But whatever.
Nettie asked if she could have a shower. Without asking why, I told
her yeah. So while she showered I made popcorn. When she was
done the two of us went down to the basement, where we sat on the
bed, naked, the bowl between us. We listened to another of the
records Nettie brought back from England. This time it was the
Jam's *All Mod Cons*. But this time there was no sing-along. We ate
the popcorn one piece at a time. Almost every kernel popped.

Nettie was bugged. I asked her if she wanted to talk about it and
she just shrugged. I went back to the popcorn. The band played on. I
looked over at Nettie and saw that she was staring at the comforter, lost
in the nothingness. When the record ended, Nettie got up to flip it. I
caught a strong whiff of Flynn's cologne. She apologized for her mood,
and I told her there was no need. She'd done nothing wrong. After that
she couldn't stop talking. This is some of what she told me:

> "He's really into working with you, y'know. Not just
> loops but features, too. But if you ask me, I think he's
> full of shit. I think if you get involved with him, you're
> gonna get fucked up so bad ...
> "I overheard Tiffany and Lance talking. Lance
> said the only reason Flynn was getting into films was so
> he could launder his drug money. Did you know he's
> got Robin working for him now? Did you know he got
> Robin so coked up he owes him, like, ten thousand
> dollars? That's what Lance said. He said she heard that
> if Robin doesn't pay up soon, Flynn's gonna do to him
> what he did to this other guy that nobody's heard from
> for the past two months ...
> "Of course, after I heard all that I began to won-
> der. So when we were doing hot knives I'm thinking,

like, how can I ask him whether or not all this shit is true? Because it's bugging me, right? But how do you do that? How do you ask somebody about stuff they don't want you to know? Especially when you don't know them that well? So I think, Well, forget it. But then he starts answering me. Only I didn't say anything, right? But he's telling me stuff as if I'd asked him! He starts telling me all this stuff about how people think his interest in films is bullshit, and how they're all just jealous because he's, like, this big-time operator. Then he starts going on about how people think he's killed this guy who owes him money. And he's so convincing. 'Cause I'm believing it, right? But, at the same time, I'm not. And for the very same reason! Because he's so convincing! Because it all just seems so contrived. But even more fucked than that is how the part of me that believes him is also that part of me that can't believe he's telling me all this without me even asking. I was totally confused. And the hash didn't help, either."

BLACK

NETTIE
(VO)
But it's *the way* he told me. The guy's *too* charming.

INT. ROBIN'S KITCHEN

Action matches monologue.

So the next thing I know we're making out. And he's doing all this great stuff with his hands and I'm getting hot and before I know it we're in the bedroom.

ROBIN'S BEDROOM

NETTIE
(VO)
He sits me down on the bed and starts taking off his

clothes, like he's stripping for me. And I mean, the guy's got this great body, right? He takes off his shirt — and he's got this nice chest, these big hunky arms — and then he pulls down his pants real slow. So now he's standing there in his briefs. And — fuck — he looks good! The guy's got this great body and this big boner poking out. And I'm thinking, If I wanna fuck this guy, why am I so afraid of him? And then — wham! — it hits me. It's like, what the fuck am I doing? And then I kinda pass out. And I'm only saying "kinda" because I can't think of another word for it, because the next thing I know the room is bright red and everything's fuzzy. So now I'm completely freaked. I reach over and turn on the lamp. Then the room goes an even deeper red. Like blood, right? I try to scream but nothing comes out. Nothing except this little croak. I mean, it's just like a dream — where you think you're screaming even though the only thing audible is, like, this little mouse fart a hundred miles away. So then I ask him, "Where are we?" And he says — and you won't believe this — but he says, "We're in my heart." Then everything sorta flashes hot, like the bed's on fire or something. And then I'm thinking, Shit! I'm having a coronary. My heart feels like it's about to explode. And I'm freaking out like I've forgotten to take my prescription or something — even though I know I did, right?

So now he's kneeling over me. And he's taking off my clothes. I look down at his cock and all I can see is the Ragnarssons' parrot. I'm not kidding. It's so fucked. Anyway, the parrot's telling me its name is Marty and I'm not supposed to give him any shit. Well, duh? So then I close my eyes real hard. And when I open them again the parrot's gone. But instead of the parrot there's this weird-looking thing, which, for a second, I thought was a crowbar. So then I look a little closer, and sure enough it looks just like one of those bifurcated kangaroo cocks I saw in a biology book once. And it's totally freaking me out, right? I mean, I don't like the idea of this thing being inside me one bit.

So there's no way. I don't even want to touch it. Then he lies down and pulls me towards him, starts sucking on my tits. Now I don't know what to do. I mean, a part of me is going: Nettie, get the fuck out of there. But then what? What if he catches me, beats my head in? And then the other part of me is going: Okay, stay put. He's not gonna stop until he comes. So I think, Just jerk him off, right? So I ask him to lie on his back, tell him I want to play with his cock. But he ignores me. Then he starts licking his way down my body. And it's so gross, because now he's just pushing spit all over me, trying to get me wet so he can fuck me with this freak cock. So I try and pull away. And that's when he grabs my ankles real hard and holds my legs up, starts rubbing himself against me. And it's so gross, this thing. I can't stand it. So I tell him I can't fuck him, that he'll hurt me. So what does he do? He reaches into Robin's night table and pulls out some lube. So now I'm really freaking out because, like, how does the guy even know it's there in the first place?

Okay, so now he's kneeling between my legs, slicking up his cock. And the guy's making a big deal of it, too. Like it's this great cock or something. Gives me this stupid grin. So I try to get up and he pushes me down. Hard. Then he reaches over and turns on the lamp. Now the room is back to normal, even though everything else is twice as scary. Because now he's talking about what he wants to do. So he tells me he wants to watch his cock go inside me, watch my tits jiggle while he's fucking me. And that's when he starts working it into me. And even with the lube it kills, right? But the guy is so strong. There's absolutely nothing I can do. But then just as quick he stops. And get this: he tells me my pussy's too loose for him. Can you believe that? Yeah, then he asks me if I've given birth before. As if that has anything to do with it! So now I'm all set to let him have it when he reaches underneath me and starts lubing up my asshole, tells me he does this to Tanya all the time and she can't get enough. Then he sticks one of his big fingers right up my butt and I swear he touched a kidney. And then he pulls it out so fast I thought he took a piece with him. That's when I lost it. I'm doing everything I can to get the fuck out of the bed, but the guy is just too strong. I am so pissed off. I start pounding him, giving him everything I've got, squeezing my ass shut. But he still manages to get it in. And it just fucking kills. It felt like forever before the guy came. And it was only then that I was able to get him off me. I mean, thank God there was lube everywhere, because everything was so greasy by then I was able to squirm away and get some fucking clothes on. That's the last thing I remember before waking up.

When I woke up he was lying beside me, dressed, reading a comic. The only thing I know for sure is that we necked. Flynn said I fell asleep as soon as I hit the bed. I still can't believe I dreamt all that in fifteen minutes. I must have been exhausted.

INT. MY BASEMENT

NETTIE

So yeah, he's probably fucking that nutcase Tanya right now. Hey — you know what else he told me? You won't believe this, but he tells me that while we were in the bedroom, you and Tanya were fucking on the couch. And you know what else he said? He said that maybe the four of us should get together one day. He said that Robin told him how much you like sucking cock. Is that true? That you like sucking cock? Fuck, I think I'd die if I ever saw you and Flynn together. I mean — the guy is such a fake.

The popcorn was almost gone. Nettie picked at the last of it, popping them into her mouth like a tiny bird. She licked her hand, then put her arm around me. "So did you?" she said, grinning, pulling me towards her. "Did I what?" I said, knowing what she meant. "Did you and Tanya get it on?" I thought for a second. I thought, No point in lying. "Well, she sucked my cock but I didn't come," I said. "Does she suck cock as good as me?" said Nettie. "No," I lied. Nettie took the bowl from the bed and put it on the floor. The light hit her crack and I saw it glisten. And I could still smell Flynn's cologne.

16.19

— Was Nettie sure it was a dream?

— That's what she said.

— Do you think she was sexually assaulted?

— Only in her dream.

— Her dream was pretty vivid.

— I suppose. But then dreams aren't illegal, are they?

— So did you and Nettie have anal sex?

— No. We just lay on the bed and listened to records. We kissed a bit. I think we'd both had enough for one night.

— When did you see her next?

— The next morning, the day she left.

17.1

Nettie and I said our goodbyes on her front steps, while her parents and Dunc waited in the car. It was pretty funny. Judge Smart in the driver's seat, staring straight ahead, taking in the garage door like a drive-in movie. Mrs. Smart must've put on an inch of lipstick. Every time I looked over that little tube was doing laps. And Dunc — Dunc was sitting behind the judge, his back turned, doing that thing you do where you bring your hands around and rub your shoulder blades, where it looks like you're necking with someone even though you're not.

Not that they bothered us. Not at all. In fact, after we said everything we needed to say — which wasn't that much, really —

we decided to follow Dunc's lead and make out. And it was funny at first, you know. Necking madly like that, putting on a show, wondering how long we could keep it going, how long it would take us to drive her folks crazy thinking of ways to intervene.

But then something happened. Because all of a sudden we were kissing like we were madly in love. It was so weird. I felt this huge burst of heat. And the next thing I know my eyes are welling up. I could've stopped it, but I didn't. I guess I wanted to share it with Nettie. I wanted her to see those tears. Because I think that's the only way I could ever tell her how much I cared about her. And you know what? She was crying, too. It was funny. And we laughed over it. Then we hugged. That's when the judge came down on the horn. Show's over.

17.2

The Saturday after New Year's Day I had a meeting at Robin's with Flynn.

EXT. MY HOUSE. DAY

I am making my way across the lawn. The sound of a door opening. Dottie, who is dressed in a housecoat, sticks her head out.

                    DOTTIE
    Psssst.

I pretend not to hear her.

                    DOTTIE
    Psssst! You little shit!

I make a quick left and meet her around back. Bengt Jr. was there to greet me. He was happy, his big tongue curling my wrist like a bracelet.

                    DOTTIE
    Fuck off, Bengt!

Dottie throws her hips into the dog's ribs. From somewhere in the house, a parrot squawks ...

PARROT

Yeah, fuck her good!

The dog skulks off, the dance all but gone from those nuts of his.

INT. THE RAGNARSSONS' KITCHEN. DAY

Dottie hands me a coffee, gives me a hard look.

DOTTIE
(to my face, angrily)
Why'd you ignore me the first time?

ME

I didn't hear you.

DOTTIE
(turning away)

Liar.

Dottie pours some Drambuie into her coffee.

ME

How's Kai?

DOTTIE

He gets out on parole next week.

She spins around quick. More eye contact. Then she reaches into a pocket and pulls out a roach. She holds it out, her hand shaking.

ME
(shrugging)

It's a roach, Dottie.

I look over at Bengt Jr., waiting by the door, cocked in the lunge position.

DOTTIE
So light it, then.

Dottie pushes the roach towards me, smudging the charcoal end against my white sweater, the one my mom knit me for Christmas. I take the joint, light it, inhale it, taste it.

ME
(passing it back)
Tastes kinda plasticky.

MY POV

Dottie is now in soft focus, as if Vaseline has been rubbed onto the lens. Her mouth is moving, but there's no audio.

INT. RAGNARSSON BEDROOM

CLOSE ON MY FACE

I am groggy. My joints ache.

ZOOM OUT

I am sprawled over the Ragnarssons' bed, my wrists and ankles tied to the bedposts.

MY POV

Dottie is sitting at her vanity, combing her hair.

ME
(weakly)
Dottie.

I turn my head the other way.

MY POV

I am looking out their east window into my mother's bedroom. She is sitting on the end of her bed. Carl is standing before her. His pants are undone. My mother is sucking Carl's cock.

I turn my head back.

MY POV

Dottie is gone from the vanity. In her place is Kai. He stands up and moves towards me. He pulls from his crotch a gun.

HIGH ANGLE

Kai grabs me by the hair, lifts up my head, and places the barrel at the nape of my neck. He fires.

MY POV

I am moving towards the ceiling, which explodes into splinters, into the blue sky above. I look behind and see my house, which is probably about the same size as the bullet I'm riding. Then I see my neighbourhood, the park, then the rest of the city. I hear a loud bang, no doubt belonging to the shot that just launched me.

INT. MY BASEMENT BEDROOM

I sit up in bed, awake.

17.3

— When did you say you had this dream again?

— Again? What do you mean "again"? Like I've already told you and you've forgotten?

— A figure of speech. When did you have it *then*?

— I had it three nights in a row — those three nights leading up to my meeting with Flynn.

— Did you have it any time after that?

— No.

— Do you have any idea what it means?

— No, do you?

17.4

So it's the Saturday after New Year's Day and I'm sitting in
Robin's apartment waiting for Flynn. Robin's in the kitchen fucking up, trying to make tea. I pick up an old copy of *Garçons de
Maroc*, flip through it loudly so he can hear what I'm doing. But
he can't. He's too fucked up. Too busy fucking up. "Robin!" I call
out. "Where's your bong?" I hear him slow down. "My favourite
song," he shouts back, "is 'Heart of Glass.'" Huh? I repeat the
question. Still, he mishears me. "Flynn's?" he says. "'One Way or
Another.' Same record."

Robin's all shaky now. He puts my cup on the table, pours out
the cream. "I thought you hated disco," I said. He gives me a hurt
look. "Blondie's not disco — it's New Wave. Big difference," he says,
passing me my cup. I take a sip, stare at Robin's fucked-up face. He'd
been doing so much coke lately it's wrecked him. I ask him about it,
and this is what he tells me:

> "It's called Bell's palsy. It's a nerve disorder. Flynn says
> it's from not eating right, but I know it's from coke.
>
> "So what happened was this: Flynn arranged a
> deal between me and two guys named Mike. It's New
> Year's Eve and I'm waiting in Max's office. The guys
> arrive and we do the exchange: an ounce of uncut
> Peruvian flake for two thousand dollars. I count the
> money. No problem. So I turn around to leave, but one
> of the Mikes grabs me in this fake-friendly way and tells
> me to sit down and do a few lines with him. I told him
> that it wasn't cool for me to do lines while working, and
> that it was definitely not cool for me to being doing
> lines in Max's office. House rules, right? But more
> importantly: Flynn's rules, too. Then the other Mike
> tells me that's okay, says he's already got permission.
>
> "The next thing I know they've got about twenty

lines cut. They hand me a bill and tell me to get crack-ing. So I do a line up each nostril, then get up to go. But the first Mike shoves me down again, tells me to do a couple more. Anyway, they made me do all twenty. And I'm totally fucked up, right? My heart's beating a mile a minute. Then they start slapping me around, threatening me, telling me stuff like, 'Ever wonder what it's like having a whole ounce shoved up your ass-hole?' Or: 'Hear the one about the guy who rubbed so much coke on his dick the fucking thing came off in the middle of a piss?' Real scary shit.

"Finally Max comes in and I leave. But I'm so fucked up after that I spend the rest of the night bent over in the can. Then Flynn shows up at about four in the morning all pissed off that I didn't sell any of the grams Tanya did up for me. I try to tell him what hap-pened and he lets me have it. Pop! Right in the cheek. That's when my face fucked up, the Bell's palsy. I know it wasn't his fault — it was the coke, right? Anyway, I decided from now on I'm gonna go back to selling hash and making movies. I'm gonna tell him today."

Robin gets up, goes over to the stereo, cues the needle. The first chords to "Jeepster." A key jiggles in the door. Then the door opens. It's Flynn. Robin cowers, skitters off to his bedroom. Flynn remains in the doorway, glaring. He doesn't move until Robin's gone. Then he walks over to the stereo and cranks down the volume knob. Doesn't lift the needle at all. Just the volume. Bolan's voice is just a whisper, the unamplified sound of a diamond on vinyl.

Flynn sits down, puts his arm around me, smiles. "I've got big plans for you and me," he says. I pull away. "We gotta talk," I tell him. "Oh, we'll be doing a lot of that over the next little while," he says. "I don't think so," I tell him. "But I do," he says, smiling, like he's just seen the future. "I don't know," I say, looking away.

17.5

— Why didn't you just get up and leave? Walk away right then and there?

— It wasn't that easy. Flynn was very clever.

— You should've made a run for it.

— Like I said, it wasn't that easy.

17.6

Flynn had a briefcase with him. And inside the briefcase was a business plan. He'd done up a binder, the same Key-Tab job I used for school. And inside Flynn's binder were all sorts of coloured pages: budgets, pie charts, statistics, pictures. He was dead serious about this film business stuff. And he'd really done his homework, too. It was scary — all that work. Scarier still was that he wanted me on board. He wanted me to be his in-house director. Because that's what he kept calling me: his in-house director. He said: "I want you to be my in-house guy." I asked him about the collective, and Flynn scoffed. "Collectives don't work."

I spent the next two hours listening to his pitch. Flynn figured by the time I graduated from high school he'd have the company well enough established that we could move to Los Angeles and work there full-time, get to the real work of making features. "LA's where the industry is," he said. "I've already got some leads on some office space. A good location. Marina Del Ray." He turned the page to some promotional photos he'd cut from a tourist pamphlet. The marina itself, a restaurant, some stores. But I had my own imagery.

I remembered my mother's reel: *The Story of This Family — So Far*. There was some footage of Marina Del Ray. There was the sign that welcomed you, then my father cleaning a fish on the dock. He held the fish up to the camera, gave it a wiggle, made a deranged kind of face. Then he turned sideways, held the fish over his head, and brought it down in such a way that it looked like he was swallowing it. Then he turned back to the camera and said something. The camera jiggled a bit. That's when he flung the fish at the camera. It blurred grey, before giving way to the top of a palm tree and the blue California sky. The next shot was taken from the car, heading north along the Port Mann Bridge, just a few miles from home.

Flynn turned to the section marked TALENT. "These are some of the people we'll be working with," he said. We flipped through maybe a dozen plastic pages, the kind you put slides in. Except instead of slides these pages were full of those little photo-booth pics you get at the mall. Tiny head-shots. Some of the scariest people I'd ever seen in my life. "If you pull out the photo," Flynn said, demonstrating, "you'll see that I've written notes on the back." Flynn handed me a photo of an angry-looking girl with feathered hair. I found the contrast between her soft white hair and hard ruddy features disturbing. Flynn nudged me. I looked over to see that he was holding out a magnifying glass. I took the magnifying glass and looked again. The girl had a sore on the corner of her mouth. "No — the other side," he said, grabbing the photo from me, turning it over.

It was the smallest handwriting I'd ever seen. Totally creeped me out. "I can usually get a hundred words on the back of each photo," Flynn said, as I read about Sandy.

17.6a

> SANDY D. 17 yrs. 5' 4". 120 lbs. Sm. tits. Sm. waist. Lge. ass. Most nights at Fresgo's. Bi-. Oral. Anal. Mlty. Good w/ big rigs. Does 40+. Bad temper. Whites only. Speaks Fr. Born in 3R, Que. No habit. Hooks for $, food too. Friends w/ Joel H., Tina F., Dee P., China C., Missy B., Tom A., Allen M., Earl H., Chris L. Shoplifts. Juvey m/v. Likes to sing (à la Suzi Quattro). Concerts. Packs blade. $ in R shoe. Baby: 1 yr. (Suzette). Joan (mom). Dad dead.

17.7

I returned Sandy and received Joel.

17.7a

> JOEL H. 19 yrs. 6' 2". 180 lbs. Fit. 7" (pencil). Lge. build. Chest hair. Strong arms. Long legs. Rnd. ass. Lge. bag. IDs hetero, but does yng. men (top, no 50-over). Liked. Sunny d.p. Fights when pushed. Born in TO. Chipper (snorts). Afts. at Austin Hotel. Friends w/ Sandy D., Tina F., Tom A., Chris L., Candace V. A., Tanya S., Noddy B., Clem, Tad 'n' Andy, Robin L. Steals cars. Guitar. No record. Dog: Zozo. Georgette (mom). Pete (dad). Ross and Autumn sibs.

17.8

It frightened me that Flynn knew so much about these people. Still, it was nowhere near as frightening as his tiny writing. I remember seeing a blow-up of the Lord's Prayer once on a postage stamp. I think it was in *Ripley's Believe It or Not.* Why would anybody do that? I thought. I was haunted by that for a long, long time. I was about to relate the *Ripley's* entry to Flynn, but he was already on the phone. It would have to wait. But by then he'd have something else for me to think about. It was always like that with Flynn. He was so quick, you barely had time to ask.

17.9

— Did you recognize any of the people in Flynn's talent pool?

— Tanya was in there.

— What about the boy with the moustache? The one in Judge Smart's study?

— That's right. He was in there, too.

— Did you ever make a film with him?

— No.

— But you asked Flynn about him. You asked him like this boy was somebody you might like to work with.

— Yeah, that's right. I did.

— And what did Flynn say?

— He said the guy was a big-time musician. But he wouldn't tell me the name of his band.

— Did you read what Flynn wrote on the back?

— No. Flynn grabbed it from me and stuck it in his pocket. The next time I looked he was replaced with someone new.

17.10

Flynn put the binder back in the case. He said he wanted to devote the rest of the meeting to capital-raising schemes. Fine, I thought. I was curious to hear what he had to say. Because by that time I'd made up my mind I was finished with this guy forever. I'd just feign interest, let him finish, then split.

According to Flynn, the best way to raise capital was by making loops and selling them to peep shows in the States. A totally stupid idea, of course. But whatever. I felt compelled to tell him why. I really wanted to stick it to him. So I told him about this article I'd read in *Hustler*, about how peep shows and theatres were on their way out because, in a couple of years, everyone would be watching pornos in their homes once these video-cassette recorders came on the market. But even more to the point: Why wouldn't he use money from some of his other businesses to bankroll production? Flynn responded by changing the topic. "No, we have to get our name established first. And the best way to do that is by making loops," he said. "But I thought we were talking about raising capital?" I replied. Flynn scowled. Not that I gave a shit. Because I had more to say. "Besides," I added, "I think porno loops are dumb. Because if you're just showing people having sex all the time, without a story around it, then you're guilty of what Angela Carter calls ..."

The next thing I know I'm seeing stars. Blood's gushing from my nose. Flynn's got me up on my feet, slapping me around the room, knocking furniture over, throwing stuff, telling me that I'm brilliant, telling me how much he needs me, that I'm his in-house director. Then he hits me again, tells me I'll make a great filmmaker one day, tells me how much he wants to be a part of it. He gives me a million reasons why I should reconsider his offer. He even says there's a place in the company for Nettie, as well. He says if I just give him the next few years of my life, then I can have whatever I want, become rich and famous — whatever. Then he throws me across the room, where I crash against the coffee table, upending it. I tell him how everything he's said thus far means nothing to me. I tell him that I don't want any of it. And the more I tell Flynn what it is that I don't want, the less I know what it is that I do. Or something like that. But whatever. That was the scary part. Not knowing. So I tell him that, too. And he just stands there, smiling. Just like my dad used to when I was a kid.

I staggered over to the couch and sat down, holding a napkin to my bloody nose. I thought maybe I should just get up and go. In fact, I began to fantasize about doing just that. How I would get up and walk out the door, catch the Arbutus bus, go home, sit on my bed, and write Nettie this great long letter about what I'd just been through, how I should've listened to her in the first place, how she was right about how fucked up Flynn really was. So yeah, I could hardly wait. And that's when I stood up. And that's when Flynn grabbed me by the shoulder and slammed me back down.

"Y'know, I hate doing business like this — I really do," he began, his voice soft. "But since you've gotten so uppity lately, I just don't see how I've got much choice." Then he sat down beside me, pulled me close. He told me how we all have to serve somebody, how even he had a boss, a boss even more powerful than him, "... someone who is capable of the most heinous things," he continued, squeezing, "someone who could explode a car, a house, someone capable of *substantial* life losses." Then Flynn squeezed me so hard I thought my ribs were gonna crack. "Now, do you have any idea who I might be talking about?" he said. "Any ideas who this boss might be?" But I could barely think. The guy was carrying on like some kind of zealot, like he was talking about God or something. I mean, could it be that Flynn was some kind of gangster for Christ?

So I told him that, and he laughed. He laughed so hard, so uncontrollably, I'm sure I could've bolted right there. But I didn't. I was *that* scared. Because what Flynn had to say next convinced me that no matter how fast I ran, no matter how hard I tried to hide, he would find me eventually. Hell, he might even kill me! So what did he say? Flynn told me his boss was none other than Kai Ragnarsson. I was stunned. In total shock. And Flynn, of course, loved it. He immediately began rubbing it in. "Y'know, if I didn't need your talent so badly," he said, "I'd love to show Kai some of your earlier work — I really would. Ha-ha-ha!" And if that wasn't enough, if that wasn't the ultimate mind-fuck, I look over at the coffee table and what should I see on the underside but this little teal sticker. And on this sticker, in big black letters: A RAGNARSSON DESIGN.

— Your life changed from that moment on.

— I suppose. But it's weird, you know. Every day after that seemed very much like the day before.

— What do you mean?

— I mean from that day on there was a sameness to everything. It's hard to explain.

— Can you provide some examples?

— Well, my mom began spending most of her time with Carl. My sister was always off with her boyfriend. School was school. And when I wasn't at home, I was shooting for Flynnskyn Pictures.

— What about your job at the fish 'n' chip shop?

— Flynn made me quit.

— What about Nettie?

— I called Nettie a couple of weeks later and she told me she'd fallen in love with this Swede. She said they were gonna be spending the summer together in London, where they both had jobs at the Tate. I can't believe her parents let her stay. I was so pissed off.

— What about the Ragnarssons?

— They just kept to themselves. Not that I went out of my way to see them after Flynn's revelation.

— And Robin?

— That was kinda sad. A couple of days after the meeting, Flynn told me Robin went to detox and found God. That's how Flynn ended up with Robin's apartment.

— Did you ever see him again?

— Robin?

— Yes.

— No.

18.1

By the time I graduated from high school, in 1980, Flynnskyn had made approximately sixty-eight porno loops. In that time we'd worked with over two hundred actors, exhausting every possible fetish, every variation of every pose ever published in *Playboy*, *Penthouse*, and *Hustler* combined. And just when I thought I'd seen it all, Flynn would recruit some new sexual oddity. The man with three breasts, the woman with the foot-long cock. But it was always the same old shit. The expectation of some new level of excitement was always offset by the predictability of the previous week's production. Commercial Photography 101. I could've been shooting parts ads for Sears. The fact that these parts moved was about as exciting as watching an oil derrick.

Every Friday, a new package would arrive on my doorstep from Kodak. And every Friday, after school, I'd go downstairs to my basement room and cut together the new loop. We had the dumbest titles, too. *Ding-Dong*, *Pie Taster*, *What a Boob!* — all Flynn's ideas, of course. But whatever. The following day I'd take the finished loop over to Robin's, where Flynn would introduce me to the cast of our latest porno-of-the-week. Then I'd make up a script — not that we'd follow it — and an hour later we'd roll film. The next morning I'd send the new package off to those oblivious technicians in New Jersey. This went on for almost a year and a half. It was easily the biggest part of my life.

Once in a while I'd get pissed off. I'd tell Flynn that I'd had it, that I was through, that I'd done my last loop, et cetera. And Flynn would take this very seriously. He'd act all concerned, tell me I was absolutely right for feeling the way I did, tell me how bad he felt for overworking me, that he was really, really sorry. Then he'd give me a little extra money, some coke — usually some coke — and the promise of a bigger say in the creative. Most of the time that was enough — the promise of a bigger say.

But sometimes it wasn't. Sometimes nothing was enough. I'd get all adamant, tell him I needed my own projects, that I was an artist or something. That's when Flynn would start in about how we were almost ready to start making features, get into some of those political themes me and Nettie used to talk about. That usually worked. Not just because I liked to be stroked but because I loved the way Flynn used to talk about me and Nettie, together. He seemed to have insight into our relationship. He'd describe it in ways I'd never thought of before. And that made me feel good, especially since Nettie and I had kinda lost touch. Only rarely did he play the Kai card.

There was this one time, though, where I came super-close to quitting. In fact, I did quit. I'm sure I did.

It was around Christmas time, 1979. My mom asked me to help her shop for Carl's present. I wanted to say no, but I hadn't seen much of my mom lately and I thought this would be a good time to catch up — being Christmas and all. Anyway, Carl had wanted a sports coat, so Mom and I went down to Woodward's on Hastings Street and picked one out. Mom had already set it aside, and all she needed was my assent. I told her it was fine, that Carl made sense in mohair.

The coat wrapped, we left Woodward's and headed west, towards the parkade. On the way my mom asked me if I knew of a place that still sold eight-tracks, because Carl had a player in his car and my mom was sick of listening to the same Doc Severinsen tape over and over again. "Why don't you just get him one of those cas-sette-adaptors?" I suggested. But Mom didn't seem that interested. "The Smarts have one; they don't work very well," she said, her heart set on eight-tracks. "So I guess they'll be deleting cassette-adaptors next," I said. And then my mom laughed. And it was really genuine, you know. Because this time she was laughing like I was a friend or something, and not just her son. Anyway, I remembered that A&A had a ninety-nine-cent bin in the back, so I said we should go there.

We're walking south on Granville Street, nearing the Birk's clock, where all the street kids hang out, when my mother says something under her breath about how sad it is that all these kids are runaways, and wouldn't it be nice if they all went home for Christmas, make their parents happy. Only she wasn't quite subtle enough, because this one girl, who was just about to panhandle us, starts laying into my mom real hard, calling her a bitch, telling her that she has no idea what her home life was like, how her mother's boyfriend used to beat the shit out of her, rape her, and "How would you like to go home to that — especially at fucking Christmas time, lady." The next thing we know we're surrounded.

And these kids were rough. Not pushing-and-punching rough — more like verbally abusive rough. It was super-heavy. Because these kids were very convincing when it came to articulating their pain. It was way too much. Way too much at once. Especially for my mom. Everyone had a story to tell. And some of these stories were similar to the ones I'd hear on set. But to get it like this, with my mom beside me — that was tough.

Looking back, though, I'm glad it happened. I'm glad my mom got a sense of what life was really like out there on the streets. I mean, I could never impress upon her how dire things were for people my age. Not all single-parent homes were as stable as ours.

If I have one regret, it's that I could never really convince my mother what a good job she'd done bringing up my sister and me. And like many of the things she was never convinced of, she was never convinced of the good in anything unless she'd heard it from somebody else, someone other than her own family. So hence Mrs. Smart. Hence Carl. And hence how thankful I was to these kids for providing my mom with this moment of difference, this moment she so desperately needed, where all she could think about, I'm sure, was how much worse things could've been for me and my sister had we not been raised right, despite the fact that my mom always felt we were stigmatized for growing up in a broken home.

There was a small opening in the crowd. I hustled Mom towards it. We were almost free when this particularly tough-looking girl jumped in front of us, frightening my mother enough that she tripped and fell. I quickly got Mom to her feet, pointed her in the other direction, and was all set to bolt for the parkade when who should be standing before us but the 6' 3" 180 lbs. 8" (thick) Donnie G. I picked up the pace, got us through the gauntlet unscathed. But not before Donnie yelled, "Hey, that old bag gonna be in your next porno?" Thank God my mom was completely distraught, because I'm sure I would've died had she known what Donnie meant.

When I gave this to Flynn as my reason for quitting he looked genuinely upset. It was right after we shot *Toe Fuck*. Flynn just sat

278

there, listened, as I told him. And it was going well, too. I sensed I'd finally gained enough momentum to get the fuck out of Flynnskyn once and for all. But just to be sure, I restated my usual reasons for quitting. And, like I already said, Flynn just listened, nodded along like I was absolutely right. When I finished I thought I'd won. It was a good little speech and I was proud of it. And I knew if I hung around for his reaction, he would invariably convince me, somehow, that I was wrong. So the next thing I know I'm out the door, skipping down the stairs. And I'm feeling great, right? Fuckin' amazing! But just as I step into the lobby, who should be coming out the elevator but Flynn. And he's got tears in his eyes. He steps between me and the doors, tells me how sorry he is. Asks me — no, begs me! — for one more chance. Just one more chance. I feel myself weaken. The guy was so persuasive. The clincher came when asked: "Would it help if I spoke with your mother?"

18.2

— But you did stop working for Flynn at one point.

— Sorta.

18.3

Graduation Day, 1980. A hot June afternoon. I'm sitting in our living room, dressed in what I'm sure is an amended version of the same powder-blue tux Dunc Smart rented five years earlier. I can't stop looking at my watch. And I'm sweating. In an hour I have to drive to Dunbar and pick up my grad partner, who — being from a school with a "maximum inclusion" policy — has been chosen for me by computer. And you'll never guess who this computer matched me up with! If you said Cheryl Parks, you'd be right. So obviously I'm nervous. More nervous than I would be if it was, say, Shawna Kowalchuk or Margie Stott I was taking to grad.

But to make matters worse, for the first time in over a year and a half, I did not receive my weekly package. Did those technicians at Kodak finally cotton on? Was I in some kind of shit? It was all too much. Making matters worse, the footage we'd shot — the footage I was expecting — was particulary nasty. So my only hope, now, was that the film didn't turn out, that it was somehow underexposed. But then again, if it hadn't turned out, Flynn would be furious anyway. So either way it was lose-lose.

Sitting across from me is Carl. We're waiting for my mom to finish wrapping my graduation present so I can rip it open and get going. Carl is staring at me. He hasn't said a word since he'd sat down. But he doesn't have to. The goof is such an easy read, such a smug fuck. And just when I think he's gonna say something predictable like "So I guess you think you're a man now" or "I suppose you'll be getting your own place tomorrow," he surprises me — the fucker. So he says, "I think it's really big of you to attend your grad after all. You've made your mother very happy." I give him a tight smile. It was all I could do. What my mom saw in this jerk I'll never know. But he did make her happy. And I suppose that's the most important thing, right? But still, I can't help but feel a little pissed off. Pissed off at Carl for not saying what I'd hoped he'd say. Because had he said what I'd hoped he'd say, then I could be *real pissed off*. And that's how I wanted to feel right now. *Real pissed off.* Then my mom walks in carrying what looks like a breadbasket. No doubt something for the apartment Carl was hoping I'd be moving to.

18.4

— A Sony BetaMax video camera!

— That's right.

— The dawn of a new era.

— I guess so. Video was being touted as the next big thing.

— But you were a film purist.

— Well, yeah. I hadn't much liked what I'd seen on video so far. It was so stark. Everything looked so ... I don't know. But then again, I'd never worked with it before, so I was willing to give it a try. I thank Nettie for that. She always kept me open to new things.

From *The Journals of Nettie Smart,* vol.17, 1980

January 1, 1980

You'll never guess who I got a letter from today! Our Boy in Vancouver! I think it's the first one ever. I couldn't believe it. I recognized the handwriting right away — even though it's changed tons since I last saw it. Nobody presses as hard as he does.

So what's it been — a year since I last saw him? Christmas '78? My last visit? Sure. Easily. And what has he been up to? Well, I'll just tuck this letter in and you can read it for yourself.

December 3, 1979

Dear Nettie,

How are you? I'm fine. I miss you. Everyone misses you! Your mother was over at our house yesterday and she said you won't be coming home for Christmas. She said your heart was acting up and the doctors said you shouldn't fly. Seems kinda strange to me. I don't know what flying has to do with anything. Don't you just sit there? It's not like they're handing out squash rackets or anything. Hope you're okay, though.

Things have pretty much stayed the same since you left. Not much change to report, I'm afraid. I suppose I could tell you about what some of your old pals have gotten up to, not that I make it my business to know. (But then again, how can you avoid it?) Most of it is just stuff I've overheard around my locker, some of which is confirmed by things I've seen — from a distance, of course.

So what have I heard? What have I seen? Well, I can tell you that your old pal Margie Stott has taken it upon herself to play the "bad girl." I'm serious! On the first day of Grade Twelve she showed up at school with pink hair — and I don't mean the pink rinse that the crumblies get at Elio's, but pink like the cover of the Sex Pistols' record! It was amazing! Obviously the last person you'd expect to be the first punk rocker at your school. She even had the safety-pin earring and the leather jacket to boot! But get this — despite the change in appearance, she's still the same suckhole she was in Grade Seven. Weird, huh? Margie Stott: good little bad girl.

Then there's Bobby and Cindy. You know about them, right? You know they've been going around since the summer? Anyway, Bobby and Cindy are the closest thing we have to a rock 'n' roll couple (if your idea of rock is the Osmond Brothers, and your idea of a couple is Ken and Barbie.) Rumour has it Bobby was offered a basketball scholarship to Puget Sound University, and he told them he wouldn't go unless they offered one to Cindy, too. Pretty big of him, I thought. Until I heard that Cindy turned them down because they refused to guarantee her a spot on the cheerleading squad. Apparently that's got the whole school divided into camps: those on Bobby's side; those on Cindy's side; and me, who doesn't give a shit. Pretty disgusting, I think. But I'm fine with it. Those two don't even look at me any more.

Shawna Kowalchuk and Alistar Chen seem to be hanging out quite a bit lately too. At least, that's how it appears to me. By the way, both of them are on the "Reach for the Top" team (along with Smith-Gurney, of course), and according to my mom they were on TV last week and beat a private school from the Fraser Valley. Mom said Smith-Gurney was amazing. She said she was amazed at how much he really knew. But back to Shawna and Alistar: I see them walking home together every day after school. And Shawna looks a lot happier now that she doesn't have to wear that boot-brace any more.

Saw John and Penny up in Kerrisdale the other day. They have a little baby. Didn't say hi or anything, although just seeing them made me curious about Mr. Gingell. Hey, the last time you were here I forgot to tell you: *I saw him*. Mr. Gingell. Yeah, I almost ran him over. So at least I can tell you he's doing okay.

And me? What have I been up to? Things have been pretty much the same since you left. I just go to school, do what I have to do. On Saturdays I go downtown, buy a record — have you heard the new Jam, *Setting Sons?* — maybe see a movie at the Cinémathèque. Sometimes I go over and visit Robin, smoke some hash. He's given up coke now, which is good. And neither of us see Flynn or Tanya any more. Those days are long gone.

And what else? Well, I've been shooting lots of footage lately. Different things. But I did start this project a little while back that you might find interesting. Actually, it's something you and I talked about doing back in Grade Seven. Remember *A Bird and a Worm?* Just kidding. No, what I've really been doing is filming all these old parts of the city, stuff that's just about to get torn down. Seems there's all sorts of new development going on and nobody's really doing much to record these old buildings. But it's not like I'm making art or anything. More documentary than anything else. Just something to do.

Oh, and one more thing: my mom asked my sister and me if we thought she should marry Carl. Yeah, and you know what my sister said? She said, "You shouldn't have to do anything you don't want to." And then my mom said, "But I want to marry Carl." And then my sister said, "So what the fuck are you asking us for?" My mom was speechless. It was so funny. My sister is way funnier than I was at her age. I don't know. Maybe you had to be there.

So I guess that's it.

Yours,
The Neighbour Formerly Known As Asshole

I don't know. As I read over his letter, I suspect there's something he isn't telling me. I can't believe his life is as boring as he makes it out to be. And I can't believe he doesn't have any friends. He's a good-looking guy; you'd think he was at least getting laid. I don't know. Maybe he isn't well. I'm sure he's hiding something from me. Not that I doubt anything he's told me. That's not it. It's just that something's missing.

But then again, I haven't been very forthcoming with him lately either. Looking back, I think I've only written about him twice since I left Vancouver. And the last time was an entry on his birthday, where I just wrote his name and a greeting. So what do I do? Write him a letter and tell him how much I miss him, how much I've been thinking about him? But that would be a lie, wouldn't it? Truth is, he's hardly ever on my mind any more.

Fuck it. Maybe I *should* send him a letter. Maybe if I told him just how bad my heart really was, he might feel moved enough to reveal something more of himself, because it's for his own good that he does. After all, it worked the last time. Though it seems a shame I have to be on my deathbed before he finally comes around. I don't know. I'll send him something.

18.6

I wasn't thrilled about the video camera, but I did appreciate the gesture. And I loved the irony! I mean, it was nice of my mom to take an interest in the very thing I was hiding from her the past two years. And even though I'd given her no indication that I might continue to pursue filmmaking — that is, I had no plans for returning to school in the fall — I'm sure she felt my interest would be there regardless of what I chose to do with my life. As well, those cameras were pretty expensive. So I made a big show of taking it out of the box, loading it up. Mom had already charged the battery.

"Here — " she said, reaching for the camera. "Can I try?" I gave her the camera and she turned it on Carl. "Carl's got something for you," she said, zooming in. Carl made a peace sign — something stupid like that — then he reached into his sports coat and pulled out an envelope, tossing it towards me — "Here." Mom reversed, set up for a low-angle shot of me opening the envelope. Inside: a plane ticket, a Eurail pass, and a thousand dollars in traveller's cheques. I checked the ticket and saw that I was leaving the following Friday

— for two months! I couldn't believe it. Fucking prick.

I turned to my mom. Did she know about this? She looked a bit tentative, like she did, like it was something Carl might've talked her into. "Excited?" she said sheepishly. I wasn't. "You did mention once that you were interested in going to London one day?" she added quickly. My poor mom. I hated Carl for putting her in this position. It was so abusive. The guy was as bad as my dad. "Well, yeah," I said. "But I said I was interested in visiting Nettie. Didn't Mrs. Smart tell you that Nettie's gonna be spending the summer in Vancouver?" My mom turned to Carl for help. She needed him to say something "So you'll have some time together before you go," he said. I couldn't believe it. I was being railroaded out of my own home. It was so *David Copperfield*. A page was turning and it felt like a sheet of metal.

18.7

— Funny how things turn out.

— There was nothing funny about it.

— Were you angry?

— Of course I was angry. My only wish was that I had more time. I could've made Carl's life miserable — I'm sure of it.

— Why didn't you just say no, then?

— I don't know. I felt so unwanted.

18.8

The phone rang. My mother went into the kitchen and picked it up. Carl had his hand over his mouth, as if to shield a yawn. But he couldn't fool me — the prick — trying to hide his laugh like that. Still, he looked a bit nervous. I could tell. So I decided to exploit that. He brought his hand down, pretending to be distracted by something out the window. I aimed the camera at his lap, watched as he worried a hangnail. Again, he brought his hand up: this time to chew at a cuticle. It made me sick that my mother had to kiss such a mouth.

I pressed Record. Carl noticed me do this and scowled, withdrawing his hand. I kept taping. I'm sure if I hadn't, he might've tried something, thrown a punch, slapped me. So I thought as long as I had the camera on him I was protected. Then my mother called out: "Carl, could you run up to the dry-cleaner's and get my dress? I've got to pop over to the Smarts'." He was more than happy to go.

Five minutes later I was alone with my watch. In thirty-three minutes I'd be leaving for Cheryl's. In less than a week I'd be out of the country. Things were moving quickly.

Now what happened next was very strange. I'd gone to the fridge to get Cheryl's orchid and was all set to leave when I heard a knock. I opened the door and who should I find but two cops in plainclothes: *the same two cops who threw me out of the Venus a year and a half before.* I couldn't believe it. They asked me if I was who I was and I said yes. Then they introduced themselves — Detectives Reese and Brown — and pushed past. I followed them into the living room, aware of my rights. Reese said sit, and I didn't. Brown made some crack about my tux, and before I could respond he told me I was in deep shit. I asked him why, and he made another crack about my tux. Reese pulled a binder from his briefcase. And the name on that binder was mine.

I laid into them: "Hey, either you're arresting me or you're gonna have to leave right now — 'cause you have no right coming into my house like this." Obviously, I was upset. I demanded to see their badges, a warrant, whatever they were supposed to show me. Then I told them I wouldn't cooperate unless my lawyer was present. Brown looked me up and down. "Who's your lawyer?" I made up a name. Reese opened the binder and wrote the name down. Then he pocketed his pen and looked up, looked me right in the eye. "I'm afraid I'll have to agree with Detective Brown," he deadpanned. "That tuxedo's one of the biggest crimes I've seen all year." Brown snickered. Reese didn't flinch. Reese was definitely the straight man here. Bad cop or not.

Too weird. I had to pinch myself. It's a dream it's a dream it's a dream, I kept thinking. Reese flipped to the middle of the binder. He motioned for me to sit down beside him. This time I did. "Do you know this man?" he said, pointing to a picture of a sleeping Robin Locke. "Yes," I said. "Name please?" said Brown. "His name is Robin Locke," I said. "When did you see him last?" said Reese. I had to think. I wasn't sure. "Around Christmas '78," I said. "Do you know anything about his disappearance?" said Brown. I shook my head. "I'd heard he was in detox," I said. "Who told you he was in detox?" I made up a name. "Marc Bolan," I said. "Who's that?" said Reese. "A singer," I said. Reese wrote the name down. He wrote: MARC BOLAN: SINGER. "Do you know where we can get in touch with this Mr. Bolan?" said Brown. "He's dead," I said. Reese wrote DEAD in brackets, then closed the binder. He turned to me: "Well, I've got some bad news — so is Mr. Locke."

Somehow I knew this. Just as I knew this visit had less to do with Robin than it did with Flynn. I checked myself: I was angry. And this pissed me off even more. I hated how my grief for Robin had taken such a back seat to my fear of Flynn. And I hated myself for this. Plus I hated Flynn.

For the next twenty-two minutes, Reese and Brown talked about the killer. Although they never once mentioned the killer's name, I knew exactly who they meant. "We're gonna need your help, son. We're gonna nail this guy," said Reese, closing the binder. "So we want you to come downtown first thing on Monday and give us a statement, tell us everything you know about Robin Locke," said Brown. "We'd ask you to come down now, but seeing as your graduation ceremony is tonight we don't want to ruin it for you," said Reese, standing up, straightening his trousers. "Yeah," said Brown, straightening his also, "you only graduate from high school once in a lifetime." I opened the door. The detectives stepped into the sun. Brown turned to me. "Besides," said Reese, "we'd hate to see that tuxedo go to waste." I could not fucking believe it. This time both of them were laughing.

18.9

— Did you ever find out what happened to the film?

— Yes, eventually.

18.10

I looked at my watch. I was late. I waited for Reese and Brown to pull out before taking off in the Falcon. I watched them turn down Valley Drive, disappear, then I grabbed the orchid and made my way down the steps. Carl had just pulled up. He was carrying my mother's dress, the one she'd be wearing at my grad ceremony. "Pretty nice, huh?" Carl lisped, holding my mother's dress against him. Yes, Carl. Now could you please move your fucking car so I can pick up my date? Carl changed his tone. He reached into his pocket, tossed me his keys. "Here — take the Caddy. You don't wanna show up in that piece of shit your mother drives now, do you?" As if I gave a shit what car I drove.

18.11

— How was grad?

— Stupid.

— What did you and Cheryl talk about?

— Nothing.

— Did you talk about the valedictory speech?

— Cheryl told me why I was chosen valedictorian.

— She told you it was a gag.

— That's right.

— She told you that the students thought it would be funny if they chose you.

— That's right. She told me that everybody thought I was a psychopath.

— You had a reputation for being unpredictable.

— That's correct.

— Why didn't you decline then? Or would that have been too predictable?

— I would've, but I got talked into it by Ms. Abbott. She said I was one of the few students in my class who had anything to say. She said it was a good opportunity for me to tell the school how I felt.

— And the students — were they satisfied with your speech?

— No. I think it went over their heads. I think most of them were hoping I'd show up with an Uzi and kill some teachers.

— What else did you and Cheryl talk about?

— That's basically it. But she did ask me if I'd heard from Nettie. So I lied and told her we kept up. Then I asked her if she'd heard anything. And she said they hadn't spoken since the homecoming party. I asked her if they were friends and she said not really. She said the only reason she was invited was because Mrs. Smart got hold of Nettie's 1976 annual and invited all the people who'd signed it. I told her she could've said no, but then she went on about how Mrs. Smart was already laying a guilt trip on her. I forget what was said after, but Cheryl got all pissed off at me and that was it for talking.

— You said: "So, how's your old pal, Cindy Carruthers?"

— That was it.

— And you did this in a particularly cruel way, like you were trying to rub something in.

— I didn't like the way she was talking about Nettie. She seemed to characterize her more as a chore than a real person.

— You made her cry.

— That wasn't my fault.

— Who's fault was it then?

— I don't know. I mean, it was weird. When I went to pick her up she was waiting on the doorstep. As soon as I pulled up she ran over to the car and jumped in. I got the distinct feeling that she was fighting with her parents or something because her father was screaming at her from the stoop and her mother was in the window doubled-over like she was crying. I think that's the real reason why she cried that day. Problems at home. It had nothing to do with me.

— Did you talk to Bobby?

— No. But you'll be happy to know he won Grade Twelve Male Athlete of the Year.

— Margie Stott?

— Nope.

— What about Shawna Kowalchuk? You danced with her.

— Yes, she was on my dance card. Supposedly another computerized thing. But probably another joke on me, no doubt.

— What did you say to her?

— I told her she was beautiful, which was true. And then she gave me the best kiss I'd ever had in my life. She had the nicest mouth.

— What about Jeffrey Smith-Gurney?

— Nope.

— Alistar Chen?

— He held out his hand and I shook it.

— What about your father? He was there.

— Didn't notice.

— Anyone else?

— No. I just wanted to get the whole thing over with. All I could think about was finding out what had happened to Robin, maybe absolve myself of the mess with Reese and Brown.

18.12

Valedictory Address

> Ladies and gentlemen, teachers and staff, members of the graduating class of 1980, good evening.
>
> In preparing tonight's address I went to the school archives and looked up other valedictory addresses. What I was looking for was a pattern, a series of clichés I could string together to prepare you for the next fifty years of your life. But I changed my mind. Too cynical, I thought. Instead I went to the Audio-Visual Room, where I booked this overhead projector. For what I really want to impart to you tonight is a model — a model that I developed while attending this school. Now, this model, I feel, belongs to all of us; and therefore I feel it is appropriate that I share it with you tonight. Because whether you know it or not, all of you — and by all of you I mean parents, teachers, and support staff included — contributed in some way to its invention. I'm calling it the Bullshit Detector, and it may very well save your life one day. So, if you please.

Where do you want to go?

What will you do to get there?   What have you done to get where you are?

Where are you coming from?

18.13

After the ceremony came the dance, and after the dance we were free. Technically, that is. Because after the dance all of us were expected to race home, change out of our tuxes and dresses, then partake in a series of carefully orchestrated activites our grad committee had spent the past year planning: the free dinner sponsored by the local McDonald's franchise, the all-night party at Foreshores Beach, the champagne breakfast the following day, a wink of sleep before going to the after-grad bash at the Hyatt, then the tent city we were expected to build on the school grounds, so those younger versions of ourselves could walk past us the following day as we woke from our graduation madness. Yuck. Of course, I wasn't having any part of it, having already experienced the better part of it from Nettie's letter back in elementary. Still, I was thankful for the excuse it provided: I had all weekend to get to the bottom of whatever happened to Robin.

Once Cheryl was dropped off, I returned home with Carl's Caddy. My intention was to change, then sneak off downtown as quickly as possible. Unfortunately, the Falcon was in the driveway. And who should be waiting by the front door, waving, but my mom. Even worse: standing beside her, the video camera in the firing position, was Carl. Needless to say, Mom was totally upset when I emerged from the car alone. "Where's your grad partner?" she called out, while Carl turned the camera towards her, recording her every disappointment. "She had a seizure," I called back, thinking fast.

So I told her all about how Cheryl had collapsed as we got into the car, how I did the right thing by sticking a pencil in her mouth, holding her head so she wouldn't smash her skull against the curb. Then, once she'd stopped spazzing out, how I took her home to her thankful parents, who may or may not be phoning tonight and thanking my mother for having such a wonderful son. By the end of it my mother was in tears. "I hope this won't put a damper on your fun," she said. To which I shrugged like it was nothing, the perfect place for Carl to stop recording.

18.14

— What else did your mother tell you before you left?

— That Nettie would be arriving the following afternoon.

— And what else?

— Just that.

— There was something else, something that Mrs. Smart told her, something she told you she didn't want to tell you until the following morning, something she thought might upset you on your grad night.

— How do you know all this?

— Just tell us what she told you.

— Okay. She told me Nettie was dying.

18.15

So Nettie was dying. In fact, she'd been dying ever since she left Vancouver, after Grade Ten. Which turned out to be the reason she left in the first place: not so much to go to some smarty-pants private school, but to be near the best heart surgeons in the world. That's what my mom told me on our steps that day, while I sat beside her, still dressed in my stupid blue tux, hardly worried about Reese and Brown any more, absolutely forgetting that I had lost another friend only months before. And when she was finished, when she told me how sorry she was, when she held me close to her as I bawled my head off, Carl had the gall to call out, "C'mon in you guys. We can watch the playback on TV."

Naturally I felt awful. But at the same time I wasn't convinced that Nettie was really that sick. Sure, she had a heart problem. And yeah, it was serious. However, I just knew that once she got back in town she would be fine, that just being here would make her better. And the funny thing was: it was the same optimism I had for Nettie that led me to believe that Robin was okay, too; that he had just wandered off somewhere; that maybe Reese and Brown were trying to con me into squealing on Flynn, because I'd seen on TV how the cops had done stuff like that in the past. I thought about all this as I made my way up to the tracks, past the brambles to that little depression Nettie and I once fucked in.

I took a joint from my pocket and smoked the whole thing myself, staring up into the dark blue sky. Even though it was evening, I could still feel the heat of the June afternoon. A seagull hovered above, and for a second I saw the sunset's red against its breast. It was a bit of a turn-on. So I listened for a minute. When I was convinced there was no one around, no trains coming, I took from my back pocket Nettie's very last letter. As I opened it I wondered if it would read any differently from the first time I read it. Because now she was dying. And because I wondered what a dying person's words might look like.

18.15a

Nettie's Very Last Letter

March 17, 1980

Hey!

Thanks for your New Year's Day letter! Sorry it's been a while. I meant to write back, but I've just been so busy lately. Not that I'm trying to make excuses or anything. Want to hear about what I've been up to?

Well, I just found out I've been accepted to Goldsmith. Do you know what that is? Probably not, right? Well, I'll tell you: Goldsmith is probably one of the best art schools in the whole of the U.K. And they want me! Yeah! But seriously, it's a really hard school to get into. And the application took ages to fill out. Still, it was worth it. They loved my portfolio, and their letter came just the other day. ACCEPTED. So I'm gonna be an artist after all. Pretty cool, huh?

I've been doing a lot of work with photography and video lately. Yeah, yeah, I know — video. Everybody hates video. But, hey — it's a new medium and I think it's brilliant. Artists from all disciplines are getting into it — performance, sculpture, painting. A couple of months ago this curator was giving a talk at St. Martin's, and one of our instructors took a group of us down to hear it. I can't remember the curator's name, but she had all kinds of video from people like Joan Joanas, Bruce Nauman, Nam June Paik. (Do you recognize these names?) But the best part was seeing

Kate Craig's *Delicate Issue*, which is this video of the artist's body shot in extreme close-up, so close in fact that you don't even know it's a body after a while. Later on, during the Q & A, somebody in the audience said they liked the work so much because of the way the body is made foreign, while, at the same time, being reclaimed through intense self-examination. Naturally, this appealed to me because I have so many issues about my own body, the way it has been controlled not only by doctors — and my own mother, for fucksakes! — but by advertising agencies and fashion companies as well, all those people who make a living telling women how they should look and dress. Do you know what I mean? Sorry, it wasn't my intention to ramble on. But this stuff just gets me so excited!

Speaking of excitement: there was a big scandal up in Edinburgh a couple of months back. The old art vs. pornography debate. Only this time it was more complicated, because it was child pornography people were up in arms about, and not the stuff you see in *Playboy*. Basically, what happened was this: A local artist took a bunch of pictures of his children while they frolicked naked on some beach, then he exhibited them in a private gallery. Two days later the cops showed up and closed the show down. This led to a bunch of arts groups getting together and putting on a series of public forums on the issue of children and sexuality. One of my instructors was asked to give a presentation, and afterwards, on his way back to his car, he was beaten up. His topic: "Advertising and the Sexualization of Children's Bodies: You Can Lust But You Can't Touch." I asked if I could read his paper, and he said I could. And it was excellent. Most of it had to do with how children are just as sexual as adults, and how the media vulgarizes that, turns them into little whores, and how this conflicts with the hysteria that's created by parents who are trying to relive their innocence through them. I think he's going to publish it, so when he does I'll make sure you get a clipping.

But that was just the beginning, because now there's a conference being planned in Manchester this summer called "Sex and Representation." And it's not just artists attending but anthropologists, media experts, historians — you name it! Sounds really interesting. I picked up a pamphlet at the Whitford the other day, and get a load of the topics: "Cinematic Pornography As Burlesque of Mainstream Hollywood: Porning In on the Biblical Epic"; "Pornography vs. The Construction of Bourgeois Taste: The Al Goldstein Story"; "The Relationship Between the Hard-core Porno Loop and the Modernist Poem: A Structural Analysis." Not bad, eh? Hopefully I'll be able to attend. Say, do you still have that photo I gave you back in Grade Seven?

Wow, now that I'm writing I feel I can just go on and on! But what about you? What have you been up to? My mom tells me she sees you from time to time, moping around, preoccupied with whatever it is you're up to. Are you still shooting old buildings? Sounds like a noble pursuit. My dad says he's been hearing all sorts of talk at the Terminal Club these days of an Expo coming to town. He says that if it ever happens, Vancouver will be rebuilt and the city will never be the same again. Something about the economic shift from a resource base to a tourism base. Make any sense to you? Are you very political these days? Hey, did you know that during Margaret Thatcher's speech last week she mentioned British Columbia's Social Credit government as a shining example of free-market capitalism? Have you heard the new Cure record yet? *Seventeen Seconds?* Pretty depressing. Are you going to university in the fall? Do you have any idea yet of what you want to be?

Well, maybe I should stop here. I'd better get back to my essay on Bacon — the painter not the philosopher. Hope you're well. I probably won't see you this summer, as I'm hoping to get my job back at the Tate. If you're ever out this way, just let me know.

You're more than welcome to stay at my granny's place in Bayswater.

By the way, I'm happy to hear you've dropped Flynn and Tanya. Cheers to Robin, too.

Yours,
Nettie

PS. There's a hit of acid behind the stamp. Purple microdot. A gift from my boyfriend, Mats.

18.16

I read Nettie's letter a second time, then returned it to my back pocket. The sun was almost down, but there was still enough light to check my watch: 9:35. I opened my fly and pulled out my cock, jerked off as I thought about all the things Nettie didn't have to say. Then I rolled over. And I guess I passed out for a while, because when I awoke I'd had the weirdest fuckin' dream.

I'm about six years old and I'm playing in my backyard. I'm pushing around a Tonka toy, a truck or something, while my parents are inside entertaining the Smarts. My sister's still a baby and I guess she's in her crib. It's a Sunday. It's summer. And I'm by myself.

So I'm roaming around the backyard, driving my truck between the flowers, around bushes, up the trees, when I hear somebody whisper my name. It's an older voice. A man's voice. And it's coming from the fence, behind a hydrangea. So I drive towards it, around the bush, where I come upon a shaded section, under the big cedar that stands between us and the Billingtons. And on the other side of the fence is Mr. Billington. I can see his eyes through the widths of horizontal plank. He calls me closer. So I go.

Mr. Billington reaches a hand through a gap between the planks. He's holding a licorice whip, swinging it around. I ask him if I can have it and he says sure. So I reach for it and he pulls it away, makes a little laugh. He says I have to help him figure something out first. I ask him what and he tells me he knows this little boy who is having problems going poop and he had read in the newspaper that licorice was really good for that kind of thing. This was news to me. Besides, I'd never had a problem with my poops. So I tell him this.

Then he said he was happy to hear that, because he would give me the licorice if I could show him what a healthy bum looked like. Because if he knew what a healthy boy's bum looked like, then he would be better able to help this boy with the not-so-healthy bum. Then I asked him why this boy couldn't go to a doctor to get his bum fixed. And Billington said that the boy's family was too poor. I thought that sounded reasonable, and since licorice was my favourite, I asked him what exactly he wanted me to do. He said all I had to do was turn my back to the fence and pull down my pants. He said it would be easy. So that's what I did. I leaned against the fence and pulled my pants down. Then his hands came through the fence and pulled them down a little lower.

I liked the way Billington's hands felt. They were smooth, the smoothest hands I'd ever felt. I liked the way they tickled my bum, they way they'd dart underneath, play with my penis. And I also liked the way they touched my asshole. Then Mr. Billington told me he was going to wet his finger and press it against me, stick it inside and feel what a healthy bum felt like. And that felt pretty good, too. Then he made me turn around and put my hand through the fence. And I really liked that. I couldn't see what I was touching, but I liked the way it felt. I asked him what it was and he told me it was an animal he sent away for, from Australia. He said when it wakes up it kinda looks like a sausage. I said I wanted to see it, but he said now wasn't a good time, that if I was good, he might show me a picture of it one day, and if I still liked it, then maybe he'd let me look at it, kiss it, put it where he's just stuck his finger.

But what I definitely didn't like was when he made me put my ear up to the fence. He tried to tell me he had this other animal that liked to eat ear wax, and that people who'd seen it thought it looked just like a tongue. But I knew he was lying. I knew it was *his* tongue. So I told him so. But he wouldn't listen. He just kept on licking. Then I tried to pull away, but he had his hands around my waist. I told him to stop, and finally he did. Which was a huge relief because I could hear my mother coming out the back door and I didn't want to get in trouble. Lucky for me I didn't.

18.17

— You're sure that was a dream?

— Of course. I dreamt it, didn't I?

— We'll take your word for it.

18.18

It was dark when I caught the Arbutus bus downtown. I had no clear plan, other than finding out as much as I could about Robin — and Flynn, too, for that matter. But I had to be careful. Flynn had such a loyal following. Or did he? So much seemed different about the city now that I'd graduated from high school. I got off at Davie and headed west, towards Robin's apartment.

I was just crossing Burrard when I noticed Robin's old pal, Tad. He was all punked up, coming out of Numbers. I waved — "Tad!" — till I was sure he'd seen me. And when he did he stopped, squinted, not sure if he knew who I was. "Hey, Tad," I said, jogging towards him. "Hey," said Tad, looking around. "So how's Robin?" I asked. Tad looked at me funny. "I really have to know," I added. Tad nodded, suggested we go somewhere.

Tad suggested Fresgo's, but my instincts said no — too obvious. Instead, we decided to walk down to Denman, to the Dover Arms, a good place to drink if you're under nineteen. I told him I'd buy him dinner and he said that was a great idea. He hadn't been working much lately because of an infection. And, as he put it himself, "When I don't work, I don't eat."

At first, I got the impression Tad was only going to tell me what I asked of him. Why should he say any more? I mean, information of any kind was like money on *these* streets. Your words had power. It was like what Nettie once told me, something she'd picked up in one of her classes, about how knowledge is a commodity. I could relate to that. And so I respected the fact that Tad couldn't be very forthcoming. Besides, I liked the way he played things. So cool. Not cool like Flynn used to be cool. But cool like you find in a new culture, where certain actions come off as sexy as the behaviours that front them. So I began with small talk, some gossip I'd heard on the set of our last loop, something about one of our tranny actors. After a while Tad loosened up. This is how it went down.

"So yeah — whatever happened to Robin?" I asked. Tad looked me right in the eye, and replied: "Robin's dead." I reached for my cigarettes. "When?" I asked, looking away, afraid of the eye contact. Tad took a swig off his pint. "A while back," he said. I pulled a cigarette from my pack. My hand was shaking. I think Tad was aware of this because when I reached for my lighter he raced me to it, held the flame up to my face. No doubt he was trying to rattle me.

I wasn't sure how much of the truth Tad was prepared to part with, but I pushed on anyway, hoping that I could at least catch him in a lie, maybe uncover something in the way he contradicted himself.

Tad didn't seem to have a problem telling me about the details of Robin's death: how he was found floating in False Creek, his body full of sleeping pills, how water rats had chewed his ears off. And when pressed, he did mention something about how Robin might have been killed elsewhere, that "according to some" he was drowned in a bathtub and dumped in the ocean a couple of days later. But when it came time for me to ask who did it, I thought for sure he'd get all cagey again.

"Do the cops know who the killer is?" I asked. Tad grinned. "I think everybody knows who did it," he answered back. "Flynn," I said. "Nope," said Tad. "Who then?" That's when Tad laughed. And it was a real scary laugh, too. Like I was in deep shit or something. "So who then?" I repeated. And with that, Tad told me it was Tanya.

But why, though? Why would Tanya have killed Robin? So I asked Tad this and he told me that Robin owed Tanya a lot of money. Apparently Tanya had fronted Robin over fifty thousand dollars in coke, and when it became clear he wasn't able to earn it back, he was offed. "So Tanya's in jail?" I asked. Tad shook his head. "Nope," he said, "they pinned it on Flynn. Happened this morning." Huh? "Yep," Tad continued, "somebody squealed."

Now I was really fucked up. But, of course, I had to know more. "So who then? Who told on Flynn?" Tad downed his pint, raised his hand for another. "Well," he began, "that's the big question, because whoever did took off quick. And they're the key witness. The crown wants to burn Flynn, but they know they don't have a case. Right now they're holding him for pandering, but he'll probably walk tomorrow." The waitress was approaching. I needed to sneak in one more question. "So where's Tanya now?" Tad reached for the menu, opened it in his lap, and told me, very matter-of-factly, that she was no doubt looking for whoever it was who ratted.

The waitress took our order. Tad selected half the menu, I stuck with lager. When she left Tad asked me if I had a dime. I reached into my pocket and gave him one. Tad took the dime, steadied it on the table, then flicked it with his finger. It spun, making a complete orbit around a pack of matches, before wobbling to a stop. He did this a couple of times. "How's Andy?" I said. Tad shrugged. "Haven't seen Andy in ages," he said, setting up the dime again, then changing his mind, flipping it instead. "Did he leave town?" I asked. Tad chuckled, looked away. All of a sudden he was up and moving. "I'm just gonna go to the bathroom — back in a sec," he said, not looking back. I activated the Bullshit Detector: Tad was flashing a .93. I picked up the menu, did the math, and left two twenties. I ran as fast as I could towards Davie, caught the first cab back to Shaughnessy.

19.1

I awoke to my name, my mother's voice calling down from the kitchen. "It's Bobby!" I shut my eyes and took a deep breath, all set to let go with something just as loud, something about my being asleep. But of course I was too late: the shush of mom's slippers, the receiver rocking gently on the sideboard, Bobby's mouth pressing on the other end. And as for all that air? My big inhalation? I yawned instead. Then I put on some gaunch and stumbled up to say, "What the fuck do *you* want?"

Bobby asked me where I was the night before, why I didn't show at Foreshores. I lied and told him I was at home reading Solzhenitsyn. He told me I shouldn't be reading "that communist shit," and that I was a liar because he phoned me three times. "Your mother said you were out partying with us." I told him that's what I tell her when I want to be alone. "Oh, so your mother's a liar, too!" "That's right," I told him. "I come from a long line of liars."

19.2

— Do you have any idea how close you are to blowing this?

— I have no idea.

— Are you aware of what will happen if you do?

— I think I have a pretty good idea.

19.3

I hung up the phone. My mother shushed towards me. She looked concerned. "Where were you last night?" So I told her I was at Foreshores, with the rest of the grad class. Then she said, "But Bobby kept phoning, he wanted to know where you were. He was very concerned." Once again, I had to think fast. "Well, Mom, if you saw what Bobby was up to last night, you would've totally understood. I mean, he was so out of his mind on mushrooms, it was pathetic."

After a light breakfast, I went upstairs to my old room, where I took watch over Thirty-third Avenue. It was almost noon, and the Smarts' Lincoln would be coming down the hill any minute. I had with me the folder Nettie gave me six years earlier, the one with the storyboards and the photo from the judge's study. I opened the folder and arranged the images over my mother's sewing table. I did this in a way that made the most sense. At one point my sister popped her head in, asked me what I was going to be wearing to after-grad. I told her nothing. Then I asked her if she wanted to see something Nettie and I did when we were kids. But she said no, she didn't have time.

A little later, Carl leaned in. "Hey, pal. Sorry to hear about Nettie. I had a sister who died at her age. Drowned. If you ever want to talk about it, I'll be around. Just letting you know." And before I could say anything, he was off, too.

The last person to stop by was my mom. But she didn't say anything. I didn't even have to look around, either. I just knew she was there, standing by the door, crying.

I looked at my watch: 12:40. Where the fuck was she? Hmm. Maybe she was going to the hospital first. I turned around to ask my mom, but now she was gone, too. When I looked back to the window, I caught a glimpse of the Lincoln as it turned onto Cypress. So I ran downstairs, got on my bike, then quickly made my way around the block. And then, for some reason, I stopped.

From behind some boxwoods I watched as the judge and Mrs. Smart got out of the Lincoln, then huddled together while Dunc lifted Nettie from the back seat and carried her towards the house. Then Mrs. Smart went ahead and opened the door. Nettie looked awful, a million times worse than she did when she returned from her surgery back in Grade Ten. As Dunc stepped up the stairs, I saw Nettie's head roll off his shoulder and hang there, upside down, her eyes wide open, her face the colour of chalk. If she wasn't so out of it, I thought for sure she was staring right at me. Fuck — was I pissed off!

19.4

— Why were you so pissed off?

— I was pissed off at everything. I was pissed off because of what was happening to Nettie. And I was pissed off because there was nothing I could do about it. And I guess I was pissed off because I'd somehow lost faith in her ever getting better.

— Any other reasons?

— Yeah, I was still pissed off over her last letter. I thought it was pretty obvious she'd lost interest in me.

— Weren't you at all concerned about your own situation? With the police? Flynn?

— Not any more. Not after seeing Nettie.

19.5

I started downtown on my bike. I'd never biked downtown before. Not that I was scared or anything; it was just something I'd never given much thought to. Besides, after seeing Nettie in her present state, I wanted to do something completely different, something new. I also wanted to resolve this whole Robin fiasco once and for all, because I wanted to get on with things, start fresh, think, for the first time, about what it was that I wanted, what I was going to do with my life.

It was pretty much all downhill from Shaughnessy. I maybe used my pedals twice. Just as I was coming approaching Robin's, a van pulls up in the space beside me. A brand new Aerostar. Written on the sliding door: BROUGHTON HOUSE FOR YOUNG ADULTS. Below, the logo: a drawing of an old Victorian house, instantly recognizable because there were only about six houses like that left in the whole West End. I remembered a couple of months back, before they kicked out all the prostitutes, as many as a dozen guys would hustle-pose the northwest corner of Davie and Broughton, just up the street from what I guess was now called Broughton House. Anyway, from where I stood I could almost see it: the nothingness that once was. I made a mental note to get some footage of those houses, for no doubt they, like everything else in the city, would soon be gone.

The van door slid open. A smartly dressed woman jumped out, scrambling like she was late for something. She looked familiar. Then she said my name and I recognized the voice. I said yes — because that's who I was.

Before I could say Tanya Suzanne, she was on me, her arms out, her hands patting at my back. She kept calling out my name, over and over, like I was something lost, something she'd been look-ing for, something she'd just found — all at once. "Oh my God, how have you been?" she said, stepping back, taking in my face. I didn't know what to say. It had only been a few weeks since I'd last seen her; but now she was going on like we were age-old buds. "Are you busy right now?" she said. "I mean, do you have time for a cof-fee?" I laughed, if only to cover the fact that I was scared shitless. Tanya was the last person I wanted to see. I looked around: the street was extremely quiet for a Saturday afternoon. I was already thinking of witnesses. Even though I knew better, I couldn't muster a no.

We walked east down Davie and found a window seat at Fresgo's. Two monster muffins steamed before us. I squirted three creams into my coffee. Tanya kept up the conversation, switching to rhetoric so she could answer her own questions. She'd hadn't stopped talking since the hug. Miles from the laconic junkie I'd once known. What happened?

Tanya told me all about how she'd cleaned herself up after they found Robin's body. How it scared the shit out of her. How they never found the killer. Then she told me about her detoxification, her ongoing involvement with NA, then AA, then NA again. "And when this Broughton House thing came up," she said, sipping, "I jumped at it. Then, after a couple of weeks, they offered me a staff position. Best thing that's ever happened. Now I'm, like, a mom to all these kids who would otherwise be shooting up, stealing, turning tricks. But does it pay as good as drugs? Course not. But hey — it's a hell of a lot more rewarding. And it's been very, very good for me. As you can see." I nodded, content just to listen. I was now convinced that this woman had nothing to do with Robin's murder. Everything Tad told me was lies. But still, I had to ask.

"So have you kept up with Flynn?" I said, lighting a cigarette, taking cover behind the smoke. "Not really!" she said, grabbing my pack, lighting one up herself. "But I hear he's doing well." Of course, this was not what I wanted to hear. Flynn was supposed to be facing a life sentence, in solitary, with armed guards outside his door. "Let's see," she began, "it's been — what? — two months since I last saw him. And, I mean, he had all these plans about getting into real estate, buying up some of these old hotels on the Downtown East side, fixing them so the old-timers living there don't have to shit in a bucket every time the toilet busts."

I nodded along, watching Tanya's face for any tell-tale tics. But no. She was telling the Flynn story like a proud sister, as if it were her own. She wanted me to believe Flynn was doing just as well as she was. But as good as it sounded, I found it very hard to believe. There was more: "So I guess he's told you he's getting out of the movie business?" Huh? But I said yes anyway. "Yeah," she continued, "he's found God. Can you believe it! Wants to do God's work from now on. Go straight. Maybe get into politics. This Expo thing's coming up and ..." Slowly I began tuning out. Although Tanya no longer posed a threat, I still felt the need to escape. Her babble was driving me crazy.

All of a sudden, Andy's name pops up. But because I was plotting my escape, I'd lost the context. However, she did say something about him being in jail. So I asked her about it. I asked her like I knew already. "Yeah, what did he do time for again?" I said, scratching my chin like I'd forgotten. Tanya seemed to shut down for a second. She knew I was fishing. She took a long drag on her cigarette, blew the smoke off the window. Then she threw me a hard look. The smoke curled back like fog. "Do you really want to know?" she said. I shrugged, even though I did. "Because if I tell you, then you're a part of it," she added. "Aren't I a part of it already?" I said, unsure about where all this was leading. Tanya's eyes narrowed. She looked like she was reading fine print. "But are you, though? Are you *really?*" she said, leaning towards me, her voice a whisper. I looked down at my muffin. Stone cold.

I listened as Tanya took me back to 1979. She told me how a bunch of kids — people like Lance, Tad, and Andy — got it in their heads that they would form a syndicate and take over Flynn's Davie Street drug trade. "So that's why I came down on Lance that day," she said, referring to the chomp she gave him on the set of *Rich Kid Gang Bang*. "But how did Robin fit into all this?" I asked. Tanya relaxed her shoulders. "That was sad," she said, lighting another cigarette. "Flynn thought he was behind the whole thing." I thought hard about what to say next. "But he wasn't?" I said finally. Tanya was slowing down, too. "No," she said finally. "Lance killed Robin and pinned it on Flynn."

Huh? Now I was really confused. And I tried to let that confusion show, too, because I was hoping that Tanya would sense this. I was hoping that she would make sense of what she'd said so I wouldn't have to ask any more questions, put myself at risk. But she didn't. She wasn't about to let me off that easy. I couldn't resist taking the next step. "So what *did* happen to Lance?" I asked. "Andy killed Lance," she said, breaking off the corner of her muffin. "So where's Andy now?" Tanya put the muffin in her mouth. She was drawing this out as long as she could. "Maybe you should ask Tad?" she said through the muffin.

A moment passed. I wasn't really sure where all this was going — and I definitely didn't want to find out. So I let go with a long shot, what I thought was the non sequitur I'd need to change the topic back to how well things were going for Tanya; but I also knew I had to protect myself, to let her know that I had friends in high places, that I better not be fucked with. I even changed my voice a bit, gave it a by-the-way kind of inflection: "Hey — did you ever come across a guy by the name of Kai Ragnarsson?" Tanya began a slow grin. The more it widened, the more I became aware that I had just answered my own question. "So you do know what happened to Andy after all," she said. I smiled knowingly, as if by chance that might help my standing. That's when I knew I was dead.

I checked my watch, made some exclamation. I excused myself, told Tanya I had to make a phone call. Tanya nodded, watched me get up. As I made my way towards the phones I asked a waiter for refills, pointing to the table where Tanya was sitting, watching me, smiling. I popped in a dime and phoned Robin's old number, once again looking over at Tanya. She smiled, waved back. When the recorded message announced that the number I had reached was no longer in service I told it that I was sorry about what had happened to Robin and that I wasn't sure what to do. The voice told me that it, too, was sorry, and that I should please hang up and try my call again. I told the voice that I would most certainly do that once the waiter came to refill our cups, that I was waiting for him to position himself in such a way that I could sneak into the kitchen, unseen, and make my way out the alley. The voice repeated itself before collapsing into a series of clicks, stopping dead on the dial tone just as the waiter arrived with his pot, blocking Tanya's view of my narrow escape.

19.6

— You wanted to get back and see Nettie.

— I had no idea what I wanted at that point.

19.7

I was unlocking my bike when who should be jogging around the corner but Flynn. The new Flynn, that is. Mr. Christian Businessman. Just like Tanya had said. He was wearing one of those thousand-dollar silver tracksuits you'd see at Holt Renfrew. And he looked positively radiant. I'd never seen anyone glow like that before.

He saw me immediately, didn't even look twice. It was as if he knew I was coming. He ran right up and stopped, held out his hand. And I shook it, just to see if it was real. "How're you doing?" he said, all smiley. "Okay," I lied. "Hungry?" he said. I was, actually. Not that I said so. "Thought you might be," he said. "When was the last time you ate?" I told him I had a piece of toast for breakfast. "Let's go to the Sylvia," he said. "Celebrate your graduation."

I didn't have much to say, which was fine because Flynn was doing all the talking. And the more he spoke about his accomplishments, his born-again status, his future plans, the more I stopped caring about whether I'd end up like Robin or Lance or Andy, or any of the number of other people he had a hand in killing. I mean, it was that boring. He hadn't even touched on anything to do with his so-called frame-up. No, all he was interested in was how much real estate he wanted to buy, how much money he gave to organizations like Broughton House, how Expo was going to revitalize the provincial economy, how he intended to run for city council one day, maybe even become premier of the province. The way he was talking he'd have no problem getting elected. Flynn had perfected a line of bullshit so irresistible he could win at both ends of the political spectrum.

"You know, the problem with you," he began, "is that you just care too much about all the wrong things." I shrugged a whatever. "You have a good mind. Why don't you put it to use. This city's on the verge of big things. *Get in now.* There's all sorts of film production going on. You could make a fortune shooting ads. I mean, forget this nickle-and-dime commie porno shit, all that porno-for-the-people you and Nettie used to talk about. No bucks doing that," he said, going back to his steak 'n' eggs. Then I remembered something. "So, Flynn," I asked him, "do you still have my copy of *The Family Dog?*" Flynn nodded. "Well, I'd like to get that back," I said, waiting for his reaction. "You can come by my place right now if you want," he said, buttering some bread. "Unless," he added, "you're worried I might kill you." I told Flynn that I wasn't, but that I hadn't ruled it out yet. With that, he laughed. And he did so in a most reassuring way, a way that implied that even if he had killed people in the past, he was no longer up to it now. So I felt okay with that. I went to the washroom and had no problem returning.

When I sat back down I saw that Flynn was reading a letter. "Who's that from?" I asked. "Nettie," he said, not looking up. Strange. "When did she send you a letter?" Flynn continued reading. Then I realized it was my letter. My letter from Nettie. I reached around behind me and sure enough it wasn't there. "It fell out of your pocket when you stood up," he said, tucking it back in the envelope, handing it over. I took the letter and put it in my pocket, all set to give him shit. But Flynn was already on his feet. "Finish your beer. Let's go," he said. So I downed it, thinking I needed the strength.

Flynn, as it turned out, lived at the other end of Gilford, near the entrance to Stanley Park. We were crossing Nelson when I told him I had yet to receive my package from Kodak. Flynn laughed. "Right," he said, "I'd forgotten about that. Those two cops that came to your door yesterday? Reese and Brown? They work for me, you know." *What!* "Whaddaya mean they work for you?" Obviously, Flynn found this amusing. "I was just curious to see if you'd turn me in or not. Which you didn't, of course. And I thank you for that. But whatever. I had Reese and Brown intercept the package." Suddenly, I didn't feel so good. It was as if I were on acid or something. Flynn continued: "I was concerned about your level of commitment ..." I reached into my pocket and pulled out Nettie's letter. "... I thought you might abandon me ..." The stamp had been removed. "... And in a way, you did ..." Flynn had taken the acid and put it in my beer. "You did abandon me ..." Of course. Of course of course of course of course.

EXT. BRICK APARTMENT BUILDING. DAY

Flynn and I are walking towards the glass entrance of the building. Flynn reaches ahead and opens the door. I step through, Flynn follows.

INT. LOBBY

A letter-carrier, a South Asian man (30s), is feeding the mailboxes. He is whistling. As we enter he turns and smiles. He is looking only at me.

LETTER-CARRIER

Hi, guy.

I smile back. Then I look over at Flynn.

ME
(VO)
Why didn't he say hi to both of us?

Flynn hurries me up the stairs.

The carpet is red and so are the walls.

PULLING ME AND FLYNN

> ME
>
> Everything's red.

> FLYNN
>
> My favourite colour.

MY POV

The walls seem to glisten, as if they were just painted. I touch my finger to one of them and my finger starts to bleed.

> FLYNN
>
> Just one more flight.

MY POV

As we step onto the top floor, everything begins to spin.

> ME
>
> Man, am I ever fucked up.

> FLYNN
>
> You can take a nap at my place.

BLACK

FROM BLACK

INT. FLYNN'S PLACE

I am standing in the middle of a room too big to belong in a small West End apartment. The room is roughly the size of Max's warehouse. In fact, it could very well be the same room except that it is painted red. At the far end is Flynn. He is standing by a door. He is waving for me to follow.

> FLYNN
> C'mon. There's some people here I want you to meet.

The next thing I know I'm opening a door, the same door Flynn had just called me from. I am in the room where Robin and I premiered *The Family Dog*. The room is dark and there are about ten people standing around watching the countdown.

FULL SCREEN: FILM LEADER

Five, four, three, two, one ...

TITLE: *CIRCLE JERK '76*

EXT. GRASSY FIELD. DAY

Five boys (12) and their dogs are walking through a grassy field bordering a river. The sound of crashing waves. One of the boys is carrying a white plastic Safeway bag. There are close-ups of each boy. The last close-up is on the boy with the bag.

CLOSE ON BAG

A *Hustler* magazine peeks through the plastic.

> VOICE
> We shot this in Vancouver.

The five boys are lying in a circle, masturbating. All of them have their pants down, magazines at their sides. Their eyes alternate between the magazines and each other.

CLOSE ON BOY #1

He is concentrating very hard. His jaw juts forward. He's on the verge of something.

I'm coming.

CLOSE ON THE OTHER BOYS LOOKING UP

BLACK

                              BOY #1
                              (VO)

        I win! I win!

THE END

Applause, bravos.

FILM LEADER

Counting down from five.

TITLE: *VENUS THEATRE*

EXT. A MOVIE THEATRE. NIGHT

A boy (16) walks up to the theatre's ticket booth. Inside the booth is
a Hindu woman (40). The boy passes her a five-dollar bill. She takes
the bill and gives him a ticket. The boy walks inside.

INT. THEATRE LOBBY

Pink curtains surround the lobby. An old Hindu man (70) sitting at
a card table. The only thing on the card table is an old shoebox. As
the boy approaches, the man motions for the boy to give him his
ticket. The boy complies. The ticket is torn in half. Half is returned
to the boy; the other half goes in the box.

The boy parts the pink curtains leading into the theatre.

FULL SCREEN

A hand taps him on the back. I turn around.

REVERSE

The hand belongs to Flynn. He is beckoning me. I turn around. We return to what was once the lobby. But now it's a room lit only by the light of a single candle. It is very hot. The walls are a deep red. There's movement, but it's hard to tell what's going on.

A MAN'S VOICE

Cut!

The lights go on.

INT. A LARGE BEDROOM

In the centre of the room is a bed. Beside the bed is a night table, where there stands a candle. Above the bed, a sign that reads: CHECK YOUR BULLSHIT DETECTOR AT THE DOOR. There are two cameras set up on tripods. A film crew lean up against the walls, smoking, sipping coffee. A teamster is stirring his Cup-a-Soup.

A very skinny woman sitting on the side of the bed. She is rubbing her face with the heels of her hands. There are IV tubes running from her arm and neck. A nurse is removing her catheter. Another is undoing the back of her gown. She takes her hands away. The woman is Nettie.

ME

Hi.

NETTIE
(tired)

Hi.

A beat.

Are you okay?

Nettie scoffs, shakes her head no. Then she lies down on her back.

I look down to see that I, too, am now naked.

FLYNN
(to me)
Basically, all we want you to do is go down on Nettie, then fuck her in the missionary position for about five minutes. After that you fuck her in the ass. When you're ready to come, pull out and come on her scar. Got it?

ME
(unsure)
Are you into this, Nettie?

Nettie nods.

ME
(still unsure)
Are you sure?

NETTIE
Just don't use more than two fingers in my ass at once.

ME
I'll just use one.

NETTIE
No more than two.

FLYNN
She's been lubed and prepped. She's all set to go.

NETTIE
(slowly adjusting herself)
Okay, I'm ready.

Are we ready on set?

Yeses from the crew.

Okay then ... Action!

I kneel between Nettie's legs and start licking her pussy. I begin to work my way in, very slowly, concentrically, eventually brushing up against her clitoris. I insert a finger. Her vagina is cool but well lubricated. I move it around. With my other hand, I trace a circle around her clitoris, then work my way out and back. I do this three times. Usually this is enough to get her attention. But she just lies there. At one point she coughs. She does this with enough force that her vaginal muscles contract and my finger is pushed out. I look up to see if Nettie's aroused. A nurse is spooning some red fluid into her mouth. I go back to licking. But this time I insert a finger into her asshole. The asshole's on the cool side as well.

FLYNN
(off)
Okay. Now start fucking her. In the missionary position. Let's go, let's go!

I open her legs, lifting them so they press against her breasts. My cock is hard and I put it inside her. I start slow, then work up to a hard clap. Her calves bounce off my shoulders. Her head is turned, her eyes are closed. She looks asleep.

I look over at Flynn. He is talking to the nurse. The nurse nods and disappears through a door. She returns just as quick with a hypodermic needle. She injects Nettie, and Nettie immediately comes alive. She is looking right at me. Her eyes are bulging.

NETTIE
Yeah, fuck me! Fuck me like that! Oh yeah! Fuck me
just like that ...

315

I begin to feel myself getting soft. The next thing I know my cock has popped out.

FLYNN
(off)

Cut! Bring in the fluff.

ME

Nobody uses fluff any more.

FLYNN

That's because everybody's a professional.

A door opens and in walks Mr. Billington and two crew. The crew are carrying a large wooden structure. A two-by-four frame with four one-by-six planks running lengthwise. It looks like a prefab section of fence. The crew hold the structure overtop the back of my legs, while Billington reaches his hand through and plays with my ass and balls. Soon, I'm back on top. And I'm fucking her. Nettie. But this time she's out of it again.

FLYNN
(off)

Okay, push her legs right back and start fucking her in the ass.

I comply. But as I do this, what do I see written on her ass but the Bullshit Detector, with Nettie's anus at the centre.

FULL SCREEN

Where do you want to go?

What will you
do to get there?

What have you done
to get where you are?

Where are you coming from?

Nevertheless, I work my way in, very slowly. I give her a hard thrust, then I pull back gently. I repeat this until I'm completely inside her. Then I get a rhythm going. The nurse sits down on the corner of the bed and gives Nettie another shot. As before, Nettie quickly comes around. But this time the nurse remains by her side.

NETTIE
(coming to life)
Oh yeah! Yeah! Do my ass like that! Yeah! Just like that ...

My thrusts get harder, faster. I feel myself ready to come. I look over at Flynn.

FLYNN
(mouthing the words)
Are you gonna come?

I nod, then start giving it. Hard. The nurse gets up. The room is very loud all of a sudden. People seem to be scurrying about, whispering. I look up to see that everything's a purple-red. The walls are throbbing. I look down at Nettie and see that she is quiet. But this times her eyes are open. There is a trace of a smile. Or is it just the muscles in her face collapsing?

ME
(whispering)
I love you, Nettie.

Nettie's face collapses even more.

I am about to come, so I pull out. I make a sound. A yell. Which is odd for me because I'm more a moaner than a shouter. But whatever. Something taps against the back of my head, something cold and metallic. I think it's the boom mike, but I guess I should've known better. I look down to see my cum dot Nettie's scar. The next spurt would be my third, and that one's always the best.

This time I went with it, my head propelling faster than any ride I'd ever been on. By the time the rest of me caught up to it, I was long gone. It was as if I passed right into the wall's flesh. That's when everything went white on white. In the distance, well behind me, the echo of something loud. A backfire.

19.8

— And here you are.

— And here I am.

— Do you know what just happened?

— I was snuffed.

— Yes. And at exactly the same time, on the other side of town, Nettie Smart passed away.

— Right.

— So what did you see when things went white on white.

— I saw Nettie and me on a swing set. We were about five years old. I think it was the first time we met, when I first moved to Shaughnessy.

— Then what did you see?

— I saw myself holding a paint-by-numbers set I'd won at church. I saw myself open the box and take out the canvas board.

— What was the image? Do you remember?

— Yes, it was a boy and a girl on a swing set.

— How did you win this paint-by-numbers set?

— It was an essay contest for the confirmation students.

— What was the topic?

— "Describe Heaven."

— Do you remember what you wrote?

— Yes, I wrote about how in heaven everything is white on white.

— How is that possible?

— I don't know, you tell me.

— We can't.

— Why?

— Because we're not finished with you yet.

— Because nobody believes in you any more, that's why.

— No. That's not the reason. And you should know better than to say something like that.

— Can I go now?

— We have a couple more questions left.

— Shoot.

— Where do you want to go?

— I want to see Nettie.

— What would you do to get there?

— Whatever it takes.

— And what have you done to get where you are?

— Everything I've told you.

— Is that where you're coming from then?

— Let me warm up with something easier.

— Okay. How old were you when you saw your first pornographic movie?

Acknowledgements

I would like to thank my editor, Maya, as well as Martha, Bernice, Skip, and John at Doubleday Canada. Thanks also to my agent, Jennifer, for introducing me to these fine people.

I am indebted to the writings of Angela Carter, Kathy Acker, Linda Williams, Caught Looking Inc., Pat Califia, and Laura Kipnis. I am also indebted to the communities of writers, editors, teachers, critics, and artists who have not only encouraged me over the course of writing this book but have made me feel good in their company as well. So: thanks to John Armstrong, Tony Burgess, Clint Burnham, Brice Canyon, Lynn Crosbie, Stan Douglas, Michael Holmes, Brian Lam, Paul Lang, Zoe Lasham, Lisa Marr, Bruce McDonald, Don McIntosh, John O'Connor, Stan Persky, Martha Sharpe, Colin Smith, Mina Totino, Scott Watson, and Cornelia Wyngaarden.

(If there is anybody reading this who feels they had an unacknowl-edged hand in this book's production [and you most certainly should, being the reader], then please add your name in the space provided below.)

I would particularly like to thank _____ .

Finally, I would especially like to thank Judy Radul, for reasons above and beyond.

About the Author

Michael Turner has long been considered one of Canada's most original, talented and versatile artists. His first book, *Company Town*, was nominated for the 1992 Dorothy Livesay B.C. Book Prize for Poetry. His second book, *Hard Core Logo*, has been adapted to radio, stage, and feature film. In 1996 he received a Genie Award for his contribution to the movie soundtrack. His screenplay-cum-novel, *American Whiskey Bar*, was produced as a live television special on Toronto's Citytv in the fall of 1998. Michael Turner lives in Vancouver.